I0734775

Murder Must Be Witnessed

Tony Read

Murder Must Be Witnessed

By Tony Read

ISBN - 978-1-906657-58-1

Spinetinglers Publishing
22 Vestry Road
Co. Down
BT23 6HJ
UK

www.spinetinglerspublishing.com

To my friend Robert Wright who gave me the idea for my third book "A Proper Country Funeral" and who has helped me in two books find a way through the mine field of grammar and punctuation.

CHAPTER ONE

The framed black and white photographs that clung tenaciously to the chipped and brittle plaster of the back wall of the Village Hall were dusty and unloved, already earmarked for the skip when the long awaited refurbishment of the crumbling building finally commenced in just over a week's time. Once people had stood before them and nostalgically remembered their childhoods, and pointed out to their own children and grandchildren elderly relatives long vanished into the grey fog of history, or small incarnations of themselves set in another time zone and on another planet; but not anymore. Nobody looked now, nobody gave them a second glance; a pictorial record of events that took place more than half a century ago was about to be unceremoniously thrown away and no-one seemed to care.

"They're so faded; it's very hard to recognise anyone anymore."

"Nobody remembers who they are; nobody gives a damn: they want ridding out."

"I wouldn't waste wall space on any one of 'em. If you like boring old photographs go to the bloody museum; you'll find shed loads of 'em there. Personally I've got better things to do with my time than stand gawping at shadows. The past is dead, it can't be resurrected, and who on earth in his right mind would want to do so anyway?"

But of course I knew better. Sometimes the past is all we have; sometimes it towers over the present like a sleeping volcano waiting for the right moment to erupt and overwhelm the unwary, sweeping away the here and now in a river of molten rage. "Revenge is a dish best served cold," so people say, but that isn't true. Revenge can be planned coldly and clinically, indeed it is better done that way, but it cannot be savoured with detached aloofness. Without a burning zeal to avenge old wrongs, even at the expense of the innocent, Revenge is an unsatisfying meal and best left untouched upon the plate.

I remember the day we celebrated the coronation of the Queen with terrifying clarity. More than anything else I remember the vividness of the colours; the sad monochrome prints destined to become landfill do not begin to tell the story. Reds as bright as new spilt blood and whites as pale as any death mask and blues so opulent and rich as to eclipse the brightest sapphires: and there was gold and silver too to banish, even if for just one day, the greyness of "Utility Britain". Somehow, despite austerity, mothers had found ways to dress their children in garish fancy dress to take part in a rough hewn tableau celebrating our history and our victory; and a little money had been found to buy prizes for those children most favoured by the judges. And there was food, plenty of food to fill empty bellies and ginger beer to drink and for the grown-ups tea and ale; all the necessary ingredients for a joyous party.

Before all that, however, we had crowned our home grown version of the Queen, dissimilar to Her Majesty only in size and weight and colour, but who could be churlish enough to make disparaging remarks about the amply proportioned Shirley Temple look alike, except perhaps my grandmother who could scour the veneer off any happy occasion with a tongue coated in acidic bile?

When I look back with hindsight it was a miracle that we were there at all, and it beggars belief that she actually allowed me to become a pirate with a crimson bandana for a headdress, an eye patch made from black felt and a little sword constructed of the finest balsa wood that could be rescued from a bag of kindling. No expense had been wasted, but it didn't matter. I was there, and for a brief while part of the general merriment rather than apart from it.

My Uncle James was expected to arrive later, and that, I suppose, was why we were present. Since the accident that broke his back he no longer lived with us, the small rooms and steep staircase of my grandmother's stone cottage were not designed to accommodate a big man, paralysed from the waist down and his ugly, monstrous, wheelchair. Uncle James now lived alone in a specially adapted bungalow amid his trophies and his triumphs and his shattered promise. Granny loved him unconditionally, he could do no wrong: I on the other hand was barely tolerated. She blamed my mother for his tragedy, and since the accident that had maimed him and killed her and her American boyfriend she took every opportunity to complain. My father was never mentioned without a sneer, but both he and my mother were untouchable, so she transferred her rage and her bitterness onto me; her burden, her cross to bear, the charitable duty that she was by circumstances forced to undertake.

Before the Second World War fortune had smiled on James; handsome, athletic and very gifted he had won a state scholarship to grammar school, and there he had excelled. My grandmother, by all accounts, indulged his every whim, even putting up with his short lived dalliances with a succession of pretty teenage girls, knowing that they were all temporary infatuations and that inevitably he would soon lose interest in them and quickly move on; the rigid discipline she imposed on me was totally unknown so far as James was concerned.

He had a good war and a lucky one, missing as he did the first two years of combat because of his age. When he was old enough to be conscripted Fate shielded him; he was brave, confident and popular, standing out from the common herd; senior officers noticed him, and twice he was mentioned in dispatches. He led a charmed life; while colleagues on either side of him were killed and injured, he survived without a scratch and left the army with a full set of limbs and senses, and a shining hero's medal to his name.

In 1944, whilst James was away fighting my mother met a good looking American called John Duke at a dance at the town hall. The story of the Yanks coming over here and stealing our girls has entered into folklore, and is so widely believed that many people think that most little boys born after 1945 came complete with crew cuts and American accents, tiny clones of their fathers, except of course most of their dads were long gone so comparisons were difficult to make. Most of these "Hollywood heartthrobs" abandoned their spawn with never a backward glance for the Annies, Marys and Graces they left behind carrying their children. John Duke didn't do that, he stayed around long enough for me to be born, and he did ask my mother to marry him, a proposal she eagerly accepted. He was a great fan of American Football was John Duke and after the war he started to play and to watch rugby, which was the nearest thing to his beloved sport that he could find on offer on this uncivilised side of the pond. He was driving home from a game in a little Morris Minor, which had seen many better days, with my mother snuggling next to him as he drove, praising him on a match winning performance and with Uncle Jim, who had been drafted into the team for one game only as an emergency replacement for an injured player also being praised for having had an outstanding match, when the crash occurred. The car they were in was confronted by a motor cycle on the wrong side of the road at a blind bend being ridden by a 17 year old youth who had played for the opposing team, still wearing his striped rugby shirt, and not thinking about anyone else on the road, who was racing back to the club house to recover some keys which he had dropped on the changing room floor. Despite the fact that he was underage the lad was drunk and travelling way too fast. My dad swerved to avoid a head on collision. The car left the road, crashed through a stone wall, rolled down a steep bank and impacted with a tree. My father and mother died instantly; Uncle James was badly injured, trapped inside the bent and twisted remains of the motor car unable to move. They had to cut him from the vehicle; he said many times after that that whilst waiting to be freed he knew his life was over and that he had prayed for the car to burst into flames and that the fire would consume his body; but even that small supplication was denied him by a disinterested and vindictive God.

The accident, as he knew it would, changed his life forever. Everything he took for granted was lost: his health, his strength, his good looks, his independence. Even his girlfriend walked away and this was his biggest loss of all; with its unerring talent for irony Fate had decreed that when he finally found his one true love he would be turned into a useless object of pity and derision, and that he would be condemned henceforth to watch in envy other people's happiness.

There was just one brief moment of hope. After initially being sure that he was permanently paralysed doctors had reassessed their conclusions and pondered that a lengthy series of intricate operations might restore some movement to his lower limbs but that came to nothing. A surgeon messed up, a mistake was made, and a final chance was lost. Today there would doubtless be an apology and a million pound out of court settlement; then there was no apology, no acceptance of any guilt, and very definitely no money on the table. My grandmother wept frequently at the fate of her only son, she never wept at all, certainly so far as I could see at the fate of her only daughter, his big sister.

Uncle James was late, so late in fact that my grandmother began to fear that he would not come and, the more the fear took hold the more impatient and unbending she became towards me. Other children were running about playing with each other, I was chained to her side, not permitted to stray an inch away from her for fear I would cause mischief, that was the case of course until she saw James, and from that moment I ceased to exist. I was free to go where I wanted in the company of whoever would put up with me. Nobody talked about "Child abuse" in those days, but once James had arrived I could have been invited to take part in the most explicit sexual games by the most infamous paedophile in the United Kingdom and she would have let me go without a second glance. Not that James was good company for her, the mental anguish he endured always made sure of that, but that day the blackness of his mood was at its most extreme. We found out later that he had seen his former girlfriend arm in arm with a radio journalist employed by the B.B.C. and it was rumoured she too was soon to be employed in the new media of television. Glamorous, well-groomed, content, she had showed no interest in, and allocated not a moment of her time to talk to the cripple who had once been her lover.

The foul mood continued for the rest of the day, stretching even my grandmother's patience to near breaking point, but he could not be cajoled out of his sullen disdain for everything that was taking place. Watching the children running, jumping and playing was agony for him and the pain was ten times worse when later in the evening the teenage boys and girls started to dance and several times he expressed a desire to leave. Granny begged him to stay a little longer for her sake. "Soon," she said, "there will be fireworks, it would be a pity not to wait for the display." Her argument prevailed, and Uncle James even began to show signs of animation and Granny felt at last he was becoming more relaxed.

As soon as it was dark enough the large bonfire that had been built on rough ground near to the football pitch was lit and scarlet and yellow flames brought new colour to the scene.

Just before the firework display commenced Uncle James declared that he was cold and that he needed to fetch a coat from the car that had carried him to the celebrations. My grandmother said that she would go, or that she would send me to get it. James snarled, "There are still some things I can do for my bloody self!" and refused all offers of help. He was away for a long time. The firework display started but still he hadn't returned: by today's standards it was nothing special, but back then it was magical to children who had never seen fireworks before. Blue and green orbs of light fell from the night sky, rockets soared towards the moon and a veritable battery of noise overwhelmed our senses. Then somebody shouted "What's that?" and we all turned round to look. At the corner of the field, a figure seated in a wheelchair was engulfed in flames. Uncle James was now the centre of attention. The smells of burning petrol and burning flesh and hair assailed our senses. People screamed, and some rushed to help, but no help could be given to him. Uncle James was beyond help; he had chosen to end his own life in the most public of ways and had burned himself to death in an inferno of his own making. My grandmother fell to the floor, stunned by events: Uncle James's torment was over, her torment and mine had leapt into an altogether more intense dimension.

CHAPTER TWO

Detective Inspector Hobson sat at the rear of the public gallery of court number 3 at Manchester Crown Court reasonably content with his lot. A verdict had been reached, a defendant had been convicted, he had been dragged from the dock screaming insults at the judge; members of the victim's family had applauded the decision; members of the defendant's family had wept and wailed, but to no end; no matter what they felt, no matter how hard they protested his innocence, in due course there would be a sentence, and that sentence would be severe; although probably not as severe as Hobson and his team of police officers would have wished to see. And it so nearly hadn't happened. When Hobson gave evidence earlier in the trial he had been attacked by the Defence Counsel anxious to prove him to be a liar or a fool and he had tried every trick in the legal textbook.

"Would it surprise you to know Inspector that you are the only person who saw the defendant discard the murder weapon when the street was full of potential eye witnesses?"

Hobson had stated that very few things in life surprised him and that he couldn't be held accountable for other people's inattention.

"Could it be a fact that at the time of the arrest there was no weapon to be seen and that the knife stained with the blood of the murder victim was brought to the scene much later by you or by one of your police colleagues?"

Hobson had retorted angrily that that was *"complete rubbish!"* and not worthy of any consideration.

The barrister had changed tack and had sought to get consensus on some peripheral facts, but he had cleverly added a small but important twist which he hoped would go unnoticed, but had his version been agreed, his client might have walked free.

The Detective Inspector was wise to the attempt; he had contradicted Counsel in clear terms and then restated the facts as he knew them to be. His testimony was an object lesson in how to deal with aggressive questioning, and he had been undamaged by the all-out assault the Defence had made upon his credibility.

The two young constables who had given evidence next had been savaged by the Defence barrister. They had crumbled under pressure, and their weakness could have sounded the death knell for the Prosecution. In due course they would learn, over time they would become robust, but in the intervening period cases would undoubtedly be lost because young officers hadn't yet acquired the experience to know when to concede and when to stand firm. Naively, many witnesses believe that the truth is a perfect shield, and that justice will finally prevail; Hobson knew this to be wrong. A trial is a game which has nearly unfathomable rules, played by egotists in front of an often partial referee, in which the self-interest of the advocates has more importance than any other outcome. The dozen citizens who make up the jury, so often thought to be the rock upon which the criminal law is founded, are pawns, manipulated by the chess Grand

Masters, frequently being sold a false version of the truth with the ease with which a door to door salesman persuades a simple pensioner to buy a product that she doesn't want and of which she has no earthly need.

Fortunately for the Prosecution, however, luck had for once been on their side. The constitution of this particular jury had been unusually strong; there had been no weak links, no people with criminal convictions, no feeble minded do-gooders unable to see evil where it exists and no fantasists incapable of staring Reality in the face and recognising that sometimes it can be cruel.

This crime of murder had been particularly horrific; an elderly lady living alone had been attacked in her own home; she had been tortured, her jewellery had been stolen, along with a substantial amount of cash. She had been brutally killed, the multiple stab wounds to her body testified as to the viciousness of the attack, and the crime scene photographs were sickening in their content. Such shocking images revolt normal people, their overwhelming reaction to inhuman cruelty is that somebody must pay, and unfortunately for the defendant he fitted the bill admirably. His shaven head and graphic tattoos which caused people to fear him as he strutted down the street, massaging his comic book conception of himself as Genghis Khan or some twenty second century mean, lean killing machine were not designed to appeal to the "twelve good men and true" who would decide his fate. If behind the facade of aggression a gentle, child-like, holy person had existed it would have mattered not. A villain had caused this tragedy, a villain had to pay the price, and he looked every inch the villain. The jurors wanted blood; they could not shake the memory of the victim's anguish from their minds, an irresistible urge for revenge spurred them on to convict.

The image of the deceased haunted them; they knew a harmless frail old lady had died alone in abject terror, her world diminished to become a tiny planet where only she and her attacker still remained. A world at war, a world dominated by a tyrant who had launched a violent incursion into a defenceless state, a blitzkrieg, total domination and a savage final solution; and for what? For the perverted pleasure the victor would take in inflicting pain, his state of arousal ten thousand times greater than when he picked up women for mundane venal sex, and for a few pieces of silver to carry off as booty.

That the defendant had failed to make a clean getaway was due entirely to the unforeseen arrival of the postman delivering a parcel. The lady was quite deaf; he knew that for a fact. She was also sweet and trusting and very friendly; she never locked her door, she had no need to, she had no enemies: and, as he had done countless times before, the postman walked into the house with a cheery shout of "*hello*" intending to place the package on the kitchen table, hoping that perhaps he might be offered a cup of tea.

The scene that met his eyes was gruesome beyond belief; the kitchen resembled an abattoir, the sadistic slaughter man disturbed in the act of bloodletting; the postman had turned and fled, pursued by the defendant, knowing that if the man caught him he would be dead. Chance had intervened, his pursuer had tripped and fallen heavily to the ground, the postman had made it to his van, and despite stalling the engine three times in his anxiety had finally succeeded in starting it just as the defendant made a grab for the driver's door. He had escaped without injury; too scared to stop anywhere en route he had driven straight to the police station and there he had told his story. He was so distressed he could only give a bare outline of events; even weeks later most of what he had witnessed remained a blur; although stood within feet of the defendant for several seconds, prior to turning and running, he never managed to identify him to the police, despite his very individual and frightening appearance.

The lack of identification of the suspect by the only eye witness had been crucial to the Defence case. D.N.A. found at the scene was explained away by a spurious story that the defendant had indeed been in the house before the crime was committed, but at the invitation of the victim herself. He claimed that he had been out walking on a hot day and, seeing the lady in her garden, he had asked her if he could have a drink of water. He said that she had invited him into the house and not only given him water but offered him biscuits from the biscuit barrel. There was not a word of truth in it; Hobson suspected that the idea had come from the barrister, or some other member of the legal team, but he had no proof: like all lawyers, a barrister was an officer of the court, and expected to act with total integrity: to allege he had done otherwise, without supporting evidence, would have enraged the judge and been entirely detrimental to the Prosecution case.

The defendant had left the crime scene on foot after the postman had escaped his murderous clutches. He had been tracked by police dogs away from the house, but the trail had been lost when he crossed a stream. It was suspected that somewhere near to that point he had parked a car, but that was pure conjecture. What was clear was that he had had the opportunity to go someplace to wash and shower and change his bloodstained clothes and shoes before once again emerging into the outside world. The clothes he took off were never found so they could not provide any physical proof that the man was a killer.

The fundamental mistake he made was to retain the murder weapon which he should have thrown away, but it was his favourite weapon of choice, which he had used many times, and unlike King Arthur, he could not bring himself to cast his Excalibur into the mystic lake. He had however wiped the blade and handle, and convinced himself that both were clean, but microscopic specks of blood had been missed, and they would prove to be his undoing.

Two days after the murder D.I. Hobson had seen him on the street. Something in the impossibly vague description the postman had given struck a chord; maybe it was simply that he looked like a thug, or perhaps it was just the fact that he was walking with a limp, consistent with having suffered a heavy fall that set alarm bells ringing but whatever it was Hobson had decided to challenge him. He had approached him and produced his warrant card: fearing that he would be searched and that a weapon would be found on him, he had fled, at one point throwing the knife under a parked car to avoid discovery. Detective Inspector Hobson had caught and overpowered him, and he had been arrested after a struggle; the knife was recovered from under the vehicle; the rest, as they say was "history."

As he waited for the public gallery to clear, the process impeded by the gargantuan grandmother of the convicted man slowly making her lumbering way to the exit door, muttering crude obscenities with every wheezing step, the contrast between this appalling specimen of humanity and the decent well-loved creature who had been butchered by her worthless grandson was so stark, that even for an experienced police officer like Hobson, the injustice of it all was almost unbearable. This common, crude monstrosity of a woman would probably one day die in her own bed surrounded by dozens of her unlovely offspring helping to ease her passage into some bizarre vision of Heaven filled with pink roses, smiling cherubs and marble angels. Her fears would be assuaged; sentimentality would wrap a comfort blanket tightly around her; how different her passing would be from that of the innocent victim of her grandchild's brutality.

Death comes to us all, and the manner in which we leave this world says much about who we are. To slip away gently, supported by caring members of one's family, controlling their grief, not wearing their sadness like gaudy cloaks, that was the best way to go thought Hobson, or to fall asleep never to wake up, that was a good way too. To die terrified and alone in pain and fear is the worst of nightmares yet that was what had happened to a helpless, well meaning, much loved lady.

In an earlier age, men like the defendant would have been publically executed and large crowds would have cheered their fate. Nobody deserved a hideous death more than this barbaric animal: if, squealing and incontinent, he had visibly shown his fear to a jeering mob, that perhaps would have been justice; but a few years behind bars, fed, clothed and entertained at great public expense; that was his actual lot; and it stank!

CHAPTER THREE

"He's a good lad Mary, a real credit to you; he must make you feel very proud."

Mary Wallington smiled as only a doting mother can. "Yes," it was true. Adam did make her proud. She wanted to say, *"He's the best son in the world, he's so good at everything it's incredible and he's so loving and so thoughtful, I'm the luckiest mum alive"*, but that would have been boasting so she simply said, "He has his moments, he's not a bad boy," but inside she was bursting with pride.

And why shouldn't she be? Adam was a phenomenon. Tall, blonde, handsome, intelligent, strong; he was a superb all round sportsman as well as being an outstanding student. Tipped by his professor at Oxford to get a first and twice voted to be the outstanding player in the University seven-a-sides, he was also extremely good at cricket; better in his mother's eyes than "Freddie" Flintoff, but with a much keener intellect, and a far greater sense of responsibility.

Where that gene came from she sometimes wondered; in her youth she had made some silly mistakes and her father, Bernard, was not known locally for his sagacity: as for Adam's father he was hopeless, although far less so than his father who had lived a whole lifetime of reckless irresponsibility. How many seventy year old men still drove too fast, drank too much and acted the giddy goat when inebriated? Mary ventured to guess that the answer would be very few. The Chairman of the local Bench had once described him as "*Derbyshire's oldest juvenile delinquent*" and frequently despaired at his behaviour. To have an ASBO at such an advanced age was almost unheard of, but Mick glorified in the notoriety. Mary longed for the day when her disreputable father-in-law departed this mortal life but feared it would be a long time coming.

With such a pedigree it was a miracle that Adam hadn't followed the family tradition and turned out vain, conceited or self-obsessed, but he hadn't. He would do anything for anybody, and everybody knew that. The girls loved him and he loved them, and he treated them gently, never roughly or unkindly, even managing to stay on good terms with most of his former girlfriends long after he ceased dating them. He could do better than Chloe, his current girlfriend though, but at the moment they made each other happy, and that was really all that mattered. How she would feel if Chloe was the one who finally took him from her Mary didn't know; she suspected she might want to scratch her eyes out.

"It's good of him to help on the church tower. Joe Lomas has properly wrecked his back, and the beehive of flowers weighs more than half a hundredweight; it always amazes me that the king doesn't collapse under the weight, particularly if it happens to be a hot day."

"How often do we get hot days in Castleton at the end of May Dick? It's usually wet enough to fill a reservoir and cold enough to turn the little girls bright blue."

"Not always Mary, not always."

And Dick was right; it wasn't always wet, and the forecast for this week was extremely promising.

Sunshine would bring the crowds, nothing was more certain than that; they came in all weathers to watch the pageant: there is something ludicrously stoical buried deep within the British character that come rain, hail, sleet and wind people still venture out in numbers to support a carnival, wait for play to start in a deluge at Old Trafford, or sing along with Cliff in a thunderstorm at Wimbledon, but this week in Castleton everything was set fair. The pubs would be heaving, the gift shops would do brisk business, the pavements would be jammed tight with pedestrians and the village would look a picture. When at the end of the procession the little girls danced around the maypole waves of nostalgia would envelop great swathes of the crowd, and the quintessential Englishness of the occasion would gladden the hearts of the watchers.

Nobody really knew when the Garland tradition first started; it certainly dated back a few hundred years, and the symbolism of it all was far from clear. The reason why it was always held on the 29th May was certain, and there was no doubt that in part the strange goings on commemorated the day the future King Charles II hid up an oak tree to avoid capture by Roundhead troops; the Cavalier costumes which the king and queen are always dressed in bear witness to that fact as does the wearing of oak leaves, which many people attending the ceremony still do. When Mary was a little girl the oak leaf protected you from harm; if you didn't wear one rough school boys would hit you with stinging nettles, but now at least that part of the ancient custom was almost never observed.

But the English Civil War was only part of a more complicated and obscure history. Why it was that for most of the ceremony the king was concealed under a wicker beehive totally covered in flowers was a question frequently asked, but seldom conclusively answered. Some said the ceremony dated back to pagan times and the myth of the Green Man, and that it was all to do with fertility and the rites of spring, but nobody was really sure. What everybody knew was that it would always continue, and that folks living as far afield as Sheffield and Manchester would come in their hundreds to witness the event, and this year Adam Wallington would play a small but important part in it.

Lucy Hobson was too young to be involved at all, but Helena, her mum, hoped that one day she might be so. She and her husband Mark were looking for a larger house, and Castleton was high on their list of possible places to live: a police inspector's salary was not great, but the Hobson's were not without money. The death of Helena's grandfather at the age of 92 had left them with a considerable legacy, and both Helena and Mark were agreed that the best use of that money would be to give their two children the best possible start in life.

Helena was a beautiful, brainy, gentle, caring creature, and Mark adored her. Even after six years of marriage he was still totally besotted by her, and she loved him in return. He had saved her from a cruel and painful death at the hands of a deranged woman, despite having been shot twice in the course of the rescue, but in a very real sense she had also saved him. His life had been on a downwards spiral before he met her, his first marriage had failed and his unsuitable first wife had then died in a car accident. The fault was entirely hers, there was no other vehicle involved, but her parents blamed him for what had occurred, and he had been subjected to a vicious campaign of slander. Heavy drinking had become the norm and soon it would have wrecked his career. Then he had met Helena, and everything had changed. Her love gave him strength and, although there were times at work when he could be forceful, aggressive and unbending in his dealing with criminals, at home he was relaxed, tolerant and forgiving. He ruled his kids with a rod of cotton wool, and even though both were still very young, they could wrap him around their little fingers: it was always Helena who had to scold them if they went too far.

Mark hadn't really wanted to go to the Garland ceremony, but Christopher wanted to be there because his little friend from infant school was going, and Helena loved to see the young girls in their white frocks festooned with spring flowers; so submissively he went along and, with the sun on his back, and the laughter of the children and the insidiously irritating, cheerful, unforgettable music tickling his ears, he was soon smiling benignly as he surveyed the world around him.

Slowly the King and Queen each mounted on massive Shire horses, followed by the village band and the schoolgirls in their white dresses processed from pub to pub. Outside each inn beer was brought out for the band; it was easy to imagine that in bygone days tipsy musicians would have become louder, more exuberant and less tuneful as the evening continued, but in recent times nobody had been arrested for being drunk in charge of a rogue trombone or disturbing the peace with an aggressively overactive drumstick and perhaps, mused Mark, despite the delicious mental picture such excesses conjured up that had never been the case.

Outside the George Inn, to much merriment and ribald comment, the larger of the two horses decided to empty its bladder; a sea of horse pee, deep enough to float the Titanic, flooded the street. Young women in open toed sandals leapt back onto the pavement; spectators like Mark and Helena, viewing the parade from the height of the churchyard safely beyond the reach of this tidal wave broke out into spontaneous laughter.

The good humour of the occasion was infectious, even the men stood at the top of the church tower caught the mood. The young man in the hooped rugby shirt waved down to the people below; he and his companions had the best seats in town; Adam Wallington thought to himself, *If I'm around next year I'll volunteer to do this again, just at this precise moment there is no place on earth that I would rather be.*

Now the time was nearly right. The King on his horse was led to the place where the maypole had been erected, and then walked back down towards the churchyard gate. A brave soul clambered onto the stone gatepost with its pyramid shaped cap and balanced precariously upon it waiting for the horse and rider to pass beneath him. He had done this many times before. Somehow managing to maintain his balance despite the odd wobble, when the horse was in the correct position he leant forward as the big animal slowly trundled toward the tower, and with one hand he seized the lid of the beehive, which he then held aloft in triumph. In due course, this pretty knot of flowers would be laid, with due respect and ceremony, at the base of the war memorial on the village green. The horse and its partly concealed rider plodded on to the church door; in a very few seconds more Adam Wallington's job would begin.

CHAPTER FOUR

When I was old enough to understand I asked her why she burned the remains of her only son when it was fire that had feasted on his flesh and inflicted on him so much pain. To my innocent eyes it seemed incomprehensible that she would choose to wreak more damage on his black and blistered body; anything but that I thought; she answered with her hand; my face bore the imprint of that slap for many hours thereafter. I didn't know then, and she never told me, that in reality she had had no choice, nor did I know how much that lack of choice hurt her.

I vividly remember the stern faced man in the black dress arriving at the cottage, a wooden cross hung from his neck, a frown set firm upon his judgemental face; God's representative on earth, or at least his agent in the poor parish that we called home. I didn't hear any of the conversation, I was sent out of the room under strict instruction not to return until my grandmother summoned me from my bedroom, but I now know that the exchange between them was as joyless as the grave. This man, who claimed Jesus as his master, and who talked in his sermons of Christian charity and forgiveness, was rigid and unbending. A crime against God and against the law of the land had been committed. The state of anguish of the perpetrator mattered not; mental health and physical discomfort had to be discounted, a tragic tale could not speak on behalf of the accused: it was a mortal sin to take your own life; the gates of Heaven were closed to mortal sinners; and the gates of the church yard would not be opened to admit the coffin of one who had disobeyed the dictates of the Almighty. Despite my grandmother's pleas and entreaties, and totally ignoring the fact that four generations of her family had served his church well and that both her first and second husbands had been churchwardens, the vicar remained unmoved; Uncle James would not be laid to rest in hallowed ground, he would not be permitted to be interred alongside his natural father and several generations of his family.

I didn't want to go, but she dragged me to the crematorium to bear witness to the passing of a life; a wicked child like me should know about the fires of Hell and learn that if I strayed from the straight and narrow path my soul would be claimed by the Devil and there would be nothing to look forward to except an eternity of torment and unhappiness. I was six years old. I had no father or mother to love me and drive away my fear. Demons would wait around every corner to attack me; Satan would set many traps. Not one ray of hope could be allowed to penetrate the shadow lands of the Old Testament.

A day or three after the cremation my grandmother collected the urn. This ugly vase containing the dust of a life tragically unfulfilled now took centre stage upon the mantelpiece; the pretty porcelain jug that had always stood there was banished to the back of a rickety corner cupboard. I was forbidden on pain of Armageddon to touch it, but I had no desire to do so lest the Devil suddenly sprang from within like a malevolent Jack-in-the-Box to drag me kicking and screaming into his unspeakably terrifying world.

For many years that urn dominated the room and controlled our sad lives. I suppose I should have recognised my grandmother's despair, and felt pity for her sorrow, but I could not. I felt nothing. If she had cared for me I'm sure it would have been different, but the gap between us, which was vast from the very start widened with time; a black island drifted away from a black continent, each land mass becoming an ever more barren place.

Under protest, and only at the insistence of the headmistress, she would grudgingly attend parents' evenings at school. Nothing bad said about me surprised her, but any slight words of praise were treated with disbelief. Teachers saw my unhappiness, saw a withdrawn and resentful child, but there was little they could do; I never went hungry, my clothes were always spotlessly clean; nobody knew the magnitude of her displeasure if I came home in a dirty or dishevelled state. Verbal abuse does not leave visible scars, but the wounds inflicted by the tongue don't heal with time; they fester and suppurate, and the toxic poison they destroy every kind thought before it is properly born. Maybe nowadays a social worker would be wise to the suffering of the child, but watching the news and reading the tabloid newspapers makes me believe that frequently the warning signs are overlooked and another innocent life is destroyed.

As for the rest of my early education, she featured not at all. She was too poor to waste money sending me on school trips, and certainly would not pay hard cash to see me perform in any concert or play. My teachers told me I had talent, the only talent she ever granted me was a talent to be wicked, and as I grew up and became physically stronger that was a talent I demonstrated to her more and more.

There may have been another way, but if there was there was nobody to show me what it was. I had no brothers or sisters to relate to, no one to stand in my corner. Nobody came knocking at our door, except a few dried out old crones to worship at her Wailing Wall. Like Moslem women in their burkas these antiquated stick insects dressed in long coats of monochromal hue would assemble in the parlour to rail against the licentiousness of the world and drink down bitter cups of tea. When the coven arrived I was excluded from their sight except just once when she thought it might be good for my moral benefit to be forced to sit in silence through a meeting; I disgraced myself by smiling. "The Devil was in the child!" I was never permitted to be with them again; humour would not be permitted to pollute the sanctity of the shrine: for this small mercy I was truly grateful.

I was joyous only when I was away from the morbid mausoleum she called home, but that joy could never be maintained. She had ensured that I had few social skills; I couldn't talk easily to others, and I was so unaware of television and of sport that I had nothing in common with the children on the street. I wasn't teased, that would have implied a measure of acceptance, and mostly I wasn't even jeered; more cruel than either of these thing was to be ignored, unnoticed by the laughing, shouting, fighting, skipping tumbling mass of humanity that was the generation of my youth.

Loneliness is a curse, and one that I have lived with all my life, although at times with effort and with dedication I have sometimes disguised the inner hermit by dressing him in a coat of "bonhomie." People never look beyond the obvious; scratch the veneer off a jester and reveal the sad recluse within; look beyond the shields of strength so many men and women carry and see the weakness cowering behind their public faces. I at least know myself, I may not like the creature I have become, but I will never drown in a sea of self-deception.

I also know who made me what I am and why there can be no forgiveness. My mother caused my torment by giving birth to me but she and my father might have gifted me a worthwhile life but for the intervention of others. The sot whose drunken antics caused the crash that killed my parents and crippled my Uncle James bears prime responsibility but Uncle James himself carries with him a substantial degree of guilt. And what of the girl who broke his heart and the surgeon who messed up his one chance of recovery, they too helped to create a desolate world for a young boy to inhabit, and they too must reap the consequences. And one more person deserves to be added to the list. The Man of God who bared his teeth, and snarled his condemnation of a tormented soul, refusing to consider for one single second my grandmother's pleas that her only son should have redemption, stoked up in her the bitterness and anger I had then to endure every single day that she lived; does not someone need to pay the price for that man's malignant obduracy? The punishment should fit the crime, and the sentence should be a life sentence. I was bequeathed such a penalty and, now as the time approaches when my foothold on the road of life becomes ever more precarious, it is my turn to leave a legacy that will be eternal. But I jump too far ahead, the passage of the boy from child to man still needs to be explained, and the "slings and arrows" that dogged his every step must be revealed.

When I was ten and a half years old I passed my eleven plus exam. I didn't really want to do so because I knew that failure would spite my grandmother, but failure would have condemned me to a life of invisibility within the mediocrity of the secondary modern school. For a short while I suppose I thought that within a new environment, and one in which it wasn't a crime to be intelligent, I might be reborn; but the naivety of youth was soon shattered by the realisation that nothing could change my state and I was pre-ordained to walk a solitary path through adolescence.

Not that she had the slightest bit of interest in my achievements, but against all the odds I started to excel in a few areas where being the school leper didn't hold me back. I discovered that I had stamina and that running came easily to me. Although not wishing to do anything for the honour of the school (if it didn't value me why should I crash my way through the pain barrier to bring it trophies) I liked the unaccustomed feeling of being a winner: for three years in a row I won the County Schools Cross Country Championship and, although I loathed the fact that I brought back silverware to an institution that looked down on me, the exhilaration I felt when breaking the tape ahead of the field was a strong aphrodisiac, although one of a very transitory nature.

The old witch never saw me race once, but that was a blessing. I didn't want her there; I think with hindsight that her presence would have overpowered my desperate will to win. My greatest fear at that time was that one day she would somehow change and try to hold me in her arms to make amends for the way she had treated me; that was my constant nightmare; her indifference defined me, her coldness was the foundation stone on which my life was set; if those everlasting certainties were taken from me I would have lost everything that anchored me in reality.

As well as running I could also shoot. I had a good eye and with the school cadet force I set records that still stand until this day. My name is on an Honours List and there are photographs hung in the school hall, but I suspect that at every Old Boys' reunion, which I have always avoided like the plague, I may be the only person in the class that nobody remembers and who nobody can describe. It is such an irony; I remember with such clarity the face of every individual who has hurt me. I have been air brushed out of every single life that I have touched, yet those who have from time to time collided with me on my journey from ill-starred beginning to unlamented end stand large in my sight and everything about them is crystal clear.

CHAPTER FIVE

All eyes now looked towards the tower. The great horse was brought to a stop just yards away from the church door, so close in fact that had the door been made of glass, its hot breath would have rendered the clear surface opaque. The animal was restless, it wanted away from this place. The man at its head tried to instil calm. "Steady boy, steady," he whispered; the beast found comfort in his words. In a few moments its work would be done. In a few moments a rope would be lowered down and attached to the cage of flowers that had for so long imprisoned the rider and it would be winched from his shoulders and hoisted to the top of the tower where it would be placed on the only pinnacle yet undecorated by Spring flowers.

"This is the bit I find quite bizarre. The whole procession must have its roots in pagan mythology and I think it's odd that everything comes to a climax at the parish church; they wouldn't let anything like this happen in the grounds of a mosque."

Helena smiled. "You're taking it too seriously Darling; it's just a bit of fun, it's timeless, it's innocent, it's nostalgic, and it makes people happy. And it's not as if the Christian church hasn't wrapped itself in pagan traditions before. Think of the date we celebrate Christmas, and how much holly and mistletoe form part of our celebrations, and all that owes far more to the Druids than it does to the birth of the baby Jesus."

"You're right as always Love, and after all this eccentric ceremony isn't the only example of weird and wonderful happenings in Derbyshire. I could take you to several places in Gamesley on a Saturday night where what takes place would make Bacchus blush with embarrassment."

"Who's Bacchus, Daddy?"

"He's nobody Poppet," said Helena, "it's just Daddy being silly," and she poked Mark in the ribs.

"Little fox cubs have got big ears Love, maybe his introduction to wine, women and S.E.X. should come bit later on in life."

***

Adam Wallington waved to the people down below. Up on top of the tower the air was fresh and, although he had companions, he had space. The people who gazed back at him reminded him of ants, except just for the moment there was virtually no movement, a static mass of humanity, welded for a second into a single entity, watching as one as he leaned over the parapet to heave the heavy framework of flowers onto the flat roof.

Not everybody in the crowd heard the shot, and even those who did largely misconstrued it as a car back firing, but everyone saw Adam's body tumble from the tower and crash down onto the path below, his arm catching the rump of the Shire horse as he fell. The animal bucked and reared in fright, the *Laughing Cavalier* was thrown from its back; people screamed in terror, the glue that had held the crowd in place dissolved. The universal fear was that somewhere close at hand a maniac with a gun was on the loose. Massacres such as those that too frequently dealt out death to the Innocents in schools in America couldn't happen here, but suddenly long forgotten place names like Hungerford and Dunblane crashed into peoples' memories, and all anyone wanted to do was to flee.

Mark grabbed Helena's hand.

"Hold on tight to Christopher!" he shouted. "I've got Lucy," but aware that her blonde curls could be a tempting target to a lunatic with an assault rifle, he lifted her from his back, and then positioning himself to the rear of his wife and children to shield them from any second shot, he pushed them roughly from the scene to the place where their car was parked. Helena's face was white, Lucy and Christopher were both crying.

"I've got to stay here Love, this is a crime scene, I can't leave it. Get yourself and the kids out of here right now before you get caught up in traffic. You'll be fine, but don't stop for anyone, go straight home, and if it makes you feel any easier keep the door locked until I get back. I'll telephone you later when I can, but don't expect to see me anytime soon; it could be a very long night."

For a few seconds Mark watched as Helena's car inched its way out of danger. Because he had acted so quickly her vehicle was one of the very first cars to leave the village, but many other people had had the same idea, and soon the centre of the village would become gridlocked by cars.

Everybody wanted to leave, nobody was prepared to give way; bumps and scrapes were occurring but were being ignored. Even if a driver was prepared to run the potential risk of a sniper's bullet by standing on his rights and demanding insurance details from an offender, nobody could be found who was prepared to risk being shouted down by an angry mob of frightened people who would see his strict adherence to the rule of Law as a dangerous impediment to their and their children's safety. The traffic chaos had the potential to get totally out of hand; it needed to be sorted quickly so that police and ambulances could get to the scene of the shooting; it wasn't going to be an easy job.

The local beat bobby, supported by two P.C.S.O's, had expected to do nothing more than explain the temporary road closures to confused motorists, perhaps deal with the odd complaint of theft of a wallet and maybe whisper in the ears of a few people who had drunk rather more than common sense might have dictated. Instead, without warning, they had been catapulted into the front line of a major incident. When Mark returned to the spot where Adam Wallington lay the uniformed officers were trying, without much success, to control the scene. A distraught woman cradled the dead body of her son in her arms, children were weeping, people were visibly in a state of shock, and any moment second, third and fourth shots could cause carnage.

The relief on the face P.C. Martin was palpable when he saw Detective Inspector Hobson emerge from the crowd.

"You've radioed in haven't you?" asked Hobson. P.C. Martin nodded.

"I'll take over here. You and one of your colleagues get down to the Main Street and try to clear a path for the emergency vehicles. Leave the other one here with me to keep the crowd back from the body; there's not much more we can do apart from that until we get more manpower."

Left with just one female Police Community Support Officer to assist him, all Mark Hobson and she could do was to position themselves either side of Mrs Mary Wallington and her murdered angel. Her screams and sobs penetrated deep into the minds of the Detective Inspector and his young companion; he at least had seen violent death before, for her it was the first time she had witnessed the ending of a life; but for both of them the knowledge that something very akin to a public execution had been staged in a sleepy Derbyshire village in front of many hundreds of people in festive mood was a deeply disturbing thought.

The minutes ticked by. Even to Mark it seemed that the second hand on his wristwatch traversed the clock face at the pace of a comatose snail, and to his inexperienced colleague it was far worse. Twelve endless minutes had gone by before the first sirens could be heard, faintly at first as the police vehicles squeezed their way down the narrow gorge that is Winnats Pass then louder and more aggressive as their progress was slowed by the cars, vans and campers that were hell bent on leaving the pretty little place that would forever in the drivers' minds be synonymous with brutal slaughter.

The last quarter of a mile took forever, indeed some members of the Tactical Firearms Unit leapt out the vehicle they were travelling in and sprinted to the spot where the body of the victim lay. They were tense, their guns were fully loaded, and they were ready to return fire should some deranged *Rambo* burst on to the scene with all guns blazing; but thankfully no such person came.

"There was just the one shot," Mark Hobson explained, "and it was bang on target. Whoever the marksman was he knew exactly what he wanted to do and what impact he wanted this murder to have; and he carried out his plan to perfection. I'm sure the shot must have been fired from the high ground near to Peveril Castle. I'm certain this was a targeted assassination. Because the killing took place in front of a large crowd I was terrified that what happened on the church tower was going to be the prelude to a massacre, but thank God I was wrong on that score."

Police numbers began to swell rapidly. A search by armed officers of the ruins of Peveril Castle and of the surrounding fields didn't flush out a man with a gun; a much more thorough search of the whole area would follow to see if traces of an assassin could be found but at least now, with a reasonable degree of confidence that they could be accomplished in safety, the other tasks that always flow from a major incident could commence. Many people had left the village before the police arrived, but many others had taken shelter in the pubs and shops to put brick and mortar between themselves and a crackpot with a rifle. The details of as many onlookers as possible who had been outside at the time of the shooting had to be collected so that witness statements could later be taken from them. Maybe someone had caught a glimpse of the killer; maybe like joining the dots in a child's colouring book snippets of collective memory could be pieced together to paint a reasonable picture of a murderer. Nothing could be presumed, a successful outcome was very far from being guaranteed, but it was beyond dispute that the effort had to be made.

Detective Chief Superintendent Stan Hardy arrived shortly after the first convoy of police vehicles and Mark briefed him with all the information that had been gained to date, which in truth was not a great deal. Dr Gerald Grimshawe, the Home Office Forensic Pathologist was now also present, and a tent had been erected over the dead body of Adam Wallington to cover the larger than life doctor and the dead student from public gaze while Dr Grimshawe, universally referred to as "*The Grim Reaper*" by irreverent police officers, carried out an initial examination. Mrs Mary Wallington had been gently led from the scene. Stunned silence had replaced screams; not a trace of colour could be detected in her face. Her eyes seemed almost as lifeless as her dead son's. She moved like a zombie, mechanically keeping step with the two police officers tasked with taking her to a place of safety. Her heart was broken, her soul had been destroyed, and everything she cared for had been lost. Years of living death lay ahead; the cruelty that had caused her tragedy was inhuman. Mark Hobson wondered what evil it was that had occurred that had caused a killer to act so heartlessly.

CHAPTER SIX

She didn't know I knew about the guns or about how I fantasised about placing the pistol to her head and blowing out her brains, but I did, and had not her unforgiving Saviour intervened I would have done so too. A date was circled on my calendar, the 10th anniversary of Uncle James' suicide, just two weeks after my 16th birthday. I had dreamed throughout my adolescent life of a day of reckoning, and it was so nearly at hand, when the chance was snatched from me by the intervention of Fate and by her massive heart attack. I wept in frustration; my abject despair at failing to wreak vengeance was taken by her withered cronies as a sign of sadness.

"The lad isn't as bad as we thought," they snivelled. Some of them even tried to wrap their sympathy around me. I recoiled from their touch. They believed I was in shock; too upset to accept a tender gesture but that wasn't the reason; their skinny hands made my flesh creep, their whining voices tortured my inner ear.

"Let him be," they said, "to grieve in his own way." I did grieve, but not for the reason they supposed.

There were two weapons locked in a wardrobe in her bedroom. The pistol was a trophy of war, taken from the hand of a dead German soldier by Uncle James and smuggled back to England in a kit bag. He had been so proud of his acquisition. It was his secret source of power. When he held it he felt like a God, knowing that he had the means to end human life at a whim. I longed to know that feeling and for her to know it too and although that can now no longer happen, others can feel the fear she should have felt; a pleasure denied to me in my youth will now gratify me in late middle age and taste sweeter for the wait.

The rifle was a Lee Enfield, standard issue to the Home Guard in the Second World War, and although not a thing of beauty, and crude in design when compared with modern weapons, it was a reliable piece of kit, unlikely to let a soldier down.

The night after V.E. Day was a riotous affair. My grandmother had danced in the street in celebration, the relief that her beloved son was no longer a target for German bullets made her leap and prance like some demented desert tribesman, high on a heady cocktail of drugs and wailing music. She raised her skirt above her knees and behaved like a wild child, unfettered for the moment by any thoughts of dignity or self-restraint. She was not alone. Other middle aged women forsook their biblical reticence to shout and laugh and show their fat or skinny legs. I have seen the photographs of their celebrations and, even though more than 6 decades have passed, I am still amazed that any of these unlovely creatures could bear to look at themselves in their shamelessness; but during their lifetimes very many did and felt no sense of embarrassment.

And if the women danced, the men got drunk, throwing off, for that one night only, 6 years of anxiety, and reclaiming for a few hours the personal freedom to act irresponsibly. The local police force kept well away, the officers of the Home Guard chose not to be on hand, and so, when someone who had probably watched too many American B movies thought it would be a good idea to fire volleys of shots into the night sky, nobody spoke against the plan, and it was carried out with noisy gusto.

Miraculously no one was hurt, friendly fire claimed no victims, and in the morning, with heads as thick as railway sleepers, shame facedly the men returned their weapons to the armoury; except that two had been lost in the excesses of the night before and could not be located.

Efforts were made to find the guns of course, but the local officers were terrified that news that rifles had gone missing would reach the ears of Area Command, and of the trouble they would be in from that fact, so it was all very low key. When no success ensued, the assumption was made that the rifles had probably found their way into the canal, and were thus effectively decommissioned, or failing that were lying rusting in a ditch to become historical remains in some distant millennium. A story was concocted involving a fire in a barn, the rescuing of animals necessitating the laying down of arms to carry out livestock, a sudden explosion as a jerry can containing petrol burst in the heat and the destruction of the building and the weapons inside it that followed on from that disaster.

Nobody checked, nobody asked questions; it was in everybody's interest to remain a secret, but of course the story wasn't true.

Propped up inside my grandmother's coal shed one weapon was found. She couldn't make up her mind what to do. She was already regretting some of her actions from the previous night, and the thought struck her if she went to the police to hand in the rifle questions would inevitably be asked as to how it got there. Tongues might start to wag. Had one of the younger members of the Home Guard, fuelled by alcohol spent a night of passion with the householder? It was ridiculous of course. Even as a child I recognised that my reluctant guardian was a sterile asexual emaciated hag, incapable of arousing the tiniest spark of excitement, even in the most desperate of men, but perhaps in a time of war insanity takes hold, and even the most preposterous of stories gain credibility.

Thinking that her personal charms might be a million times greater than they actually were, she panicked. To maintain her reputation, to avoid even the slightest whiff of scandal she removed the rifle to the safety of her wardrobe, and there she kept it hidden until James returned. He would know what to do. He would advise her on the right course of action to follow.

"It's too late to do anything now Mum, just keep it locked away. There's a Red Peril just over the horizon, and Stalin will be ten times worse than Hitler. Who knows, we may yet need to defend ourselves against a foreign invader.

She believed his ill-informed utterances and heeded his advice, and even was pleased when somehow he acquired live ammunition for the weapon. The ludicrousness of a feeble old witch confronting a Russian tank with an ancient rifle was entirely lost on her. I should thank God that I apparently got my mental faculties from my father; I'm sure as hell they didn't pass down the female line.

The day the doctor pronounced her dead, before any of the self-important social workers or interfering do-gooders who so repelled me, as I have already said, came to take charge of the situation and dictate to me how I should live my life and make unilateral decisions about what should happen to her property, I entered her bedroom and removed both guns from her wardrobe. Her clothes smelled of mothballs, and when I touched them inadvertently, whilst reaching into the wardrobe's deepest recesses to seize the rifle, my skin felt the sting of nettles and it seemed to me that the very fabric of her dresses were steeped in poison. Had it not been for the fact that I didn't know how long I would be left on my own before unwanted intruders arrived, and that I had to get the weapons safe, I would gladly have set fire to her rags and burned down the house and every memory in it.

I have kept them hidden now for more than 40 years, but from time to time their hiding place has changed. I have made sure that they were dry and that the mechanisms were well oiled and free from rust. Wrapped in blankets they slept a deep and peaceful sleep, but finally the time came for them to be raised from their slumbers. The moment was right, the consequences of brutal disregard for anyone's feeling except their own are now clear. My long march through the country of Despair is nearly done and soon it will come to a shattering conclusion. Along the way I have seen Hope die, not a merciful quick death, but agonisingly slowly, like a patient riddled with cancer, it has dragged itself towards a painful end. The bony fingers of Resentment have gripped my throat and wrung every drop of human emotion from my brain, their jagged nails piercing my skin, seeking to draw blood. To prise them from my neck before they kill me, I needed the remedy of Revenge.

Planning and then carrying out a first act of extermination has loosened their hold upon me, and I find that I can breathe more freely. What happened in one sleepy Derbyshire village is just the beginning, but what a beginning it was! A death sentence set against a pageant of history, witnessed by a multitude of little people, stunned into silence by the brutality of the act; from Derbyshire to Dubai, from Castleton to Canberra the story has made headlines across the globe

The myth of Ye Olde England has been exploded. Bloody reality has usurped whimsical fantasy. The first chapter in a new narrative has been published, and when the story is complete it will shock the world and bring me closure; but that is not the point. Guilty men and women will have been punished for their sins. Not directly, that would have been too merciful an outcome, but they will have seen people who are dear to them destroyed in very public ways. At first they will not know why the innocent had to suffer, but the reason will be ultimately revealed, and they will then have to live with the knowledge that it was their crimes that condemned their loved ones to become human sacrifices.

Nobody paid attention to a scruffy old bloke walking a dog on an exposed hillside. Nobody noticed him drop down behind a wall to seek out the weapon he had previously concealed under a heap of fallen stones. Not one person saw him point the rifle at the church tower, or witness the remarkable steadiness of his aim. I knew that I had just one chance to make my plan succeed, but I never doubted that I would hit the target. I did however worry that I might mistime the shot and that my victim would fall backward onto the tower, which would have entirely spoilt the visual impact of the scene; but fortune favours the brave, and everything worked out to perfection.

As he bent over to grab that ridiculous cage of flowers, his weight was well forward from the parapet. He thought it didn't matter because he had gripped a pinnacle with his left hand, but when the bullet struck his instinctive reaction was to release his hold, and when he did so Isaac Newton was yet again proved right. All eyes were fixed on the falling body. I ducked further behind the wall and, taking the weapon with me, crawled along its length for more than a quarter of a mile before hiding it once more, this time under a pile of old fence posts which were rotting away in a corner of the field. From there I made my way home, blending in with the crowds of people escaping from the drama that had just unfolded; I left the dog to make its own way home, not caring if it made it or it didn't. The crying of the children was music to my ears. I hope to hear this lament many more times before the next twelve months have passed; it is a sound I shall never tire of listening to.

CHAPTER SEVEN

Detective Inspector Hobson's office at Burrdale Police Station was universally referred to as "The Broom Cupboard" because of its less than generous size. Just big enough to shoe horn in a small desk and office chair, 2 fairly uncomfortable padded seats, a battered grey filing cabinet and a small wall mounted bookcase, it didn't offer its usual occupant much by way of luxury. Apart from the PC and monitor on the D.I.'s desk it would have looked familiar to any stray ghost from the 1940's seeking to deliver to a senior officer a report on the activities of "Fifth Columnists" or the illicit trading of "Black Marketeers"

Not that this small room was any indication of lack of status or esteem. All the rooms at Burrdale police station were economically proportioned; even the office of Sub-Divisional Commander Chief Inspector Martin Mullis was barely big enough to swing a cat, unless a very small Manx kitten was selected and some clever way was devised of hanging on to its non-existent tail prior to aerially rotating it around the room. Over the years many complaints had been made about the lack of facilities, and from time to time plans had been drawn up for large extensions to be built, but for one reason or another, usually cost, all had ultimately come to nothing. A new plan was now on the table. Centralisation was the name of the game; the writing was on the cell wall for Burrdale nick and in five years time nobody could feel confident that it would still exist.

D.S. Pete Bennett knocked on the door as he entered the small office, but not until he was halfway into the room. If it was inconvenient the D.I. would tell him to "Get lost until later". The two men got on well together; Hobson wasn't obsessed with his own importance and enjoyed banter with the lanky detective sergeant; both men liked and respected each other, and each knew that when the job demanded 100% commitment to the task in hand there would be no shortfall in the degree of effort each would expend to try to get a just result.

Hobson looked up as his most experienced detective breezed into the room.

"Jesus! Don't you ever knock properly Pete? What if you'd found a half-naked Big Rita draped across my desk?

"She wouldn't fit in here Gov; little Tracey the typist might have been a possibility, but given the fact that you've already bagged the best looking girl in town, I was reasonably confident that I wouldn't walk in and find you shagging the office bike".

"Point taken Pete. I've actually just been reading the report on the bullet that killed Adam Wallington and I've got a question for you. You live locally. What's radio reception like in Castleton?"

"Not brilliant: but there are worse places in Derbyshire, why do you ask?"

"Because I don't think some people in the Castleton area can have heard the broadcast on the BBC."

"What broadcast was that?" asked Bennett perplexed, "I've got no idea what you're talking about."

"You know. The one in 1945 when Mr Churchill told the nation that we'd thumped the Nazis and that after nearly 6 years of warfare, hostilities in Europe were finally over."

The look on Pete Bennett's face was one of incredulity.

"The best thing you can do Gov is to find a quiet room, have a lie down, and keep taking the Happy Pills."

"I don't need to do that. It's this report that's got me thinking. The clever lads at the Firearms Lab have discovered that the bullet that sliced Adam Wallington's heart in two is probably about 60 years old and that a World War II British Army issue rifle must have been the weapon of choice."

"Not the type of firearm that features large in today's crime reports is it Gov? I can't remember the last time I read about a professional hitman reaching for his trusty Lee Enfield to take out his unsuspecting victim."

"Neither can I. I suspect it was a good few years before I was born so I think it's bloody strange and, although I know this sounds completely bizarre, I'm wondering if it is remotely possible that the assassin could be roughly the same vintage as the rifle."

"I don't see how that could be possible. We know that the shot was fired from the hillside below the castle. It's an undeniable fact that there were several hundred people in the village square. Nobody saw anybody running away, and for Christ's sake how quickly could a octogenarian sniper leg it in any event?"

"You're absolutely right as usual Pete, but in one sense I think you're also wrong on one important point. You poured scorn on the idea of our killer being a sniper, but I think that is exactly what he was. He only needed one shot to complete his task, which to me indicates he is an outstanding marksman. He's got nothing wrong with his eyesight, and he certainly ain't suffering from Parkinson's or any nervous tick, so I have to concede that we're not likely to be looking for an 80+ year old Rambo, but I'm sure our killer isn't young, and I do think his choice of weapon is significant. All this is pure conjecture of course, and it could be he used this rifle because that was the one choice open to him, but in my mind I see a ceremonial sword being unsheathed and then being put to good use before a multitude of worshippers."

"The priest at the altar sacrificing a first born child, I think you been watching too many old films on telly, but funnily enough I can also see exactly where you're coming from. Like you, I think what happened in the churchyard in Castleton was a carefully planned and impeccably staged piece of street theatre."

Both men gained a considerable degree of re-assurance from the fact that there was a high degree of consensus between them, but both would have been the first to admit that supposition, conjecture and theory counted for very little and that hard evidence was the only thing that mattered, and that commodity was in very short supply.

Yet, despite that firmly held belief, when Detective Inspector Hobson and Detective Sergeant Bennett entered the Incident Room, examples of evidence were everywhere to be seen. Photographs of the victim and the crime scene filled an entire notice board, and large photographs of the opposite hillside, pin pointing places from which the fatal shot could have been fired took up most of a second notice board. Careful calculations had been made by experts; the trajectory of the bullet had been meticulously worked out, and it was beyond doubt that much of what was on display would form an important part of any prosecution case that might subsequently be brought.

And of course there was much more. It was a fact that eye witnesses to the shooting itself were extremely thin on the ground, very few people had been looking away from the church tower at the time of the shot. Two couples thought they recalled a man walking his dog across the slope below the castle, but neither of them could remember anything about his appearance. About the dog's appearance there was a degree of certainty. "It was a black and white Border Collie, we're pretty sure about that," said a middle aged couple from Nantwich; "Our daughter Tracey once got bitten by one when we were out walking. Nasty little dogs! We've never trusted 'em since. What type of beast snaps at a child just because she pulls its tail?"

A very sensible one, thought the officer taking the statement; wisely he chose not to share his view with the witnesses.

"A flippin Border Collie! How many of those to the square mile do you get in this part of Derbyshire?" grumbled D.I.

Hobson. "It will be like looking for a needle in a bloomin haystack, and probably to no good effect; I've never yet come across a killer who has combined taking a life with giving Fido his early evening constitutional."

"Bess," said D.S. Bennett, "it'll be called "Bess", no-one calls a Border Collie "Fido".

But if nobody saw the man who fired the gun, a great many people knew the victim. It came as no great surprise that members of his close family were effusive in his praise; that was nearly always the case. Mark Hobson remembered the case of a sadistic pervert, who ended up being convicted on 16 counts of Rape on 5 different little girls, all aged under 12, who had been portrayed by his immediate family as the embodiment of all things pure and good, and a certain candidate for canonisation by a future Pope; and such misjudgements of character were all too common.

"Even when evil stares them in the face, some people are so fucking blinkered that they can't see the wickedness in front of them, despite the fact that it would be obvious to any half-witted moron that what they're looking at is a sadistic piece of shit," D.S. Bennett had said at the time, appalled by the wilful refusal of the rapist's family members to recognise the truth.

The thing that did surprise the two officers was the extent to which people who were not at all well-disposed to the Wallington family exempted Adam from their general condemnation.

"His granddad is the biggest arsehole under the sun. He's always thought he can get away with anything; very liberal with his promises, utterly useless at keeping any of them. Bad breeding stock generally leads to bad progeny but somehow that lad turned out well despite his ancestry."

"His father's always been a total waste of space, virtually everything he's done he's messed up, I could never understand what Mary saw in him, and his grandfather Michael is an arrogant pig. He's the most selfish man I've ever met. He never thinks of anybody but himself. He believes he's so witty and so clever, and even at his age he thinks that he's God's gift to women. He makes my flesh creep; a geriatric Peter Pan, without a single responsible bone in his body. I tell you I was distraught when our Jenny announced that Adam Wallington was her new boyfriend. But he couldn't have been nicer, he was considerate, kind, loving and gentle; I was very sad when she broke it off with him. He was gutted, I could see that, but it's a terribly dated thing to say in the 21st century, he behaved like a complete gentleman. I never thought I would shed a tear for any member of the Wallington family, but I wept buckets when I heard that Adam was dead."

"They say "like father like son", but in Adam Wallington's case nothing could be further from the truth. It's as if common sense and decency skipped two generations and then landed fairly and squarely on the shoulders of young Adam. Why he had to be the one who was taken from us I can't begin to understand. There isn't any justice when good kids are gunned down and old bastards like his granddad go on forever and ever."

And those comments were just a few amongst many. Nearly everyone in Castleton had a tale to tell about Adam. His former teachers, his school friends, his neighbours, and even casual acquaintances all sang his praises with a sincerity that Mark Hobson and Peter Bennett found compelling.

"The lad doesn't seem to have had an enemy in the world," said Hobson, "and yet he's been publically gunned down in front of a great crowd of people. There has to be a reason for that. Surely there has to be a dark side; nobody could be as perfect as people say he was."

"Maybe not," replied D.S. Bennett, "but you are dealing with witnesses who we would normally regard as being truthful, law-abiding, honest and hard-working. I personally will be extremely surprised if we find anything at all to tarnish the reputation of this particular golden boy."

CHAPTER EIGHT

For the first time in years the sun that had smiled on the Peak District over the late Spring Bank Holiday weekend had not then fled into hiding at the start of June to be replaced by the usual cool and damp weather that normally heralded the onset of a Derbyshire summer, but instead it had lingered happily for the whole month. In July it had continued to show a marked reluctance to depart; even the advent of the long school holidays hadn't issued in a change to cold monsoon conditions, and for the foreseeable future the barometer seemed to be set fair. If the hot spell persisted for much longer hose pipe bans would become the order of the day. Already the grouse moors above Glossop had been on fire, the hills around Buxton were tinder dry; every day that passed without rain heightened the risk of imminent calamity; everything it seemed had a price, and beautiful summer weather potentially came at a high cost.

The regulars at The Royal Albert were certainly feeling the heat, primarily because the extension being built at the back of the public house had for the time being taken from them the ability to fling open the rear doors to allow air to rush into the small public bar. In due course the pallets of bricks stacked against the existing wall would become empty, and the obstruction to the doorway would be gone, but until the brickies had completed their task the situation wasn't going to change. The restaurant and lounge bars were unaffected by the construction work being carried on outside, but this was little comfort to the pub's darts and domino players.

Pub games were not wanted in the smarter parts of the inn; they had to be restricted to the hot and sticky back bar, and as temperatures soared, the tempers of the players became increasingly frayed. Prior to the start of the season, knowing that building work would cause disruption, there had been some debate about whether a team should be entered in the Summer "Darts and Doms" league. The vote had been very much in favour of participating: for most of the middle aged men who made up the majority of the players, the thought of not having a bolt hole to run to on a Monday night to escape the eagle-eyed suspicion of watchful wives was a loss they couldn't begin to contemplate. Now some of these men were beginning to believe that they had made a bad choice. The season was however nearly half over, the teams kept chalking up unexpected wins, loyalty to the cause dictated no one should jump ship at such a critical stage of the competition.

"I've had enough of this blasted heat," moaned Raymond Baker, a plasterer by trade and also a volunteer fireman, "I've been called out 3 times in the last 10 days to tackle fires on Kinder, and I'm just about done in. Two of them were definitely started deliberately. What is it about hot weather that makes fucking lunatics start fires?"

"It's the same thing that sparks off riots in the inner cities," said Alan Nadin, a recently retired police officer. "Have you noticed that you don't get many public order situations when there's a cold wind howling and it's chucking it down with rain?"

"I wish it'd chuck down with rain tomorrow; it would make my life a great deal easier."

"The folks organising Buxton Festival wouldn't necessarily agree with you Ray," countered Bill Adamson who owned a hardware shop, "They say the fine weather is causing record attendances."

"They've not got to work in it. They don't know what life's like in the real world. There's a hell of a lot more to it than putting on obscure operas that nobody round here have even heard of. It's bloody elitism in my view. People come from all over the country to listen to stuff that hasn't been performed for centuries, and there has to be a bloody good reason for that. Its folk saying look at me, *I've got taste not like the rest of you ignorant shits*, but I bet you 95% of the stuck up bastards haven't actually got a bleedin' clue about what the hell is going on on stage."

"It's not only stuck up bastards who attend the festival Ray. Lots of ordinary people do. My wife Jackie is going to an afternoon talk by Edward Cartwright, and she's certainly not stuck up, and I think a lot of other people from round here will be doing the same thing."

"Local boy made good eh? A scrawny kid from Dove Holes somehow gets lucky and finds himself at RADA. He gets a bit part in a T.V. mini-series: by chance he's spotted by an American film director who is looking for a nerdy Englishman to play a particular role. For some bizarre reason, totally unrelated to merit, the film is an overnight success. Little Eddie becomes big in America and then one day surprises everyone by showing the world that he can string a few sentences together without the aid of a script writer. He puts pen to paper, writes a hundred thousand words of drivel and comes up with a best seller. And now he's back home lording over the rest of us, but some people remember what a prat he was in his youth. He's cornered the market in crap that's for sure and he's made an absolute fortune along the way: I can't understand what anybody sees in him."

"He's not that bad Ray, but in any event you're not part of his target audience, His stuff is aimed at middle aged housewives looking for a bit of romance. The most romantic thing you've ever done is buy your missus a washing up bowl for a Valentine's Day present."

"The old one was buggered, it was leaking badly, I couldn't have her wasting hot water could I now Alan?"

"It's not just middle aged housewives who think he's great: a lot of teenage boys and girls think so too, or at least that's what my niece Penny tells me; she's going to interview him on Wednesday for *Look North West*. If the weather stays like it is I think she'll do the interview outdoors, probably just outside the Opera House to emphasise that he is part of the festival. She's quite nervous about it, she's only just started with the BBC. If the viewing public take to her then she'll be well in, but if they don't...."

"She'll be fine Bill," said Alan Nadin, "She's a pretty girl with lots of personality, what's not to like about her?"

"I hope so Alan, it's what she always wanted, she takes after her Granny in that respect, and maybe if she gets lucky she might end up with a halfway decent career."

"And what does her Nana think about it all?"

"It's quite hard to say Alan. She's pretty frail nowadays, and she may be showing early signs of dementia. I think there's a lot of pride, but there's also a little sadness. Her life in the spotlight was quite short lived; when she became pregnant with Penny's dad that was it. You couldn't have both a career and a family in those days, so her happiness at her grandchild's success is tinged with a little bit of jealousy."

Who was it said "knowledge is power"? I have no idea, but whoever it was he had a point. Without knowledge we are feeble, with facts at our disposal we are empowered. Good teachers disseminate knowledge, bad teachers deal in second hand information. Life is the greatest teacher of all, and death is the greatest learning tool. Long ago I learnt Life's most important lesson; I learnt from the bible to know my enemies. I know them very well. I think about them constantly but, like lambs awaiting slaughter grazing in the field, they have no thoughts about what lies ahead and certainly they have no memories of me.

Who needs knowledge most? Is it the surgeon performing open heart surgery, or the scientist trying to discover a cure for cancer? Maybe you think it is the lawyer trying to save an innocent man from the gallows or the general preparing his bloody battle plan; but you would be wrong. Knowledge is needed most by the blackmailer and the gambler; charlatans and rogues cannot survive without it; all of these would drown in a sea of ignorance, but voyaging on an ocean of enlightenment they sail supreme.

I heard the prattle in the public house and it pleased me to hear what was said. Edward Cartwright, "The High Peak Heartthrob", is to grace us with his presence. That fact I already knew, but to discover he intends to stand in a sunlit square and share with his adoring public the wisdom of his years, that piece of information set my brain on fire. The loud mouthed fireman, for all his stupidity, was right about our prodigal son. He was weird as a child, a skinny pathetic youth who thought himself above the common herd. Even innumerable smacks across the face could not dent his belief in himself, and behind him every step of the way was his adoring mother. She called the pupils in the village school "animals", she blamed the teachers for not protecting her precious son, her constant bleating to the local newspaper did nothing to improve his popularity, but ordinary kids were made to suffer as a consequence. Had he been born a halfwit or a cripple what happened to him would have been cruel and undeserved, but because she shouted from the roof tops that he was "special" and "uniquely gifted" she guaranteed that he would be mocked and verbally abused by the sons and daughters of quarrymen and farm labourers. A little humility could have made a huge difference, but she, like so many besotted women I have known, was incapable of showing humility so far as her offspring was concerned. The blinkers that once limited my grandmother's vision when she looked upon my Uncle James were worn by Edward's mother, and no doubt will be handed down the generations to every mother of a son.

Maybe isolation caused him to become an actor; reality was perhaps too hard for him to accept, yet had he not been so smugly self-obsessed it could have been a different story. Self –obsession is a cardinal sin, it ruins lives: years ago I watched a heartless woman destroy a man in order to follow her own over riding ambition.

When he is interviewed on Wednesday it will be the first time in 15 years that he has returned to his roots; the lure of money is probably the reason why he has come, although he could be intending to tell the world how badly he was treated to help publicise a new work of fiction. He may condemn for all time his place of birth, and if he does then the bitterness which will be created will do me no harm. But I suspect a different intent. I think he wants to shine like Christ in a medieval painting standing on high while lesser mortals pay homage to him. Whatever is his aim I can promise you that when he talks to the girl in two days' time millions of people worldwide will hear him speak and then watch in disbelief as a small but indelible piece of history takes place before their eyes.

CHAPTER NINE

Frank Oakes stood transfixed, his three dogs sitting obediently by his side. Why their master came here day after day they didn't know, it offered no sport for them, but they waited until he signalled that it was time to move on. His solitary vigil had become routine, and even the noises of the diggers and of crashing masonry no longer disturbed the animals, but every noise and crack and rumble seemed to make the man who fed and cared for them shake with anger.

He had once felt so differently, and his pleasure at having money had been immense, but recently something deep inside him had changed. He hadn't become a socialist, he despised any belief that stifled ambition and which tinkered with the mechanics of society. There were always winners and so there were always losers. Ability was not shared out equally amongst people, and if you had a special talent or skill or drive it was only right that you should succeed and enjoy the rewards of your success. If some people wasted their opportunities, making themselves unemployable and sentencing themselves to lives on benefit, then chose to squander state handouts to finance drug or alcohol addiction why should responsible hard working citizens have to pick up the tab for their insane decisions? But flaunting one's prosperity, that was another matter and, when money was used destructively, that was wrong. It caused heartache and distress, and right now the ache his heart felt was almost unbearable.

When his parents had sold the farm he had rejoiced. A yoke of servitude had been lifted from his shoulders, the need to follow in the footsteps of his father and his grandfather had been removed; a hard life of toil governed by the weather and the seasons had been avoided; and as a family they had lived well on the proceeds of the sale.

Money had allowed him to pursue his own interests. It had financed his time at university, and given him a spending power far greater than that of the average student. He had been young, carefree and rich, and for decades thereafter he had regarded his student years as the happiest days of his life.

The little antique shop he had established in the late 1970's to put his book learned knowledge to practical use had flourished, and at the height of the Thatcher boom he had made enormous profits. Even the leaner times he had experienced since then had been far less extreme than for many of his contemporaries, and never once when there had been a downturn had the litmus paper of his politics turned from blue to red.

What had changed however was his view of the past. Over time nostalgia for his childhood years had unexpectedly wormed its way back into his sub-consciousness. For months before the terrible events he had witnessed had begun his mind had been drawn back to the solid 18th Century farmhouse that had been his home for the first 17 years of his life. Sometimes the smell of a log fire would awaken his dormant senses and he would be transported back to the old fashioned kitchen where all his meals had been eaten seated at a heavy oak table. He remembered the smell of wet dogs and drying coats impregnated with the aromas of the cattle sheds, and although the perfume wasn't sweet, there was something surprisingly wholesome about the scent. He heard the logs crackle in the grate, and saw the flames illuminating the horse brasses that hung on leather straps on each side of the mantelpiece. Over the fireplace, on two hooks screwed into a rugged beam he remembered his father's shotgun and the strict orders from his mum and dad never to touch it, and the excitement he felt the first time his father let him come shooting with him, and the thrill and the guilt he felt when he killed his first rabbit. As he daydreamed he would find his mouth salivating and the glorious smells of baking pastry and fresh made bread would overwhelm his senses and the taste of fresh picked raspberries and cream straight from the cow would make him weep for joy. And now it was all gone.

The man from Accrington who had made countless millions by inventing and marketing computer games had been an unknown quantity when he attended the auction, but he had blown every other potential purchaser out of the water. Old money based on property values and on extravagant salaries had turned out to be no match for the monster that is the World Wide Web; and so a man with no breeding and no taste and without an ounce of empathy for the traditional values of the countryside had become a rural landowner. The farm house, which had already been turned into a luxury £2,000,000 dwelling by an intervening owner who had converted the original building into a dream home to satisfy the desires of any overpaid footballer's wife by adding 3 bedrooms, a huge games room and a kitchen fit for a 21st century palace, he regarded as a hovel. He had grandiose plans for a 10 bedroom mock Georgian mansion and so the whole site had to be cleared. Everything was reduced to rubble. The new kitchen extension with its granite worktops, Canadian Oak units, incredibly expensive floor tiles and its Aga still in situ was smashed to pieces by a wrecking ball; and even though Oakes had no love for the modern additions that had cheapened the integrity of his former home he had been appalled at the destruction he had witnessed.

When the main part of the centuries old brick farmhouse suffered a similar fate he had been physically sick and when the farm buildings were attacked he felt dispossessed. His roots were being ripped from the ground by an alien invader; his family history was being ruthlessly expunged. Had he had with him an assault rifle he would have shot, without hesitation, the men destroying his past, although the person he really hated was the arrogant insensitive sod who had commissioned this carnage and, had he been able to lay hands on him, his rage was so great that he would have gouged out his eyes with his bare hands before tearing him limb from limb.

But he had no firearm and no means of delivering vengeance so, as he had done every single day since the workmen had arrived on site, he had stood on the public footpath that ran through fields at the side of the farmstead, and stared, and taken photographs and silently called the new owner and his insensitive Storm Troopers every bitter, unkind name his mind could dredge up from the gutters of obscenity.

His presence had eventually registered itself on the minds of the workmen. They had asked him what he was doing. He hadn't replied. His silence had unnerved them. They told him to "Clear off," and once a hand had been raised. He had warned his potential attacker that he had a tape recorder hidden in his pocket and that every word he had said had been recorded. He had threatened him with court action if he even laid one finger upon him. Up until that moment the claim he made was false, but thereafter he had always been equipped to record any insulting comment that might be directed towards him.

The incident had been reported back up the chain of command, and on the next day the owner himself had blustered onto the scene.

"Are you some sort of fucking weirdo? What are you doing here day after day in all sorts of bloody awful weather? You're a fucking lunatic. You're upsetting my men. Now just fuck off before I call the police."

"I'm on a public footpath; I've got every right to be here. I belong on this land, you don't. You can't bully me. I intend to come here every day. When your fantasy mansion is complete and you and your family and your mega rich friends are enjoying a barbecue or splashing about in your king sized swimming pool I'll be the spectre at the feast. You think you can buy the world with money, but you can't buy happiness. One day everything you stand for will crumble into dust, then Nature will cleanse this site of every excrescence you have heaped upon it."

It had felt good to utter those words, and everything he had said he had meant, but it had been a mistake. Men like the millionaire from Accrington treat the Law as a commodity. The solicitor's letter he had received had accused him of harassment and of besetting their client's property. It demanded that he cease immediately or face a court injunction. He had taken his own legal advice, and had been appalled to discover that every action that was threatened would be supported by the court.

It was a terrible realisation, and after it he had felt defeated. The enormity of the injustice haunted him; he could talk of nothing else. He became a bore; everyone in the Royal Albert would groan when he set off at a gallop to complain about the evil of excess.

"Your family brought it on themselves Frank. Your mum and dad were happy to sell up and to make a huge profit, and I don't think they'd have done that if you had expressed a desire to stay put. You could have hung onto your legacy, instead you all plumped for the easy life. You can't blame anybody else. A lot of people in here think you're damned lucky, and certainly I for one would gladly swap bank balances with you."

"It's not about money Bill, it's about having all your childhood memories torn down. You can point out to your kids the house where you were born and one day they may point out to their kids the house where granddad was born;

I can't do that. There's nothing left for me to show my kids. It's like I never existed, I feel cheated out of my best memories."

"You cheated yourself Frank, or your mum and dad cheated you if they sold against your wishes, but can we change the bloody record, we're all sick to death of hearing about your problems."

He stopped going to the pub after that. He stayed at home, to the annoyance of his wife and he fantasised about seeking revenge. When he slept at night and sleep didn't come easy now, he dreamt about retribution and redemption. In dreams he undid the damage that had been caused; in dreams he humiliated the odious entrepreneur who had become his Nemesis; in dreams he returned everything to the way it had been before; but dreams don't have muscles and sinews with which to reconstruct buildings, or physically change history, so Accrington's computer games tycoon had continued undaunted with his project to create a tasteless pseudo stately home, no longer routinely observed by a bitter, angry man.

Only two people had offered him comfort. One was Mary Wallington, who seemed to understand the extent to which he was grieving, and he had looked forward to talking to her, but she was now totally absorbed by her own grief for her son and was poor company. Each meeting between them now only served to exacerbate both their sadness, and hence contact between them had come to an unhappy end.

The second person who appeared to have some inkling of the depth of his misery was his part time gardener, Tim Bradley, a shy man who lacked confidence, but with a flair for gardening, who nurtured his plants and seeds with true devotion. He understood that bushes and shrubs needed to be well dug in, and in a simplistic view of life knew people should be well dug in too, although he had neither wife nor children to give him strength and bind him to one place. In a strange way, since the demolition of the farm Oakes viewed him as a kindred spirit. The thought did not please him; Tim was too gentle and too diffident for his taste, but at least he seemed to feel his pain, and to understand that no amount of being told to "pull yourself together man" could change, in any way, the degree of anguish that he felt. As cold winter had metamorphosed into sizzling spring and baking summer his mood had become ever more disturbed.

CHAPTER TEN

"Over 200 people spoken to, over 200 ingenious theories, and we're still no nearer discovering a motive. Most victims we come across have got something about 'em which explains why they were killed but with Adam Wallington there's nothing at all. If some enterprising individual with time on his hands had carried out a poll to discover who was the most undeserving person to experience premature violent death Adam Wallington would have topped his list by a country mile; the lad seems to have been a saint, everybody loved him; nobody has a word to say against him."

"And yet he's the one who is no longer with us, and his death was a dramatic public spectacle. Whoever killed him was prepared to run enormous risks to carry out a public execution that speaks to me of intense hatred, and seems totally at odds with the accepted wisdom that Adam was a thoroughly likeable decent kid."

"I agree Gov, but that's the situation we're in. Isn't it fucking ironical that in the one case where all sections of the public are bending over backwards to help the police, not a bit of hard evidence has been forthcoming."

"It's the way of the world Pete. Even when we thought we'd had a bit of a lead on the Border Collie, it turned out to be nothing. The local men whose names we were given, who regularly walk their dogs in the evening both had impeccable alibis and, in any event, when was the last time in your recollection when a J.P. or a District Judge last stood in the dock indicted for murder?"

"Doctors can turn out to be killers, why not lawyers and court officials?"

"No reason at all, but they don't do it without a reason, and a reason is the one thing we patently don't have."

Detective Inspector Mark Hobson and Detective Sergeant Pete Bennett were reviewing the evidence obtained to date in respect of the "Castleton Garland" murder and finding it sadly lacking. For over an hour they had sifted through statements and reports obtained so far in the hope that they might spot something that had been overlooked, but to no discernible effect.

"There isn't any good news is there Gov?" moaned the increasingly frustrated detective sergeant.

"Not yet Pete, but on the plus side we haven't had another killing, and when this murder first took place I was more than a little afraid that it might be a prelude to a killing spree."

"There's still time for that, tomorrow we could be scraping up corpses from the pavement like rotten fruit on a windy autumn day."

"You're not helping me feel any more relaxed Pete. There could be mayhem tomorrow, but perhaps every day that passes without incident makes that possibility a little more remote."

***

Penny Adamson had done her research, far more than was strictly necessary to carry out a four minute on screen interview with the movie star cum author she was about to meet. She knew that she would not be able to use 99% of what she had read, and that the best she could hope for was a flashing of unnaturally white teeth, a plethora of platitudes about a "quaint little theatre", shameless plugging of his new book and perhaps some totally sanitised reminiscences of an idyllic childhood in sleepy Derbyshire; but it hadn't been like that. She would have much preferred to play the part of a ruthless investigative journalist, and strip away the candy coated myth from an altogether more bitter life, but that was not her remit, and if she wanted to make it big on T.V. she would have to deliver just what the producer wanted. If he had told her to carry out the interview dressed in a golden bikini, whilst being sprayed with the famous Buxton Water she would have cheerfully done as she was told, but inside it rankled that she couldn't show the viewing public that she was more than just a "trolley dolly of the airways" and that she had hidden depth. She had toyed with the idea of dropping one mildly uncomfortable question into the mix to see what would come from it, but if Edward Cartwright took exception to anything she said he would in all probability terminate the interview immediately, and simply turn on his heels and walk away. The producer would be incandescent, he would scream at her like a demented banshee telling her that she'd "blown it", and that would be the end of her career before it had properly begun. She was determined that that wouldn't happen.

The man she was about to allow to polish his own ego had been a snivelling wimp, teased and made fun of by the other children, pushed on by a besotted mother for whom he could do no wrong; but, in fairness to him, helped by a decent brain; this ambitious "mother's boy" had made it all the way to Beverley Hills and become a global phenomenon. She had a much better pedigree. She was popular; she was good looking, with a first class degree in English from Leeds University, and with the benefit of a grandmother who had worked in television at probably the most exciting time in its history. If she played her cards sensibly, and didn't try to get too much too soon, she might become an A List celebrity in her own right. The thought struck her that sometime in the future she could write a book, an autobiography perhaps, or even a novel, and that one day it might be her standing in front of the Frank Matcham designed Opera House, answering lightweight questions from some pretty little wannabee. She looked at the publicity photograph of her famous interviewee; *don't worry little man,* she thought, *your secrets are safe with me.*

Turning her attention to her own appearance, which she scrutinised in great detail, she examined her image in an ornate full length mirror; not a hair was out of place. Her eyes sparkled; her skin was perfect; even the bright sunlight of a July afternoon would not reveal some hidden flaw. The pretty summer dress she had picked to wear flattered every curve of her body. In her head she could hear her Uncle Bill telling his mates in the pub *she looked pretty as a picture, she's going right to the top is that girl,* and she was sure that none of the middle aged men to whom he relayed his opinions would disagree with him. She looked at her watch, it was almost 3 o'clock. Showtime was about to begin.

***

Forward planning, that is always the key. To know what you want and then to work out how best to achieve it, that is the way to succeed. The Castleton Garland ceremony is the same every year so on one level I had plenty of time to plan, but please remember it was only a fortnight before this year's event that I discovered that the Wallington boy would be stood for all to see on top of the church tower. He was always the "who", and the "why" had been set in stone for decades, but the "when" had been extremely difficult. To begin with I had toyed with the idea of ending his life while he played rugby, but with so few people generally watching the matches, such a plan would have failed a crucial test. I had resigned myself to wait until he was the guest, or better yet the best man or groom at a big wedding, but when that would be could not be predicted, and the uncertainty as to whether this would ever happen I found unsettling. Fate, and an old man's bad back gave me the chance I was after, and the rest, as I have a tendency to say is "history."

But history is an ever changing concept, and things yet undreamt of will one day become part of the common psyche. For the second time in a few short weeks I am about to write a new page in one personal history by tearing out many chapters in another. I have a free hand to create and to destroy and I intend to use it well.

I have made my decisions. Some were incredibly easy. I hold the moral high ground, so it is from that vantage point I have to act. Looking down on the world below from the bell tower of a place of worship makes me feel like God and, like him it is from above that my wrath will be visited on the sinner; and is there not an irony to be noted in that the victim and not I has chosen the exact spot upon which a life should end?

The difficult decisions were those relating to small details of my plan. I thought long and hard about how I could gain entry to the tower without being seen. In the end I trusted in human nature and what many might think of as Sod's Law. I realised that to become invisible I had to shine a spotlight upon myself. Try to creep into a room unnoticed and without fail someone will see you and every head will then turn in your direction; sneak down the street in the shadows and you travel with a day glow placard round your neck screaming to every Tom, Dick and Jenny that you meet "Look at me, Look at Me;" conceal yourself behind a mask or by wrapping a scarf around your face and the whole world will take note of your progress. It is inbuilt within every man and woman on the planet to stare at that which they believe is being deliberately hidden from them.

The converse is equally true. The man who enters a room, wearing his egotism like a gaudy cape, seeking to be the centre of attention, is the person everyone tries strenuously to ignore. I have seen groups of friends shuffle into a tight scrum to bar access to some well-known boasting bore. I have witnessed families avert their gaze from punk rockers and from painted Goths, and if later asked to recall who they saw out and about on the street, unless they are prompted otherwise, they will completely forget the sad specimens of humanity who have tried their best to stand out from the common herd.

Everyone needs good fortune, and I was lucky that repairs were being carried out to the fabric of the building, although temporarily in suspension awaiting the allocation of additional funding. Dressed in a Hi-Viz jacket, and wearing a white hard hat, I carried lengths of plastic downspouts and stacked them alongside the door. On my hands I wore rough gloves, ostensibly to protect them from harm, but really to make sure no fingerprints were left. Into one tube I forced a bung, and then slid into it my vintage army rifle, concealing it totally from view. I carried it to the church door and, picking my moment, I slipped unnoticed into the dwelling place of Jesus. Within seconds I was climbing the tower, wedging the doorway to the tower closed behind me so nobody could follow and, discarding my safety jacket and helmet on the stairs so that I would not be seen, I ascended to the gallery. There I waited patiently for my time to come. I had a perfect view. I saw the BBC camera crew arrive. I heard the squeals of adulation, and moments later the idol of the crowd was waving to his adoring fans. An interviewer strode towards their hero, her hand outstretched to meet him. I swear I could hear his heart beating. I picked up my weapon and carefully took aim. My blood was ice; my hands were steady as the rocky crags outside. This was my chance to complete another chapter in this saga of revenge. I did not flinch, I squeezed the trigger gently, making sure I did not jerk the weapon; on the stroke of three o'clock I fired.

CHAPTER ELEVEN

It was Helena who unearthed a possible clue as to the history of the weapon that had been used to send Adam Wallington to a tragically early grave; it wasn't copper bottomed evidence, the police don't usually get that lucky, but it did reveal a potentially productive line of inquiry. It came about because Helena had volunteered to help at Christopher's school, and was discovered purely by chance.

Christopher was way too young of course, but the older children at the primary school were learning a little about life in 1940's Britain. Nothing too gory, no rotting corpses, or mass exterminations or atomic bombs, these revelations would come later when they were in secondary school, but instead an insight into what it was like to grow up at a time when food was rationed, everyone "dug for victory", movement between places was restricted, identity cards had to be carried at all times, and the amount of light on the streets at night depended upon how generous the Moon was inclined to be with her favours.

The children had learned about "evacuees" and "make do and mend", and had been taught some of the playground games from half a century ago. Contrasts had been drawn between then and now, and, in simple terms, it had been explained to them how the freedoms they all took for granted had been hard fought for by their parents and grandparents.

"Community spirit" had been described as being "really important", and the fact that even in times of peril and uncertainty, people had maintained their ability to laugh and to find ways to amuse and entertain themselves had been a constantly recurring theme. The last lesson before the half term break had specifically examined the ecstatic celebration of victory that had spontaneously erupted on V.E. Night. A first-hand account of some of the events that had occurred had been written down 40 years later by one of the members of the Home Guard who had been carried away by the unbridled joy of that momentous occasion. He had set pen to paper to record a personal history to give to his grandchildren so they could understand where their roots lay, and how they had become the people that they had become; part of his narrative had recounted his experiences as a teenager growing up in a world at war. It was in this part of his narrative that a long forgotten secret was revealed.

There was much to admire in what he disclosed, and the way in which men too old or too young to fight still tried to do their bit was almost heroic, but when he recalled what he had done when the BBC told the nation that the war in Europe was over he became shamefaced, admitting in the course of a mad 24 hour period he had got drunk, lost his rifle, and perhaps also his virginity, although of that fact he could not be sure.

"It wasn't just me," he wrote. "I know at least one other chap did the same thing. It was one of the worst offences a soldier could commit, and afterwards I was scared I'd be in big trouble. And I should have been, but fortunately nobody wanted to make a fuss. The officers made up some explanation which satisfied Area Command, they were worried that they could have been accused of dereliction of duty, and given the general euphoria of the time it was far easier for everyone to accept a cobbled together story rather than making waves. I learned a lesson though. I never drank too much again, and I was always careful to look after my property after that. I've tried and tried to remember what I did with it many times since, but my mind's a complete blank. I'm pretty sure I just put it down somewhere and forgot about it. Maybe somebody found it, we'll never know, but it's not an episode I'm proud off. I do know I woke up in a strange bed, lying next to a woman old enough to be my mother, being sick all over the bed sheets, and then being literally thrown out of the house."

Helena had asked if she could copy the relevant pages of the self-penned autobiography, which the school had been more than happy to agree to, and had shown the copy to Mark when she returned home.

"It may be something or nothing Darling," she said to him, "but suppose he's right and somebody did find his gun and decide to keep it. Everybody seems to have been very willing to accept that the missing rifle no longer existed, people stopped looking for it, it would have been an embarrassment if it had been found because then it would be obvious that someone had lied. Is it possible that after nearly 60 years it has emerged and that this is the weapon that was used to murder Adam Wallington?"

"It is Love, it surely is. You've done a brilliant job. Now all you need to do is find a diary containing the confessions of a middle aged *femme fatal*, listing her sexual conquests of drunken adolescents in wartime Derbyshire, and we might be on to a winner."

"No, that's your job" joked Helena, "I'll let you look for geriatric sex kittens, I'll content myself with getting us all some tea."

***

Sex was very much on the mind of Edward Cartwright, although the images his mind was creating were nothing like those that Detective Inspector Mark Hobson had visualised when he thought about the events so vividly described in one man's recollections of the past. The more his brain had tried to decide the real significance of his wife's discovery, the more he had become convinced that from a single and perhaps totally understandable act of carelessness, terrible consequences could now be flowing, despite the fact that more than 50 years had elapsed without anything of note occurring. His mind painted a picture of a nervous youth waking up in a confused state, to find himself lying on a bed alongside a woman 30 or more years his senior. The realisation that in a drunken state he had perhaps allowed himself to encourage her sexual advances, or worse yet had forced his clumsy attempts at sex upon her must have appalled him. Had he even committed rape? Mark Hobson thought this unlikely because in his extremely intoxicated state the chances of the man maintaining an erection must have been nigh on impossible, but the possibility couldn't be completely ruled out. More likely an inability to perform had been a lucky escape for both parties, although it also could have been a cause of frustration to one or the other, or the pair. He had joked with Helena, setting her the task to find a diary, or some piece of written evidence to reveal who this woman was, but as he relaxed in his armchair after the evening meal he had become sure that this was no laughing matter. A soldier, even a naive young member of the Home Guard would not abandon his weapon without cause; a teenager struggling to reach sexual maturity might well put down his gun if enticed into a house by a woman seemingly giving him the chance to cross the Rubicon from boyhood into manhood. This was all fantasy of course, but if anything like that had actually happened that night, it was probable that the woman was a great deal more sober, or at least more used to alcohol than an inexperienced boy struggling to prove himself a man would have been, and could well have seen and remembered exactly what he did with the gun. She could easily have gone back for it and retrieved it as a thing of value, and kept it, or sold it on, and finding who she was could be the start of a paper chase that could lead a person following it across the decades to the present day. Mark Hobson certainly made that journey in his mind and had spent the rest of the evening trying to work out the practical steps that could be taken in the 21st Century to discover her identity.

Edward Cartwright, on the other hand, was wedded to a simple plan, and was not going to let other thoughts get in the way of it. In the States he was what his grandmother in Dove Holes would have called a "Matinee Idol." In simple terms this meant that young girls were in the habit of throwing themselves at him, and he was not in the habit of refusing them. Back in the land of his birth things were different. He seemed to attract just two classes of female, namely pre-pubescent girls who had to be treated as out of bounds, and romantically inclined older women, most of whom got their excitement in life from reading his books, or watching "bodice ripping" yarns on television or at the cinema. The trouble with this second category of British women was that, unlike their American cousins, they did not possess beautifully manicured teeth or expensively coiffured hair and chose to wander in a world of make-believe because they couldn't attract the Heathcliffe, or even the Quasimodo of their dreams.

The girl who was about to interview him was much more to his taste. She sparkled in the July sun, she was bright and lively and intelligent and athletic, and without doubt ticked all the boxes for a one night, or even a one week, stand. He had spoken to her on the phone to arrange details of the interview, and had found she had an appealing voice. There was something particularly attractive about a well-modulated, softly spoken English voice that made most of the American voices he was used to listening to sound strident or superficial or both. Perhaps there was also something of himself that he recognised in her; she was ambitious, as he had always been, and she wanted, like him, to be famous; that put him in the driving seat: if he couldn't charm her to his bed then all his RADA training and his movie acting was worthless, he knew that was not the case. He pondered a little on the best way to play her. He decided that it would look best if he revealed a vulnerable edge, stressing his humble origins and showing how close he sometimes came to being overwhelmed by his success. That strategy had worked before in Los Angeles, there was no reason why it shouldn't work in Buxton.

After the interview he would invite her to take tea with him, such a very British thing to do and if he appeared a little anxious it wouldn't harm his cause. He would ask her how she thought the interview went, it would elevate her status if she was the one giving rather than seeking re-assurance. The predominant emotion he should display on camera should be his delight at being back amongst friends and family: the bitterness with which he one day intended to expose the meanness, stupidity and narrow mindedness of the people who had ruined his childhood was, for the moment, best left unrevealed. If he was nice, she would be putty in his hands and if he floated the idea that a girl like her could easily become a star of American day time T.V., and that he was the man who could pull strings for her, then it was a dead certainty that she would willingly succumb to his desires.

He glanced at his Rolex watch, the time to perform was at hand. He checked his appearance in the mirror and was content with what he saw. If this had been a film premier in New York, Vancouver or Cannes he would have done a lot more, but for regional television in the U.K. it was more than adequate. Knowing that any second the cheers of the crowd would ring in his ears and that his adoring fans would rush forward to try and touch him, he had been assured that none of their sticky hands would ever reach his body; he stepped into the warm sunlight to milk the applause.

CHAPTER TWELVE

The fatal shot rang out exactly at three o'clock. The cheers that had greeted the Hollywood actor had begun to subside. A beautiful young reporter had stepped forward to speak to the star. The television cameras were rolling, and in seconds calls for quiet would be bellowed across the square in front of Buxton Opera House and there would be complete silence, or at the very least extraneous noise would be reduced to an acceptable background level. Then it happened. There was a loud bang, the sound bouncing off the tall buildings next to the Old Hall Hotel and then rebounding off the facade of the Edwardian theatre before fading into nothing. For a split second there was absolute quiet, and then the panic set in. Some of the members of the large crowd started to scream, many others started to cry. Edward Cartwright's face was white as alabaster, his mouth gaped open as if his jaw had become unhinged. Blood splattered his cream Cashmere sweater. At his feet the body of a stunningly beautiful young woman lay bleeding on the pavement. It had taken the blink of an eye to cut short a life filled with so much promise; and all the time the T.V. camera had rolled; the cameraman too shocked to even move.

***

The first report of the murder was radioed into Buxton Police Station less than 60 seconds after the shooting had occurred; the 999 calls took a few more moments to arrive, but certainly, in a very short time indeed, it was known that a major incident had occurred, and that somewhere in town a man with a gun was on the loose.

He had killed once, it was perfectly possible that he could kill again; the public had to be protected; the police had to act quickly to preserve evidence and to restore calm, but at the same time they too needed to be protected, and to be equipped to return fire if they came under attack.

Detective Inspector Hobson was sat in his office telling Detective Sergeant Peter Bennett about the intriguing history that Helena had uncovered and asking him for his thoughts about the significance of these revelations when the news of the murder was received at Burrdale Police Station. The crime was obviously one that had been committed in Buxton, but even from the outset, similarities were being drawn between this death and the recent killing in Castleton. In both cases a single shot had been fired, in both cases the murder had taken place before a large crowd of onlookers, and in both cases the victims were young, intelligent, local people; although there were already suggestions being made in some quarters that the intended victim this time had been a high profile celebrity, and not the little known T.V. reporter who had been in the process of interviewing him. In the course of time, probably in a very short space of time, the apparent link between the two crimes would become substantially stronger than it was at present, or much more tenuous. If the fatal bullet matched the bullet that killed Adam Wallington it would prove almost beyond doubt that the killer of Adam was the same person who had struck with such deadly effect here; if a different weapon had been used it didn't mean that there had to be a different killer, but it made that possibility much more likely. Hobson and Bennett set off immediately to go to the scene of the crime.

They arrived less than 20 minutes after receiving the call. A semblance of order had been restored. Officers in uniform were keeping the crowd well back from the spot where the victim lay. An ambulance was on hand to remove the body after the pathologist had carried out his initial examination. Screens had been erected to afford the deceased a degree of dignity in death and in due course she would be taken away, with proper solemnity, to a place where a post mortem would take place. Armed officers were stationed at various points around the square and nearby buildings were being searched, so far to no good effect. Whoever had carried out this despicable crime had melted away into thin air, leaving nothing behind him except a legacy of eternal sadness for one grieving family.

"There ain't no sodding God is there Pete?" Mark Hobson was fighting with his emotions. "This girl left home this morning thinking that she was on the verge of something big. I've met her family, they were so proud of her, and in an instance she's been snatched away from them. I can't begin to imagine how they'll cope with the grief, and the worst thing is that this wasn't a tragic accident; this shooting was carefully planned and deliberately carried out. It's an act of total lunacy, everybody adored her, and it's bloody unbelievable."

"I never truly thought there was Gov, and horrific events like this confirm my belief, but it could be she wasn't the intended victim. Edward Cartwright I'm told is in the process of packing to go home, we need to put a stop to that little game right away. He believes the bullet was meant for him, he just wants away; and in many ways he does make a more logical target."

"Why's that Pete."

"Well, he's world famous. There are some people round here who resent his success. I've been told a few times since it was known that he was going to attend the festival that he was pretty unpopular when he was at school, and folks round here have long memories. I think the killer had visions of the shooting being broadcast around the world; he probably never thought that the police would seize the tape for evidential purposes so that most of the real dramatic stuff wouldn't be shown on air. I think our killer wanted his Jack Ruby moment, although unlike Jack Ruby he clearly doesn't want to be caught."

"Do you think that it's likely that the animal who butchered this poor girl is the same person who shot Adam Wallington, because if it is then this is not the end. He's got other people in his sights, and until he's caught every public event in the Peak District has got to be treated by the police as a place where murder might happen."

"Why do you say that Gov?"

"Because he needs crowds of people to witness his acts of madness. He's making statements to the world, and he'll keep on making statements until in his own mind he has finished his blood soaked story."

***

"You can't leave at the moment; the British police will want a witness statement from you. You've got to stay here until after they have spoken to you."

"I'm not staying here, and that's final. If they want to talk to me they can fly someone over to Los Angeles and I'll talk to them there in the safety of my own home."

"Just think how that would damage your reputation Edward. The British public won't like it if you just turn and run. A pretty young girl has been murdered for Christ's sake. You owe it to her family to try and help the police. If you scuttle back to the States your name will be mud; you'll be called a coward, the tabloid press will have a field day, and the two million dollars you earned in the U.K. in the last 12 months will dwindle into a pocket full of petty cash." So spoke Edward Cartwright's literary agent, as she tried to persuade the reluctant star to stand his ground.

"I can make that money back in one low budget film. I should never have come here. I hate the place, and I hate the people. One thing is certain; I'll never set foot in Derbyshire again."

The fruitless attempts at persuasion were interrupted by a knock on the hotel bedroom door.

"I'm not talking to anyone." Cartwright screamed at his agent. "Tell whoever it is to get lost." Shaking her head, she left the heroic actor hastily throwing clothes into a suitcase and went to see who it was who wanted to gain admittance. She came back a few minutes later with an envelope in her hand.

"It was the hotel porter with a message for you; maybe this will convince you to change your mind; it was apparently left at the reception desk at shortly before 3pm by a young girl, she said it was urgent, but in all the excitement that then followed he forgot about the note until a few minutes ago"

"Why can't the stupid little bitches leave me alone? You open it and if it's just another starry eyed teenage whore get rid of it; even you can manage to do that without my help. I hate every last one of them. Why do so many ghastly school children think that they can have a part of me?"

"They pay your wages, without them you're nothing!"

"Bullshit," snarled Cartwright. "If you want to keep yourself in a job I suggest you remember what your place is and don't presume to give me any unwanted advice!"

The literary agent did as she was told and opened the letter; as she read it a less than charitable smile flickered across her face.

"I strongly advise you to take a look at this, the writer of this note obviously knows you very well."

Cartwright angrily snatched the piece of paper; as he started to read the words on the page, the colour left his face and his hands began to shake.

"IF YOU ARE ABLE TO READ THIS IT WILL MEAN THAT I HAVE FAILED AND THAT A ONCE IN A LIFETIME OPPORTUNITY HAS BEEN LOST, UNLESS YOUR DEATH ALTHOUGH NOT INSTANANEOUS IS NONE-THE-LESS INEVITABLE GIVEN THE GRAVITY OF YOUR WOUNDS, IN WHICH CASE IT WILL BE GOOD FOR YOU TO KNOW HOW MUCH YOU ARE DESPISED, AND HOW MUCH BETTER THE WORLD WILL BE WITHOUT YOU. TO KNOW THAT YOUR DEATH WILL BE APPLAUDED BY MANY PEOPLE WITH THE SAME ENTHUSIASM THAT AIR-BRAINED BARBIE DOLLS HAVE SHOWN WHEN THEY HAVE SQUEALED THEIR LOVE FOR YOU WILL BE A BITTER PILL TO SWALLOW, AND WITH NO HOPE OF AVOIDING YOUR INEVITABLE FATE THAT MEDICINE WOULD BE THE BEST THAT I COULD PRESCRIBE.

THE WORST THAT COULD BEFALL IS THAT DESPITE ALL MY PLANNING AND MY UNDOUBTED EXPERTISE, I HAVE CONTRIVED TO MISS MY TARGET COMPLETELY AND THAT THE BULLET WITH YOUR NAME WRITTEN ON IT HAS LANDED HARMLESSLY AMONGST THE SHRUBS OR IN THE GUTTER. IF THAT IS WHAT HAS TRANSPIRED THEN NOTHING ABOUT THE EVENTS OF TODAY WILL PRICK YOUR CONSCIENCE, AND LIKE THE SHALLOW PIECE OF SHIT THAT YOU ARE, YOU WILL SIMPLY TRY TO PRETEND THAT TODAY NEVER HAPPENED AND EXPUNGE FROM YOUR MIND THE NARROW ESCAPE THAT YOU HAVE JUST HAD. BUT KNOW THIS, IF YOU DELUDE YOURSELF THAT EVERYTHING IS JUST DANDY YOU WILL LEARN TO YOUR COST THAT THAT

IS VERY FAR FROM THE TRUTH. YOU MUST ALSO UNDERSTAND THAT IF YOU ENTER INTO A STATE OF DENIAL YOU BANISH YOURSELF FOREVER FROM THIS ISLAND. YOU MAY TODAY THINK THAT ROOTS MEAN NOTHING BUT A TIME WILL COME WHEN YOU WILL WANT TO BE BACK HERE TO MOURN A DEATH OR CLAIM AN INHERITANCE. WHEN YOU DO I WILL BE WAITING. TOMORROW, NEXT WEEK, NEXT YEAR I WILL BE A RECEPTION COMMITTEE OF ONE AND I CAN GUARANTEE THAT THEN YOU WILL KEEP YOUR DATE WITH DESTINY.

ALL OTHER OUTCOMES ARE ONES THAT I CAN LIVE WITH, BUT WHETHER YOU CAN BEAR THE STRAIN REMAINS TO BE SEEN, BUT I DOUBT IT. IF I HAVE CAUSED YOU INJURY I PRAY THE PAIN WAS SEVERE AND CONSTANT; IF I HAVE MARKED YOUR SMUG FACE I AM GLAD OF IT. IF BY MISCHANCE AN INNOCENT BYSTANDER, BE IT MAN, WOMAN OR BABE IN ARMS, PERISHED AT THE SCENE THE DIRECT CAUSE OF THAT TRAGEDY IS YOUR EXISTENCE AND THE VILE PERSON YOU HAVE BECOME. THE BLAME FOR THIS DISASTER CAN BE LAID FAIRLY AND SQUARELY AT YOUR DOOR, AND I WILL MAKE IT MY MISSION TO ENSURE THE WORLD KNOWS OF YOUR GUILT.

IT MAY TAKE YOU A LONG TIME, BUT I PROMISE YOU REALISATION WILL COME, AND WHEN IT DOES YOU WILL DISCOVER THAT A CLEAN KILL TODAY WOULD HAVE BEEN THE KINDEST THING THAT COULD HAVE

HAPPENED TO YOU. I HOPE THAT HAS HAPPENED, A FINITE END WOULD HERALD A NEW BEGINNING, BUT SOON I WILL KNOW FOR SURE.

YOU HAVE NO SOUL TO ROT IN HELL, BUT YOU HAVE A MIND THAT CAN DROWN IN ITS OWN FEAR. IF YOU STILL LIVE YOUR HAPPY DAYS ARE OVER, THE NIGHTMARES AND THE SLEEPLESS NIGHTS ARE JUST BEGINNING.

"I knew it, I just knew it. Some maniac is trying to kill me. I want an armed guard, I want to be taken away from this place of bedlam in a bulletproof car with a motorcycle escort and I want to be on a plane to a civilised country in the next 24 hours."

"I thought the U.S.A. was the world leader when it comes to gun crime, are you sure you'll be safe there? Personally I'd prefer to stay and take my chances here," said his agent unsympathetically.

"You're as mad as the rest of them", exploded Cartwright, "Just get on to the police and demand that I have proper protection right away, and make it clear that they're not dealing with some nobody from the council estate. Their task is to safeguard the life of a very important person; if I don't get the level of security I need there will be hell to pay."

"What a surprise!" commented the agent, "while I'm away making phone calls I suggest you don't have a drink of water; the state you're in, you might inadvertently turn it into wine and it wouldn't look good if you ended up pissed before the police arrive."

"Just get it fucking done!" he screamed picking up a magazine from the table and hurling it towards her as she left the room to carry out his instructions.

CHAPTER THIRTEEN

"That note just about proves it, doesn't it Mark?" Detective Chief Superintendent Stan Hardy was sat behind his desk being briefed by Detective Inspector Hobson about the latest developments in the Penny Adamson murder. "The poor girl wasn't the intended victim after all. Does that make it better or worse for the family to cope with do you think? To know that she wasn't hated by someone must be a relief, but on the other hand the fact that she died for no reason whatsoever must make it doubly hard to stomach."

"I don't know, Sir," admitted Hobson, "but I don't know if your initial premise is right either. Forensics have confirmed that the gun that killed Adam Wallington is the same weapon used to take Penny's life. When Adam was killed we now know the murderer was over 400 yards away from his victim; the fact that he hit his target in precisely the right place, and exactly the right moment to achieve the dramatic result that he did is a clear indication that our killer is a highly talented marksman; I doubt if any of our firearms trained officers are anywhere near that good. I've watched the footage of Penny's shooting over and over again, and it's brought tears to my eyes, but at the moment she was hit she was standing at least 2 feet away from Cartwright; an interviewer would never be right in the face of an interviewee, even in a highly charged political interview, which this wasn't. The distance between Penny and St John's bell tower, which is where we are sure the rifle was fired from is about a third the Castleton distance from which he shot Adam. To miss by as much as he did at that range is, to my mind unthinkable. He's a crack shot. It just wouldn't happen."

"Maybe he was distracted by somebody in the crowd," said Hardy, "there were a lot of people milling about, and one of them could have moved suddenly and spooked him."

"I don't think so Sir, he's too focused to allow that to occur. I don't believe he would have fired at all if he couldn't have been sure of getting the result he wanted."

"Then, assuming the anonymous note sent to Edward Cartwright was genuinely written by our assassin, and of course we have no way of knowing that..."

"Well there are certainly no fingerprints on the paper," interjected Mark.

"Why would he write to Cartwright telling him he was the intended victim and verbally abusing and threatening him in the manner that he does?"

"To throw us off the scent; to send us on a wild goose chase; but I do think there is a genuine dislike for our A-list celebrity to throw into the equation."

"Well, if Adam and Penny were the intended victims all along, it must follow that there has to be something to link them together in the killer's mind mustn't it Mark?"

"That has to be correct Sir, but as yet we have no idea what that might be. Adam and Penny did know each other, it's a small community and there's only 18 months difference in age between them. They went to the same school, and briefly attended the same youth club. We've not yet been able to talk to Penny's close relatives; they're so shocked that they can't think of anything other than the loss of a beautiful daughter and sister. It might be weeks before we can chat to them about her social contacts. If we tried it now all we'd get would be a bucket full of tears, and if they thought we were doing anything to undermine her character they'd throw us out of the house and never talk to us again."

"I understand that Mark, but what about school friends and work colleagues, can they give us any useful information?"

"They have one or two mutual acquaintances. They were both sporty, and I think they have been to a couple of parties together. They got on well, they probably classed each other as "mates", but it seems they were never an item. Apart from his university pals Adam's closest friends were from the rugby club; Penny was still close to some of her classmates and they liked going out for meals and girlie nights out in the clubs in Manchester. Adam liked to keep things local. Neither of them appears ever to have fallen out with anyone, or if they did there is no record anywhere of that having happened. They both seem to have been highly talented, likeable, decent kids with great potential and attractive personalities; that's why everyone is so overwhelmed by their deaths."

"Have either of them ever had a connection with Edward Cartwright that we know of?"

"Penny's mum knew Cartwright's auntie, and they were quite good friends. She died about 3 years ago; Penny's mum went to the funeral. Needless to say the Hollywood superstar wasn't there; but that's the only link that we can find."

"I see," said Hardy. "Not much to go on there. Does Cartwright himself have anything to say on the topic?"

Mark Hobson nearly exploded with indignation. "He's an arrogant little shit, why couldn't he have been the one who died? He's a self-obsessed maggot with a ludicrously inflated idea about his own importance;" and Hobson went on to tell the Detective Chief Superintendent about a meeting that had taken place between Cartwright and D.S. Peter Bennett.

"He wanted a police marksman to be deployed to guard him the whole time he stayed in the U.K. He demanded a bullet proof car to convey him to the airport and police outriders to ensure that he didn't have to stop en route. He also suggested that he should be allowed to bypass airport security and be allowed to board his plane immediately on arrival. Pete told him where to get off, but he did say every step was being taken to keep him safe. Cartwright wouldn't be convinced so he's currently shitting himself, but he is also milking his situation for all it's worth. There is no doubt that he wants to ensure that his departure, whenever it comes, attracts maximum publicity. Exposure worldwide on prime time news would do nothing to harm his celebrity status."

"What did he say about the case?" asked Hardy.

"Well first of all he didn't want to say anything at all, and he was refusing to make any kind of witness statement. Pete was having none of that. He told him he was a material witness and that he should co-operate. He made it crystal clear, as only Pete can, that he would need to attend any Crown Court trial, and that failure to do so would lead to a warrant being issued for his arrest. Off the record he also made it clear that he would personally ensure that the American news media would be fed pictures of Penny Adamson and given an idealised profile of her life, and the senseless killing of such a lovely girl would be highlighted for all its worth. He went on to promise Cartwright that he would label him a coward and stress how his refusal to assist the Prosecution in such an important case as this was being viewed by her family and the British public at large as totally despicable. The Yanks are big on public duty. Pete assured him that by the time he had finished with him he'd rank way below the Ayatollah Khomeini in the popularity stakes. Cartwright got the message, but of course, Sir, if anyone was to inquire Pete would deny that any of this was actually said."

"Understood," said Hardy, "Pete can sure ruffle a few feathers when he puts his mind to it."

"After he knew he had no option but to speak to us Cartwright couldn't stop talking. He's come up with a 7 page witness statement most of which is entirely irrelevant to what we need to know. He's named 16 specific individuals who he suspects might have sent the letter to him. All of them are people he was at school with. Most of what he alleges amounts to no more than a bit of name calling and maybe a couple of playground fights, but he's convinced that some or all of them have conspired together to blacken his name and perhaps kill him. Two of the people he regards as suspects are now members of this force; another is a leading defence solicitor in Sheffield, and a girl he is particularly vitriolic about is now a Church of England vicar in the West Midlands. The annoying thing is that we will have to investigate all this bullshit because there just might be a grain of evidence mixed in with all the rubbish that he's told us. Pete, as you can imagine, is not at all impressed Sir."

***

 Believe me I am sickened by her death. I have feelings like any man, and I would have been proud to be the parent of such a girl. I have cried myself to sleep knowing that I have extinguished such a promising light. Nightmares wrench me into consciousness. I see her falling, as in slow motion to the ground, a look of terrified amazement on her face. I try to console myself that her death was instantaneous and that she felt no fear or pain, but the look that she gives me in my dreams belies that fact. My body shakes with grief as I watch her blood spread slowly across the pavement. Maybe the spot where she was executed will become a sacred place, already the square outside the Opera house is carpeted with flowers and countless cards expressing sorrow. The message left by her friends tug at my heartstrings, and the anger that underlies the sorrow is so strong that it frightens me. I am truly hated now, and with just cause, I ache with grief. Part of me yearns to beg forgiveness, maybe they will erect a memorial stone at the place where she perished and where the blood of the martyr stained the earth red. One day perhaps I could do penance there but it would be pointless; nothing can ever redeem my soul.

But have I even got a soul? For me to have a soul there must be a God and I was abandoned by my Creator at the moment my mother died; when I most needed his love he was absent. I have no joyous memories, only bible blackness and supreme intolerance. Surely nobody could win a battle against such odds.

God hates me. Only a vengeful uncaring God could gift me a life pre-ordained to cause such heartache. I had no free will; if the guilty are to be held to account, and He demands his day of reckoning, then the innocent must pay the price. Through their deaths sins will be repaid, a life of torment is the sentence they will bear. One day they will learn everything, and they will understand how completely they are responsible for the destruction that has been unleashed. To know, with absolute certainty that their selfishness has destroyed the lives of people they cherished is knowledge that cannot be borne; maybe they will expedite their journeys into Hell by slashing their own wrists and terminating their presence on Mother Earth.

If soon every detail of their foul deeds has to emerge from the shadows of Evil, you may wonder why it was I wrote to Edward Cartwright, who though contemptible is not a player in this game of death. The answer is self-evident. The time is not yet right. At this moment it is better to scatter confusion onto fertile ground, and to use diversionary tactics to lead investigators down a long and winding trail to a dead end. They will soon suspect that he appears to be the missing piece in a complicated jigsaw. There is much about his character that is odious, and one day he will be tried in the court of public opinion, but he is largely irrelevant to my unfolding story. Still, it would be good to see a pathetic self-deluded peacock plucked clean of his feathers. To bring him down may give me the strength to carry on; at least he would not be another innocent person to weigh down my conscience. I have no choice but to complete the task I have started. Next time I will not look into the face of the sacrificial lamb; I can stand no further pain; instead I visualise the faces of the authors of my tragedy, and perhaps find salvation in their sadness.

CHAPTER FOURTEEN

Frank Oakes had felt unwell on the day of the murder; he had withdrawn into his bedroom and demanded to be left alone and so it wasn't until the early evening news the next night that he had been made aware of the dreadful things that had occurred less than 5 miles from his home. When he first saw the bulletin he felt sick. The night of the murder the story had dominated the national news, relegating to second place a plane crash in South East Asia which had claimed over 200 lives. No doubt if all the passengers had been British it would have been different but, in so far as was known from the sketchy details available, only 6 U.K. nationals had died, and none of them had come from the leafy suburbs of the Home Counties. It wasn't that the T.V. producers consciously judged the lives of foreigners to be inherently less valuable than those of white English middle class people, it was a realisation that if a tragedy happened far away from home some viewers tended to think that it had no impact upon them. The dramatic death of a very attractive young reporter, on home soil, while she was in the process of interviewing a celebrity ticked any box that could be prescribed; and even though the murder itself wasn't shown in graphic detail, the shocking realisation that such a crime could take place in an oasis of culture in the heart of England was both disturbing and thought provoking. Even 24 hours after the event, and with reports of suspected genocide in a central African state, the story remained a major theme for all the news channels.

Frank was aghast. *In all my life,* he thought, *nothing like this has ever happened before. The world has gone mad! What's changed so dramatically in the last few years?*

And the more Frank thought about it the more he was sure that he knew the answer. Local families weren't always virtuous or law abiding, he was too worldly wise to believe that, but they didn't generally resolve their differences by turning Buxton into Dodge City or Castleton into Boot Hill. Both Penny and Adam had been good kids, that was the universally held consensus and he did not demur from it; but even if they hadn't been, even if someone had good cause to hate them, if he was local he would have gone about it differently. A knife in the chest or across the throat, a blow to the back of the skull with a blunt instrument, a hit and run accident, perhaps in a stolen car, all these ways of killing he could accept might have been employed by somebody native to the High Peak, and the list was by no means complete, but the use of an ancient weapon in a public place that was alien to the psyche of upland Derbyshire. The maniac responsible for these two deaths had to be an outsider, and Frank knew the outsider he suspected it to be.

Video games were frequently violent, immoral and exploitative. Frank seemed to remember once having read an article in a tabloid newspaper linking the video games industry to organised crime. The bastard who had demolished his former home had made millions from pedalling his anti-social, addictive rubbish without apparently worrying for one second about the harm he was causing to impressionable youngsters. Before his arrival in the High Peak rural Derbyshire had been a peaceful, wholesome place; now it seemed anything but. It could just be coincidence of course; it could be that the arrival of his Nemesis had nothing to do with the terrible things that were going on, but Frank didn't believe in coincidence. The world seemed blind to the threat this man posed; something had to be done, and he was the man fate had decreed should do it.

His first action had to be to make his theory known, to point the finger at the man he believed had commissioned these murders. He was sure in his own mind that he wouldn't have done the job himself. Any man who could demolish a £2,000,000 luxury house, without at least stripping out the valuable fixtures and fittings had enough money to burn to meet the heating needs of a small town for the foreseeable future. Such a man would pay an expert to carry out the assassination; he would undoubtedly not bloody his own hands. In any event the man was not a shooter; Frank had no doubt that that was the case. He was too volatile, too impulsive, and too ill-disciplined to be a crack shot; his father's prowess with a shotgun gave him the insight with which to judge, and his own experiences on the university shooting range confirmed his unequivocal verdict.

The gaping black hole in his theory was "motive", and that would be very hard to discover, but someone had to make the effort. And there was one thing Frank was completely clear about in his own mind, and in this respect his thoughts were a lot closer to those of Detective Inspector Mark Hobson than anyone could have predicted. He was sure the killer had not missed his intended target when Penny

Adamson had died; had the Derbyshire D.I. known his thoughts were being shared by an embittered obsessive, he might have started to have serious doubts.

There was only one place to start promulgating his argument, a place where he hoped to find a degree of support, a place from where rumour could spread. Rescinding his self-imposed edict of permanent exile Frank put on his coat and, with the determined zeal of a crusader marching against the Infidel, he set off, at a brisk pace, to walk the half mile distance from his house to the public bar of the Royal Albert Hotel.

***

The mood in Burrdale was sombre. Photographs of Penny were being displayed in the shop windows, some framed in black and set amongst white flowers to signify mourning, and everywhere there were notices from the police asking that anyone who might have seen anything suspicious should contact them with any information they might have, no matter how inconsequential that information might appear to be. In Buxton these notices were even more visible because it was from the crowds of onlookers that small specks of recollection might be teased about the time immediately before the fatal shooting: in Burrdale the hope was that somebody might just have seen a person behaving oddly near to Penny's home, or even in the busy local coffee shops and bars where she had sometimes socialised.

Not that they were busy now. Restaurants and coffee houses had seen a 60% drop in customers since the fatal shooting and in many of the bars and pubs the story was the same one. Whilst an insane killer with a gun could be stalking the towns and villages of the High Peak there was very little incentive for people to venture beyond the safety of their own front doors. It would soon change; if nothing else happened people would soon forget, and fear would be stowed away in some dark cupboard in their brains to lie gathering dust until the next shocking event snatched it from obscurity and propelled it back into the limelight.

One person who was not present in any pub was Bill Adamson; tragedy had drawn the whole Adamson family together; nobody could comprehend, nobody could understand, and none of them could yet face the outside world; Penny's parents, Bill's brother and his wife were in such a state of shock that he doubted if they would ever be able to do so again.

Raymond Baker had ventured out, but in a sullen and angry mood, and Alan Nadin had looked in the "Albert" to seek out Bill and pass on his and his wife's condolences. Like many women in town Jackie Nadin had cried when she heard the news. There was nothing anyone could do; words couldn't lessen the impact this crazy act of slaughter had had, but words were all anyone had, and friends of the Adamson family wanted to let them know how devastated they were to hear of Penny's death and to offer what little support and comfort they could.

The 3 other people in the public bar were not intimately acquainted with the Adamson family, although all were not entirely unknown to them. There were two members of the dominoes team who didn't really have much contact with Bill, and so were largely unmoved by the tragedy, and the third man looked as if he had drifted into a closed world by accident, and why he chose to remain drinking alone in such depressing company might have been a topic of conversation in happier times. It was into this miserable gathering that Frank Oakes propelled himself.

"I've worked out who the bastard is who shot Penny Adamson," he announced, his voice quivering with emotion as he spoke. "I know who is to blame for this unspeakable outrage." Ray and Alan looked at Frank with incredulity; how could he claim to have such knowledge! The two detached members of the dominoes team briefly ceased their chat about the shortcomings of the Government to lend an ear: the third man was seated too far away to pick up every single word that was spoken, but if anybody had been paying attention to him it would have been obvious that he was straining to hear precisely what was said.

"I never expected to see you in here again," said Raymond Baker, "and I can't say you've been much missed, but if you've got any information that could lead to the arrest of the murderous swine that shot Penny, then you're welcome, and I'm sure Alan Nadin will know what to do with it." Alan didn't speak, but he nodded his head in agreement.

Sometimes speaking loudly, sometimes dropping his voice to a near whisper when dealing with the most sensitive parts of his tale, Frank started to reveal his theory. He railed against the computer games industry, which he likened to legal pornography. He explained why he was sure that the death of Penny hadn't been a tragic mistake, quoting his own experiences as a target shooter to support his conclusions, and making stark comparisons between the state of anxiety that had now seized the whole Peak District, and contrasting that with the more relaxed, joyous feelings of well-being that were usually apparent in the gardens of Buxton and in the small hamlets and villages that lay within a 5 mile radius of Burrdale. With a flourish he then named his suspect, keeping his listeners in suspense for several seconds, like a T.V presenter announcing the result of a talent competition.

"Mickey Shah! You fucking arsehole! You come here when everybody is grieving about the senseless killing of a beautiful young girl! You claim you can reveal the name of the killer! You get us on tenterhooks, and then you trot out the same old mantra about how unfair the world has been to you, and how wicked the man is who knocked down your family home, the one which you and your parents gratefully got rid of for a huge sum of money many years ago. Mickey Shah may be a greedy bastard, with no redeeming qualities, but there isn't a shred of evidence to suggest that he has anything to do whatsoever with Penny's death. I'm just glad for your sake that Bill Adamson isn't here; he'd probably have given you a smack in the mouth to fucking shut you up. Can't you see how stupid talk like this would upset him? I suggest you piss off to whatever planet you come from and take your crackpot ideas with you. That's the best thing this fool can do isn't it Alan?"

The retired C.I.D. officer didn't reply, but a nod of his head signalled that he did not disagree.

"So you are just going to sit idly by and not lift a finger to stop him" roared Oakes, "is this what the world has finally come to? Well the two of you may not care how many more kids get killed, but I flaming well do! I'll stop the bastard myself, even if I have to shoot him. I can handle a gun you know, and I know where I can get one; I won't be afraid to use it; just you yellow livered apologies for men wait and bloody see!"

"On your bike Oakes," retorted Baker, "book yourself into a mental hospital; it'll save the cost of getting two doctors to come and section you!"

CHAPTER FIFTEEN

The evidence was clear. Both fatal bullets had been fired from the same gun. The report went into great detail and Mark Hobson could have bored DS Bennett rigid by reading out all the points of similarity which had lead the expert to come to the unequivocal conclusion that he had, but there was no need. It was accepted by everyone that the weapon that had fired these bullets had been used twice, to deadly effect; whether it would be used again with similar result only time would tell.

"Our absolute priority has to be to find this bloody gun! Surely to God somebody must have seen something! A rifle's not a hand gun for Christ's sake; you can't just stick it in your coat pocket. It was brought to the church and it was taken from the church. It didn't take us long to work out that the bell tower was the probable vantage point of the killer. It wasn't there when we searched the building, it hadn't been hidden in the grounds otherwise we would have found it. It didn't vanish into thin air; nobody waved a wand to make it disappear; somebody carried it, and whether or not people realise it, somebody witnessed it being removed."

"Very likely Gov," said Pete Bennett, "but whether the penny will ever drop is a very open question."

"Has anything been received in response to the notices? They're on practically every bloody lamppost; surely they must have had some impact?"

"Not much so far Gov, but it's still early days. Give 'em time, they may yet yield up something."

"Time is a luxury we haven't got Pete. The "perfect son" and the "perfect daughter" have been killed in cold blood. Every parent and grandparent in the county is screaming at us to find the murderer. If we hang around twiddling our thumbs, waiting for results to be handed to us on a plate, then we'll be crucified by the press, and rightly so."

***

One man who wasn't sitting about waiting to be crucified was Mickey Shah, he was looking for a saviour in the form of the Derbyshire Constabulary. His complaint to the police was totally unexpected.

Since he had moved into his monstrous mock-Georgian mansion he hadn't made the slightest effort to integrate into local society. There had been parties at his home for his uncouth friends, which had prompted complaints about noise being received by the police, even though his nearest neighbours were nearly half a mile away, and the manner of the driving of some of the flash cars that had visited the property had been little short of reckless, but that was all anybody had seen or heard of him and his unruly disciples. The outside world was not worth considering and probably beneath contempt, that had been his assessment of his neighbours, and as for the local police he regarded them as Keystone cops in Noddy cars who were risible in their ineptitude; but now he wanted their protection.

He was forthright in his demands. He claimed that that "weirdo" Frank Oakes had threatened to kill him. "The idiot has been shooting off his mouth in a local pub and now I've received an anonymous note telling me "I'm next." The moron's a total lunatic. He used to stand outside my property day after day, no matter what the bleedin' weather, and he proper put the wind up some of my builders. I had to get a lawyer to threaten him with court action, which seemed to do the trick, until now."

And Shah had other allegations to make against the man. "The bastard's been seen with a gun near to my house. One of the village idiots told one of my lads, who told me. I don't know who it was but my lad didn't think he were pissing him about. The cretin's a dangerous fucking nutter, and I want him locked up."

The overbearing manner of the Computer Games king was profoundly irritating, and D.S. Bennett, who took details of the complaint, would have loved to tell him to stick his allegations and his unsigned message some place where the sun didn't shine, and that nobody at Burrdale nick was going to lift a finger to help until he showed considerably less arrogance than he was doing at present, but of course he didn't do that. He assured the verbally energetic tycoon that his complaint would be reported to his senior officer, and that there would be a thorough investigation by the police. Immediately after Mr Shah left the police station, Pete Bennett sought out Detective Inspector Hobson to put him in the picture.

"It may be nothing at all Gov," he said. "Alan Nadin was present in the pub when Oakes had his outburst, and he didn't take the threat seriously, but if he has been seen with a gun then we're duty bound to look into it."

"Does this man Oakes have a shotgun licence or a firearms certificate?" asked the D.I.

"Not anymore," was the reply. "He used to have a legal shotgun, but he handed that in a few years ago. He's never applied for a firearms certificate, but he bragged in the pub about being a crack shot at university. Alan thinks this is true; and there was a gun club at his college."

"Then we need to get hold of a tame J.P. and ask him to issue us a warrant under S.46 of the 1968 Firearms Act and then you and I can pay the talkative Mr Oakes a visit."

***

She still wasn't happy. He'd never known her walk out in a strop before, but when he disappeared into his bedroom on what turned out to be the day of the murder she had done just that. She had tried to discourage him, but he hadn't listened. Leaving home just after The Archers finished, she had driven into town to visit her mother before going shopping in a local supermarket; Frank knew what his wife and her mum would talk about, and he was sure he wouldn't receive any compliments from either party. Before she left she had urged him to pull himself together and he had ignored her. Consequently, when she returned, she had chosen to sleep in the spare room that night. He could have done anything that day and she wouldn't have known or cared; even three days later they were hardly speaking; it didn't look if hostilities would end any time soon.

Sitting like a reluctant Trappist monk in his own home, afraid to breach her edict of silence, he was brooding about the unreasonableness of women and the rigour with which they held grudges when he was disturbed from his contemplation of the woes of the world by a loud banging on his door. He opened it, and was amazed to find himself confronted by two plain clothes police officers.

"Mr Frank Oakes?" the first one said. "My name is Detective Inspector Mark Hobson of the Derbyshire Constabulary, and this is Detective Sergeant Peter Bennett; we have reason to believe that an illegal firearm may be hidden within these premises and I have with me a warrant issued under The Firearms Act 1968 which allows me to enter your home and search for such a weapon, and which permits me to use reasonable force to do so should you seek to prevent me: I'm sure that isn't going to happen is it Sir?"

Frank's mouth twitched like that of a rainbow trout pulled from fast flowing waters on an angler's hook, just prior to being dispatched to Fishy Heaven by a stout stick.

"Illegal firearm!" he stuttered, "I don't have an illegal firearm, this is just ridiculous!"

"Then you have nothing to worry about on that score then, do you Sir? But I will also need to speak to you about some of your recent public utterances and that might be an altogether different matter."

For the next hour Frank sweated as the search was carried out. The uniformed officers who had arrived shortly after the two detectives were thorough. Wardrobes, drawers, chests and cabinets were all searched revealing nothing. The loft proved empty of any suspect weapons and the garden shed, although containing axes, pruning knives, sickles and grafting spades, all of which could kill a man if used inappropriately, did not surrender a venerable Lee Enfield rifle from within its depths: and all the while the search was going on Frank's wife was glaring at her husband who she held totally to blame for this unwanted invasion by the forces of law and order. When the search was finally concluded the detective inspector turned to face Frank.

"The fact that we haven't found a gun doesn't mean that you're not still a suspect. You could easily have concealed one elsewhere than at your home; and if you have, take my word we will find it; but for the present I have no evidence to arrest you for any firearms offences. I now need to question you about certain threats you are alleged to have made against Mr Michael Shah; I also need to confirm your movements on the afternoon that Penny Adamson was killed."

Oakes made a sideways glance at his wife, the look of panic on his face was clear for all to see.

"I can't help you Frank," she snapped; "remember you took yourself off to the bedroom and didn't come out for over 24 hours. I went shopping and to visit Mum; you could have done anything while I was away. I can't pull you out of any hole that you've dug for yourself."

"So you have no alibi for the time in question? That could be a big problem for you Sir. So what exactly did you do whilst your wife was out?"

"I paced up and down, I tried to read a book, and mostly I just sat."

"And of course we only have your word for that, don't we Sir? It's looking increasingly likely that you are going to have to accompany me to the police station for further questioning, but before I finally make up my mind on that score I want to ask you about your relationship with Mickey Shah."

"There isn't one. I think he's an uncouth parasite taking advantage of mentally deficient kids who buy the rubbish he produces. He's an absolute shit, and I hate him."

"Now that's a statement I am prepared to accept. Do you accept that you made a threat to shoot him in the public bar of the Royal Albert, and before you answer that I should tell you I have a very reliable witness to this incident?"

Frank didn't answer but nodded his head; his wife gave him a withering look and called him a "bloody fool."

"Mr Shah has received an anonymous note that simply states "You're next!" Mr Shah believes that this is a promise to make him the third victim of a person who has already murdered two people. I think his logic is impeccable. I'm asking you straight out, did you send Mr Shah that note?"

"Certainly not!" blurted Oakes, trying to keep calm, but failing miserably.

"Well I think this warrants more investigation. I need you to attend the police station for further questioning. Are you willing to accompany me voluntarily to allow this to take place or will I have to arrest you and take you there in custody?"

Oakes looked as if he was about to burst into tears.

"Go with him voluntarily Frank," said his wife. "It looks better. I don't know what's the matter with you is these days; why can't you keep out of trouble?"

It was then there was a knock on the door. Oakes, who was standing closest to it, opened it in a daze. Tim Bradley was standing on the doorstep.

"It's not a good time Tim," he stammered, "Can't it wait until later?"

"It can Mr Oakes, but it will only take a couple of seconds, and it's the second time I've tried to speak to you about it. It's about that dead tree in the hedgerow I called round on the afternoon that that poor lass was killed in Buxton. I knocked on your back door, but you didn't answer. I know you were in, I saw you through your bedroom window pacing about the room, but you didn't come down. All I want to know is what do you want me to do with the timber when I take it down. Do I cut it up into logs and stack them close to the house or would you like me to deal with it in another way?"

"What time was it that you called?" asked Mark Hobson. "Please think very carefully, this could be extremely important."

"I remember exactly," said Bradley. "It was ten minutes to 3 pm. I know that for sure because I got a phone call at home at half past two which I was waiting for and that then dragged on for 15 minutes, which was longer than I thought it would. My kitchen clock gave me the exact time. I came straight over here after the call finished and that always takes me 5 minutes."

"Are you sure of all this?" questioned the Detective Inspector.

"Absolutely!" replied Tim Bradley.

Hobson turned to Frank Oakes.

"If Mr Bradley is right, you have an alibi, Mr Oakes, certainly as regards having any direct involvement in the death of Penny Adamson. It's not possible for you to get from here to the bell tower in less than 10 minutes, and even if that were so you would have needed considerably more time than that to get ready to do what you had to do. I still intend to speak to you about your behaviour in the public house, but that will now do at some other time. You've had a very lucky escape Mr Oakes; you nearly landed yourself in a whole heap of trouble. I suggest you listen to your wife in future and keep your mouth closed and your nose clean."

CHAPTER SIXTEEN

"Are you sure that Oakes's alibi is genuine?" Detective Chief Superintendent Stan Hardy was quizzing Mark Hobson about the unproductive search of Frank Oakes's property and the last minute lifeline he had been thrown by the revelation of Tim Bradley.

"We'll it wasn't a set up job Sir, of that I've got no doubt. Oakes was in a state of panic, I'm sure about that. When I told him he'd have to come down to the station with me to be questioned further, he turned grey; he couldn't have faked that. If he'd known all along that he had a Get out of gaol free card he wouldn't have looked like that. Bradley's intervention was a bolt from the blue; I'd stake my life on it; ask Pete Bennett if you want a second opinion, I know he thinks the same way as I do."

"So unless he can perform miracles, or he's got a Star Trek transporter room in his cellar he's in the clear as regards Penny Adamson's murder: he doesn't have a transporter room in his cellar does he Mark?"

"He doesn't even have a cellar Sir," said Mark laughing. "I wouldn't totally cross him off the list of suspects; as far as we're aware he doesn't have an alibi for the Adam Wallington killing, but if we are correct in our assumption that the same man is responsible for both deaths, it does make him a pretty long shot."

"Witnesses at Castleton saw a man with a dog just before that murder; we've never found out who that person was; does Frank Oakes own a dog?"

"Well his wife's got a poodle Sir, well two poodles if you count Oakes as one, and he's got a couple of terriers, but they certainly don't have a border collie so we can't tie him in on that score."

"So our first decent shout at a suspect has turned into a whisper," said Hardy, "pity about that, the Chief Constable is getting very worked up about this case. He needs a bone to throw to the press otherwise his neck and our jobs could soon be on the line."

The D.C.S. and the D.I. then spent the best part of an hour considering the options currently available to the police. After considering the poor response to the posters to date, Stan Hardy decided that there should be a wider appeal to the public.

"I'll get on to the B.B.C. to see if we can get a spot on Crime Watch and you can have your two minutes of stardom appealing for information. Given the publicity this case has already had they'll jump at the chance, and who knows, we could get lucky; it's worked before, there's no reason why it shouldn't work again."

"As you wish Sir, but wouldn't you like to do the appeal yourself?"

"I'd sooner stick a wasp up my arse Mark; you've got a pretty face, this is your baby."

"Thank you Sir," responded Mark, "I just wish I had the same option."

Another area of expansion for the inquiry was then discussed.

"We've found no links at all between Adam and Penny except for the unsurprising fact that they did know each other and that whilst they were not close friends they got on very well when they bumped into each other. They weren't star crossed lovers; nobody has jilted anybody or broken up any marriage or serious relationship so far as we are aware; they both had lots of mates; their friends were friendly with each other; there's no gang warfare, and not an ounce of animosity anywhere to be seen."

"But there has to be a connection in the killer's mind Mark. Perhaps we've been concentrating too much on the immediate past; maybe we need to go back a generation or three to get to the root of this matter."

"I totally agree Sir, and I think there's one more thing we need to consider. If the fan letter sent to Edward Cartwright was designed to throw us off the scent by bringing into the picture somebody who could lead us down the long road to Nowhere, and if the report of Oakes being seen with a gun is fabricated, and we've got no way of checking that at present, then the killer or somebody else is deliberately throwing red herrings into the public domain to make our job a damn sight more difficult than it needs to be. Mickey Shah isn't best pleased that we haven't locked Frank up and he's no longer busting a gut to help us; his information was third hand. He now says he can't remember which of his men spoke to him, and he can't be bothered to do our detective work for us, so we're pretty well stymied in that regard. I don't know if all of this is pure conjecture, and everything might be as it appears to be, but to be honest, I don't think it is."

"Well our job is to wade through half-truths and lies to find golden nuggets of fact. You've got a pair of wellington boots haven't you Mark?"

"Black, size 9: I've also got a pair of waders if the murky waters of fabrication and invention get too deep," laughed Mark.

***

The builders carrying out the renovations at St John's church were perplexed. It wasn't a big problem, well it wasn't a problem at all but it was perplexing. Building materials disappearing from the site was unfortunately a common occurrence, and no longer routinely reported to the police. Unauthorised waste being dumped was also a frequent irritation and there were times when the fly tippers found it quicker to ignore waste skips and leave their piles of rags, broken bottles, building debris and sometimes much worse scattered across the ground for others to pick up and dispose of, which was the cause of many expletives; but what had happened here was something very different. A number of lengths of plastic soil pipes had been stacked outside the church. They were in good condition, and to any person who glanced in their direction they looked as though they were intended for future use in the building restoration. The police had not viewed them as in any way unusual, and had merely checked them to ensure nothing was concealed within them, and nothing had been discovered.

Somebody gifting a building contractor several lengths of quality plastic piping, now that was unusual and warranted further inquiry; the site foreman certainly felt that was so. He sought out the young curate who was standing in for the incumbent for a couple of weeks while he made his annual pilgrimage to the gambling temples of Las Vegas. He informed him of his findings. The curate, being a bright young man who balanced faith in God with living in the real world a great deal more successfully than many of his older colleagues, and was only too well aware that a killer had entered the beautiful church in which he worked to snuff out one of his Saviour's most lovely creations, wondered if in any way the two events could be connected. He wasn't sure, it was probably nothing, but to be on the safe side he decided to report his suspicions to the police.

****

Detective Inspector Mark Hobson was taking 10 minutes to carry out a much needed tidy up of his desk when the Reverend Jacob Lindley arrived at Burrdale Police Station; papers were strewn across the floor, a pile of law reports, borrowed from the C.P.S. over the last few weeks, was doing a very creditable impression of the Leaning Tower of Pisa, a small but wilful tub of paperclips had decided to throw itself onto a chair, and just at that moment the D.I.'s office looked as if it had been struck by a not inconsiderable cyclone. It wasn't usually this messy; no police officer of ability could afford to be disorganised, but even at his best Mark Hobson was never going to be a contender for "The Clear Desk Copper of the Month Award." His untidiness didn't bother Detective Chief Superintendent Stan Hardy; too often these days, far more time than he thought was strictly necessary, was spent by young officers trying to conform to the latest dictates from on high on office neatness rather than getting down to some bona fide police work. He had no complaints about Mark Hobson on that score, but the world was changing rapidly. Soon paper files would be a thing of the past, soon all information would be stored upon computer, and every desk top would gleam so brightly that it would dazzle the eyes of anyone unwise enough to even glance at it. He comforted himself by remembering that he had only 5 more years to go before he could retire on full pension. He hoped he would reach retirement before I.T. turned on its head a world he had known for over 30 years.

Mark Hobson shared many of these feelings, although in his case the time before he could jump ship was considerably longer than 5 years. He was just about to corral the errant paperclips back into their plastic container when the knock on his door occurred. The interruption was unexpected and Hobson turned quickly towards the noise, accidentally bumping into his filing cabinet as he did so. The Leaning Tower of Pisa took the full force of the tremor. It tottered for a moment, and then it tumbled to the ground. In the Detective Inspector's eyes the root cause of this unnatural disaster was the untimely arrival of the fresh faced young clergyman; when he left his office to meet him, feelings of

Christian charity were not utmost in his mind, and mumbling to himself about wishy washy bible bashers he grumpily made his way to the inquiry desk.

He was pleasantly surprised to find that the Reverend Jacob Lindley fitted none of the usual priestly stereotypes. He was athletic, personable, down to earth, and not on the least bit happy clappy. He shook hands with a firm grip, there was nothing feeble or effeminate about his handshake, and he didn't beat about the bush.

"I'm Jake Lindley," he told the Detective Inspector, "I'm standing in for the Reverend Harold Peters while he's away on holiday. As I think you know we're having some building work done at St John's; it had been temporarily suspended to wait for additional funding, but that's now in place and everything is back on track. One of the builders told me about something a little bit odd today; in view of the terrible tragedy that occurred so close to our bell tower, and the possibility that that may have been the place from where the fatal shot was fired, I thought it would be better if I told the police. It may be nothing at all, and totally unconnected with the ghastly murder you're investigating but...."

The Curate then proceeded to outline the workman's discovery to the ever more excited Detective Inspector. A Lee Enfield rifle would easily fit inside a length of soil pipe, and if some sort of bung was inserted in either end it would be completely hidden from view. A man dressed in a suit carrying a single length of piping would attract attention, but a builder repeatedly carrying lengths of pipe to a construction site would attract no attention at all. In Mark's mind it was beginning to look as if the mystery of how the killer got the gun to and from the church had finally been solved. And of course, these pipes could be a fertile source of evidence. The assassin hadn't had much time to plan. The final details of the T.V. interview hadn't been agreed until shortly before the date set for it to take place so once those were fixed, and a positive weather forecast made it obvious that there would be no need for a plan B, he had to act quickly. Mistakes could have been made. All the lengths of piping would need to be checked for fingerprints and for D.N.A. Building supply merchants would need to be contacted to see if details of a purchaser could be unearthed, and the murderer must have had to use his own vehicle or trailer to carry the soil pipes to the edge of the graveyard; unless of course he had used a hire vehicle. If the van used was a hire van then details of the driver and a copy of his driving licence had to be on some Rental firm's files; if it wasn't rented then somebody might have recognised it; and surely if somebody did they would come forward if the urgency of the need to do so was made clear by the police. There was another thing too; the man as well as the van needed to look the part; he had to look like a typical builder's labourer, if there was such a thing. A pristine Day Glow waistcoat, a shining unmarked hard hat wouldn't look right. In an effort to blend in the killer might have had to beg, borrow or steal well-worn safety equipment items from somewhere; and if he had then this was potentially another very productive line of inquiry.

CHAPTER SEVENTEEN

Mick Wallington's reaction to his grandson's death had been decidedly odd. For weeks he had seemed unmoved by, or even indifferent to, the tragedy that had robbed the world of a talented young man; almost as if the dramatic events had failed to register in his mind. He had attended the funeral, and thankfully had not done anything inappropriate, but he hadn't talked to anyone and had left immediately after the event.

"He can't think about other people, even when they need him most," complained Mary Wallington's sister, bitterly, "He doesn't, seem to give a damn about Mary! Do you know the heartless sod hasn't spoken to her once since Adam died, and it's been nearly 3 months? He's a selfish, thoughtless unfeeling swine."

But belatedly things had changed. Like a delayed action bomb, the full horror of the murder had finally exploded into his consciousness. He had "coped" with the disaster in exactly the way Mary most feared he would. He had hit the bottle big time, and done nightly circuits of the town pubs crying, sighing, shouting, swearing and making drunken promises to avenge the killing of his most precious grandchild. Strangers taken in by his grief were moved by his sadness, and would listen sympathetically to his extreme ravings; locals who knew the man better were less inclined to pity him; many were sure that this was just another example of Mick seeking the limelight, and exploiting other people's unhappiness for his own ends; but even they gave him more tolerance than was usually allotted to him.

"For Mary's sake we just have to let him shoot his mouth off," explained Raymond Baker. "She's got enough on her plate at the moment, she can do without her friends turning against the man she is unlucky enough to have as a father-in-law."

Seven days into his one man wake, Mick finally got around to visiting his daughter-in-law. He was only partially drunk when he arrived, and hence slightly less extravagantly grief stricken than might otherwise have been the case. He embraced her in a bear hug Big Daddy would have been proud of, he pledged undying support in her hour of need, and he swore by her God that he would not rest until Adam's killer was found and brought to justice. Words poured from his lips in a sentimental torrent; it was amazing that so many clichés could flow from such a shallow source. Mary felt like screaming, and battled against an urge to run from the room in tears and lock herself in her bedroom far away from the cacophony of meaningless sound; she controlled her desire to do so and instead waited in near silence for the downpour of worthless promises to abate. Eventually it subsided, and Mick finally left, satisfied in his own mind that he had done the right thing.

***

His visit to the parents of Penny Adamson 5 days after her death did not meet with the approval he had expected. He had learned from his tardiness with regard to Adam; he now knew he should have acted sooner; he was determined not to make the same mistake a second time. But his venture was ill-fated from the outset, and very short lived. He had no close affinity with them, and just because many years before he had had a short term relationship with her grandmother, when she was in between boyfriends, cut no ice at all. It had only lasted a few weeks whilst she was coming to terms with the fact that her previous boyfriend had been seriously injured in a road traffic accident, and it had been based on a deception. He had seen her emotional state, thought that she was a good looking girl, and had leapt forward to comfort her, sensing that in her unhappiness there was an opportunity to fill a void. He had conveniently not told her his true identity, instead using the name of a cousin who was currently serving with the British Army overseas; it was a clumsy deception, bound to ultimately fail, but he had reasoned that by then he would have won her heart. He had vastly overplayed his hand. When she learnt his true identity, and discovered that it was his drunken driving that had been the direct cause of the crash that had maimed her former lover, she had exploded with rage and thrown him over in dramatic fashion; his superficial charm had started to wear very thin in any event; he was already unable to compete for her affections with the man from the BBC who seemed to offer her a glittering future. All this, however, Mick had reasoned was history; the noble nature of his visit was self-evident, and proof that he was a changed man, surely he would be welcomed with open arms; nobody would want to reject his message of sympathy would they?

Never were a man's good intentions less productive. He was treated with suspicion the moment he arrived on the doorstep, and when he started to behave as a grief stricken doting relative that was too much to bear. His transparent insincerity and his tactless parroting of inappropriate platitudes nearly drove Penny's father to distraction; he hadn't yet buried his lovely daughter and here was this thoughtless imbecile causing trouble. He called Mick "a pathetic waste of space" and threatened to "kick his arse down the road unless he forthwith got off his property". Mick was appalled that his good will pilgrimage to bring comfort to a bereaved family had been so vehemently denounced. Over the next few days, many times in many pubs, he railed loudly against the self-destructive stupidity of people who reject genuine offers to help, particularly when the person making the offer could do so much to right a horrible wrong. He persisted with this theme until he was finally warned by several landlords that another word on this topic would see him immediately and permanently barred from their premises.

***

During this period the antics of the "Burrdale Braggart" had come to the attention of the local police, and had caused Detective Inspector Mark Hobson to look for a possible link between Mick, Adam and Penny which could explain why a ruthless killer had acted as he had. All his efforts came to nothing. He found no tangible connection between the two fine young people and the reprobate who had by this time driven to distraction half the population of the town. Mick had barely featured in Adam's life when he was a child, and he had never featured in Penny's. He had never exerted influence over either of them; he certainly had never been the puppet master who pulled their strings to control their every movement. At no time had he persuaded them to act irresponsibly, unpleasantly or illegally, or to do any act that could have harmed a third party or benefitted himself.

***

But bad as they were, the antics of the "Hollywood Heartthrob" were perhaps even more unedifying than those of the "Burrdale Braggart", and to Detective Inspector Hobson and the Derbyshire Constabulary a great deal more annoying. Having reluctantly made a witness statement to the police, he had been allowed to leave the Peak District to return to his home in the United States, which was the only place he claimed to feel safe. It was with incredulity therefore that, less than two weeks later, Mark Hobson learned that he was back in England, staying in the most expensive suite at the Dorchester Hotel in Mayfair. He had a new project to announce. A film version of his early life was to be made by an American T.V. company and was almost certain to be snapped up by the B.B.C. Edward Cartwright was promising that it would be an explosive "mockumentary", fearlessly shining the spotlight on the pettiness, cruelty and narrow-mindedness that was rife in the sleepy towns and villages of rural England. His valiant fight against bullying would be a major plank of the story, and the way his super-intelligence triumphed over the Neanderthal prejudices of ill-informed yokels would be a recurring theme within the film. The police and other authorities could expect harsh treatment when the story of the self-confessed "Boy Genius" was told, and viewers would be informed that everything depicted on film was based on truth.

"Our best lawyers have already approved the script," announced a spokesman for the television company. "There will be no grounds for any legal complaint, but undoubtedly some people may recognise themselves, and will probably not like what they see. A child actor has been selected to play the part of young Edward, but Edward himself will take the role when he arrives at manhood. We will be filming in Derbyshire", the spokesman continued, "and Edward will be present, but he will have round the clock protection provided by some of the top security advisers money can buy. We dared not leave issues of his safety to the over-stretched and underfunded resources of the British Police."

"He's an annoying little twat, isn't he Gov? I'm half minded to take a pot shot at him myself to see how good his so called security advisers are;" lamented Detective Sergeant Pete Bennett, "he's come back here to stir up as much trouble as he possibly can, and what's more he's being paid an absolute fortune for doing so."

"I'd be happy to pass you the bullets," said Hobson, "but you never know, his presence could be a blessing in disguise, if he irritates other people as much as he irritates us, something might happen that could assist our investigation. This may all be a publicity stunt on his part but it could backfire horribly on him if, despite my doubts, he is a genuine object of a killer's intentions.

CHAPTER EIGHTEEN

White Van Land had proved to be a barren kingdom for Derbyshire Constabulary. Within the geographical area of the High Peak nearly every large village or small town had a Van-Hire business that needed to be investigated. Some of these were little more than a one man outfit, operating on a very small scale; others had fleets of vans at their disposal, but all needed to be checked. If you threw into the mix that Burrdale was roughly equidistant between the two large cities of Manchester and Sheffield, the number of outlets soared; and of course there was no guarantee that the killer had restricted his search for transport to a 25 mile radius.

"It could be sodding anywhere," complained Detective Sergeant Peter Bennett, "a straw coloured needle in a haystack could be easier to find."

The Building Supplies Merchants who sold work clothing also inhabited an infertile realm. Bricklayers, plasterers, carpenters, plumbers and labourers had all bought work boots, over trousers and heavy duty jackets, as had ordinary members of the public, but to date all the purchases that could be traced back to an individual had been acquired to fill a genuine need.

"I don't think that we're looking for new stuff anyway;" commented D.I. Hobson, "a well-scrubbed, immaculately kitted out builder's labourer would stand out like a bacon butty on a vegetarian menu. Everything about our man had to be ordinary, that way he could just merge into the background after he'd done his dirty work. You kill a beautiful young woman who has never done you any harm and then just saunter out of the picture as if nothing unusual has happened. What type of man can do that?"

"A psychopath Gov, a fucking psychopath," responded D.S. Bennett bitterly.

***

Unlike the sterile worlds the police were currently exploring, the world of Constance Cartwright had just become a great deal more bountiful. Edward was back in the United Kingdom. Edward would sometime soon return to the home of his birth. She felt thrilled. It would be the last time he would do this. He had promised her he would build her a new house using some of the global receipts from the film to pay for it, and in a place far removed from the rugged Pennine hills. She would have liked that place to be Los Angeles, but a move to America had never been on the cards; but maybe a home in Prestbury, or some other upmarket Cheshire village might be a suitable alternative. She picked up one of the many photographs of her only son that were on display throughout her cottage and she smiled; in it he was about 8 years old.

Such a pretty boy, she thought. A blessing that came to me late in life; to successfully become pregnant and then to deliver a beautiful baby in your 41st year, that's an achievement, particularly when the child is as special as my son has turned out to be.

She was interrupted in her musing by a loud banging at the door. None of her friends would knock in such a manner; feeling more than a little threatened, she made her way into the hall.

The man on the doorstep was tall. He had a red face, he looked angry, and maybe a little inebriated; in fact, he looked as he nearly always did. What business Mick Wallington had with her, Constance could not begin to imagine.

She opened the door, but positioned her body in the space created; Michael Wallington could do his talking on the doorstep, he was not wanted inside the house.

"Good afternoon Mick," she said, "What brings you here on this beautiful July afternoon?"

"It's your bloody son," he boomed, "back here to make trouble for people like me. Well, you can give him a message from me, Connie. You can tell him that if this trashy film he's making shows me in a bad light, then he'll be fucking sorry. I know things about him that he would very much like to keep secret. It will only take one phone call to the Daily Mail to dump him in deep shit, so if he has got any sense of self-preservation he'd better mind his P's and Q's."

Connie gave her visitor a withering look.

"How dare you come to my house making threats," she screamed in his face. "Just clear off out of it: if you're not gone from my doorstep in 10 seconds I'm calling the police."

Mick's face turned to flame.

"You've just made a bad mistake, Lady," he snarled. "You and your dickhead son will live to regret this day!"

***

Mick Wallington was not the only person interested in the plans of Edward Cartwright; the imminent return of Burrdale's most famous son was also exciting the editor of the local newspaper.

"There's mileage in this story," he told his reporters. "We've got boots on the ground; I want interviews with anyone who knew Edward Cartwright as a child who might have a tale to tell. If we do the groundwork properly, we may be able to put together a piece that could be syndicated to the Nationals."

Had they known of these instructions, it is possible that both Mr Michael Wallington and Mrs Constance Elizabeth Cartwright would both have had feelings of extreme unease.

***

If the search for evidence to identify the suspicious hirer of a vehicle or purchaser of heavy duty work clothes was getting nowhere fast, the efforts of Mark Hobson and Pete Bennett to try to discover who it was that had told Mickey Shah that Frank Oakes had been seen in possession of a rifle was also not progressing well. The self-made millionaire couldn't have been less interested in helping the police. He now claimed he could not even remember who had been working for him from one day to the next. He employed casual labourers to bolster his team of builders, as and when required; he thought that it was possible that it may have been one of them who had raised the alarm. If it was, then by now it was likely that he had returned to Poland or Albania, or whatever tin pot Eastern European state he had come from. Shah told Hobson that the police were wasting their time and that they hadn't a hope in Hell of locating the missing witness. When the detective inspector told him it would be in his best interest to cooperate with the police because his life might be in danger, Mickey Shah had been scornful about the degree of protection the Derbyshire police could give him. He had state of the art security cameras and burglar alarms to protect his mock-Georgian monstrosity, and he had men in his employ who had experience in the field of personal security; he neither wanted nor needed any help from a penny ha'penny organisation like the local C.I.D. Mark Hobson could have cheerfully smacked him in the face, but wisely he restricted himself to advising the obnoxious entrepreneur not to take the law into his own hands. Mr Shah denied that was his intention, but he left the detective inspector in no doubt that if he discovered who it was who had passed false information to him, that person would be in rapid need of a one-way ticket to a far off destination, and a swift change of identity.

***

Mick Wallington was on his fourth pint in as many pubs, and was in full flow. At last he had a new subject to rail about. The tragic death of his grandson no longer occupied his mind, the dreadful murder of a pretty T.V. reporter no longer seemed worthy of his attention, the full force of his invective was now being turned towards the film star Edward Cartwright.

"He's a miserable little shit," he bellowed. "He's come back here to throw crap at us; bloody Broadmoor will look like a temple of sanity in comparison to what he portrays this place to be. On screen we will all be depicted as slobbering sex maniacs or pig ignorant thugs; well I for one ain't going to stand for it. I know stuff about his fuckin family that could sink him. I've already warned his stuck up bitch of a mother to rein her whelp in, otherwise he's in big trouble. Lots of people would pay good money to know what I know about him."

"You know sod all Mick, you're talking through your backside as usual. A couple of pints and you're off exploring Cloud Cuckoo Land; just give it a rest, or go somewhere else to peddle your ridiculous fantasies," retorted a disgruntled Raymond Baker.

"You've have no idea what I know Baker. You won't be laughing so loudly when people are paying me good money to buy what I have to sell."

"And pigs might fucking fly," laughed Baker. "Just piss off, won't you Mick, there's only so much surrealism people can put up with in the course of one night."

Most of the people in the pub supported the bluntly put suggestion that Mr Wallington should go elsewhere for his next drink. Private conversation had been nigh on impossible whilst "The Braggart" held the stage. Everyone had been forced to listen to the intemperate monologue;

most of the people present had simply wished it would come to an end. One listener however had paid rapt attention to every word, and near the end of the tirade had slipped quietly into the car park at the rear of the pub, and from there he had made an anonymous phone call on his mobile.

Mick was sulking now, and resentfully silent. Even though the noise pollution had dramatically declined with the temporary closing of the orator's mouth, the regulars in the pub were still destined to enjoy a little more of his presence. He had stormed towards the exit door immediately his exchange with Raymond Baker terminated, and a collective sigh of relief was about to burst forth, only needing the slamming of that door as Wallington left before stepping out into the cold, when a well-meaning buffoon waylaid him and tried to calm him down. The sigh of relief turned into an audible groan at this intervention; people just wanted Mick gone. Even though he was no longer indulging a public rant, his mere presence in the room meant that nobody could relax.

This state of limbo existed for another 20 minutes before he finally departed. The misguided attempt to placate him had failed; he would go to where people appreciated him, he wouldn't be back there in a hurry. The landlord and his customers could all go fuck themselves, for all he cared; they were of no further interest to him. He had a valuable commodity to auction, what did he need with them? What he did need though was another drink. It was now dark, which had to mean it was well past 10pm; despite extended licensing hours many of the local pubs closed early in midweek. The Bold Centurion was not one of them, however; he would be sure to get a drink there. Despite not having a torch Mick set off down a narrow, unlit path, bordered on both sides by high hedges and in the shadow of several tall trees, which was a recognised short cut to his next port of call.

It was almost pitch black, the moon was young and low down in the sky and the stars which twinkled above did little to illuminate the track. Using his arms like a cat uses its whiskers to feel both sides of a restricted space, and also to help him keep his balance he hurried down the path. He had a long walk in front of him, although in broad daylight the 400 yards would have seemed a short jog, and strangely he felt uneasy. Suddenly behind him, he heard whispering voices followed by the stamp of heavy feet. He quickened his pace, those following him quickened theirs. Panic started to set in, whoever was behind him intended him harm. Mick felt like a hunted fox being doggedly pursued by an angry pack of hounds. He started to run, for the first time in decades, thankful at least that the path was straight; a pinprick of light appeared, if he could just make it to the end before they caught him he would be safe. The doors of The Centurion would be just yards away; surely he would not be followed into the building.

The speck of light grew bigger and bigger. Not since his rugby playing days, over 50 years before, had he run so fast for so long. His legs ached, his chest hurt, his lungs gulped down air, every fibre of his body was telling him to stop, but to stop would be fatal. He glanced behind him to see if he could catch sight of his attackers, they were still in darkness, but he could clearly hear the pounding of their feet. They hadn't gained on him as much as he had feared; just 50 yards separated him from sanctuary. He would make it! He would escape the violent beating they intended for him. He quickly glanced behind him once more, now he could see two men charging after him, but they were still over 70 yards behind him, the gap was too wide, they wouldn't catch him, providing his heart kept on pumping. He turned back to look toward the place of his salvation and ran slap bang into the baseball bat being wielded by a huge shaven headed man who was clearly no stranger to violence.

CHAPTER NINETEEN

Night after night sleep is denied to me. I dare not close my eyes because, when I do, my brain seizes the opportunity to create pictures of a dead woman's face. She was young, with so much to live for, and I took her life. I have become a monster, and although I had no other choice but to do what I did, I am tormented by feelings of disgust and self-loathing.

When tiredness finally overwhelms me, I dream the same bloody dream. I am a priest dressed all in black, a stern judge of all human frailty, a ruthless dispenser of harsh justice. Pity and compassion are alien concepts to me, and guilt can stain the hands of several generations. She stands before me accused of being the cursed child of a heretic. I see fear in her face when it dawns upon her that she must pay the penalty for coming from a diseased bloodline. She tries to protest that she cannot be held responsible for her ancestors' crimes. I ask her who else is there to take the blame. She cannot tell me. I turn to holy writ and tell her that the "sins of the father" cannot be ignored. She grabs the hem of my robes and begs for mercy, then reaches up to touch the holy cross that hangs around my neck. The crucifix is razor sharp; her fingers bleed as she tries to grasp it. That is a sign from God that her prayers have not found favour. Roughly I push her from me and thrust her from the sanctuary of the temple onto the violent streets below. An angry mob surrounds her and beat her with sticks and jagged stones. Her screams eventually fall silent. Nothing of her beauty remains, a work of art has been destroyed, an icon has been smashed, only a photograph now exists to remind the world how beautiful she once was.

I should be rejoicing that a just punishment has been imposed, instead I find myself weeping at the ending of a life unfulfilled. The wicked disciple of Lord Jesus Christ, who with a stone heart refused to let my grandmother bury her son in his churchyard, tells me that I have done well. His approval is the one thing I cannot stomach. I am tainted by his righteous evil. In despair, I put my hands together and pray for the forgiveness of my sins; the angels and archangels screech their derision at my plea. I stand before St Peter, as the girl stood before me, and I beg for absolution; the Gatekeeper of Heaven has deaf ears. An indictment listing my many failings is read out. A punishment is handed down. My sentence is one of eternal damnation. Struggling and pleading for Christ's mercy, I am chained against my will to the bony crone who gave my mother birth and to the hideously burned body of her only son.

I wake up with a scream, in a cold sweat, but with a face the colour of the fires of Hell, and from then on I cannot sleep, but pace the room, wearing the carpet threadbare as I do so. I talk to myself and tell myself that I will only gain a measure of serenity if the killing stops but, if it does, then that must mean that all that has gone on before was pointless, and surely it is a bigger sin to kill wantonly, and without reason, rather than to carry out a pre-ordained and carefully thought out retribution. I know this must be correct; so why do I agonise about it.

Looking so intently into her face before I pulled the trigger was a big mistake as I already have made clear. It is not one I will repeat. I will aim for the heart and ignore the head, and as I fire I will imagine that I am a small boy, and that the person I am ridding the world of is the person who injured that helpless child and not the scapegoat for my wrath. Before the next time comes I will wipe the last vestiges of compassion from my mind. By doing that some deluded folk will say I risk destroying what believers call a soul, but all religion is fantasy and has no place in the real world.

Yet, despite that obvious truth millions of people worldwide still adhere to outmoded doctrine. Throughout the last two millennia confused simpletons have committed atrocities on behalf of Allah and of Christ and a host of lesser Gods. Torture, banishment, brainwashing, blackmail, hypnotism and supernatural claptrap, these have been the tools of imams, rabbis and priests, and even now, in the twenty first century, when religious mumbo-jumbo means so little to most normal human beings, across the world people are daily suffering death, persecution and punishment for their blind faith. How these people cannot see that Religion is the mother of Cruelty and the grandmother of Corruption is a mystery that I cannot begin to understand. The stories that the Bible and the Koran tell us are primitive fiction, which have no place in the modern world, but human nature has an inherent need for make-believe. We all have sagas to relate; some worthy, some less so; I have an unworthy tale to tell you which you may perhaps find instructive.

A woman, no longer in the first flush of youth, for all intents and purposes left upon the shelf, identified a particular handsome young man as the person who should father her a child. She wasn't dog rough as men sometimes label unglamorous women, indeed she was not unattractive in a superior sort of way, but she looked down on ordinary people and believed herself to be above the common herd, hence she was not loved by them, nor ever had been.

The young man she selected for the role was clever, gifted, handsome, well-educated and, unbeknown to her, shallow. She was too old, too plain, and too aloof to ever have appeared on his radar, so it was never likely to be a match made in Heaven; but never-the- less she pursued him relentlessly. At first he didn't notice her, then he tried to ignore her, then he tried to rebuff her, and finally, when everything else failed, he listened to her proposition.

She did not want love, that would be a distraction, marriage was never an issue; indeed she was adamant that she didn't want any form of relationship. All she wanted was a child she could nurture and mould into becoming a successful person on her terms.

Some wine was drunk, all bought by her, and after much discussion, and some hesitation, a deal was struck. In return for the sum of £1000 (a tidy sum at that time,) to be paid in advance, the man agreed to have unguarded sex with her, and if she became pregnant then a further £1000 would be handed over: should the first attempt to create an embryo fail; then repeat fees of £500 per time would become payable, the act of copulation to take place at the optimum time of each calendar month. Other than the initial £1000 bonus for a job well done, there would be no additional payments on offer; the young man would also have to agree to renounce all claim to the child, and to keep the details of this agreement a permanent and closely guarded secret.

The deal was financially attractive to him, despite the fact that he was rich, particularly so if there wasn't initially a successful outcome; the woman herself was a far less attractive proposition; however he had a scheme to deal with that particular stumbling block.

A date was agreed, and both parties went to a quiet hotel to carry out their plan. He feigned nervousness, and insisted he must have a little alcohol to calm his nerves. He insisted she drink too, which she was happy to do so. His wine came straight from the bottle to the glass; her wine had a secret additive. He appeared to become "merry", she became more noticeably "drunk", albeit they both had drunk the same amount. Struggling to undress herself, she eventually more or less collapsed onto the bed, and then he undressed himself and slid under the duvet beside her. Her later memory of events was poor, but given that she didn't want emotional attachment, she regarded that as no bad thing; but she was aware that rough sex had taken place.

She was lucky, she became pregnant after that first encounter, thus saving her embarrassment, and also money, and she later gave birth to the child she longed for. The baby boy became her project, and in many ways that project turned out exactly as she would have wished: in many ways, but not in every single one. As the child grew up, he failed to take on many of the physical traits of his father. If she was disappointed she never said so and indeed marvelled at the fact about how surprising and gloriously unpredictable Nature could be; the young man knew that the true explanation was far from unpredictable.

When first he had consented to take part in this sex for money plan, he had worried that his ambivalence to her physical attractions might rob him of his chance to make money. A jolly jape had been worked out, a joker had been played, and a substitute had been fielded; the winning goal, the hole in one, had been scored by a ringer. In return for £250 another man had done the actual deed. From the standpoint of the two "conspirators" the initial "coupling" turned out to be too successful, thus ensuring there would be no lucrative repeat fees. The "substitute" was particularly bitter that this moneymaking scheme ended so prematurely; it wasn't in his nature to accept setbacks gracefully. The £250 he received for 5 minutes of exertion was spent within just 7 days; Mick Wallington has never known the meaning of self-restraint.

As for the identity of the woman who went to such extremes to bear a child, that is surely obvious. Constance Cartwright designed her own baby, or at least she thought she did, and if her son did not match the blueprint it seemed not to matter. She remains blissfully ignorant of the trick that was played upon her, and for the time being it is better if that situation continues. Mick Wallington was about to use his knowledge to blackmail Edward Cartwright. He figured that in America a sordid tale of sex for cash and the exposure that the Golden Boy was sired by the 47 year old town rapscallion, would cause the fans to turn their backs on their idol and the T.V. channels would drop any plans they had to tell his rags to riches story. He may have been right about that, but I'm not sure that that would have been the case, but whatever the outcome, the tabloid press and the T.V channels in this country would have then focussed on the life of the person who tossed the story into the public domain. His past anti-social acts would have been rigorously examined, and no doubt the drunken act that killed 2 people and so badly maimed a third that he chose to commit suicide in a dramatically public way would have made the front pages. From there it is possible that the victims of Wallington's recklessness might have themselves become the subject of inquiry, and had that occurred there was a risk that some way along the line I might have featured in that narrative. That was a risk I couldn't take. Mick had made powerful enemies. When he started to tell the world in his drunken state that he knew stuff about Cartwright, I had to act. A short phone call was all that was needed, but Mick had to be delayed a little while so that those with the means to cause him harm could gain the time they needed to find him and inflict their pain. He was easy to delay, and happy to talk to any person who he thought might be on his side. He had his message to relate; as did the men who would shortly meet him. The message that they brought was as brutal as it was clear; Mick's life is not in danger, that would have spared him the anguish that is yet to come, but from now on he will be terrified of his own shadow and too frightened to reappear upon the public stage. Edward Cartwright will be pleased to think he has been silenced, and Mickey Shah – who so readily believed a lie that was fed to him – will also be content, and that will be enough for now.

So now you have learned about phone calls and falsehoods, and that Mick and Connie were for just one night an "item", which is more than the stuck up Mrs Cartwright knows, but of course there is still a third party to reveal. I think perhaps you should hang in suspense a little longer before the final name is made public. Could it be Alan Nadin, or Frank Oakes, or Tim Bradley or Bill Adamson? Maybe Raymond Baker is the man, or maybe Mickey Shah is not the newcomer to these parts that he seems to be. Think hard, jump to what conclusions most appeal to you. All may be revealed the next time I speak.

CHAPTER TWENTY

"He's in a pretty bad way Gov. He's got a fractured jaw, 3 cracked ribs, a broken wrist and a lump on the side of his head the size of a goose egg. His mouth is all wired up. He can only take food through a tube, he's lost his 2 front teeth, and it will be a long time before he can talk properly, not that it is likely that he would be willing to talk to us in any event."

"The poor old sod Pete. I know that there are quite a few people in this town who might think that it couldn't have happened to a more deserving bloke, but he's 75 years old for Christ's sake, surely to God nobody that age should have to undergo the beating that's been handed out to him."

"I wouldn't take issue with that Gov," replied Detective Sergeant Bennett, "it just takes the edge off my anger a bit knowing what a loud-mouthed prat he can sometimes be."

"Nobody's going to disagree with you there Peter, but prat or not, he still shouldn't have suffered in the way that he did, and we need to find out why the things that happened to him happened, and more importantly who was responsible for causing them."

"I think the "why" is pretty clear when you look at all the circumstances. He'd been ranting in the pub about Edward Cartwright, and how he knew stuff which would cause him a great deal of bother. Cartwright wouldn't like that, and neither would the people who promote him. He's got private bodyguards watching out for him; one phone call to them and that would be it. A good kicking is a sure fire way of guaranteeing that people don't talk out of turn in future; perhaps it's in that direction that we should be looking."

Detective Inspector Hobson looked doubtful.

"Maybe it is Pete, I certainly wouldn't rule it out, but at the same time what happened to Mick was pretty crude and unsophisticated; I think Cartwright's men might have had a little more subtlety about them. Is there anybody else who you think might enter into the picture?"

"Not that I can think of Gov," replied the detective sergeant.

"Well, I've got another possible candidate for you," continued Mark Hobson. "Just suppose for a moment somebody told Mickey Shah that it was Wallington who made up the story about Frank Oakes being seen creeping around near to his house with a rifle in his hand. Shah's first reaction would be to report the incident to us because that would land Oakes in very deep water. If it then became apparent that it was a cock and bull story that would make him very angry. It was worth his while dealing with us when he thought that Oakes might end up in court, but generally speaking Shah doesn't like the police poking into his affairs. He was prepared to let us interview him when he thought that interview would be a nail in Oakes' coffin, but when he realised that wasn't going to be the case, he would have been mortified that he had let us speak to him for no good reason. From choice he would keep us at arm's length, and the fact that he let us get up close and personal when there was no possibility of any advantage accruing to him would have left him feeling pretty pissed off. He's got thugs working for him who wouldn't think twice about kicking the shit out of an old man; in fact they would probably think it was good sport. I know this is all pure conjecture, but do you think there might be some mileage in this line of inquiry?"

"There might be Gov," admitted Pete Bennett. "Certainly we'd be fools not to follow both lines of inquiry at this stage."

***

And the inquiries were vigorously pursued, but ultimately to no good effect. Edward Cartwright vehemently denied any knowledge whatsoever of Mick Wallington, and thereby, if he was telling the truth, demonstrated a complete lack of motive. Whether he was being honest remained a live issue, but having lived away from the Peak District for so long, his story couldn't easily be disproved. The professional "minders" the T.V. Company was paying big bucks to, to look after their star performer, were used to being questioned. They were experienced in their trade. They weren't the sort of men to be intimidated by police interrogation, denials of wrongdoing tripped easily off their tongues. To outwardly appear to be fully cooperating, to apparently bend over backwards to assist the police, whilst in reality making sure that nothing of consequence was exposed was a skill they had perfected over many years of practice. Hobson and Bennett had had no illusions; they had known from the outset that interviewing them would be an exercise in futility, but the metaphorical banging of heads against a brick wall was unfortunately part of every detective's daily routine.

The men who worked for Mickey Shah were far less intelligent than those who guarded Edward Cartwright, but they were just as tight lipped as their American cousins. It was "bloody ridiculous" to suppose that any of them had anything to do with the assault on Mick Wallington, and if the police thought otherwise they were "talking through their arses." Mr Wallington didn't owe their employer money; neither was he going about slandering him or threatening to expose him. If the victim had been Frank Oakes then on paper it might have been a different matter, but even then they were adamant that only words of warning would have been used, and that violence would never have been on the agenda.

Mark Hobson was as sceptical of their denials as he had been of Edward Cartwright's and his hired hands, but he had no evidence to accuse them of lying, and so, for the time being, they all had to be regarded as suspects against whom no immediate action could be taken.

***

If one honest witness had been present at the scene to point an accusing finger in any particular direction, then it might have been a very different picture, but at the time Mick Wallington had been giving a very good impression of a punch bag there had been nobody outside The Bold Centurion to take note of the brutality. When the baseball bat crashed into his face, fracturing his jaw, and dislodging 2 of his front teeth, he had screamed like a harpooned whale, but nobody except his attackers had been around to hear his squeal of pain. When seconds later the two men who had chased him down the alley enthusiastically joined in the affray Mick was already a broken man, too traumatised, and in too much agony to be able to utter an intelligible sound. He thought he was about to die; he had never experienced so much pain; every breath he took was agony to such a degree that now utterly defenceless and incapable of movement, he prayed that the next blow when it came would forever put him out of his misery.

"He's lucky to be alive," commented D.S. Bennett. "It's only by the grace of God that he's still here. Two young chaps left the pub to go for a curry and caught the very tail end of the punch up. They saw two men kicking what they first thought was a bin bag, and then they noticed a third bloke standing nearby with a lump of wood in his hand. The penny dropped, they realised that what they were actually witnessing was somebody being beaten up. They were brave lads, braver than a lot of people might have been. They shouted at the men to stop, the three thugs could easily have turned on them, and for all the lads knew they could have been tooled up. Fortunately by this time the men had accomplished everything they wanted to achieve, so rather than seeking confrontation they just walked off back down the path and disappeared into the darkness. Apart from being able to tell us that 2 of the men were masked, that all of them were big, and that the bloke with the lump of wood, who they only saw the back of, was a skinhead, they've not been able to give us any useful descriptions. There is no

CCTV at The Bold Centurion, the street lighting at that location is poor; the presumption has to be that they left the scene in one or more vehicles, but if they did nobody saw them depart."

"Did either of the lads follow them at all? Can somebody at least tell us in which direction they went when they got to the other end of the footpath?" asked the DI.

"Neither of them did Gov; one of the lads is Giles Sterndale, he's a medical student at Leicester University; his grandfather was a surgeon at the M.R.I and his father is a practising G.P.in Macclesfield. He attended to Mick whilst his mate dialled 999. He almost certainly saved his life. Mick was in such a state of shock that at one point he stopped breathing. I don't know exactly how he did it, I think mouth to mouth resuscitation may not have been possible because there was too much blood, but somehow he got him breathing again, then the paramedics arrived and took over, and luckily for him he has survived."

"But not with a tale to tell eh Pete? I bet you any money that even when he is well enough to talk, Mr Wallington will not be saying a single word to us."

"Nothing could be surer than that Gov, but we will still have to go through the motions."

CHAPTER TWENTY ONE

The Reverend Jacob (call me Jake) Lindley was in the process of going through the church accounts of St Catherine's Lower Burrdale, a task given to him by the Rural Dean, who was aware that he had briefly studied accountancy before realising that his true vocation lay in the field of religion. They did not make pretty reading. Income over the past 25 years had steadily declined; not so much on paper, but disastrously in real terms. Money bought so much less now and everything was so very expensive. The price of central heating oil had gone through the roof, electricity bills had rocketed, and nowadays it seemed that even the most minor repairs to the fabric of building ran into thousands of pounds. The congregation had dwindled to next to nothing, and with an average age of just over 70 years, most of the pensioners who worshipped there could not afford to put more than a few pence onto the collection plate each week. The situation couldn't continue; something had to be done, and that something inevitably had to be closure.

Once it had been very different. Once a struggling parish could have looked for support to its neighbours, but not anymore; even the big churches in the big towns were feeling the pinch. Just for a second the Rev Lindley pondered on why it was that the Anglican Church was shrinking so dramatically, as were many other Christian denominations, but in the cities, mosques were often nearly full to bursting point, and there was dynamism about Islam, which his church totally lacked. There was perhaps a dangerous level of fanaticism in some places too, which was the downside of the passion the Imams could instil in their flock, but just at the moment he would have given anything to be able to tap into that mood of excitement and demonstrate to the people of Lower Burrdale that the Anglican Church was as relevant and necessary today as it had been 100 years ago.

That St Catherine's Church had once thrived was clear from the quality of the original Victorian build, and the high status tombs and monuments that could still be seen in the sadly neglected graveyard. That the numbers who prayed there had once been great was obvious from the books of old photographs that could still be found in the vestry. Men wearing trilby hats and women, mostly wearing long black coats, or shapeless floral printed summer frocks if the occasion was a church fete or a Sunday School outing, had gathered in abundance to take part in whatever event was taking place, and although smiles were in relative short supply mostly these snapshots seemed to capture groups of people happy enough with their lots. Many of the pictures had faded with age, or taken on a sepia hue, but it would still be possible for anyone who might remember any of the persons involved to positively identify those individuals. Not that a lot of people looked at them now, the last time the albums had been touched appeared to have been several years ago by a man seeking to research his family history.

One thing was abundantly clear. People in the years immediately after the Second World War may have been poorer then, but there was more genuine faith. A good proportion of people still tried to give a tenth of their weekly income to the church, and even those who couldn't afford that gave as generously as they could, and not just little bits of small change that was the norm in the 21st Century. Over the years St Catherine's had received a goodly amount of donated cash.

Another thing that was equally clear was that that cash hadn't always been wisely spent. At times various incumbents had promoted their own pet projects. In the late 1960s, one vicar had championed the cause of Christianity in Central Africa to such a degree that a totally unrealistic proportion of the church's yearly income had been sent overseas. Later it had been discovered much of that money had found its way into the pockets of corrupt officials and only a tiny percentage of it had reached its intended destination.

The minister who followed him had been a very different character. He had argued that a parish room should be built in part of the Churchyard and had persuaded his Parochial Church Council of the wisdom of this scheme. He had claimed to have contacts in the building trade and that he could find someone who would do the building work at a fraction of the usual cost, and to an extent this turned out to be true; the only problem was that the builder used low quality materials and cut corners at every turn; this money saving solution had later cost the church thousands of pounds it didn't have to put right the botched cowboy job that had been carried out.

But perhaps the biggest problem of all had been the overbearing personality of some of the clerics. Between 1949 and 1965 the Reverend Matthew Hardman had lived up to his surname and ruled the parish with a rod of iron. He had also kept a scrapbook of his many pronouncements that had appeared in the local paper. Rock and Roll was "intrinsically evil," miniskirts were "the garments of the whores", interfaith marriages were "a betrayal of Christ", self-harm and suicide were "mortal sins", adultery was "the worst sin of all", Sunday Trading was "an attack on Christian values" and there were many other examples of his intemperate views. The Reverend Jacob Lindley saw the Reverend Hardman as a self-opinionated bigot; the Reverend Hardman, if he had still been alive would have proclaimed himself to be a "warrior in God's army," and denounced the Reverend Lindley as a "dangerous revisionist."

And of course his rigid stance on so many issues hadn't been universally admired and from time to time there had been a cost. There were a number of letters contained in a box file marked "Complaints" that gave testament to that conclusion. Gentle pleading letters from people wanting to remarry in church following a divorce had been replied to aggressively. It hadn't mattered if there had been gross domestic violence, blatant desertion or even the other spouse's adultery, the reply was always the same. Rejection is a bitter pill to swallow, but judgemental rejection is intolerable. Over the course of his 16 year tenure as parish priest there had been 23 occasions when he had refused to marry divorcees.

Sadly, over the same period there had been 35 suicides, and grieving relatives had begged to be allowed to hold a church service to remember their departed loved ones. Hardman had been as inflexible as granite. The woman who killed herself rather than descend into complete dementia was "a coward who disobeyed the 7th commandment;" the young boy who was bullied unmercifully because he had a speech impediment, "deserved no special treatment"; even James Rowbotham, a crippled war hero, who ended his life in a dramatically tragic way felt the wrath of the vicar's cutting tongue. The man was "a weakling before God," and by taking to himself the power of life and death he had "circumvented God's will."

"If God had wanted him dead, then he would have died in the war, or in the car accident; that hadn't happened, therefore God didn't want it. To go against the wishes of our Lord was a passport to eternal damnation."

On occasions the unkind language of his refusal had led to anguished letters being written to the local papers, and over the course of time the vicar's intransigence had cost his church many legacies.

If all the money that would have been freely given had there been just a little tolerance and compassion had actually been bequeathed to this church, thought Jacob Lindley, then there probably wouldn't be the gaping hole in its finances that there is today.

Two or three specific examples stood out. When the local bank manager had jumped from a railway viaduct near Glossop, killing himself and causing a 3 car pileup as terrified motorists tried to avoid running over his mangled body the incident had made the National News. He had been diagnosed as suffering from clinical depression and he was also in a lot of pain from an incurable back injury. For 20 years he had been a sidesman at the church, an enthusiastic fund-raiser and a devout member of the congregation. It had counted for nothing; the man was denied a Christian burial in the Rev. Hardman's church. His widow was enraged. She wrote a letter to the Bishop to express her disgust, and to explain that as a result of the Reverend Harman's appalling attitude she had revoked her current will, which had left everything of value she possessed, including a 5 bedroom detached house, to the church, and that the R.S.P.C.A. would instead benefit from her generosity.

There were other examples too. The mother of James Rowbotham felt similarly aggrieved. The value of her estate was considerably less than the value of the estate of the bank manager, but the estate did include a cottage, so was by no means negligible, and many hundreds of pounds could have been available to swell the church coffers.

And there were at least 7 letters in a similar vein. Jake Lindley wondered why it was that, once upon a time, so many of the men called to serve the church had been so intolerant, doctrinaire, self-important and in many cases misogynistic. For too many of them the sexual act between men and women had been unclean, and the spiritual father of the Lower Burrdale church had been one of them. Intolerance of all human frailty was in his D.N.A; the only saving grace that could be found was that, unlike too many of his colleagues, at least Reverend Hardman seemed to have been unmoved by the innocent charms of some of his choristers. For what it was worth, the stern enforcer of God's will had been an excellent theologian; Jacob Lindley thought that it wasn't probably worth very much in the eyes of his Creator.

***

It had been the source of much unhappiness to the Adamson family that Penny's funeral had had to be delayed to await a coroner's ruling. Because she had been murdered in cold blood there was a massive on-going police investigation to try to discover the identity of and then to arrest her killer. An inquest had been opened and adjourned, but that had taken 12 days to arrange because the Coroner wanted to take charge personally, and not leave it to his deputy. At some stage in the future, it was hoped there would be a criminal trial followed by a jury verdict. In the meantime the Coroner could easily have ruled that Penny's body should not be disposed of until after the conclusion of that trial, leaving only the option of a memorial service to be held in the interim. It would not have been the same thing as a funeral, and the healing process would have been held in abeyance. Whether with the death of one so young and beautiful there could ever be said to be a healing process was by no means certain, but months or even years in limbo would have greatly added to the family's distress. Fortunately he had not done this, and had permitted burial to take place, which was what the undertaker had predicted would be the decision, but none of the Adamson family had wanted to start making arrangements until they were sure that they would not have to be abandoned.

 Now they had the go-ahead. The coroner had felt that because the circumstances of Penny's death were recorded on video tape and it was 100% certain that she had been fatally wounded by an assassin's bullet, given that the P.M. report indicated that she had been an active young woman in perfect health, there was no need to postpone the funeral. He had come to a similar conclusion some months earlier with regards to the remains of Adam Wallington, and nobody thought in either case that there would be any grounds at all for defence barristers to challenge the basic circumstances of their deaths. He had however stipulated in Adam's case, as he had done in Penny's case that cremation should not be an option, leaving open the possibility of both bodies being exhumed if in the course of any trial the Defence convinced a judge of the need to re-examine them. Arrangements had finally been made; Penny was now to be laid to rest 26 days after her life came to such an abrupt end.

The persons who had been hit the hardest hit by Penny's death were of course her mum and dad and younger brother; they were devastated by her loss; right now it seemed utterly impossible for them to contemplate any kind of a future without her.

Sheila Adamson too had been overwhelmed by grief, and in some ways the loss of her granddaughter hit her hardest of all. When Penny had got the job at the B.B.C. Sheila had been thrilled, although at the same time it had re-awakened the sorrow she had felt when her own media career had been cut short, and though she tried to avoid it there had been a touch of resentment that the world was opening up for this young woman when it had so abruptly closed for her. She had tried to be philosophical; she had consoled herself that in her declining years she would at least get the pleasure of experiencing vicariously her grandchild's moments of success. Her death seemed like a double blow. Having once seen her dreams snatched from her grasp by the accident of pregnancy, now it seemed even the consolation prize of watching somebody she cared for living those dreams was also being denied to her. It was so unfair! Why did God have to be spiteful? Maybe if her thought processes had been a great deal more organised than they now could be she could have viewed her situation more objectively, but complex problems now baffled her, and unravelling multi-layered emotions was entirely beyond her.

***

"If Penny's death was the intended outcome all along, then we will need to have plain clothed officers attending her funeral service just in case her killer decides to put in an appearance. I don't think that there'll be any sort of incident at the church," commented Detective Inspector Hobson, "but we can't take any chances. I do think it's possible that if our murderer wanted her dead, he might also want to be present to witness her body being laid to rest."

"You mean he'll behave a bit like an arsonist returning to the scene of a fire he has started so that he can get all excited when a big red fire tender arrives?"

"Exactly so Pete, exactly so: I think we'll have to borrow some C.I.D. officers from outside the area so that their faces aren't known locally, that way if he does put in an appearance our man won't be deterred by a police presence."

"But without some local knowledge how will they know what to look for? Grief sometimes causes people to behave very oddly, any excess of emotion could appear strange, as could any apparent lack of emotion; and to someone who didn't know it might be a signal to investigate further. We don't want to end up nicking a distraught cousin or half cousin on suspicion of murder."

"We'll have local officers present as well to pay their respects and they'll be highly visible. Our man won't be phased by that, he'll expect them to be there. If he attends the service, and it's a very, very big "if", he'll probably place himself out of their sight line. I'm going to be there as well, and I'll probably stand out like a sore thumb, that won't matter a jot. What matters is that we get this one right, that there is someone on hand to make sure no unfortunate mistakes are made, but who can give the O.K if a genuine suspect is spotted."

CHAPTER TWENTY TWO

"Dr Brodie says you can have 10 minutes with Mr Wallington, but if he starts to get upset then you must stop your questioning; he nearly died when he was attacked, if he gets agitated it could trigger a relapse: is that perfectly understood?"

"Yes nurse," replied Detective Inspector Hobson, "we'll be as good as gold with your patient, won't we Pete?"

"Aren't we always Gov," replied Detective Sergeant Pete Bennett; there was something about the expression on his face that made the nurse think that that was not necessarily so.

The two High Peak detectives had been awaiting the doctor's permission to speak to the "Burrdale Braggart," and were now about to ask him about the events that had led up to his hospitalisation. Neither officer was particularly optimistic that anything worthwhile would be achieved, but they weren't oracles, and great results had sometimes sprung from unpromising beginnings. On the other hand disastrous outcomes had sometimes followed on from fantastic initial interviews, so wise officers never counted their chickens in advance of hatching; which was always a sensible approach to take. Armed with a substantial degree of scepticism, and suitably modest expectations, they entered the room Mick Wallington was languishing in.

He looked a complete mess. His face was badly bruised and swollen, one eye was completely shut and his jaw looked as if it had been clumsily assembled using Meccano; he appeared the picture of misery. For a moment Pete Bennett was tempted to ask him if he was auditioning for a part in a new James Bond movie as a sidekick to the villainous Jaws, but wisely he controlled that particular urge.

Mark Hobson introduced himself and his colleague, expressed the hope that the patient would soon be feeling better, and asked him if he was prepared to answer a few simple questions about the events surrounding the attack on him that had caused so many injuries. Wallington nodded his head and mouthed that he would do his best.

Predictably perhaps, his best turned out to be poor. He was able to confirm that he had been attacked by three men wearing dark clothing. He claimed that two of them were masked; he now wasn't sure about the third. He was clear that the man he almost ran into had a baseball bat and that he had struck him with it and he thought the other two men also had weapons of some type. He stressed that all the men were tall and well-built to such a degree that D.I. Hobson started to wonder if they were renegades from a Land of Giants, and that was about it. He had heard the men speak but couldn't remember anything they had actually said, nor whether any of them had regional accents or other oddities of speech. Both Hobson and Bennett were left feeling that Mick was not telling the whole truth, but that much of what he said could be correct.

When Mark Hobson questioned him about peripheral matters the assault victim became a lot more evasive. It was put to him that it was a matter of record that, before the attack, he had been proclaiming to the World and his wife that he knew secrets about Edward Cartwright that could destroy him; he denied that was the case; he did admit to getting a little drunk and saying one or two mildly derogatory things about the Hollywood teen idol, but that was all. When Detective Inspector Hobson started to press him on this point and to demand to know exactly what it was he knew about Cartwright Mick refused to answer. He started to hyperventilate, he complained about pains in his chest, he pressed his panic button and that was the end of the interview. The two Burrdale detectives left the hospital feeling that although they may have been fed some crumbs of truth, the main meal had eluded them.

But if Mr Michael Wallington couldn't or wouldn't tell the police his secrets, perhaps it was possible that they knew a lady who would do so. A visit to the home of Constance Cartwright was quickly arranged, and within the hour both officers were knocking on the "Superstar's" mum's door to see if she could fill in some of the many blanks in Mick's story.

Mrs Cartwright was politeness itself, and outwardly pleasant and cooperative, but underneath the facade of a genteel English woman Hobson believed she was a She Wolf, who would do or say anything that was necessary to protect her son. She claimed that Wallington had come ranting and raving to her house and made non-specific threats to damage Edward; she was adamant that he neither said nor hinted what it was he claimed to know that he thought would mortally wound Edward.

"I just sent him on his way with a flea in his ear. Everything he said was preposterous; just the babblings of a self-deceiving alcoholic. He couldn't know anything because there is nothing to know; Edward's life is a matter of public record, there are no skeletons in our cupboards."

Towards the end of the interview D.S. Bennett commented that it must have been difficult to bring up a child on her own, which led D.I. Hobson to ask about the whereabouts of Edward's father. Mrs Cartwright became quite coy, but with a little gentle prodding she revealed that Edward was the result of a one night stand with a man she could not name; she did say that so far as she was aware this man was now dead and had some grounds to believe he had been involved in a very serious car accident.

***

"They both know stuff they aren't telling us about," Detective Inspector Hobson said to Detective Sergeant Bennett. "Wallington knows exactly why he was beaten up like he was, and Mrs Cartwright isn't the type of woman to have a one night brief encounter behind the cowsheds with an itinerant organ grinder."

"I didn't know you were into innuendo Gov," laughed D. S. Bennett, doing a very passable impression of Kenneth Williams extolling the charms of Matron, "but I take your point entirely. She wouldn't open her legs for any Tom, Dick or Harry; whoever Edward Cartwright's dad is, it wasn't just a bit of casual sex, I'll bet a pound to a penny that that weren't the case."

"So we need to discover who the super stud is who fathered Burrdale's brightest star, but before we get side-tracked doing that, we need to find out who was responsible for the attack on Mick, and to my mind after today we ain't much nearer to doing that than when we started."

"Perhaps Giles Sterndale could help us Gov, he's a bright kid and he's not connected at all to Connie or to Mick so far as I can tell; perhaps he can give us a few more facts than his initial statement contains, unadulterated with the half-truths and obfuscation that others have been content to fob us off with".

"He's a lovely lad Love, not a bit arrogant, although he has every right to be; I think he'll make a great doctor. It made such a pleasant change to speak to such a clever, uncomplicated genuine bloke," Mark Hobson explained to his wife in the kitchen of their house as she prepared the evening meal.

"Mick Wallington and Constance Cartwright are hiding things from us," he continued, "of that I'm absolutely bloody certain, but when Pete and I spoke to Giles Sterndale it was like a breath of fresh air. Unfortunately, he wasn't able to add that much to his original statement except, crucially, he thought that one of the guys who assaulted Mick might have been foreign. Mickey Shah employs foreign workers as cheap labour; I'm wondering if it could have been one of his men."

"It sounds like a good enough theory to me Darling."

"It is Love, but the snag is that he isn't the only one round here who does that; some of the larger farms round here could use migrant labour, and Edward Cartwright has got private bodyguards flown in from the States to protect him; there is no reason why it couldn't have been one of them."

"And of course you're not likely to get much out of them are you Pet?"

"We've got more chance of platting sawdust than getting a sensible reply from any one of them," replied her husband bitterly.

"Did Giles Sterndale have anything else to say?"

"Not really Love. We ended up just talking about medicine. Do you know that when he qualifies, he'll be a third generation doctor? Both his dad and his granddad are still alive. His father's still practising as a G.P.in Macclesfield, and his granddad was a surgeon here at the local hospital before moving onto higher things at the M.R.I. He started life as an army doctor in the Second World War. Apparently he was good at his job, but with an appalling bedside manner; fortunately he made very few mistakes because if he'd been accident prone he'd have had problems; there was very little about his character that would have persuaded any patient to hold back. Giles did say that a man like his granddad wouldn't survive in today's N.H.S. Nowadays people look for legal redress at the drop of a hat and ambulance chasing lawyers get rich on the pickings. It's a sad state of affairs. In my view there are too many flaming lawyers; it's about time the Government ordered a radical cull of the legal profession."

At that point Mark and Helena's two young children burst into the room and put an end to their father's musing before he extended his drastic remedy to encompass social workers, civil servants, politicians of all political persuasions and tabloid journalists. Now it was the children's time to claim their daddy's attention whilst mummy finished off making the tea; and Mark loved it. He had a beautiful wife, two gorgeous kids, he was a happy family man, and in the end that was all that mattered in his life.

It was only much later, after the children had been tucked in bed and read a bedtime story, while Mark and Helena were relaxing together with a glass of wine that the conversation turned again to the murder case he was investigating. Remembering how Helena had unearthed a family diary at Christopher's school, which had contained the confession of a young home guard soldier, Mark asked his wife if she could remember the name of the child who had brought the journal into school. Helena replied that she would have to check to be sure, but she thought the diary had been brought to school by a little girl called Alicia. She couldn't remember the girl's surname, except that it sounded Polish, but she knew that her uncle was Frank Oakes.

"He might be the best person to speak to," she said. "If it is the little girl I'm thinking of both her parents have high powered jobs and can be difficult to get hold of. Frank Oakes is very local, and given the fact that the last time you met him he was terrified that you would arrest him, I shouldn't think he'll give you any trouble."

"You can bet good money on that," laughed Mark.

***

And unlike the forecasts of most pundits Mark Hobson's prediction hit the nail on the head. Frank Oakes bent over backwards to be helpful. He confirmed that Alicia's diary had been written by his late father, and that the story of the rifle contained in it was true; it had become the stuff of legend at family dinner parties and the tale had been told and retold to entertain relatives. His dad had been far less forthcoming when asked about what exactly occurred in the woman's bedroom, maintaining the account in the diary that he woke up not actually knowing what had happened. He had always refused to name the lady concerned, but from what he had said Frank had surmised that she lived in a small terraced house close to the junction of Quarry Street and Canal Street. That was all he could tell the Detective Inspector; it wasn't much, but it was enough; a search of the Electoral Roll for the period offered good prospects of answers, and if that didn't work, there were other documents held by the Local Authority which almost certainly would do so.

In the event the task turned out to be straight forward. There were only half a dozen properties near enough to the road junction that could possibly fit the description that the police had been given. Canal Street and Quarry Street were in the industrial part of town; all the houses at that location had been built as workers' cottages in the mid 1880's and were all quite small and insignificant. During the Second World War two had been badly damaged by fire and had remained semi-derelict until the early 1960s, two more were occupied by elderly couples whose active sex lives had long since passed them by, one was lived in by a quarry foreman, his common law wife and their 6 children, and the final property was home to a middle aged widow and, when they were not overseas fighting abroad, or working away from home as part of the war effort, her two adult children. This was the only house where there would have been enough privacy to have permitted illicit sex to take place unnoticed, and where the single occupant was still young enough to enjoy a bit of rough and tumble. The woman's name was Mabel Agnes Rowbotham; a quick check of the records confirmed that she had died of a heart attack in 1969 having outlived her daughter who died in a car crash by 24 years and her son, who committed suicide in 1953 by 16 years. The son died without issue. The daughter, it seemed, had an illegitimate child fathered by a U.S. airman, but no trace of that boy appeared in the Register of Birth, Marriages and Death.

"And so the search for a missing weapon goes cold once more" grumbled Detective Sergeant Bennett. "On the basis that his mum and dad weren't married, I searched the records against the name Rowbotham, but none of the entries I could find fitted the bill. I then searched against obviously American sounding surnames in case the kid was registered in the father's name, but again without success. So what is our next move then Gov?"

"We keep on looking Pete, we've added one tiny piece to the jigsaw by discovering the I.D. of the person most likely to have found the missing rifle, and that has to be progress."

"If you say so Gov, if you say so," mumbled a less than convinced Detective Sergeant Bennett.

CHAPTER TWENTY THREE

"Man that is born of woman hath but a short time to live and is full of misery, he cometh up and is cut down like a flower" intoned the parish priest at the beginning of the desperately sad occasion that was Penny Adamson's funeral.

Bleak words for a bleak day thought Mark Hobson; and spoken far too soon in one young woman's life; and everybody here except perhaps one man must be of that view.

The small church was full to overflowing, and quite incapable of accommodating the number of people wanting to attend the funeral. Speakers had been erected to relay the service to the hundreds of mourners who had been unable to find room inside the building. T.V camera crews and reporters from several news channels added to the throng and they at least could be professionally detached from the events of the day and contain a degree of composure. Not so the many residents of Burrdale who stood in silence as the funeral orations were read out. Many people were in tears, and many more were on the verge of crying. The route the hearse had taken was strewn with flowers thrown by onlookers onto the hearse as it slowly made its way to the church. The outpouring of emotion mirrored that displayed by the vast crowds of people who watched the passing of Princess Diana's funeral cortege. Public demonstrations of grief were a relatively new phenomenon: Detective Inspector Hobson wondered if they were necessarily a good thing. People cry too easily nowadays he thought, it cheapens real grief, but even the hard-nosed detective had been close to tears when Sheila Adamson had talked about her dead granddaughter.

Dressed in an expensive black suit, which had once fitted her like a glove, but which now hung loosely across her shoulders and emphasised that the wearer had shrunk with age, looking thin and frail, the seventy seven year old lady had to be helped to the lectern by two middle aged men who were probably relatives. Her hair was now snow white, although immaculately groomed, her joints were stiff with age, but although her face was lined, she still had good bone structure, and it retained many of the elements that had made it beautiful. If the congregation had been able to see photographs of this old lady taken when in her early twenties they would have thought that, at that age, she bore an uncanny resemblance to her murdered granddaughter whom they had all come together to mourn.

For what seemed like an eternity, she struggled to compose herself, so overcome was she by grief, but then, hesitantly, and with a voice charged with emotion, she began to address the congregation.

"My beautiful, beloved granddaughter Penny was somebody everybody loved. She was kind, generous-hearted, and as bright as a button. She held the world in the palm of her hands; when she walked into a room, she brought the sunlight with her. She touched the heart of everyone who knew her, and made even the grumpiest man or woman feel that the day was better for having met her. She capti…capti…capti…"

Here Sheila struggled to remember the word, and it seemed as if her hymn of praise for Penny would be cut short, but one of the men with her whispered in her ear, and she was able to continue.

"She captivated us all with her personality and her wit. She was reaching for the stars and they were within her grasp, then as her fingers closed around her dream, she was taken from us.

"I think about her every hour of every day, and when I close my eyes at night I hear her voice calling me and I wake up expecting to see her smiling face; but she's not there! I cannot begin to compre… compre… comprehend the insanity that has snatched her from this world. Why a madman has destroyed someone so lovely and so blessed is a mystery, but by that act of cruelty he has destroyed my life, and damaged, perhaps irrep… irrep… irreparably, so many innocent lives as well. "Only the good die young"; why does that have to be? What is the world coming to if it allows such wickedness? A monster from the depths of Hell has unleashed his fury, and has created Hell on Earth for me, and for all Penny's family and friends, and done so for no reason and that is the saddest thing of all. My days are filled with misery; I miss her so much, I…" and at that point Sheila burst into tears and despite comforting arms being wrapped around her shoulder, she was no longer able to continue with the eulogy.

And she was not the only person who failed to complete her homage to Penny, the occasion was too much for one of her friends who had intended to share some childhood memories of a feisty little girl, but who broke down almost before she started, and there was a sense of despair that hung over the whole congregation that was tangible.

That despair seemed to intensify when the coffin was carried from the church to the grave. Many people sobbed quietly and many more shed silent tears; even the vicar struggled to keep his emotions in check, and the words "earth to earth, ashes to ashes " never before came so hesitantly from his lips. Moments like this tested even his faith. How could an all-seeing, benevolent Saviour of the world allow one so gifted to be brutally gunned down?

Mark Hobson stood respectfully silent towards the rear of the crowd, other plain clothed officers did likewise; the only thing to distinguish them from the rest of the mourners was that their heads were not bowed, and their eyes were scanning the churchyard to see if anything even vaguely suspicious was taking place.

They saw absolutely nothing. Nobody seemed to take an unnatural interest in the tragedy reaching its climax being played out before their eyes, no-one secretly tried to photograph the scene with a compact camera or a mobile phone, although unbeknown to the mourners the police were recording proceedings from the anonymity of a dark blue unmarked van. The T.V. crews were off course openly filming absolutely everything, to the distress of many among the crowd.

The police had made a list of names they thought would be attending the funeral; notable absences might be worth investigating, but there were none; no relative had declined to be present, none of Penny's friends had excused themselves, and indeed it seemed as if the whole population of one small Peak District town had turned out to say a sad farewell of one of their own. The only thing that soured the sombre occasion from Mark Hobson's point of view was the unnecessarily large bouquet of expensive orchids, brought to the church by a minion of Edward Cartwright with the cringingly sentimental message attached to it. The card read, "The stars tonight will be brighter with your presence, and the angels will make sweeter music; your light will always shine on us." It was signed with the flamboyant signature Edward Cartwright; even a visually impaired onlooker with cataracts would have had no problem reading that particular signature; nobody could be left in any doubt who had sent this floral tribute. The Hollywood superstar hadn't felt able to attend the funeral itself, despite the publicity opportunity, there was too great a degree of risk, but he had instructed his lackey to place the flowers in the most prominent position possible to ensure that they would be noticed by all of the camera crews covering the sad event.

***

After it was all over, and the besieging media had decamped en masse to move on to the next scene of tragedy or disaster that fired their imagination, Mark Hobson remained in the churchyard where he was joined by Detective Sergeant Bennett. He had declined the invitation to join Penny's family and some of the other mourners at what promised to be the saddest of wakes, and instead was now looking at the messages of sympathy attached to the vast mounds of floral tributes that had been placed alongside the grave and spread out across a wide area of lawn, covering the dark grass with a myriad of white, blue, red, yellow, pink and orange flowers. The costs of theses wreaths and bouquets must have run into many thousands of pounds, and within a week they'll all be dead thought Mark Hobson, maybe there is a better way to remember a loved one, but if there was he couldn't think of one except perhaps a charitable donation and that did not always meet an innate need to publicly express heartfelt sorrow. In any event Helena had insisted that they should send flowers as well as placing money in an envelope, and he trusted implicitly her sense of right and wrong.

"It's a bad day" murmured Pete Bennett, "and we haven't really gained anything from having a police presence, have we Gov?"

"We haven't Pete, but who knows? It's possible the uniform officers may have deterred a maniac from committing a further atrocity, we will never know, but if they have then it will have been worthwhile, and the fact that we didn't pick anybody out from the crowd doesn't mean the killer wasn't among us; something in my guts tells me he certainly was, but perhaps today was the time to plan his next move, and maybe he just watched and waited, and enjoyed the spectacle of the police using manpower to no good effect."

"Are you sure that that feeling wasn't just indigestion?" joked D.S. Bennett, then feeling that today humour was out of place, he added, "so that means you are definitely expecting another incident at some time?"

"Sadly I am Pete, but where and when is a closed book to us at present."

***

But in a house not too far from the church, a person who had been at the funeral was already planning his next move. From its hiding place under the floorboards of his bedroom he had removed a laptop computer and was busy typing a letter; his more expensive Sony computer sat unused on his desk, that was the one which was always on show, that was the one he played computer games on and occasionally wrote inconsequential letters. Letters that mattered, letters that would be left unsigned, were never written on that computer; in the unlikely event of someone wanting to search his computer for evidence of misuse they would be wasting their time; there was nothing incriminating that could be found upon it.

Carefully, he worked and then re-worked the document he was preparing; every word had to be exactly right, every word had to have dramatic impact; this document would not only be sent to a named individual, but copies would also be sent to the police and the local press. It was vital the world knew who was to blame for the death of a talented young woman. What impact his missive would have he didn't know, but he could guess and he could hope. Satisfied at last with the result of his labours, he attached the Lap Top to the printer and printed off 3 copies of the letter. He then shut down the computer and returned it and the printer to their secret hiding place. Tomorrow he would make a journey and buy stamps. The day after tomorrow the named individual should receive a neatly printed envelope and the day after that, maybe when there had already been some sort of dramatic event, the other intended recipients would get their copies. He didn't of course know what dramatic event there might be, but he did know he expected it to be significant.

CHAPTER TWENTY FOUR

The more he considered it, the more Jacob Lindley worried about the plight of St Catherine's church. What would its fate be if, and more probably when, it was closed and ultimately de-consecrated. The most likely outcome was that it would be put up for sale by auction and purchased by a builder or a property developer and turned into a substantial detached dwelling or perhaps several dwellings if a clever architect could come up with an appropriated design. He didn't know, but he believed that the facade of the building might be listed, or at least protected by planning restrictions, so total demolition maybe wasn't an option, but undoubtedly a building that had once been holy would at best become a parody of its former self. Given that it did possess a more than adequate car park domestic use might not be the only option; there was a real possibility that it could be bought and transformed into a place of recreation to begin a new life as a restaurant or a gym or a retail outlet; and that saddened the Church of England vicar.

It wasn't that he was prejudiced against other religions, he was a strong believer in multi-faith co-operation, but there was that inside him that felt it would be wrong if this Christian site was acquired by a devout Muslim or a practising Hindu and turned into a curry house or an Indian restaurant from which to dispense ethnic food, and perhaps ethnic religion too.

I am being very narrow minded he thought, the world is changing, and I have to accept that it is, never-the-less he couldn't feel happy that another Anglican church was likely soon to be permanently closing its doors.

I blame the arrogance of past generations for causing this crisis, he mused. If some of the men ordained by various bishops at different times had shown humility and true Christian charity and not behaved so irresponsibly and egotistically, one pretty little church would not be on the verge of disappearing into the pages of history.

If only people cared it might be a very different matter, he rationalised, but patently in the 21st century, very few people did. The idea struck him that in the not too dim and distant past, one person had searched all the records in the vestry to trace a family history; maybe that could be a way forward; genealogy was becoming a hugely popular subject to study; in the 21st century more and more men and women seemed to want to look into the past to trace their ancestry. Every church had its records; if more people could be persuaded to use them as research centres or reference libraries that would be no bad thing, and if the church welcomed the seekers of knowledge with open arms and did everything it could to facilitate their searches, it was possible that some of them might develop a desire to become involved with the church in other ways and so, in a novel manner, more people might be brought into the fold.

I wish I knew who the person was who carried out the personal research, he thought it might be possible to build on his experiences, and in some way to encourage others to follow his example. I'll do my best to discover who it was, you never know what might be achieved by highlighting the endeavours of one man to trace his past; a suitable heart-warming tale of discovery could bring great rewards.

It was approaching midday two days after the day of Penny's funeral. The weather couldn't have been nicer. Visibility was perfect, there were a few fluffy clouds in the sky, but the day was set fair, the sun was high in the sky; it didn't dazzle drivers or pedestrians with its glare. There were no parked vehicles or other hazards for anyone to be aware of, and nothing to cause the slightest difficulty for either motorist or other road users; in fact conditions could not have been better for everyone who was out and about at that time.

The man driving the Ford Focus was not travelling quickly; he was consciously keeping his speed down below the 40mph speed limit on that stretch of road to avoid putting points on his driving licence. He had a clear view of the old lady on the pavement walking slowly towards him. He was a little surprised she was by herself, it was nice to be out and about on such a glorious day, but if she had been his mother he would have felt happier if someone had been with her. However the lady seemed fully alert and was concentrating on his approaching vehicle, and he was 100% certain that she would not be taken by surprise as he drove past her.

He must have been no more than 15 feet away from her, travelling at 38mph according to his speedometer when suddenly, and looking straight at him, she leapt out in front of his moving car. He was too close even to swerve, although that was what he tried to do, and he slammed on his brakes in an emergency stop, but it was to no avail. The point of impact was just to the left of the centre of his vehicle. She was flung high into the air and catapulted over the car landing with a sickening thud some 30 yards behind it. She never stood a chance; it was obvious from the moment of impact that nobody could survive such an accident.

***

"The driver's in a state of shock. He just kept repeating "She was looking straight at me, She was looking straight at me," there's no fault at all on his part. Skid marks indicate that he wasn't exceeding the speed limit, he had new properly inflated tyres on his vehicle, his car had just been serviced, his brakes were in good order; he's blaming himself for the death, but there was nothing he could have done."

"So it was either suicide Gov, or Sheila Adamson was a lot more gaga than anybody realised" surmised Detective Sergeant Bennett.

"That's just about it Pete," replied D.I. Hobson, "and I don't think Sheila was anywhere near to losing all her marbles. She stumbled over the odd word at the funeral, and she was very emotional, but everybody was in a state that day: it wasn't just her, and I don't believe that within 48 hours her mental state could have deteriorated to the extent that she no longer knew what she was doing."

"Then she killed herself when in sound mind, and we have to try to find out why."

"Exactly so Peter, exactly so," agreed the Detective Inspector.

And as soon as the police started looking the answer became obvious. Sheila had been pretty subdued since the funeral, and not very talkative, but apart from a desire to be allowed to keep her own company, and an understandable tendency to allow her mind to wander back to happier times, she had been otherwise O.K.

On the morning of her death, her cleaner had found her up and dressed when she arrived, and perhaps a wee bit brighter than she had been on the last occasion that they had met. The cleaner had made coffee for both herself and her employer before she started work, as was her usual practice, and as they finished their drinks the postman had arrived and the cleaner had brought the letters through to Sheila. After that she had left her alone while she went upstairs to commence the big task of dusting and vacuuming the bedrooms and changing the bedding on Sheila's bed. It had taken over an hour. At one time when the Hoover was temporarily switched off, she had thought she heard sobbing downstairs and she had listened intently to see if that was correct. The sobbing had not been repeated and the cleaner thought that she had just imagined it, or maybe it was the wind, and she had carried on with her work. She hadn't heard the front door open, and it was only when she felt an unusual draught that she realised Sheila had gone outside, not bothering to close the door behind her.

Hard upon that realisation had followed the squeal of brakes, the dull sound of collision and just seconds later the screams of the car driver. After that everything had seemed to merge into one, the wailing of sirens, the shouting of paramedics, the crying of witnesses, the buzzing of police radios and an overwhelming feeling of helplessness and regret. Nobody could comprehend why Sheila had done what she did, but later when the body had been moved, the road had been re-opened, and the police visited the home of the deceased it became crystal clear why these tragic events had occurred.

It was the cleaner who found the letter crumpled up in a ball besides Sheila's chair. Right from the opening words, it was evident that the unkind words it contained were the cause of the dramatic suicide of the frail old lady it had been anonymously sent to.

Yesterday in church, it read you complained to the whole world that you did not know why your granddaughter had been murdered. You said the death sentence passed on her must be the work of a maniac, and you stated that a young woman with so much to live for, which is true, was killed without reason, which is false. Nothing happens without cause; there was a reason for her execution. Her death was not a random malicious act of spite; it is vitally important that you know why she had to die and who should properly be blamed for her death.

If you want to discover who signed her death warrant look into the mirror and you will see. Yes the fault, Dear Sheila, lies with you. I will not tell you yet exactly which of your actions caused these terrible events, but in time all will be revealed and until the time of revelation you should search your conscience to try discover what mortal sin it was that condemned Penny to die. And know this too, that knowledge cannot be our secret; it will be shared with all your friends and family. People will point fingers at you and snarl "She is the whore who killed her grandchild; she is the tart who brought down vengeance upon an innocent head. Do not be fooled by her tears, she destroyed a beautiful, clever girl just as surely as if she had slit her throat. Her immorality was the root cause of this tragedy; if she had not sinned a lovely, vibrant young woman would still be with us.

By your actions you condemned me to a life of Hell on Earth, I now repay that compliment. It is your turn to begin to know how barren life can feel.

Rest a while in Purgatory, before you make your way to a place of eternal pain. Live with regrets for the rest of your joyless life, you uncaring, selfish, wanton slut.

CHAPTER TWENTY FIVE

The letter addressed to the Divisional Commander of the High Peak Area of Derbyshire arrived the day after Sheila Adamson's suicide. It had been posted in the Hillsborough area of Sheffield and there was nothing unusual about the envelope. The letter itself was an exact copy of the one that had been sent to Sheila, and had obviously been printed off at the same time, so although the contents were new to the highest ranking police officer in North Derbyshire, they weren't new to Mark Hobson and Pete Bennett, neither were they new to Detective Chief Superintendent Stan Hardy who had been shown the original document at a very early stage. What was new however, was the brief explanatory note attached to this copy of it. Headed "Reasons for Penny Adamson's death" it informed the reader that the attached letter had been sent to Sheila Adamson to rip away the layers of self-deceit that she had wrapped around herself for more than 40 years. It hinted that in due course more information would be forthcoming, and it implied that as well as the police other people might also have been provided with copies of it.

"And that's what worries me most," snapped D.C.S. Hardy. "If the press get hold of this story it will be all over the front pages; there were enough of the bastards covering Penny Adamson's funeral; if they pick up on the fact that Sheila's suicide is a direct follow on from that event this place will be crawling with dozens of Mr Murdoch's merry men. I want to try and keep a lid on things for the moment, if we possibly, possibly can."

But predictably that was a vain hope. The editor of the Burrdale Advertiser was a responsible enough man, and generally very amenable to police requests for co-operation, but this was too good a story to suppress. He was quite happy to hand over the letter he had received accepting that the document itself could be evidence, especially if it was found to carry fingerprints or D.N.A. (which nobody thought to be very likely,) and he was even prepared to print only certain details of the letter to avoid causing Penny's family any unnecessary distress, but he was not prepared to forego the chance to run a story suggesting that the suicide of a respected local woman had direct links to the murder of a beautiful girl that had been front page news worldwide only a couple of weeks before. He also had his contacts in Fleet Street, and there was no way he was not going to make full use of them.

"I just hope the tabloids don't doorstep the family, and that they show a little restraint and compassion, but given the track records of some of their attack dogs, I can't be hopeful that that will be the case" grumbled D.C.S. Hardy.

"They're not called "gutter press" for nothing Sir," replied Mark Hobson. "There will be a feeding frenzy for sure, and there won't be very much we can do about that."

***

And of course that turned out to be the case. The Adamson family felt like prisoners in their own home; it seemed like their world was falling apart. To lose a mother and a daughter in the space of a few days, when one had been murdered, and the other had been driven to commit suicide in a dramatically terrible way was unbearable. Penny's father, Robert looked as if he had aged 50 years overnight; Penny's mother, Maureen couldn't stop crying, her younger brother Alan didn't seem to know if he was living in this world or the next, and for all of them their futures, which had been so badly wounded by Penny's public execution now seemed to have been dealt fatal blows by Sheila's death. The only crumb of comfort, if it could be called that, was because of the despair inside the house they were largely oblivious to the media throng now encamped outside their front door. A uniform police constable had been posted just outside their threshold to ensure that no rabid newshound hammered on the door or windows to try to extract a comment from the grieving relatives, or even to snatch a photograph of them in their distress.

Letters of condolence were beginning to arrive by the sack load, which the family were too shocked even to look at, but because the killer had chosen to use the Royal Mail to outline his intentions to Sheila and also to involve the police and the press D. I. Hobson realised it was possible that he might also wish to contact the family, maybe to gloat, maybe to threaten them, or in some way ratchet the level of their unhappiness to explosive levels. For that reason, and with the consent of the family (they would have consented to almost anything at the time, so detached from reality they had become) all the letters were being vetted by the police. The detective inspector had ordered that only the most cursory glance be given to letters and cards which were signed and hand written; he had no wish to pry into the private world of family torment, but that printed messages, or unsigned correspondence should be looked at in more detail: he wasn't necessarily expecting that there would be such letters, but it was a precaution, and in the end it turned out to be a wise one to take.

The note itself was short. It was type written in the same font as the other letters, and it was unsigned, and bizarrely, to some small degree, it attempted to offer a little re-assurance.

"How some fucking psychopath can imagine for a nanosecond that anything he writes could alleviate the pain he has caused his victim's family beggars bloody belief" roared an incandescent Detective Inspector Hobson, "we've got to get this maniac put away for good; he's mad enough to do absolutely anything, he's got no sense of fucking reality."

What the letter actually said was simple enough. It promised Robert Adamson that no other members of his family would be hurt; it stated that a debt had been "paid in full" and thus no further action was required against him or anyone closely connected to him. It did caveat that by saying that the extent of his mother's sinning would have to be further revealed before the file could be finally closed, but there was nothing he or any of his surviving relatives needed to do in that regard. It did express satisfaction at Sheila's dramatic death, but there it also expressed regret about having to impose a penalty on Penny. "She was innocent of any crime except association with her grandmother" it continued. "Her death was Sheila's punishment, and it was sad that such a beautiful and talented young woman had had to pay the price for a loved one's immorality." It was these words of regret that really enraged Mark Hobson.

"I totally agree with what you say Mark, but saying it and doing it are two different matters; where do you think this note leaves our investigation? Does it help us to see any more of the bigger picture?"

"I think it does Sir," said the Detective Inspector. "The family has heard directly from the killer that in his eyes Penny was innocent of any crime. I don't know if we should believe a single word he says, but if it is true, the reason for her death was to punish the real object of his hatred in the most devastating way he could possibly imagine. This would explain why nobody has a bad word to say against the girl, because there isn't one to be said. She didn't have enemies, except for one very dangerous man who intended to use her murder as an instrument of retribution; nobody else had the least dislike of her, and as I now see it, this case has never been about personal animosity towards Penny; I think we've wasted hundreds of man hours looking for a motive that was never there.

I'm also wondering if the same couldn't be true of Adam Wallington. Everybody we spoke to told us what a nice lad he was. I think we thought that was too good to be true, but we were wrong. I think that it's been a mistake to look for a link between Penny and Adam, one doesn't exist except on the most superficial and meaningless level. I believe that our killer used Adam's murder as a means to an end, just as he did with Penny."

"Then are you saying that the real target of our man's anger was Mick and not Adam Wallington," asked Detective Chief Superintendent Stan Hardy, "and that it is in the links between Mick and Sheila where the answers may lie?"

"I'm saying exactly that, Sir," replied Hobson; "I would bet money that if he hasn't already done so, Mick will be getting a letter. The problem we have is that with Sheila we found out about it immediately because she was so upset when she got it that she dropped it onto the floor before stepping out onto a busy road in order to end her life. If Mick has already received a letter he may not be prepared to admit it, and if he won't talk to us it will be much harder for us to find out anything about it, unless the killer has also sent us a copy, or intends to do so in due course, and I don't know if that is his plan. "

"Why do you say that?" asked the slightly puzzled Detective Chief Superintendent.

"I don't know," replied Mark, "it's just a gut feeling that I have that he wants Wallington to suffer more. I'm pretty confident that he is the person who set up the attack on him, and I think that may be just the beginning. I don't think he has shown his full hand. He's playing a game with Mick, and at the moment, not all the chess pieces are on the board. He is being very careful not to reveal too much at this stage in case he lets slip something that will bring it to a premature end. I think this is just the softening up process; he may have set the ball in motion by writing a letter, but if he has got extended plans to really turn the screw on him then that could still be a little way down the line."

"So what is your next move then Mark?"

"Pete and I are going back to have another little chat with him in his hospital bed; you never know, it is conceivable that he may already have started his personal journey to Damascus; and if he has then that could radically alter everything."

***

Sadly for the police, however, Mick was no St Paul and his hazardous journey towards self-knowledge was currently on permanent hold. It was obvious that he was a worried man, who was drowning in a sea of self-pity, and his bruised and battered body ached all over, which made him tetchy and irritable. He had also realised that having once unleashed the forces of evil by talking too loudly whilst on drink, it was not in his best interest to talk about subjects which couldn't withstand public scrutiny; he was therefore not co-operative when the police came to speak to him for a second time.

"No," he said, he hadn't received any letters. "Why should I? I've got absolutely nothing to hide," although even he realised that that bald statement would never be believed.

He stated he was sure that he had done nothing that might anger his grandson's killer. He could only imagine that a lunatic had believed Adam was his enemy; he wouldn't accept for a moment the thesis that it might have been his and not his grandson's conduct that was the root cause of the trouble. He did accept that for a period of weeks over 40 years ago, he had briefly dated Sheila Adamson, but that was so long ago as now to be meaningless. He admitted that the relationship had ended in acrimony, and sadly he felt Robert Adamson still held a grudge: this he regarded as silly after all these years, but he couldn't be held responsible for other people's lack of charity could he?

The theme of the questions then changed to become a probe into exactly what it was he knew about Edward Cartwright that he thought was so damaging to him. Again he refused to answer and was just as stubborn and bloody-minded as he had been on the last occasion when he had been grilled. Detective Inspector Hobson and Detective Sergeant Bennett left the hospital feeling even more frustrated than they had done before. They requested him to let them know if he did receive any threats or any anonymous letters; he swore he would do so, but both Hobson and Bennett knew that was not going to happen. Mick was not a man who could easily be made to feel guilty, unlike Sheila Adamson, but neither he nor the police knew that at that moment, somebody he was acquainted with was planning to fire an Exocet missile into his squalid world of ego, and mortally wound him with the payload of truth that it carried; if anyone was going to be stripped of his self-delusions and shown the ugliness of his life to date, that person was going to be Mick Wallington.

CHAPTER TWENTY SIX

The project that Christopher's school had been doing on the lives of ordinary people during the Second World War had excited Helena, and re-awakened in her an interest in local history which had been dormant for most of the last 6 years. Being pregnant and becoming the mother of 2 young children during that period had of course placed huge demands on her time, but she knew there was another reason why she had shied away from night school classes and local history societies, but now it was time to move on. Helena had mentioned to another young mum that she was toying with the idea of learning a little bit more about that period of Burrdale's history. She in response had told Helena that she had just joined the Burrdale Social History Group that had recently re-formed after a gap of nearly 3 years and she suggested that Helena go along with her to one of their meetings to see if it might also be for her.

Despite having made the first move, and knowing that she had to forget the past, when the offer was made she had been hesitant. The memory of John Winston was still fresh in her mind and her husband's belief that given time that man would have engineered a sexual encounter with her seemed very well founded. Mark knew that Helena would have rejected the lecturer out of hand; he trusted his wife implicitly, but that hadn't been the point; he had worried about the man's reaction to being turned down; obsessive men, particularly men with highly developed senses of their own self-importance, don't take kindly to being rebuffed: in his time as a policeman Mark had dealt with a number of nasty indecent assaults and 2 rapes which had followed on directly from a woman's rejection of a man's advances.

But John Winston was no longer on the scene. His laptop computer, believed to have been hurled into one of the local reservoirs by the local history tutor to destroy its memory had never been recovered. There was no available evidence to prove that the teacher had purchased child pornography online, although many people had their suspicions, but he had made some admissions about watching legal soft porn, and Mark suspected that his computer might well have contained 1000s of images and numerous video clips of deviant sexual practices; but nothing could be proved and the tutor had not been charged with a single offence.

The people of Burrdale, however, had made a decision. Many of them believed that Winston had developed unsavoury links with disgraced ex-councillor Tony Patterson, who was currently serving a 10 year sentence for photographing and then circulating his vile pictures of depraved middle aged men having sexual intercourse and doing other unspeakable acts of a grotesque nature with children who from their size, weight, and lack of maturity, the police believed to be aged between 7 and 10 years old. Winston also had the additional burden of being the nephew of Crawford Winston, who had been convicted of a number of indecent assaults and acts of gross indecency with young teenage girls and was known personally, on one occasion, to have watched him having sex with an underage Virginia Brocklehurst from which event two terrible tragedies had been born. The death of Lucas Norton and the murder, many years later, of Virginia herself had both stemmed from that one act of voyeurism, and the town was now not willing ever to forgive or to forget.

The collective judgement of the people of Burrdale might have been a touch unfair; Winston himself had only been a child when that incident took place, and he could never have dreamed what dire consequences would flow from that one act of sexual curiosity, but in reality that mattered not. The finger of suspicion had been pointed; a verdict of guilty had been passed by the townspeople; and a universally agreed sanction had been imposed. John Winston had been shunned by virtually everyone in town; the very mention of his name had been enough to cause usually mild mannered people to launch into tirades of abuse, 3 times his home had been damaged by objects being thrown at it and on every public toilet wall in Burrdale obscenities had been scrawled about him; most were excessively crude, one or two were remarkably funny.

Perhaps it was because he had once enjoyed a celebrity status that the anger had been so intense. Even some of the mature middle class ladies, who for years had attended his night school classes and seen their tutor as a charismatic charmer, had turned against him; forgetting how much over the years they had enjoyed his flirtatious comments and witty innuendos. When the stories about him began to circulate they were aghast. Before all of his problems commenced Winston had been able to make a joke if there was ever any physical contact between himself and a student and the class would have roared with laughter when he used a clever double entendre to explain away the incident, but that became history. It had ceased to matter that he had made learning easy; it was of no importance that his classes had been fun, now these ladies believed that every slight and often accidental contact there may have been now amounted to indecent assault. It was unfortunate the celebrity tutor's fall from grace had coincided with a new age of sexual Puritanism. Attitudes to a slap on the bottom or a quick touch of a breast were no longer a subject for humour, (perhaps that had always been the case, but the message had got lost somewhere during the 1970's) but the licence that men like John Winston had enjoyed was now a thing of the past. Helena Hobson knew that her husband believed that, in the not too distant future, some very public figures would find themselves having starring roles in sex offences trials and that their stellar status, which had shielded and protected them for years, would ultimately be the means of their undoing; she didn't know if this prophecy would turn out to be true, all she knew was that on matters such as this, his judgement was very seldom wrong.

She had asked Mark if he thought that it might be a good idea to become involved again with the local history group and whether he would mind if she took a couple of hours a week to get a break from the kids and pursue a new hobby. He had been fully supportive of the idea. He didn't tell Helena that before he gave his answer he had carried out checks to discover the current whereabouts of Winston, and that he had learned that the man was now believed to be somewhere in Thailand or Cambodia, with no plans to return to the U.K. He also didn't mention to Helena that he had run checks on the backgrounds of most of the members of the group to see if anything of concern was revealed; fortunately nobody had been identified as a risk, and he was as sure as he could be that his wife would be completely safe.

So it was, with his blessing, and not knowing what precautions he had taken before he said "yes" that Helena started to attend the weekly meetings of the B.S.H.G.

She was relieved to find that the members of it were pleasant, earnest and well-motivated. The tutor was young and well informed, with an obvious passion for his subject, but without the flamboyance of the unlamented Mr Winston; he was also reputed to be gay, and this fact might slightly have influenced Mark when he was weighing up potential risk for his wife.

His subject, which dovetailed quite nicely with the little project the primary school had been involved in, was Social Attitudes and Behaviour after the two World Wars. He was particularly interested in highlighting how ordinary people had responded to a number of specific circumstances in the ten year period after 1918 and the 10 year period after 1945, in particular focussing on the differences that could be observed; he also was keen to note what, if any, threads remained constant in the two control periods.

He looked at how families had dealt with issues such as illegitimacy, single motherhood, adoption and the treatment of orphans in the decade after bloody conflict. In the 1920s the biggest cause of single parent families had been the deaths of tens of thousands of young men in battle. Many had married their sweethearts whilst on home leave, sometimes by way of special licence, and many others had intended to get married until Fate in the form of a machine gun bullet or poisonous gas had intervened to thwart their plans. Most of the babies born in these circumstances were loved and wanted, but some had been stigmatised as bastards by the straight laced guardians of sexual propriety that every town and village seemed to possess; these "well-meaning" people had no doubt been the main reason why some innocent infants had been abandoned on church or orphanage steps by young women too frightened to risk a public shaming by the self-styled pillars of the community.

Immediately after the Second World War the situation had been different. Because so many American troops were stationed over here, and so many of our young men had been fighting abroad, short term relationships had frequently developed between G.I.'s and local girls, and unfortunately pregnancies had resulted from casual acts of sex. Babies born in these circumstances were generally unwanted, and many had been put up for adoption to avoid scandal; sadly others had been got rid of in less humane ways, and it was only the lucky ones who found love and protection in a family home. Some of these were "unofficially adopted" by relatives of the mother's family living far away from her place of birth.

Another marked difference the lecturer had noted was that after the 1st World War, particularly in small rural communities, there had been a marked reluctance to involve outsiders in family affairs. A solicitor would be consulted if a person wanted to leave a will, and for some people with money, to defend them in court if accused of a crime, but those occasions were few and far between; money was tight, legal aid was non-existent, the ordinary working man was probably awkward when speaking to professional people. The lecturer then related a number of instances where children, who had been born in wedlock and properly registered at birth then lost their fathers when still at a very young age through illness, accident or misadventure. In some cases the young widow had struggled to cope alone, but quite often, probably out of necessity, she remarried and not infrequently had further children in a very short space of time. The first born child would take the surname of the new husband, and would be universally known by that name despite the fact his birth certificate said something completely different. In an age when few people went abroad, and a large proportion of the population didn't drive, nobody saw any need to change the record "There were," said the lecturer "cases where some men and women never knew their true surnames for the whole of their lives."

There was something very sad about that state of affairs, thought Helena. Children have a right to know the truth. It seems so unnatural for them to be left in ignorance.

"After the 2nd World War," he continued, "that problem became a lot less common place. People were used to State scrutiny having lived through a period of conflict. For nearly 6 years everyone could expect to be stopped on the street and have their I.D. challenged, informal family arrangements no longer had the same effect; while there probably was still the odd time when incorrect details were given and accepted as genuine, to a much greater degree than before officials demanded proof before they would be satisfied that any individual was who he claimed to be."

And on balance, that was probably a good thing, rationalised Helena.

CHAPTER TWENTY SEVEN

Mary Wallington had agonised for 3 days: she knew what the compassionate thing to do would be and if Adam had still been alive she would not have had a moment's hesitation. He might be an old rogue, she would have thought, but he is my father-in-law and Adam's granddad, and he is in hospital in pain, I must visit him. Tragically, however, Adam was dead, and with him had died much of her ability to care; when you added in the manner of Mick's behaviour immediately after his grandson's death, which had certainly not raised his standing in her eyes, and his antics before he was assaulted, she had little cause to feel well disposed towards him. Once upon a time, on a good day, she might have been willing to view him as a loveable reprobate, but now she thought of him as a loud, selfish, shallow wastrel who nobody in their right mind would want to help; but despite all those feelings, he was family, and try as she might she couldn't stop herself from feeling guilty about deliberately ignoring him. Being unable to come to a decision herself, she decided to seek the opinion of the one person who wasn't a relative, to whom she had once been a source of re-assurance; she also hoped that if his advice was to go to the hospital he might take her there in his car. Public transport was almost non-existent; in recent years Adam had been her chauffeur; she hadn't touched a car herself for the best part of a decade since the accident on black ice, which had severely dented the family Renault, and which had totally destroyed her confidence in driving.

Frank Oakes was pleased to see her, he had missed the chats they used to have, and he was glad that now she needed a favour she had turned to him. The only problem was that he was currently walking on crutches, having severely sprained his ankle, and for the next few weeks was totally unable to drive.

Frank told Mary that the choice could only be made by her. He said that she shouldn't feel guilty if she decided to pretend that Mick no longer existed, that she didn't owe him anything, and that nobody could blame her if she completely shunned him, but, there was a caveat.

"Nobody would think ill of you if you did," he continued, "but I worry that you might think ill of yourself and that could cause you pain. I could quite happily walk past Mick in the gutter and not give him a second glance, but you've got something of the Good Samaritan in your D.N.A., you couldn't do that, so maybe the best thing to do is to visit him, but be resolved in your mind the extent to which you are prepared to try and assist him, and don't budge from that no matter how much he tries to persuade you to do more. Give him an inch and he'll take a mile, he'll try to take advantage of you if you let him; be aware of the risk at all times."

Frank apologised profusely that he couldn't personally drive Mary to the hospital, but he said he would ask his gardener/handyman Tim Bradley to take her there; he explained Bradley frequently borrowed his pick-up truck to collect purchases from the local shops and that he was therefore a named driver on his insurance certificate; he also sometimes drove his Jaguar but that was currently being repaired following a minor shunt in which it had sustained rear end damage. If she didn't mind travelling in a Mitsubishi truck then that was transport sorted out.

The Reverend Jacob Lindley was feeling nervous, although he couldn't exactly say why. As part of his campaign to get people involved in the fight to save St Catherine's and to promote the use of the building as a place of study he had taken to the airways and the local press; he had also put up a number of posters in strategic places around the town asking for anyone who thought they might like to study the church records and memorabilia to get in touch with him and, also, if anyone had already examined the archive material or they knew of somebody who had, to either email him at the email address provided or to write to him at an address set out below. Jake had made it clear he was particularly interested in speaking to recent searchers of the records to find out what their experience had been like and to listen to their views about how facilities could be improved. His imminent interview on High Peak Radio was just another small step along the way; he didn't know exactly what to expect, and rather feared the prospect of being mauled by a Jeremy Paxman look alike but with a temperament that made Paxman seem like a fluffy kitten by comparison.

As it happened, the young lady who he met did not have a diet of red meat and in no way did she resemble a food starved jackal. She was attractive and helpful. She explained that the interview would be pre-recorded so that it could be edited to remove all unnecessary umming, arrghing, coughing and pausing thus making it sound more professional and easier to listen to. She then made him a very nice cup of coffee and gave him plenty of time to relax before recording actually commenced.

Jake had written a script, and by and large he managed to stick to it, and after some early hesitancy he soon warmed to his task and within a very short space of time was in full flow. It didn't take long, but it said everything that needed to be said, and after it was over the interviewer complimented him on his fluency. It's probably flattery thought Jake, but it's still quite nice to be flattered by a pretty little girl like this.

***

Mary's journey to the hospital was completely uneventful. There was little conversation, her driver was not the talkative type, and that suited her; nor was he the type of man who liked listening to loud music, although he did sometimes turn on High Peak Radio for its local news and travel information. The journey was also not a long one in terms of distance, but it could take quite a time if it coincided with the local schools disgorging their children, or with the rush hours at the beginning and end of the day, but at 1.30 pm on a normal school holiday type day traffic conditions were generally light, and today was no exception.

When they got to the hospital the car park was full, and although one or two spaces did start to appear they were all too small for a large pick-up truck. Mary's driver told her he would drop her off near to one of the entrances to the hospital, and would then cruise around until a suitable space did become available, and that after he had parked up he would come up to the ward either to wait for her or to tell her where the truck could be found and then return to it to wait for her there. He expressed a dislike of hospitals, and hoped that if there came a stage when he could no longer withstand the super-heated atmosphere of the ward, and chose instead to banish himself to peace of the driving cab, she would understand.

The girl at the inquiry desk was helpful. Mr Wallington was on Ward E4 on the second floor. Strictly speaking visiting time didn't commence for another 25 minutes, but nobody would mind if she wanted to go up straight away.

When she entered the side room Mick was in she was shocked at his appearance. She had expected to see facial cuts and bruising, but she hadn't expected to see him looking so pale, or even frail. For the first time when she stared at him lying on the hospital bed the thought struck her that he was an old man, not an indestructible Hell-raiser who would probably live forever to the great annoyance of more virtuous contemporaries.

It was obvious he hadn't seen her arrive; his eyes were closed and he appeared to be asleep. Had it been her mother, or somebody she felt close to, she would have leant over and kissed him, but because he was who he was she couldn't bring herself to do that. She coughed quietly and gently touched his hand, and with a start he woke up into consciousness; she thought that she could see fear in his eyes.

"Mary," he stammered, "is that you? It's kind of you to come and visit me."

She thought that she could see embryonic tears. His lack of bravado and his apparent gratitude touched her. It was the right thing to do she told herself, I've never seen him like this before, he's a lonely, silly old man who has suddenly realised that he needs people who care for him close at hand. Inside her breast compassion started to grow. I will do what I can to help him in future, she thought, I'm really all he's got left; I can't turn my back on him now.

She stayed with him for nearly an hour, it was longer than she intended to, but she didn't want him to be left by himself when all the other patients had visitors; to be seen by them as a man who nobody was bothered about had to be a ghastly experience; she had nothing else to do, her time was cheap, and he appeared glad of her company.

It was only when her chauffeur arrived at the door that she realised it was time to go. She told Mick she would try and visit him again while he remained in hospital, and that when he was allowed home, she would be quite happy to pop in and help him with the housework until he was back on his feet and also cook him a few hot meals; and when she said that he just broke down in tears. As she left, she bent down and kissed him on the forehead; he squeezed her hand tightly, and she knew that he had changed.

On the journey home Mary pondered if she had been a fool, and whether out of pity she had offered too much; she concluded that if Mick really had become a better person then the answer was "no." Her driver never once interrupted her train of thought; in the background High Peak Radio played quietly; the Reverend Jacob Lindley softly made his plea for information to its many listeners.

CHAPTER TWENTY EIGHT

"We've called him a psychopath and a f-ing maniac Love, and he probably is one, anyone who can slaughter two innocent kids who have never personally done him the slightest harm can't be right in the head; but there's more to all this than simple insanity. He's specifically picked his targets, and chosen to butcher them in the most public of ways. If it was just random shooting, at Castleton in particular, he could have had a field day; the opportunity at Buxton was less because he was so much closer to the victim and if he carried on shooting from the bell tower he would have been spotted very quickly and he could easily have found himself cornered inside the church."

"I'm sure you're right Darling," replied Helena, "but if he isn't just killing for killing's sake, what could his motive be?"

"The obvious one is revenge Sweetheart, but I think it is a very particular type of revenge; the letter to Penny Adamson's dad made that clear, he's imposing a terrible penalty on the innocent to punish the guilty; it takes a very disturbed mind to dream up such a savage sentence; but just think how you and I would feel if somebody tried to hurt one of our kids to get back at me."

"Just don't even go there," shuddered Helena, the thought too shocking to even contemplate, and seeking to divert her husband's thoughts away from that horrific possibility she asked him if he had any theory about what might have driven the killer he was hunting to commit such acts of savagery.

"That's the million dollar question, but unfortunately I don't have a million dollar answer. I think the cause is historic. I think that something happened either during or shortly after the 2nd World War that left him permanently scarred. When we do find out who it is, and we will find him, my bet will be that we discover he was left psychologically damaged by some big event in his life. Given the state of the world today, and I suppose thinking about Tony Patterson and the sort of men he catered for it could be to do with child sex abuse or something like that, but I could so easily be wrong about that."

"Given the very nature of the crimes he has committed, and the fact that he seems to have then departed the scene so quickly and with such stealth, that's got to mean that he must have been pretty young when whatever it was occurred; I can't see somebody in his late 70s or even older being able to do that."

"Neither can I Sherlock," responded Mark. "To achieve what he did, and to get away with it, he would have to have a level of physical fitness far beyond that which you would expect to find in most septuagenarians."

"Well, if finding a person at the moment seems like an impossible task, are you any closer to finding the murder weapon?"

"We aren't Love, we really aren't. I thought after we'd spoken to Frank Oakes that we were making progress, but it came to a dead end and -"

At that moment conversation was interrupted by the strident demands of the telephone bell.

Two minutes later, when the call ended, Mark turned to Helena.

"I've got to nip down to the station for a bit Darling, I'll try not to be long, but there's been a development that Pete Bennett thinks might be significant. I'm not holding my breath, it'll probably be nothing, but we're due a bit of good luck, and maybe today will be the day we get some. Pete tells me Alan Nadin is with him and he thinks that maybe we could be on to something."

It took Detective Inspector Hobson less than 8 minutes to arrive at the nick. When he got there it was virtually empty. Now rumoured to be earmarked for closure within the next 12 months very little money was being thrown at it, and it was becoming a cold, drab, uninspiring place: retired Detective Sergeant Alan Nadin was always sad when he visited it in its current state of neglect.

"It used to be buzzing in here," he said. "There was so much going on when I were a young copper. The old place knows that it hangs under sentence of death; you can feel the unhappiness in every office. They say it will make Derbyshire Constabulary more efficient if it centralises operations. They pretend a shiny new building in Buxton is the way forward; but it's not about that; it's all to do with budget cuts and has bugger all to do with efficiency. You mark my words, if it closes that will only be the first step. Give it 10 years and there will be no local police stations left, and the copper on the beat will have become more and more detached from the local community because ordinary folk will feel the next generation of bobbies have absolutely nothing in common with them. If it has to close, then I think it would be better for everyone now if they sent in the wrecking ball sooner rather than later, so that the sodding architects and builders can make their packet cramming in as many chicken coops as they can squeeze onto the site. It's always the same way; the bastard developers make a fortune at our expense putting up little cardboard houses that are absolutely identical to each other and that nobody wants, but nobody can do anything to prevent."

"The outline plans, which still have to be approved, show there will be 12 starter homes, some of which, judging by the measurements, might just be big enough to accommodate undersized dwarves," said Mark Hobson, "just as long as none of them have the desire to swing Tiddles around by the tail; but I suppose it's what they call progress in today's 'Cool Britannia.'"

D.S. Pete Bennett snorted in disgust.

"Oh God I'm sorry Alan," apologised Mark, "if Pete gets started on this subject we'll be here till midnight, and I've just given him the perfect lead in, he'll be rabbiting on now for hours and hours."

"I'd need days if not weeks," laughed Pete Bennett, "but maybe a change of scene could distract me from my work, what say we adjourn to the Royal Albert and there Alan and I can tell you what we have found out over a decent pint of beer, and do it in more comfortable surroundings."

That suggestion was warmly received, and sat in comfortable seats in a quiet corner of the main bar out of earshot of other customers, Pete Bennett and Alan Nadin told Detective Inspector Hobson their tale. It appeared both men had been in the back bar of the pub they were in, reminiscing and having a quiet drink when an argument had developed between Raymond Baker and a man who they thought to be one of Mickey Shah's occasional employees.

"Ray's a good bloke," said Alan, but he's always been a bit of a hothead; I find it a little bit ironic that somebody of his temperament has chosen to be a volunteer fireman; when he loses his rag he goes as red as a beetroot and sometimes you think his head is about to burst into flames; well that is what happened last night."

"So what actually occurred?" Mark asked.

"Well we couldn't exactly hear," replied Alan Nadin, "but the chap he was talking to said something about Ray's dad. "It was as if someone had lit the blue touch paper on a rocket; Ray just went berserk; he grabbed the other lad by the throat, and it looked as if an almighty fight was about to kick off; that was when Pete and I stepped in."

"I think I heard the word "bastard" interjected Pete Bennett and there were a couple of other insults that I didn't quite catch, but from the look on Ray's face they definitely weren't complimentary."

"Bastard is a sensitive word so far as Ray is concerned," said Alan Nadin, he then went on to explain why that was the case.

"Ray's very protective when it comes to his old man" he added. "He gets very upset when people slag him off."

"And the trouble is the "bastard" allegation is true" interjected Detective Sergeant Bennett, "his old man is illegitimate, and everybody in town knows that fact."

Pete Bennett then went on to explain that Raymond Baker's father was born just after the end of the 2nd World War. He said that his mum, Raymond's grandmother, who was now dead, was at the time of his birth a naive young woman who had found herself pregnant and abandoned in the autumn of 1945.

"There were all sorts of rumours about who the father might be," said Bennett, "the best bet seems to be that it was probably an Italian P.O.W., but it could have been a G.I. or maybe a Polish fighter pilot. One thing is certain: The father, whoever he was, wasn't blonde, and Ray's dad is so swarthy that the Italian theory has the most credence, but when he was a little lad somebody came up with the idea that he may have been an American mixed-race marine. Certainly some of the kids at school used to wind him up by calling him a "nigger"; it wasn't a taboo word then, but it wasn't very nice and when they did that he used to get very upset. Despite everything he turned into a pretty decent chap, but he never forgot the jibes and they must have hurt him; Ray goes ape-shit if anyone does anything to remind his old fellah of his unfortunate past."

Mark Hobson's mind was whirring. There wasn't the slightest bit of evidence to support a theory, and he had absolutely no grounds whatsoever to arrest Raymond Baker, or anyone else, on suspicion of involvement in the murders of Adam and Penny; but suppose a caring but hot-headed son was minded to try to pay back the people who had mocked and jeered his innocent father? It could be total rubbish. It could be that nothing could be further from the truth, but for the first time in a long while Mark Hobson was sensing that maybe some of the pieces of the jigsaw were finally falling into place.

"Good news Mr Wallington, you can go back home this afternoon." The young doctor with a beaming smile and impressively mangled vowels had no doubt that he was the bearer of glad tidings. Mick was not so sure. He had the suspicion that in reality the hospital had decided that it needed his bed for a more deserving case, and that his welfare was very much a secondary consideration, but much of his natural cynicism had been beaten out of him by the paid thugs who had attacked him, and in a way he would not have expected he now found himself less eager to argue with people than had once been the case. Perhaps it was only a temporary phase, perhaps it was just an understandable lack of confidence which would disappear when he felt fitter and was back in his own place, but oddly he didn't think it would.

It was what was waiting for him that really bothered him, or rather what was not waiting for him that he found scary. He had nobody at home to talk to, nobody to notice if he was alive or dead, nobody to care for him, nobody with whom to share a joke or a moment of quiet enjoyment. He had always despised those things. Relationships, other than short term sexual relationships in which he was the master, and in which he could turn commitment on and off with the flick of a switch, he had always viewed as an encumbrance. To have to consider the feelings of other people had always been too onerous a demand even to contemplate. I can come and go as I please he had thought, nobody tells me what to do; for the first time in his life he found himself doubting the benefit of complete independence.

The thought struck him that his daughter-in-law Mary had promised to look in on him and to help him get back on his feet again. She was a good girl, his son had been lucky to find her. I have ignored her, I have taken her for granted, he thought. I have been a fool. I need somebody to talk to and maybe even to care for me a little. I have been given a chance to change my life: I mustn't mess up this last opportunity.

CHAPTER TWENTY NINE

The greetings card sent to Frank Oakes on the occasion of his birthday did not bring a message of congratulation; instead it promised that the next year of his life would be a very uncomfortable one. It contained an explicit threat that the sender would soon reveal to the world at large details of a grubby little contract that he had entered into 30 years before. It accused him of taking Connie Cartwright's money under false pretences and claimed that, contrary to her belief, the writer knew that a D.N.A. test, if one was ever carried out, would prove conclusively that he could not be the father of her son. It concluded by announcing that very soon Connie herself would be getting her own greetings card which would explain to her how she had been duped and suggest that she should demand her money back as services had not been rendered as required. It also provocatively stated that the story was far too intriguing to stay out of the public domain; although it left open the door to the possibility of widespread publicity being avoided if the result of Connie's failed attempt to produce a designer son dug deep into his pockets and withdrew a sufficiently large wad of banknotes to satisfy the needs of the situation.

Who could know such a thing, thought Oakes, there can only be one person, and that person must be Mick Wallington.

The card received by Constance Cartwright 4 days later couldn't really be classified as a greetings card at all, unless the picture of the white lily and the words "In deepest sympathy" had taken on a whole new meaning, which Constance seriously doubted. It purported to mourn the passing of a dream. It told her the son she had tried to create was a mark of her failure, not a symbol of her success. It mocked her for being so gullible, it sternly reprimanded her for allowing herself to get so drunk that she did not know who had had sexual intercourse with her all those many years ago or how many times semen had been ejaculated into her body. It even raised the possibility that more than one person could have had intercourse with her that night, although it specifically excluded Frank Oakes from that possibility. It accused Connie of behaving worse than a whore, and without even having the justification of poverty or ignorance to mitigate the offence. It speculated about how much damage could be done to Edward's reputation, particularly in those parts of the United States where Mom and apple pie reigned supreme and God gave out a sugar coated message to encourage the well-scrubbed, well-heeled faithful (but definitely not for the benefit of Hispanics, Negroes, Jews or Moslems.) If it became known that his mother had paid to have sex with a man who had found her so repellent that partly for a crude joke, and partly because she excited him so little, he had called in a stand-in to do the dastardly deed.

Connie was beside herself with fury and with dread. Doubts that she had managed to suppress for nearly 30 years now broke free from their cage. When Edward was a little boy she had frequently looked at him to see if she could see any likeness developing between him and the handsome man she had chosen to be his father. There had been none: now she understood why. Frank Oakes had a lot to answer for. A face to face confrontation was inevitable, but not today; if she could have laid hands on him at that moment she would have scratched his eyes out, and that would have been a dangerous thing to do. If she injured him, or if she publicly exposed him the story would go global, and that could not be allowed to happen. The hateful postcard seemed to offer the prospect that if enough money was paid by Edward the story could be contained; not that anything that the person who had sent her the card said could be taken at face value.

Like Frank Oakes, she suspected that the sender of this vile missive had to be Mick Wallington. The dreadful thought struck her with the force of a blacksmith's anvil thrown by a pumped up Geoff Capes that the most likely sire of her son had to be the "Burrdale Braggart"; the only crumb of comfort she had was that Edward had not inherited any of his most obvious physical characteristics; it was a very small crumb indeed.

That crumb of comfort lasted only a moment before it was swallowed up by the realisation that in order for Edward to pay off a potential blackmailer he would have to be told the whole truth.

When he was a little boy and he had asked about his father, she had invented a story that he was an American lawyer who she had met while she was on holiday in Italy, and that she had fallen madly in love with him. She had told Edward that he was rich, and handsome, and very intelligent and that she had been swept off her feet by him. She said that they had had a week of passion before reality kicked in. She had a job to return to, and it turned out that he had a wife in New Hampshire, and that he had hopes of making a career in politics. They had embraced and they had parted, never to see each other again. Soon after she arrived back home, she discovered she was pregnant and she had made the conscious decision never to tell him to protect him from scandal. When she told this story she made it sound like a romantic dream, and Edward had been swept along by the romance, and indeed had seemed relieved that his father was a man of distinction, and not a member of the common herd. How he would react when he discovered he had been lied to, she didn't know. How he would respond to her pleas for forgiveness she could only guess, although tolerance of his fellow human beings was not one of his strongest traits. Whether he would agree to pay money in return for silence was far from clear, and even if he did she feared that her relationship with her cherished child could be forever damaged.

Mortified by the prospect of rejection, terrified that she might be permanently cut adrift from the young man she had dedicated her life to, she sank down on her knees in the corner of the room, and she howled.

***

The Reverend Jacob Lindley was feeling quite disheartened. He had had no idea about what the response to his appeal for information and for public support on High Peak Radio would be, but he had hoped it would be large. He had also anticipated that the feature in the local newspaper would generate a degree of interest and that the effort he had put into creating and putting up eye catching posters would prove to have been worthwhile.

So far that did not seem to be the case. Seven people had telephoned him, five had e-mailed and five more had written to him at his home address. Seventeen responses from a local population of over ten thousand was hardly a cause for celebration, and was particularly disappointing when he knew how much care he had taken to ensure his message was phrased in exactly the right terms.

The lack of e-mails wasn't surprising, he hadn't expected too much from this method of communication. Most of the people he had hoped to reach were old, although some flattered themselves and defied logic by labelling themselves as middle aged; but if these people had unrealistic expectations of living for 120 years like the occasional Russian peasant or Tibetan monk then maybe they were entitled to regard 80+ as not ancient; the Reverend Lindley was not at all convinced. Had his target audience been teenagers then it would have been a different story. Young people were taught computing skills at school and would willingly embrace new technology, but for their parents and grandparents it was different, and they were largely unaware of the phenomenon which was the World Wide Web. One day he told himself, and probably one day very soon, everyone will be signed up and octogenarians will be expert at sending electronic mail, but just at the moment older people are apathetic or even antagonistic to the I.T. revolution.

The lack of significant traditional post and the very few calls to his telephone land line did upset him; he looked for reasons as to why this might be; the fact many of his carefully crafted posters had been torn down might have something to do with it. Kids with time on their hands do some very stupid things, he thought, but why do they take such perverse pleasure in spoiling things for other people? Even making allowance for the fact that the youngsters whom he suspected of being responsible were unlikely to be church-goers, and that therefore St Catherine's had less importance to them than the local "offie" or Skateboard Park; he felt aggrieved. An unusually cynical thought crept into his mind unbidden. If the people who run the venues where kids congregate were marketing the Church of England, it might be a whole lot different. After all, if they can convince themselves that black is white and that spotty adolescents barely out of short trousers are old enough to legally buy booze, surely they could do the same for organised religion and make Faith seem like fun?

Whatever happened to family loyalty? he mused. Many of these children will have grandparents whom they love. Surely they can see what the loss of a much loved local church would mean to them, why couldn't they have remembered that before they started ripping down my posters? But that's the way of the world now. Maybe I was naive to think I could garner enough support to make a significant difference; I was obviously wrong; well that's it, my campaign to save St Catherine's is at an end.

At that moment the voice in his head chastised him for lack of courage, and the Church of England vicar resolved to continue the fight rather than run the risk of alienating his God.

CHAPTER THIRTY

Detective Chief Superintendent Stan Hardy was a reasonable man. He could see the effort that was being put into trying to solve the Castleton and the Buxton murders, and he was sure that Detective Inspector Mark Hobson and the other officers attached to the case were doing their level best to bring it to a successful conclusion.

I've got a strong team in place, headed by a very capable officer. We've got enough bodies on the ground to be effective, although it would be nice to have more, he thought, and yet we are struggling to make progress. The thing that was lacking, which was vital to every successful investigation was "Luck", and "Luck" was the one thing no amount of money could buy or expensive state of the art high tech equipment could create. Unfortunately the general public, usually egged on by a hostile tabloid press, didn't seem to understand the difficulties the police operated under. It was very easy to throw unfounded accusations of inertia, inefficiency, idleness or idiocy at targets like a local constabulary, and it was almost inevitable that some of the mud would stick. Not in the cheeriest frame of mind, he telephoned Mark Hobson to arrange a meeting to discuss the latest developments in the case.

"It is a bit like wading through treacle at the moment Sir, I readily admit that, but I do think we are beginning to unravel some of the threads. We know now that Penny Adamson was killed solely to cause pain to a member of her family, and not because of anything she had specifically done which is a fairly unusual set of circumstances. If instead of being a young woman she had been a little girl living with unhappy, warring violent parents it wouldn't be that uncommon; sadly unhinged fathers sometimes murder their offspring to spite their estranged wives, and in extreme cases, mothers kill their children prior to committing suicide to get back at an unfaithful partner, but Penny was a happy girl, adored by her parents so she doesn't fit that pattern. In any event, it seems that her grandmother was viewed by our killer as the villain of the piece; he said as much in the letter we recovered from her house immediately after the old lady threw herself under a car. The problem is that despite our best efforts, we can't find anything in her past life that could have triggered such a terrible revenge."

"She worked for the BBC didn't she Mark? Is it possible that through her work she managed to anger somebody in the criminal fraternity?

"I should seriously doubt that Sir. She wasn't an investigating journalist or anything like that; so far as I can find out she was a continuity announcer or something very similar to that. Everything she said on air would have been scripted, I really can't see any way at all how she could have angered some Mafia godfather to the extent that nearly half a century later he still bears a grudge sufficient to want to totally destroy her life: even if you allow for the fact that such a person might now be the proud owner of a Queen's birthday telegram it would be a pretty long shot. In any event Sheila only worked for the BBC for a couple of years before she had to give up work to bring up a baby."

"I take your points," said Hardy, "I was just clutching at straws in any event."

"I think we all are Sir and, in one sense, I don't think you're entirely wide of the mark. We know the motive is historic, we know the killer regarded Sheila as "an uncaring, selfish, worthless slut", because he said as much in his letter, and I think that attitude is the key. I am sure we are not looking at a career criminal; my bet will be that when we find him we will discover that he has very few, if any, previous convictions, but we are looking for a man who in his own way is as ruthless as any gangster. Our biggest stumbling block is that there is nothing at all that we can find out about Sheila's early life which remotely suggests that she was an easy lay; in fact quite the contrary. She seems to have demanded high standards in men, and very few of the lads in town seemed to measure up to them. I suspect there must have been casual boyfriends, but we don't have any idea about who most of them were. The only time when she appears to have dropped her standards was when she was in a distressed state of mind following an R.T.A. which badly injured her then boyfriend; he was so badly hurt that it doomed their relationship; while she was grieving there seems to have been a very short lived affair with Mick Wallington, which came to an abrupt end as soon as she realised what a jerk he actually was. Soon after that she met a chap who worked for the British Broadcasting Company, and in a comparatively short time they were engaged and then married."

"Do you think it is possible she used her sexual attraction to advance her career – in other words, is it possible that she set out to sleep her way to the top?"

"That's entirely possible Sir, but if she did her plan went off the rails when she became pregnant, and it is not beyond the realms of probability that somebody found out and there were consequences which ruined lives, but I think we would be extremely lucky to discover any details at all after all this time."

Ah Luck! thought the senior detective officer in all of the High Peak, that word again. I am beginning to get a little fed up with thinking about Luck, when it offers us so very little assistance.

***

The letter from Burrdale Local History Society was unexpected, and very, very welcome. He should have thought God moves in a mysterious way, but instead Jacob Lindley thought this could be a game changer, why didn't I think of this before. Its contents could not have been more straight forward. It told the young vicar that his appeal for people to get involved in the fight to save St Catherine's by using it as a centre of research when not required for religious purposes had breathed new life into a long dormant plan to write a "History of Burrdale and its families since the end of the English Civil War." The date of Charles 1st's execution was a significant one because Burrdale's only historical figure of note had been a prominent Royalist and had paid a heavy price for his allegiance when Oliver Cromwell came to power.

It's so obvious, he thought. If I had used any logic I should have seen that to get people using the church as a base for a big project is the way forward, and if we combine that with providing a self-service tea and coffee stall so that they can obtain refreshment whilst they work that has to be a worthwhile plan; and if we can also broaden the church's appeal to attract people wishing to rest their weary legs after a day's shopping, or to become a venue for young mums doing the school run to then get together for a social chat the results could be very positive indeed. He wondered about the possibility of one day setting up an Internet Cafe, which would demonstrate how forward thinking the Anglican Church was, but there were moral and theological issues involved, and whether the Bishop would sanction such a bold scheme was very far from certain. What was certain was that the Parochial church council for St Catherine's backed the plan as it currently appeared on the table, and the Reverend Lindley had been instructed to reply to the local History Society, expressing approval of the scheme as proposed.

Very quickly things had then snowballed. Letters had appeared in all the local newspapers, and the chairman of the Burrdale Local History Society had been interviewed on High Peak Radio. More posters, this time prepared by the Burrdale L.H.S. had appeared on notice boards throughout the town, and these had been much more striking and professionally done than Jake's own efforts. The only cloud on the horizon was that many of these new posters had also been torn down; indicating that one person at least did not like the plan; but his or her opposition had mattered not, the message had got across.

The message had certainly been received by the members of the Women's Institute. Once the idea of providing tea, coffee and biscuits from a self-service table had been approved, it had been Jacob Lindley's responsibility to look for volunteers who would keep it well stocked and who would be agreeable to coming in each night to tidy and wash up and to empty the Honesty Box so as to remove temptation from the Ungodly.

A number of ladies had raised their hands, and a weekly rota had been drawn up; one of the people whose name appeared on the rota was Mrs Mary Wallington.

***

Mary Wallington's father-in-law was surprised how happy he felt. He still had the marks of the savage beating he had received, and sometimes at night Fear and Rage still held him in their grip, but not as firmly or as constantly as had been the case a few short days before. His natural tendency to watch out for himself and to push his personal interests above everything else had not been entirely knocked out of him, but it certainly had been cowed, and there were times when he could now look at the world without putting himself in the centre of the picture. Something had changed; somehow his attitude had mellowed, and he realised that this was all down to the generosity and kindness of his son's wife.

Such a transformation hadn't come without a cost. Mary's deep sadness over the death of Adam now touched him in a way that it hadn't done before. For possibly the first time in his life he felt real grief; that was an uncomfortable sensation, and one which he would have preferred not to know, but he was beginning to understand that in the real world, a world not dominated by him, there was joy and despair in equal measure, but that when life was good it was much better than that which he had known before. He still had dreams of making it big, he was still sure that he had valuable information he could sell, but now embryonic scruples were starting to develop, and his conscience if not yet shouting from the rooftops was at least beginning to whisper in his ear and persuading him to curb his rashest moments.

With Mary's help I am becoming a new man he thought; he was amazed just how much that prospect appealed to him.

***

"What the hell is happening to this town Vicar?" Bill Adamson was on the verge of tears. For the first time since Penny's murder and Sheila's suicide, he had forced himself to get back to a kind of normality and to meet people in the way he had always done before tragedy struck his family. His wife had prodded him to go out. "We can't live our lives behind closed doors forever Love, " she had said, "some form of life still goes on outside, and like it or not, we are part of it. Summon up the courage and just pop out for half an hour. If you can do it, then maybe we can learn from your example."

So it was Bill found himself in the back bar of the Royal Albert. He had almost drowned in the sea of sympathy that had washed over him the moment he entered the room. He had been about to turn and hurry away, but the young vicar had seen his anxiety and had gently parted the waters and led him quietly to the bar.

"I don't know Bill," the Reverend Lindley had replied to Bill's question, "I don't know if God does either, but perhaps he does have a purpose and we are all just too blind to see it."

"What purpose could your God have that involves so much evil?" asked Raymond Baker. "I know that God doesn't exist, but if he did, the fact that within a few short weeks he has permitted 3 horrible crimes to take place would say a hell of a lot about his supposed compassion."

"I wish I could answer that," mumbled his representative on Earth, "but I am afraid like you I really don't have any idea."

"It says everything about religion doesn't it when lovely kids like Bill's niece and Adam Wallington get wiped from the face of the planet and a seventy seven year old lady is driven to commit suicide when shite like Mick Wallington survive. Any decent omniscient being would at least have taken the chance to rid the world of a worthless piece of garbage like him."

"He may have changed, Raymond" interjected retired police officer Alan Nadin. "He came in here for the first time since he was released from hospital a couple of days ago. He drank lemonade, he sat quietly in a corner, he hardly spoke, but when he did it was in a very moderate and sensible way; it is just possible he is trying to turn over a new leaf."

"Bullshit!" responded Baker belligerently. "Once a gobshite always a gobshite; he may end up pulling the wool over all of your eyes, but he won't succeed in doing that with me. At some stage I guarantee you that I will be able to show you that he is still the same waste of space he always has been; just you wait and bloody see."

<h1 style="text-align:center">CHAPTER THIRTY ONE</h1>

"You fucking lied to me! You told me my dad was fucking special, and now you're telling me that you don't know who he was, but that he could be the biggest arsehole in England!" Edward Cartwright was incandescent; his anger so intense that anyone standing within 50 yards of the Hollywood actor needed a heat screen for self-protection; Constance Cartwright was well within the danger zone and without anything at all to shield her from her son's wrath.

"You said my dad was somebody! You claimed he was clever, cultured and charismatic! You implied that you were swept away by a real life Prince Charming, and now I find that you paid a man to have sex with you, and that he took your money then drafted in the village loudmouth to perform the act of procreation for him. Were you so repulsive that you had to bribe people with cash before they would fuck you? They'll love all this in Hollywood; with one unbelievably stupid act you have probably ruined my career; you've got a lot to answer for haven't you mother?"

Connie was crying so much she could hardly speak; her head whirled, she felt dizzy, her whole body was shaking, and if she hadn't been able to clutch the back of a solid wooden chair she would have collapsed to the floor. She tried to speak, words were hard to formulate; eventually she cried out, in a shrill and terrified wail.

"Edward, oh Edward, it wasn't like that. I just wanted a child to love, I wanted a beautiful baby boy, but I didn't want to become the property of any man. That's how things were in those days. If you were a wife or a mother you were seen as belonging to your husband. Nobody had the vision to look beyond the mundane. I knew that if I was not restricted by the lack of ambition that was endemic in the local male population I could raise a child to achieve the universe; and you have done that Darling, and you've done it all with your own talent, but I have worked tirelessly to help you, and I have sacrificed so much just to see you succeed. I'm so, so sorry my Darling; please don't be cross with me; I can't bear it when you are cross with me."

"Cross Mother! I've got every right to be fucking cross! Even if what you planned had any merit, you fucked everything up by getting so drunk that you don't know who took advantage of you. For all you know my father could have had some congenital disease which he has passed on to me, or he could have the I.Q, of a brain damaged dung beetle, and he could yet have left me with a legacy of ill health and under-achievement. And that's not the worst bit. The worst bit is that somebody knows, the worst bit is that some bastard is laughing at me behind my back, and it's going to cost me a pretty packet, and hours of time, which I haven't got to try and prevent him from destroying everything I have ever worked for."

"Oh Edward, darling, stop it, stop it! I can't bear to hear you talk like this. We can get through this I promise you, we can come out stronger for the experience; we -"

Edward Cartwright cut his mother short. "We can't do anything Mother. We don't exist anymore. I'll sort this my own way. Right now the best thing you can do is to fuck off before I'm tempted to hit you. I suspect it will be a very long time, if ever, before we meet again."

Mark Hobson had finished his evening meal; the children had been tucked into bed; he had read them a much loved story from a well-thumbed book of fairy tales and had played about with the ending until he was reprimanded by his 5 year old son.

"Read it right Daddy," he had instructed his errant father, and put on a very cross face. Mark loved to tease his children; the bedtime stories and the good night kisses were precious moments to savour. Wistfully he thought, make the most of these days, they won't last forever. An awful lot of him wished that they could.

He had come downstairs and now sat in an armchair opposite his beautiful wife Helena. She was everything that he had ever dreamed of, and even when things weren't going well at work, or he was trying to sort out the aftermath of some sickening crime, she was the glorious, gorgeous beacon who lit up his darkest thoughts.

Tonight was one of those nights, when, despite his best intentions always to leave his work back at the office, he couldn't stop thinking about the Adamson and Wallington families and the double murder he was investigating; Helena instinctively knew when he was worried.

"It will all come right Darling, you know it will, and things always look blackest just before the dawn. You will solve these horrible crimes; I have every confidence; after all, like the Mounties, my husband always gets his man."

"I'm not so sure" joked Mark, "maybe I need to join the Royal Canadian Mounted Police but I can tell you I think there is still one hell of a journey for me to travel before this case is finally resolved."

"You'll find the answers sooner than you think Love, you always do; something will click and then that will be it."

"Maybe, maybe not," sighed Mark. "I've got this strange feeling that somewhere out there, probably hidden in some archive is a photograph, or a letter, or some other piece of documentary evidence which will give me all the answers I am looking for; the trouble is I have no idea where I should start looking for it, or even how long it will be before that most basic of building blocks has been unearthed."

"See what tomorrow brings" counselled Helena, "for now let's just snuggle together and watch a film and forget about your work for the rest of the evening."

"I'm already suffering from total amnesia," laughed Mark, only too happy to agree to his wife's proposal.

***

"You may not believe me, but I still think every day about the death of Penny Adamson. I truly regret that her death was inevitable and that I had to be the person to take her life, but how else could Sheila have understood the grossness of her conduct? I wrote to Penny's father intending to offer him a degree of comfort, to tell him that his lovely daughter was no sinner and that none of his surviving relatives need live in fear, but it seems my olive branch has been spurned. He had to know that his own mother signed his child's death warrant by her inconstancy; he had to understand she was Jezebel, but out of respect for him I played the gentleman and spared him the lurid details. Now I am tempted to reveal the ugly truth, but Sheila is dead and can offend no more, so out of misplaced kindness I will let the matter lie. Sheila should have lived longer with her guilt, but it is some comfort to know that her regret and self-loathing were so great that she raced to end her life in the manner that she did. I think if you die when your mind is anguished the pain may last for all eternity, but more likely thoughts rot with the decaying body or burn like wisps of writing paper in the crematorium oven. What is beyond dispute however, is that the written word can be a deadly assassin.

The time has come for my pen to kill again. This time my letter, when complete, will not be sent to the guilty party, but to someone else; that is a stroke of genius. The guilty party will be blissfully unaware that another person has learned the truth, but that shield of ignorance will soon be shattered by explosions of resentment and recrimination. What will result from the mayhem is impossible to predict, but whatever comes to pass the pain that will be felt will be so much the worse because it is totally unexpected. Wound a Leopard at its fiercest and it will feel pain, wound it when it is in the process of changing its spots and the shock will be much greater. Will history repeat itself? Will another villain take the coward's way out? Only time will tell; but if it does, then I will rejoice that a Category One offender has fled into the past tense; and if that does happen then half my grand design will be complete. What will then follow? I can tell you that another event, more dramatic and more shocking than anything that has gone before will shake this community to its roots. "How could he do such a thing?" the newspapers will howl. If some wordy hack or self-righteous editor could live a blighted life they would understand, but in due course I will make it easy for them, but not until every loose end has been tied in.

The police are at their wits end, they cannot begin to imagine what they are dealing with, and most likely they never will. I do not worry about them. If I have a worry, it is the meddling of the self-important fools who are trying to create a historic narrative. I thought that the removal of their ridiculous posters would have denied their half-baked scheme the oxygen of publicity it needed, but I was mistaken. The project masterminded by the pushy curate has taken flight, and now every would-be Simon Sharma is trawling through old records and fading photographs to find some hidden gem. If I am to sleep more easily the source material has to go; it helped me understand so much about the criminals who stole my life, it could help others in their quest to understand me. I have my plans, remedial action will soon be taken and the world will be appalled by what it sees.

CHAPTER THIRTY TWO

My poor, uncomprehending Mary,

I know so much about you. I know that you have asked yourself a million times why your precious son Adam had to die, and now the time has come for you to have answers.

I will begin with words of consolation. Nothing in Adam's character led to his downfall; the boy was exactly as he seemed; and even if your maternal pride was a little excessive, and his virtues were not as great as you believed (no son's virtues ever could be), he was clever, honest, gracious, loving and considerate, and his qualities should have brought him success and contentment. He had no hidden flaws, or at least none that I have ever heard about, and it is a total tragedy that I had to strike him down.

So having exonerated him from blame, the question has to be where should the responsibility for this disaster lie? I have to tell you that a little of it rests upon your shoulders; you chose to marry a man of limited talent and from a tainted bloodline, and by doing that you guaranteed that forever afterwards you and your children were at risk. Had you selected a different partner that would not have been the case; I am sure you and your issue would have prospered; the qualities that made your son such an impressive young man undoubtedly came from you, and would have been as potent, if not more potent if he had had a different father. In fact, I am sure that would have been the case because there would have been no defective genes to throw into the mix.

Comfort yourself with this thought, however: I regard your culpability as minimal; I do not want to shift any of the blame away from the one person whose actions sentenced Adam to death and you to a life of eternal sadness.

You may now be asking yourself who that person could be, but in your heart, I am sure you already know. The person you are now befriending, the man benefitting from your generosity of spirit is the monster whose actions long ago decreed that his grandchild was doomed to die a violent death.

Yes Mary, the architect of your tragedy, the villain who penned this tale of revenge and retribution is none other than Michael Wallington; and do not doubt even for one second that, but for his flawed character, your son would still be with you now. I swear that this declaration is completely true; Mick is the fiend whose presence on Earth has led to murder and to mayhem.

I am sure you are wondering now what it was that amoral rogue did to incur my eternal hatred; the list I fear is endless. When Adam was alive you were as aware of his shortcomings as any woman, you were sometimes irritated, sometimes frustrated, occasionally amused by his more obvious failings; but those failings were symptomatic of a deeper malaise. In his lifetime the man who you are now trying to help recover from his injuries justly inflicted by the agents of a person he has wronged, cared nothing for the feeling of other people. His selfishness and irresponsibility have caused pain and sometimes death. I am sure you must have guessed that his sexual appetite was voracious. Would it shock you to know that on one occasion he fucked an unconscious female? Oh dear! I have used a bad word in front of a follower of Jesus Christ, that was wrong of me, and yet there is no better word to describe intercourse without love; but now I remember a better one, although it is another 4 letter word. The word is "rape" and in the eyes of the Law your father-in-law would today be classed as a "rapist."

There is so much more that I could say, and if I were to write it all down it would fill a 6 volume novel, but it is better to leave some things hanging in the ether; if you can bring yourself to speak to him, maybe he will have the decency to fill in some of the gaps, but knowing this man as I do I wouldn't hold my breath.

Finally can I give you one small piece of advice? I have heard a rumour that he is trying to change his ways; that the "Hail fellow well met", "Fuck your daughter for a fiver" bragging, boasting egomaniac is seeking to embrace humanity. Don't be deceived by his tears or his lies, he is your Nemesis, he represents everything that is bad in your life, he destroyed your child, never forget that for a single second.

***

Mick Wallington had woken early, and instead of his usual vain attempt to re-conquer sleep he threw the duvet from the bed to remove any temptation he might have to linger in his warm pit. If his life had been the subject of a "Fly on the wall" documentary, no doubt anyone who had witnessed his usual ill-tempered battle to put off the moment of rising would have been amazed at his behaviour, but feelings were beginning to stir in him which he had never known before.

It wasn't love, clearly that would be entirely inappropriate, Mary was young enough to be his daughter, and in any event she was very far removed from any image he might have had of a potential soul mate; but it was a sudden realisation that he enjoyed her company. In his mid-70s he was finally beginning to understand that he needed other people, and that the best way to have decent human contact with his fellow man or woman was to engage properly with them rather than to always place himself at the centre of the universe.

Today was one of the days Mary had set aside to visit him, and he was surprised just how good that made him feel. What he valued most was her conversation. Before he had fallen asleep last night the obvious fact had struck him that the less time she had to spend doing housework, the more time she could spend talking to him. He had resolved that before she arrived, he would clear up most of his usual mess and that that the kitchen would be straight, pots and pans would be washed and the living room would be clean and tidy. Forgoing breakfast, he had set to work, and in fairness to him he had done a half way decent job.

It's not perfect he thought, but it is a damn sight better than it was.

The next thought he had was that he would buy her a small present, a little gift with no strings attached; there could be nothing wrong in doing that. The trouble was what to get her. He thought about flowers, but they presented a problem; a small bunch would look cheap and penny-pinching, a large bouquet might appear O.T.T. and laden with a meaning that they simply didn't possess.

He considered cosmetics or perfume, but both these ideas he abandoned almost immediately; scent and cologne would be too personal, and in any event he didn't know what products might appeal to Mary. A bottle of wine would be the easy option, but she didn't drink a great deal, and a gift of alcohol might say more about the giver than perhaps was wise. Eventually, after wracking his brain, he settled on the idea of a pretty houseplant, perhaps in a striking ceramic bowl; if he chose well it could be tasteful, and at the same time understated, and it would have an element of permanence that cut flowers never could possess. With a spring in his step he left his home and strolled down to the local florists. He entered the shop and carefully looked at what was on display; he also enlisted the help of the girl behind the counter and she proved to have very good judgement Eventually a nice little pink plant in a Portmeirion bowl was selected. It wasn't cheap, but that was how it should be. Pleased with himself, he paid for his gift and left the shop feeling well satisfied with his work.

When he arrived back home after buying the gift, and after he had satisfied himself that the place really did look presentable, he turned his attention to himself. He looked in the mirror, and was decidedly unimpressed with the image that stared back at him. He looked seedy and overweight and not to put too fine a word to it "scruffy". It would be an hour at least before Mary arrived; he could do her the honour of at least looking half way decent; he decided to make the effort. First he went upstairs to his wardrobe to decide what to wear. His initial idea was to put on a clean pair of black jeans and a long sleeved black and silver striped shirt, but then he changed his mind, partly because the jeans were too tight, partly because the dark colours emphasised the greyness of his thinning hair, and partly because wearing those clothes he would be "the Dandy Cock", the old Mick, the person who was wanting the world to look at him and to take notice: Mary wouldn't like that. Eventually he selected a smart pair of light grey casual trousers, which he teamed with a pale blue shirt and a dark blue jumper. He looked conventionally respectable, if a little self-effacing. There was nothing about his outfit that could cause Mary, or anyone else, any disquiet.

Next he showered and shaved, taking good care not to nick himself with the razor; he also found time to trim the unwanted foliage from the tips of his ears and which also peeped out from inside his nostrils. How come I can grow hair in abundance in places where nobody wants it, he thought, yet in the places where it is needed it's a bloody desert. It was a matter of profound regret to him that his once luxuriant locks were now becoming brittle and thin, but that was Nature's way, and he didn't have the money or even the inclination to think about a hair transplant.

The remedial work having been finished, and now dressed in clean clothing, in an unusual state of preparedness Mick went down to the kitchen. He got out 2 china mugs that were always kept for best, checked to see that they were unmarked, found a matching jug into which he poured some fresh milk and a little bowl and he tipped a small quantity of sugar straight from the packet into it, making sure it contained no black specks of coffee picked up from contact with damp teaspoons. He placed all of these items onto a colourful little tray which he placed on the kitchen worktop and then sat back and waited for his guest to arrive.

***

"The place was like an abattoir Love, there was blood everywhere, I've never seen a man bleed so much and still be alive," Detective Inspector Hobson was describing to his wife the carnage he had seen that afternoon at the home of Michael Wallington.

"Apparently she just went berserk. Mick had been looking forward to the visit, he'd even tidied his place up to make it look nice, but the moment he opened the door she produced a boning knife from her handbag and flew at him. She was screaming at him, "You killed him! You killed him" and Mick was squealing in fright. He's got severe lacerations to both his arms, numerous scratches and small puncture wounds to his chest and abdomen, a deep wound to his upper thigh and several cuts to his back. He is very lucky to still be with us. I think the only reason he has survived is that Mary isn't a big woman and many of her blows must have lacked power. At present he's in an intensive care ward; the doctors say his wounds will probably all heal in time, but he's in a state of total shock, and they are not sure if he'll ever recover mentally from his ordeal."

"Poor man," said Helena, "and poor, poor Mary, She's such a nice woman, she wouldn't hurt a fly, I can't believe she's done everything you say she's done."

"She's probably in a worse condition mentally than he is," replied Mark, and she's got self-inflicted wounds to both wrists. After her initial frenzy subsided the enormity of what she'd done seemed to sink in, she tried to take her own life, but fortunately the paramedics arrived before she could bleed to death and they managed to stem the flow. She's now in a secure ward at the local hospital. The doctors say she's currently in no fit state to be interviewed. If she hadn't been so badly injured, she would already have been sectioned: it's all so very, very sad."

"It's a good job the ambulance got there so quickly," commented Helena, "otherwise you could have been looking at two dead bodies when you arrived."

"There was so much yelling and screaming going on that half the street heard it. In less than 5 minutes we had received no less than twelve 999 calls; it was obvious that something pretty dramatic was happening; the call-handlers acted very swiftly, and in just over 4 minutes the first ambulance was on the scene. It took us a couple of minutes longer to get there, but inside 10 minutes Mick and Mary were both in the care of paramedics, and we had secured the crime scene."

"What caused Mary to act in the way that she did?" asked Helena. "There has to be a reason why she behaved in such a violent manner?"

"There is Love," replied Mark. "We found a screwed up letter in her handbag; it told her that young Adam would still be alive but for the actions of his granddad. It couldn't have been more specific; Mary's in a pretty fragile state, and that letter seems to have tipped her over the edge, particularly as recently she has been doing what she can to get Mick back on his feet again after his bad beating up. Something inside her head snapped. She went to her kitchen drawer, picked out a very sharp knife, and then went round to Mick's house to kill him. But Mary's not the villain of the piece, and actually neither is Mick; it's the lunatic who sent the letter who is really to blame."

"Sheila Adamson got a letter just before she threw herself under a car didn't she Darling?" queried Helena. "Do you think both letters were written by the same person?"

"Almost certainly yes," replied Mark. "Both letters use the same font, both have a similar style to them, and both were sent with the intent to cause trouble."

"And the writer has certainly succeeded in doing that, hasn't he Darling? The sooner he is locked up out of harm's way the safer everyone round here will feel. I know when I do the school run tomorrow; the sole topic of conversation at the school gate will be who's going to be next."

"I wish I knew," sighed Mark, "but I'm sure there is going to be another killing, and that is a very, very sobering thought."

CHAPTER THIRTY THREE

The high drama that had left two people with multiple stab wounds, and in very precarious emotional states would certainly have caused the Reverend Jacob Lindley to ponder whether there was any comfort he could bring to either tormented soul, but at present the incident had not been widely reported, and so, for the time being, he knew nothing about it. His mind was on other things, and he was wrestling with a dilemma. He had just been asked if he would lead the prayers at the War Memorial on Remembrance Sunday, and he was very happy to do this, but he was aware it could also be something of a poisoned chalice. For several years there had been arguments in town as to precisely when the laying of wreathes should take place, and feelings had run high. The Reverend Lindley and the majority of the ordinary people in town who did not attend church regularly believed passionately that this should take place at 11am to coincide with the ceremony at the Cenotaph in London, and in the knowledge that most towns and villages in Great Britain were also holding their Remembrance Day services at this time; a sense of being one with the Nation in mourning the war dead, and giving thanks for their courage and their sacrifice; that was what these people wanted to feel.

But there was another point of view. For the very best of motives the incumbent at the Parish Church, his parochial church council, and some of the members of the local Royal British Legion wanted to see the lengthy formal ceremony take place within the church at 11am. The Market Square in Burrdale in November could be an unforgiving place, and if the very young and the very old could be protected from cold winds and driving rain, which were not uncommon occurrences in the Peak District of Derbyshire, then surely that had to be a good thing. The trouble was the people who waited outside in the square for the ceremony to finally take place often stood for unnecessarily long periods getting soaked to the skin and chilled to the bone, and were left feeling like poor relations to the main event. It was also a fact that Burrdale had three World War II veterans who were not Christians, and one of these was a decorated war hero; it seemed very unjust that these fine old gentlemen were being forced to accept a minor role in the events of the day.

After years of sometimes bitter dispute a compromise had finally been reached. It was now agreed that the service in church should start half an hour earlier than had previously been the case to ensure that it could continue in exactly the way it had always done, but that it would finish in sufficient time for the whole congregation to exit the church, and re-assemble at the War Memorial by 10.55am to swell the ranks of people waiting there to participate in a solemn act of remembrance. It was proposed that there would only be one hymn, and that would not be one that had previously been sung in church, and that prayers would then be said. The "Last Post" would be played, flags and banners would be lowered to honour the fallen, and after 2 minutes silence, wreaths and floral tributes would be laid. It was so simple and so rational it beggared belief that agreement couldn't have happened earlier, but still not everyone approved;

there was some in the local church hierarchy who did not look kindly on the changes.

Well tough, thought Jacob, what we are doing is the right thing, and that is all that matters.

But the dispute over Remembrance Sunday wasn't the only thing on the curate's mind. His pet project to save St Catherine's was gaining momentum, and despite a few problems early on with the tea and coffee table and some errors in the cleaning rota, everything was now running smoothly. Much of the good work to ensure the success of the scheme was due to the heroic efforts of Mary Wallington.

She's a true Christian, thought the Reverend Lindley, she's been through so much and yet she can still think of others; what a shining example to us all! When the time finally comes she will have earned her place in Heaven. His only real difficulty was that it was proving hard to demonstrate to the Bishop that, so far as St Catherine's was concerned, there had been a sea change. If I could do a comparison between the situation as it has been for the last 5 years, and the way things are now, he thought, I might stand a chance, particularly if I can prove now that as well as greatly increased numbers, the experience most people get is vastly different to what it was before. I really must find somebody who searched the records and had a miserable time doing so to make my point. The trouble was identifying any such person was proving difficult, but recently he had been given a couple of names to look into, and he hoped that at least one of these would bear fruit.

***

"At least with Mick we're looking at a man who made enemies, that must give us a bit of a starting point," D.I. Mark Hobson was discussing the possible motives of the writer of the unsigned letter to Mary Wallington with D. S. Peter Bennett, and trying to put a positive spin on the situation the police were faced with as they tried to unravel the tangled threads of this most complex criminal investigation.

"The trouble is that there are so many possible candidates that it will be a bugger of a job trying to pick out a winner" retorted the less than convinced detective sergeant.

"That's as may be," added the detective inspector, "but let's not put ourselves off before we begin; shall we both jot down a few names and see which, if any of them, leap off the page as genuine suspects?"

It wasn't difficult to unearth possible perpetrators; almost any member of the Adamson family could qualify as a legitimate contender and Constance Cartwright and her son Edward couldn't be ignored either, particularly as Edward was also a prime suspect for arranging the brutal attack on Mick outside the pub only a couple of weeks before.

"And don't forget Mickey Shah" said Mark Hobson. "There is some anecdotal evidence that he believed it was Mick who fed him false information about Frank Oakes being seen with a gun near to his property. That led to him making a complaint to us, which in turn exposed him to police scrutiny and he certainly didn't like that; he'd be only too pleased to punish Mick for his impudence."

"And what about Oakes himself?" queried Pete Bennett. "If he thought Wallington had lied about him to Mickey Shah, which had then led to his home being raided, and himself nearly getting arrested, that would give him a credible motive to get back at Mick."

"It would," agreed D.I. Hobson," but he doesn't appear to have had any reason to write to Sheila Adamson, and I am convinced that both anonymous letters were written by the same person, and I think that that person is also our killer. If that assumption is correct, then Frank Oakes is out of the frame: he has an alibi for the shooting of Penny, I'm absolutely sure that it wasn't a put up job between him and Tim Bradley, I would stake my life on that, unless I really am a totally pathetic judge of character."

"You're many things Gov," laughed D.S. Bennett, but even I wouldn't accuse you of being that."

"Your ringing endorsement of my talents overwhelms me Pete," responded Mark "You're beginning to mellow; keep on like this, and pretty soon people might stop calling you a cynic."

"No chance Gov!" retorted the Detective Sergeant. "With you around I'm always going to have something to be cynical about."

It was after the banter had subsided, and both men had considered in details all the possible suspects they could think of, that another name was added to what had become a very long list.

"Try this one for size," said Pete Bennett. "What about Raymond Baker? He's not a bad bloke otherwise Alan Nadin wouldn't be mates with him, but he's got a fiery temper, and he can be a bit of a hothead. He's always pretty outspoken about Mick Wallington and he's not averse to conflict if he's in the wrong mood. He nearly started a punch up in the pub last week, and he is touchy if people say uncomplimentary things about his dad. I heard rumours that his dad is currently very poorly, and that Ray himself may also be quite ill."

"That's an interesting thought Pete, and worthy of some consideration. If the lad is under a lot of pressure at the moment, particularly if he is sensing time is running out for his father, and maybe for himself, he could be trying to resolve a few grievances before Old Father Time puts an end to his innings. The problem is that while all this makes an attractive little theory, there is absolutely no evidence whatsoever to support our contentions."

***

Constance Cartwright looked unwell, everybody said so. She had lost her sparkle, she no longer bubbled over with pride, and she no longer seized every opportunity to talk about her wonderful son. There were people for whom this was a blessed relief, but her friends were starting to worry about her. Without Edward at the centre of her world, what did her world contain? The truth for many people who observed her was that it didn't contain a great deal. Her friends tried to support her, ask her what was worrying her so that they could try and help, but that just brought angry responses of "There's nothing wrong with me," and "I'm fine! Now please mind your own business!" All their well-meaning advances were rebuffed.

In the last fortnight she had become a virtual recluse, only venturing out of necessity to buy food or post letters, and she didn't pick up her phone, although if it had been Edward's voice on the answer phone then that would have been a different matter; but it never was. She longed to hear him speak, and had repeatedly tried to telephone him, but he never picked up, and if the messages she left for him were being passed on, which she seriously doubted, they were being stubbornly ignored. She had tried watching video tapes of some of his T.V. appearances to ease the pain, but that only seemed to make things worse; and she frequently ended up in tears. There seemed to be no prospect that things would ever change.

She knew who was to blame for her unhappiness, and it wasn't herself, nor was it Edward, although she was seeing in him a cruel streak which she hadn't seen before, and that distressed her greatly. Little seeds of anger were beginning to germinate, and once she had heard herself saying "I made you and I can break you", but she had been appalled at that notion, and lashed herself mentally for ever thinking that way. The idea of seeking to attack her own son had been banished to the dark recesses of her mind, but it hadn't died, and one day might yet make a re-appearance.

But for now she had another target, for now there was just one man who had caused the rift between her and her golden boy, and that man was Frank Oakes; it didn't matter that he had kept a secret for over 30 years, it didn't matter that her problems existed because some malicious person was raking over history to cause mischief, and that Frank might also be a victim; all that mattered was Frank Oakes had taken her money, sneered at her behind her back, conspired with a reprobate to humiliate her, and left her a figure of fun in the mind of any ne'er-do-well he had chosen to confide in. His behaviour had been intolerable, he had to be punished; the only question was how.

She ruled out the possibility of a face to face confrontation; even though she had calmed down just a touch from the white heat of rage she had felt when she first read the anonymous letter, she still could not be sure that she could keep her finger nails from gouging deep cuts in his face if he was in range, and if a screaming fracas took place in a public place that spelled danger to her and her uncaring son. She wondered about a private meeting, whether at his place or at her's, to confront him with his treachery and to seek financial recompense for his duplicity, but that was too cold and too civilised a response to contemplate; the last thing she felt at this moment was "civilised".

It was as she was writing another pleading letter to Edward, begging for forgiveness and imploring him to give her a final chance, knowing full well that it would never be read, that the thought struck her that there was one person who would not ignore her words, and for whom they might have a devastating effect, and that person was Mrs Frank Oakes. Abandoning in mid-sentence her latest epistle to her stone-hearted child, she started to rough out a missive to this unfortunate lady. It would take a long time to complete, it had to be perfectly crafted, and the despicable behaviour of her husband had to be thoroughly explained to have maximum impact. Other people had used words to make ticking time bombs; it was her turn now, and she would create one which she hoped would have huge destructive potential.

CHAPTER THIRTY FOUR

It had started off so very promisingly. One of the two people whose names had been given to the crusading curate, after an initial bout of reluctance, had agreed to meet and talk with him. He had stipulated a time and place, and he had met with Jacob Lindley in a quiet public house approximately 6 miles away from the Peak District town of Burrdale; this was not entirely convenient for the Reverend Lindley, and he had found the refusal to meet in town a little odd, but it had been a pre-condition and, if he wanted the conversation, then he had to agree to the man's stipulations.

When they met face to face, at first the omens seemed positive, and the man had shown a great deal of interest in the fight to save St Catherine's, and he had paid particular attention when the young vicar had explained, with great enthusiasm, how much use the archival material was now getting.

"I didn't think there was so much stuff in there," he had said, and the curate had replied, "Neither did a great many other people, but you probably noticed two large cupboards, which most people assume contain prayer books and vestments, but which are actually stuffed to the gunnels with parish records going back more than two centuries, and hundreds of old photographs and newsletters."

Jacob Lindley had explained that although much of the archive material had been stored there for decades, recently it had been added to by the addition of records from the village hall.

"When it came to the crunch the managing committee felt guilty about just throwing everything away, so they took it down to the church and stuffed it into the cupboard on a couple of empty shelves making them creak under the weight. One day soon volunteers are going to sort through everything, and catalogue what they find; they are very excited about the prospect of doing this. The Local History Society believes that there could well be enough material to create a detailed history of Burrdale from the time of the Napoleonic Wars to the present day. It's a wonderful prospect, and one which I am sure you, with your interest in local history, could become heavily involved in."

He had expected the man to jump at the chance, but he hadn't done so. Jacob Lindley wondered if time was the issue, and if the man didn't feel that he had enough free time to do the project justice. He had said he was sure that he would not be expected to do anything more than that which he felt entirely comfortable with, and he had suggested a visit to the church might allay any doubts that he might be having on that score: he also made it clear that the he thought that so far as he personally was concerned he didn't anticipate that more than this one session would be necessary to cover all the points he wanted to raise with him.

"That's all there is to it," he had said cheerily, "so are you content to go along with that? I am more than happy to put down on paper all your comments, and to prepare a draft letter to the Bishop in your name. You would of course be able to alter or omit anything you didn't feel entirely comfortable with; so have we got a deal?"

To his surprise the man had indicated forcefully that they hadn't. "I don't agree," he told the Reverend Lindley. "Local history isn't really my thing." He had added that he had only consented to meet him out of courtesy, and that now he felt himself being pressurised into doing something he didn't want to do and which wasn't in his best interest. Jacob Lindley thought that this statement seemed to be at odds with the man's earlier intense interest in the project, but the stranger had refused to change his mind. All the curate's pleas for cooperation fell onto deaf ears. He felt angry and frustrated; it had been a completely wasted afternoon, and he now begrudged the £5.80 pence he had spent buying the man drinks.

***

The headlines in the local papers were fairly muted, and in all of them there was an element of sympathy for the alleged offender; the attitudes they publicly expressed reflected the views of the residents of Burrdale, who regarded the incident at Michael Wallington's home as a personal tragedy for Mary and to a lesser extent for Mick himself. It was perhaps inevitable that this would be the case. Mary had earned their respect; her support for good causes, her tireless work on behalf of the church, her likeability and common sense, and her devotion to her family all now weighed in the balance in her favour. It seemed to be universally accepted that she had been driven to act as she did by the evil machinations of a cold blooded killer, and she had been used by him to further his own twisted agenda. There was far less sympathy for Mick, who it was generally felt had acted at best inappropriately and at worst irresponsibly for the last 5 decades, and maybe it could be said that his chickens were coming home to roost; but even for him there were some who had noticed a change in his behaviour latterly and who felt sorry that a man who seemed genuinely to be trying to mend his ways had been so savagely attacked in his own home. Not everyone agreed. Raymond Baker was not one of these people. When, in trying to gauge the public mood, a reporter from the Burrdale Advertiser had approached Ray, as a local resident, for his comments on Mary and Mick; he had described Mary as a "saint"; the four letter word he used to describe Mick was not one a decent family newspaper was happy to publish.

The national newspapers had shown no such restraint, and the tabloids in particular had predictably chosen to use sensational and lurid headlines.

The Sun had headlined its story "Murder victim's Mum takes Bloody Vengeance". The Daily Star had been more succinct, choosing to run with a single word "Bloodbath" and The Daily Mirror, seizing on a comment made to one of its reporters by a local vicar, had trumpeted "The Revenge of a Good Christian." What had then followed in all of these three newspapers had been highly dramatised accounts of the tragic happenings that had taken place in the sleepy High Peak backwater of Burrdale. Words like "frenzied," "slashed," berserk" littered their descriptions of events. Mary had "screamed like a banshee," Mick had "howled like a wounded animal," and there had been plenty of other unhelpful and inaccurate similes to keep even the most gruesome of their readers happy. There was no balance; reasonable men like Stan Hardy and Mark Hobson profoundly regretted this lack of restraint, and Helena Hobson was so appalled by this lack of understanding and compassion that she penned letters to the editors of these three journals complaining about the way the story had been carried. Mark agreed with all her comments, but had said that they would do no good, and might even rebound on them as a family if the press got the idea that a senior police officer was biased in favour of a violent offender, should these matters eventually come to trial. Reluctantly Helena agreed with him, and her well-crafted, eloquent letters were never sent.

Detective Chief Superintendent Stanley Hardy and Detective Inspector Mark Hobson were meeting to discuss progress in the Wallington and Adamson murder case, and were doing so against a backdrop of mounting public disquiet and increasingly shrill demands from the Chief Constable to "Get something sorted soon!"

The good news was that more officers had been found who could be added to the inquiry, and that had to be a bonus. The bad news was that the Chief was now expecting a quick resolution of the case so that the newspapers could get the headlines they were praying for. A result would also give him a respite from the whining criticism of local politicians who were beginning to pain his ears on a regular basis and clog up his in tray with their ill-informed accusations of incompetence and inertia. Sir Walter Thurlow was not a crusading police officer: all he wanted was good publicity, and he liked to bask in the limelight and take the credit for success when things went well, but he hated criticism, and if an investigation became protracted he rapidly became impatient. His love of the news media easily turned to loathing, and he would make a great show of cracking the whip to demonstrate his desire to get the crime solved. It didn't matter how well the case had been handled to date, all he was interested in was a name on a court list; right now in this case he wanted to see somebody arrested on suspicion of murder, and it didn't much matter who that person might be. Fortunately, Stan Hardy and Mark Hobson didn't share this lack of particularity.

"We were able to interview Mary Wallington in hospital Sir," explained DI Hobson, "but it could only be a short interview to see if she had any idea who it was who might have sent her the letter, which of course she hadn't, and to ascertain if there had been any other letters or phone calls relating to Adam's death, which again of course there hadn't. I intend to carry out a longer interview under caution later on today. She is still very upset, but the doctors no longer feel that she is unfit to be questioned at length."

"And then what?" queried the DCS.

"Well Sir, unless the C.P.S. advise me otherwise I was thinking of charging her with the unlawful wounding of

Michael Wallington and then bailing her with conditions to attend court in twenty eight days time. I don't want to apply for a remand in custody, she isn't a threat to anybody else, and to be honest Sir, I feel desperately sorry for her, as do most of the people in this town."

"She may not be a threat to anyone else Mark, but is she a threat to herself? The very last thing we need is another suicide. The Chief would go apoplectic, and the self-righteous scribes who write for the tabloids would have a feeding frenzy if there was another death."

"I don't think there will be Sir. She's got a sister who she's very close to, and who is worried sick about her. I'm sure she will keep a far closer eye on her than any prison warder could possibly do, even with the help of twenty four hour CCTV. I know volcanoes can erupt more than once, but in Mary's case that's highly unlikely. She regrets what she's done, she feels bitterly ashamed, she's frightened to death about what is going to happen to her, but she's not the type not to face the music, that's just not her way."

"Fair enough then," replied the Detective Chief Superintendent, "providing the C.P.S. are happy then so am I."

There was one further point for the two officers to consider, and that was the Chief Constable's insistence that whatever was done from now on had to be eye catching and newsworthy.

"He wants to be seen to be pulling out all the stops," explained DCS Hardy. "We've got more men we must make use of them. I'm thinking about another round of house to house inquiries and getting the Burrdale Advertiser on board to make sure we get maximum publicity. The Chief also wants posters and leaflets and anything else that we can think of to show the world we are actively seeking a killer. Cost isn't an issue, although I wouldn't bet that it won't become one at some future date. Can we get something to the printers in the next 24 hours? It might all turn out to be a waste of time, but until the shit hits the fan it will keep our big boss happy."

"I'll get right onto it Sir," replied Hobson, "but like you I'm not convinced that we'll get anything out of this exercise except some bobbies with blisters and a big bill for printing and copying."

CHAPTER THIRTY FIVE

It was a little after 10.30 pm that the fire was first noticed. A team of men from the Royal Albert were returning to their local after a darts and dominoes friendly match with the Black Greyhound in the nearby village of Chapel Middleton when the flames were spotted. All of the passengers on the minibus borrowed from the 1st Burrdale Scouts for the night to transport them to and from the match had been drinking, but none of them were very drunk. The driver, Tim Bradley, was stone cold sober. He would have much sooner have spent an evening at home watching Poirot on T.V. rather than sitting miserably waiting for his noisy passengers to finish their drinks and return to the coach, but that hadn't been an option. He had been unable to withstand the pressure that had been put on him to volunteer his services since he was a known teetotaller, and it had been recognised by the players that even unremarkable self-effacing men had their uses, if they avoided the need for someone who normally enjoyed a drink having to remain depressingly abstemious on a lively pub games night. He had morosely sipped his pint of orange and lemonade for more than 2 hours, and had not been wonderful company. When he was actually cajoled into playing a game himself because the team were one man light, and when he then lost that in spectacular fashion, he felt that this evening couldn't have been much worse.

He had been wrapped up in his own thoughts when he heard somebody shout out "Fucking hell lads look! The church is on fire!" He had brought the bus to an emergency halt and as he drew to a stop, it was he who saw a man run from behind a gravestone and into the darkness of the churchyard at the side of the burning building: nobody else witnessed this and afterwards one or two people reflected that the power of alcohol to deaden the senses had been clearly demonstrated by this episode.

By the time the coach had stopped the vestry at St Catherine's was well alight, the fire hadn't yet reached the main body of the church, but without the quick intervention of the fire brigade, that position would soon change. The windows were cracked and blackened, and the heat was intense: had it just been a small blaze the men from the Royal Albert might have tried to force an entry to put out the flames, but there was far too much smoke and too much searing heat ever to think about doing that. 999 calls were made to the fire brigade and to the police on mobile phones, and the group of friends watched transfixed as the vestry burned, whilst they waited for the emergency services to arrive.

***

It took eight minutes for the first fire tender to appear, which was longer than the target time the Derbyshire Fire Service set for itself, but not by very much. Flames were now shooting from the vestry roof and it was obvious that roof joists and trusses were well alight, and that urgent action was paramount, but this turned out to be harder than it should have been because the centuries old sturdy church door was locked preventing easy access to the building. If this fire had been started deliberately, then the arsonist must have had a key, and had locked the door when he left the scene of his crime. The only logical reason for doing that had to be a belief that the heavy oak door would be a barrier to anyone seeking to put out the fire, and a conviction that every second's delay would lead to a greater degree of destruction; but this was just speculation. The cause of the blaze couldn't be predicted at this stage; faulty wiring or defective electrical equipment could hold the key, but the only thing that mattered at the moment was putting the fire out and saving as much of the fabric of the main building that could possibly be saved.

It took over an hour for the fire to be extinguished, by which time the roof of the vestry had almost completely collapsed. To a limited extent the fire had also spread to the main part of the church, but structurally that remained sound, with only a few overhanging eaves needing to be replaced. Inside the building the problem was much greater; smoke had damaged paintwork, including 2 frescos, and water had damaged pews, carpets, hassocks and sacred books.

***

"It doesn't help your campaign to save this place does it Reverend?"

The senior fire officer present at the scene was talking to a visibly upset Jacob Lindley, who had arrived at the stricken church after having received a phone call from a nearby resident. The excitement was largely over by the time he got there and apart from the smell of smoke in the atmosphere and the smouldering roof timbers there was not a great deal to see. The numbers of spectators had dwindled to a handful, and even the few people who were left were now drifting away. The police had taken contact details of potential witnesses, including all the members of the Royal Albert's darts and dominoes team; they would be spoken to individually in due course, and anyone with any potentially relevant information would be asked to provide a witness statement. There had not been the manpower to record evidence at the scene and in any event, most of these men had been making sideways glances at their watches, desperately wanting to get back to their home pub before the landlord called time for the night. Statements made when witnesses feel under pressure are rarely comprehensive, even if the pressure is being entirely generated by the witnesses themselves.

"No, it doesn't," responded an unhappy Church of England curate. "Maybe it won't be a fatal blow; but that said, it's certainly something those wishing to keep this place alive could have very well done without. Have you any idea how the fire may have started?"

"It's much too early to say," replied the fire officer. "I can tell you this though: the fire must have been burning for at least an hour before it was discovered, which means that it had to have been started no later than 9.15pm."

"And you have no idea what caused the blaze? Can you even say if it was by accident or design? If it does turn out to have been deliberately set alight that would be absolutely tragic; it's such a beautiful building, and it means so much to the people hereabouts; I don't know how some of them will cope if this turns out to be arson."

"I wish I could rule that out Vicar, but I am afraid I can't. There are aspects of this fire that do appear to be suspicious, and we have to treat it as such. It doesn't necessarily follow that there won't be an innocent explanation, but if I were you, I would be preparing myself for some bad news."

***

I don't know if they will conclude that a crime was committed, I think it likely that they will. My belief is that they will think that the seat of the fire was amongst piles of folders temporarily stacked on the floor under a wooden table and, if they do that, they will be correct. They may also find melted candle wax in that location and conclude that lighted candles were used to start the blaze, but candles in a vestry are like books in a library, you expect to find them there, you would be amazed if there weren't any and, as everybody knows, wax melts when heated, and so its presence may not be viewed as suspicious. Almost the entire roof has collapsed so there will be tons of debris to sift through and thousands of waterlogged scraps of paper to examine. It will be hard for investigators to be sure what really happened, and I sincerely hope that that will be the case; but in reality what really happened is straight forward.

The cause of the destruction of the vestry was the presence of the eager men and women who used it to compile their many lists, catalogue their photographs and read every line of every notebook and parish document. Meticulous record making can cause danger. Nobody should seek to discover all History's secrets; many things are better left buried in the sands of time. And what made it doubly dangerous here was cross-checking. One person looking at a page can miss a vital point, particularly if his eyes are tired after a day of staring at bad handwriting or reading small print, but if fresh eyes on another day re-examine it, the likelihood is that what was overlooked once will be noticed the second time around.

If I had had a year to go through every item stored in that small room, I have no doubt that I could have discovered and removed everything with the potential to do me harm, but that was never an option. I am sure I might have been able to grab odd moments here and there to get undisturbed access to the archive, but what good would that have done me? There would also have been an ever present risk that my renewed interest in the records would have attracted unwelcome attention and comment.

In any event I have been told that I do not have a year. The moon faced young doctor broke the news to me last week, but it is something I have suspected for a long while. I think she expected me to break down in floods of tears and, if I had then she would have tried to quench the intensity of my grief by drowning it in a sea of platitudes, but I do not fear my own mortality, and she was disappointed. A clock is ticking inside us all, what is so shocking or surprising when we find out that is true? I have been given 9 months more life at most upon this earth. Somewhere in this realm a woman no doubt conceived at the very moment my doctor put on her black cap and pronounced sentence upon me. If she is right, a newborn child may gulp down its first lung full of air at the very same time that I take my last: there is symmetry in the universe, and that is an undeniable truth.

As yet I have no pain, or at least none that cannot be held at bay by the ingestion of pills, which is good because I still have so much more to do. For the time being I can still move with ease, I can control my limbs, my hand is steady and my body does not shake, but who can say how long that situation will remain? There is unfinished business to complete. For one more unsuspecting soul a date with death is ringed upon the calendar; another life is destined to become tragically unfulfilled.

After the death of Penny I did not know if I had the strength to continue, but if I did not it would have served no purpose. For her sake, it was clear I had to remain true to my resolve so I have had to conquer self-doubt and carry on to the bitter end. The guilty must pay the price, and live with the terrible knowledge that their evil actions led to the killing of the Innocents. A terrible "Age of Enlightenment" awaits them and the world will soon see how their shallowness and callousness ruined lives. Their Hell will be on Earth, mine may be in another place, but I will have finally seen justice done, and that must be enough.

CHAPTER THIRTY SIX

As far as Constance Cartwright was concerned life couldn't get any worse than it was at present, and then suddenly it did. The Burrdale Advertiser had been running a feature it called "Romantic Gestures" for about a month, and it was asking its readers to write in and tell the paper about the most romantic thing their partners had ever done for them. The idea had sprung from an article it had published about a couple who had celebrated 75 years of marriage and the revelation that the husband had proposed to his wife from the stage of Buxton Opera House in front of a packed auditorium. The paper pointed out that although public proposals are not rare, and seldom newsworthy, back in the 1930s it had been a very different matter. The Advertiser had invited its readers to send in accounts of their most precious moments, offering a prize of dinner for two at an exclusive restaurant for the best story, and they had been inundated with responses. What had been intended to be a one off feature had now run for 4 weeks and the paper already had enough material for at least another 8 weeks.

It was the letter from a Mrs Susan Oakes that really incensed Connie. Her beautiful memory was of her husband asking her to marry him on the dance floor of the Palace Hotel in Buxton, and as such was not sufficiently unusual to be a contender for the top prize, but it was the date when this took place that most shocked Constance Cartwright.

On the very night Frank Oakes should have been fulfilling his contractual obligation to her, after he had encouraged her to drink to excess, and when she had become half comatose, he had slipped away to meet his fiancée, leaving her to the none too tender touches of the local loudmouth. This couldn't have been a spur of the moment decision; it had to have been pre-planned, probably for days, if not weeks. Had he used the money she had paid him for his services to buy an engagement ring for his sweetheart? She didn't know, but it was a very real possibility.

And it wasn't as if Susan Oakes was a particularly attractive young woman. A simple, homely girl of modest intelligence and very little style; and that was being generous to her.

And he could find it in his heart to court and marry her, she thought, yet he found the prospect of spending just one night with me so abhorrent that he treated me like a piece of meat and gave me to a degenerate fool to use me as he pleased.

Fury took a firm grip on her. Her only thought was to get even with the despicable cad who had abused her. Had Connie been able to think clearly she would have realised that characterising Oakes in this way made him sound like a villain in a 1940s B movie, but in a way that was exactly how she saw him, and all she could do was plot revenge. Poor deluded Susan Oakes obviously thought enough about her man to share the story of his devotion to her with the world. She had to be made aware of the true nature of the beast. Connie pulled open the top drawer of her bureau with such force that it nearly ended up on the floor, and it was only as it was about to topple that she realised the danger and she just managed to prevent the mishap occurring. She pushed the drawer back in far enough to prevent catastrophe, and when it was properly balanced she removed from it a pad of writing paper. She opened this up and looked at the carefully crafted letter she had penned to Mrs Susan Oakes and then decided not to send because it might be too dangerous to do so. She picked it up, read it, and then tore it into a hundred tiny pieces that then landed on the carpet like confetti. It was too bland, too circumspect, too lacking in emotion, too controlled. Seizing another piece of paper from the pad she began to scribble furiously. No stone would be left unturned, no sordid detail would be omitted; Mrs Oakes would learn the whole unvarnished truth.

She was surprised how easily the vitriol flowed from her pen; none of her friends would have dreamed her capable of such rage, but it was as if all the bitterness and hate that had been festering in her brain from the moment she first learned of her betrayal had now erupted onto the page and she was powerless to stop it.

Nothing was kept concealed, no opportunity to blacken Oakes's name was overlooked, and even if Susan Oakes had been as naive as a virgin with Down Syndrome the message would have got through.

If she is still with that unprincipled swine by this time tomorrow night she thought, I will be amazed.

She was desperate to get the letter dispatched but, realising that to have maximum effect it had to be clearly legible, she forced herself to type out her accusations onto an A4 piece of paper. When it was done, she folded the letter and placed it in an envelope; she didn't sign it, her identity was unimportant; his iniquity was all that mattered, and for that he was going to be severely punished.

***

It had been a stupid thing to do. Frank had told himself that to revisit the site of his old house would only upset him, but he had gone there all the same. Nothing that was left was recognisable. Even the copse of tall trees at the rear of the property, where rooks had once roosted was no more. Mickey Shah had paid a price for ordering them to be felled, in blatant disregard of tree preservation orders, but a five figure fine was chicken feed to the Computer Games millionaire. He had had to pay court costs, which were substantial, and he had been instructed to replant the wood, but giant oaks take centuries to mature and so for his lifetime his view across the valley would be unobstructed, and that was what he had wanted to achieve by cutting down the 200 year old giants. Rich men always win thought Frank, forgetting for the moment that many of the inhabitants of Burrdale would have included him in that privileged class of people.

He had stared at the mock-Georgian monstrosity, which had replaced his childhood home, and it had brought tears to his eyes. It always did. To compound his misery Mickey Shah had seen him standing on the footpath and had gesticulated towards him in a particularly course and vulgar way. What an ignorant, arrogant sod he was, a man with no breeding, no taste and no eye for beauty. It was appalling to think that such a person could trample roughshod over good taste and decency, but do that he most certainly could. The one thing that consoled Frank was that, at last, Susan seemed to understand his pain and accept that he was not merely wallowing in self-pity, but was overwhelmed by a deeper, irresistible sense of loss which he could not overcome. She hadn't always been so sympathetic, but now he knew when he returned home she would try to comfort him, and that thought sustained him.

"Dear Mrs Oakes,

We have never met, and yet I pity you. You have the misfortune to have married a vile degenerate man who has no moral conscience and no sense of honour.

You wrote a letter to the local paper, sharing with its readers the most romantic moment of your life. You saw Prince Charming on the dance floor, but the man who held you in his arms and asked you to be his wife had earlier that same evening spent time with me. I was unmarried, and I had no wish to be so, but I was desperate to have a child. Your husband seemed like a well-educated, intelligent man, and he was certainly good looking, a fact that he was all too well aware of. I mistakenly thought he would be the ideal father for my baby. I came to him with a proposition. I would not have done this if I had known he was soon to be committed to another woman. He never once mentioned that he had a girlfriend. Despite being a wealthy man, who could have so easily declined to become involved with me, he jumped at the chance of easy money, and a deal was done; which must tell you a great deal about his character.

We met in a small hotel, I will not bore you with the details, and because I was nervous he gave me alcohol to drink before the act of procreation was attempted. I strongly believe that my drink may have been drugged; I know that there are drugs now available that could be used in the circumstances I found myself in, but whether any existed then I cannot honestly say. What I do know for sure is that he undressed and climbed into bed alongside me. What happened then is a blur. I was barely conscious so I have very little memory of intercourse taking place, although I do remember feeling a man's penis slide into my vagina and experiencing rough force as he ejaculated his sperm into my body. It was very clinical and, I think, very quick. Then I was left on my own.

I became pregnant, which was what I wanted, and I thought your husband had kept his part of the deal, but when my child was born it bore no physical resemblance to him or to me. I looked for reasons why this might be, never considering the most obvious answer of all. I rationalised that my son perhaps took after a grandfather or a great grandfather, which was an unbelievably stupid thing to do.

I was completely wrong. I have learned recently how your husband used and abused me. He allowed me to believe that he would help me. He agreed to be the father of my child on the basis that no call would be made on him for any support and that our deal would always remain a closely guarded secret. He took my money, £2000 in total, which was a fortune 30 years ago, and then he hatched a plan to humiliate me. He slid quietly from my bed while I was still in a daze and ushered in a drunken lout to do the deed on his behalf. I was nothing to him but a piece of meat. He allowed me to be raped by his unspeakable accomplice, and whilst that crime was being committed, with his treachery still in the forefront of his mind, he hotfooted it to you to make his great romantic gesture.

You married a monster, a perverted, dishonest wretch. You cannot trust a word he says; he is the embodiment of greed and immorality. Save yourself whilst you can. If you stay with this piece of human garbage you will be forever tainted by his sin.

The first things Frank noticed when he returned from his dismal vigil at his childhood home were the two suitcases in the hallway: the second thing he noticed was the look of thunder on his wife's face.

At one level, it was obvious without a word being spoken. She was leaving him, with no intention ever to return. On another level, it was completely incomprehensible. Why would she do such a thing? There had been no friction between them when he left just 2 hours before, and there had been no contact with each other since then. There was nothing he could have done in the intervening period that could have precipitated such a crisis. The colour drained from his face, his right hand took on a life of its own, and he struggled for breath as he tried to understand the nightmare that was starting to unfold. Words failed him. He tried to speak. His mouth flopped open and closed like a fresh caught fish gasping for air on the river bank, but no sound issued from his lips; then with a howl of anguish he managed to scream the single word "Why?"

Susan didn't answer. She thrust a piece of paper into his hand; a letter typed in bold black font. His hand, which had shaken before now went into overdrive; it was sometime before it steadied enough to allow him to read the script, and an eternity before its brutal message sank in. Tears cascaded down his face. He tried to beg his wife to stay. He pleaded that it was all so very long ago. He begged for one more chance. He promised that he was not the man he had been 30 years ago. He tried to remind her of the good times they had had, but throughout it all Susan Oakes remained unmoved.

A taxi then arrived outside. He briefly thought of blocking her passage, or grabbing her suitcases so she couldn't leave, but she gave him such a look of fury that he backed away.

"I will send someone to collect the rest of my things tomorrow," she snarled at him, "and if between now and then you lay one finger on them then you will be sorry! Now get out of my way. I never want to see you again. My lawyer will be in touch very soon. I want the house, and I want half of all your money. You brought all this upon yourself by your unbelievably degenerate behaviour."

With that, she turned and started to stride out of the door, but before she crossed the threshold she turned to face the wretched man who was disintegrating before her very eyes.

"Who was it?" she screamed at him: and in his miserable state he told her.

CHAPTER THIRTY SEVEN

The Derbyshire Fire Brigade was convinced that the fire in the vestry at St Catherine's Church had been started deliberately. No electrical items had been left plugged in, all the light switches had been turned off, and so there was no credibility to any theory that an electrical fault might have caused an accidental blaze.

But that said, many of the tell-tale signs of deliberate arson were missing. Paperwork, carpets, curtains, chairs and tables; none of these items had been soaked in petrol or some other accelerant; and this was not usual if a fire had been intentionally set. The Chief Fire Officer in his report speculated that the arsonist may have been put off the idea of creating an immediate inferno because of the very real risk that such a blaze would be noticed quickly, as would the presence of anyone running from the scene. In the circumstances, he concluded that the offender must have chosen another way to start the fire, allowing it to build slowly without being seen, and allowing him to put some distance between himself and the building before it was engulfed in flames.

After looking at all the available evidence the C.F.O. was of the opinion that cupboard doors had been opened, and that reports, photographs, documents and folders had been unceremoniously pulled from the shelves and either strewn across the floor or spread out in depth across the central wooden table.

The person responsible for the crime he believed had then placed lighted candles in candlesticks among the heaps of documents so that when they burned down sufficiently their naked flames would caress bone dry paper with predictable results. It was likely that short lengths of candle had been chosen to minimise the length of time it would take for them to do their work. The culprit must then have left the church, locking the main door behind him, and in all probability concealed himself somewhere not too far away to watch the drama he had created unfold before his eyes. This would not be untypical behaviour, particularly if the arsonist had mental health issues or a personality disorder.

Once the fire in the vestry of St Catherine's Church had been extinguished, and the Chief Fire Officer was satisfied that there was no risk of anything re-igniting, the building had been handed over to the police, but nobody had been permitted to enter it until the remains of the roof had been removed, and an official from The Health and Safety Executive had pronounced the building safe. Then, and only then, Scientific Support Officers had been allowed to commence their search to discover the cause of the fire and, after they had done their job, police officers in blue overalls had been given instructions to begin the tedious and dirty job of bagging up fire damaged and waterlogged paperwork so that it could be properly examined at a later date. Van loads of material had been removed and taken to the old garage at the back of Burrdale Police Station. Once upon a time that had been home to police patrol vehicles, and routine maintenance had been carried out there, but a strategic re-examination of resources had led to the establishment of a Centralised Road Traffic Department, housed in purpose built premises several miles away, and this had put an end to local control and servicing. For years now the garage had remained largely empty, or been treated as a dumping ground for redundant equipment; nothing had been done to convert it into a more usable space; that cost money, and money wasn't going to be thrown at a police station that was probably scheduled for closure. But now, for the moment at least, it had a purpose; it provided a secure, if Spartan place where the recovered material could be laid out on trestle tables and then meticulously examined.

The C.F.O. thought it possible that the man the driver of the coach had seen in the shadows could be the man responsible for setting the fire; maybe he had tarried too long, or maybe he had revelled in a sense of danger, both were perfectly reasonable premises, and ones which Detective Inspector Hobson was quite prepared to consider.

***

"The more I think about all of this Pete, the more I become convinced that the fire at St Catherine's is linked to the murders we are investigating. It wasn't a random act of criminal damage, nor was it an attack on the church itself by some sort of religious nutcase. If it had been an attack on Christianity in reprisal for an attack on a mosque or a synagogue or a Hindu temple my bet would be that the altar or the pulpit would have been deliberately targeted, but that didn't happen. I think the vestry was damaged because it contained historic documents. When nobody was bothered about them, their existence wasn't a problem, but now, because there has been so much publicity, and there are so many volunteers currently ploughing through the paperwork, it has become one. Somebody is afraid that someone will unearth a letter, a document or photograph that will reveal a secret he wants to keep hidden. My gut feeling is that whatever he is concerned about relates to a period either during or shortly after the 2nd World War, which is the time when a rifle, which could be our murder weapon, went absent without leave."

"So what's the plan then Gov?"

"We use some of the extra manpower Sir Walter has given us to sift through every soggy bit of paper that can be rescued from the vestry to see if we can find a few more pieces to stick into our increasingly complicated jigsaw."

"A nice job, and a long shot, the lads doing the sifting are going to be calling you a few names under their breath."

"They can call me anything they want, Pete. We're fighting a battle against someone who has already killed two outstanding young people to make a point, and there's no way I'm going to leave any stone unturned in my efforts to prevent him killing again."

"I can see where you're coming from," responded a slightly unconvinced Detective Sergeant.

***

It was the talk of the town. Connie Cartwright always claimed she never listened to gossip, and that idle chit chat and low level scandal mongering held no interest for her whatsoever, yet she had been eager to learn about the disappearance of Frank Oakes because that story excited her.

It had soon become common knowledge that his wife had left him, although not many people knew the reason why, and Burrdale was awash with unfounded rumours, some of which were more fanciful than others. What was universally acknowledged was that he had taken the break up very badly. There had been a scene at his house when Susan's brother and father had called there to collect her things, but both were of statures that made brick outhouses look decidedly undersized and in addition her brother was a two times winner of the Northern Counties Iron Man competition. Frank had blustered then he had capitulated and let the men enter his house and take what they will; he hadn't even protested when some items, which had been left to him in his auntie's will, were wrongly included in their haul. He had listened without responding to the verbal insults that had been thrown at him, but when they left he had cried like a baby. He felt emasculated, victimised and worthless.

After that incident he had withdrawn into himself. For three days he had remained holed up in his home and had refused all human contact. The paper boy had found yesterday's paper still in the letter box on two consecutive days and he had asked the newsagent what he should do. The newsagent had instructed him to push the papers completely through into the house, even though they then could clearly be seen lying on the floor through the glass door panel and might give a would-be burglar cause to believe that the householder was away. Prevention of Crime officers would definitely not have approved of this advice, but they couldn't charge for the unread journals whereas the newsagent could, provided they had been pushed inside the building.

Eventually, after four days Frank emerged. He wasn't wearing a coat, he had no bag on his back or luggage in his hands; the forecast was for wet and windy weather, but seemingly undeterred by that he had been seen striding out across the moors heading in the general direction of the Derbyshire/Staffordshire border.

All this was music to Connie's ears. At least the man who had so vilely taken advantage of her was being made to suffer. She hoped that he might die of exposure and that his body wouldn't be found until maggots had started to gorge on his flesh. It wasn't a nice thought, but then again he wasn't a nice man.

***

Members of the Mountain Rescue team with their rescue dogs searched the high moorland for the missing man while volunteers criss-crossed the lower slopes searching for the unhappy Frank. Alan Nadin was one of these, as were other regulars of the Royal Albert; Raymond Baker was not one of them; he was in no fit state to help. As Alan later remarked to Mark Hobson in passing over a quiet pint in the pub after a futile day's searching "He's not on this planet at the moment Mark. His dad's riddled with cancer, the doctors don't think he'll last the week, and Ray's just had it confirmed that he's got cancer too, and the odds are he will probably be dead himself within twelve months." Hobson made genuine expressions of sympathy, but never-the-less filed the information he had been given in the section of his brain that was totally pre-occupied with the Wallington and Adamson murder inquiry.

***

It was the telephone call that Constance Cartwright received from a reporter from The Sun that brought home to her, in the most dramatic way possible, how unwise she had been to have sent that letter to Susan Oakes. Had she realised that Frank would tell Susan, who the sender of the anonymous letter was, and had she understood that Susan would hate her for making the revelation just as much as she would hate Frank for his immorality she would never have sent it; but hindsight is at best an unhelpful gift. Susan had gone public. Susan had contacted The Sun telling it that she had a story which she felt could become a worldwide blockbuster. She had shown them the letter and they had paid her a five figure sum to be allowed to use it. Now the newspaper wanted to know her reaction to the story that was about to be published. Distraught, she had put the phone down, but from that moment on it had never stopped ringing until she finally unplugged the wretched thing, but that did nothing to bring her peace of mind..

Horrid men and women with cameras and tape recorders had started to gather outside her house; they had knocked loudly on her door, and when she had refused to answer it they had even shouted through the letter box demanding a statement. Hell on Earth had arrived; the reporters and photographers camped outside seemed to Constance to have become chattering demons, waiting for the right moment to leap out at her and sink their talons into her unprotected flesh. The image of a painting by Hieronymus Bosch muscled its way into her mind. She was going mad, she was being tortured by the media; and the sad truth was she was the author of her own downfall. For a moment her thoughts turned to Frank Oakes. Somewhere amongst the heather his body might be laying awaiting discovery, or in anguish and despair he might be sitting alone waiting for cold and hunger to drag him towards a final end. She found herself wishing she could swap places with him; her despair was total, nothing could be worse than this, but she was about to be disillusioned.

She put on the television to take her mind off the catastrophe that had befallen her only to see a picture of Edward emerging from the doors of a hotel being jostled by a crowd of T.V. reporters demanding that he talk to them. He was accompanied by a large man in a grey suit who Connie surmised had to be a lawyer or a minder. She was right. Edward never spoke, but his companion read a short pre-prepared statement.

"My client, Mr Cartwright, is appalled to discover the truth about his own birth and the truly disgusting role of his mother in this unpleasant saga. He of course is a victim of her revolting behaviour, and he shares the indignation and outrage that the public feel about her unprincipled actions. Until yesterday he had no knowledge of any of these events.

His mother has consistently lied to him throughout his life and he is devastated by her deceit. He wants both the world and his mother to know that he no longer considers himself to be her son, and that all contact between them is forever severed. Mr Cartwright will not be making any further statements about this matter. In a very real sense it is as if his mother has just died, and he needs some time alone and undisturbed to come to terms with his grief."

***

But if the news for Constance Cartwright was uniformly black, and if the words of the lawyer had destroyed all hope within her, news for the Derbyshire Constabulary had just become a whole lot better.

Firstly, Frank Oakes had been found alive. He was in a very poor state both mentally and physically, and it would probably be days before he was fit enough or rational enough to answer questions, but one day he would be so.

Secondly, Detective Sergeant Peter Bennett had been told about an anonymous tip off. Because of what was said, and the decent amount of background knowledge that was revealed he didn't think that this was just a mindless hoax. It gave the police a name. It suggested that the man who had set fire to St Catherine's church was also the man who had sent the letters to Sheila Adamson and Mary Wallington. The name was a total surprise, but then again, nothing about this case was turning out to be normal. Perhaps finally Lady Luck had decided to shine on Detective Chief

Superintendent Stan Hardy, and Detective Inspector Mark Hobson.

CHAPTER THIRTY EIGHT

If the fire at St Catherine's was a bitter blow for the Reverend Jacob Lindley and a major obstacle to those people who were trying to persuade the Bishop to keep this pretty little church open, there was at least some joy for him in another potentially contentious area.

The arrangements for this year's Remembrance Sunday parade were running surprisingly smoothly. Everybody was in agreement. There was none of the complaining or moaning or bitterness or acrimony, which had so marred preparations in previous years. Everybody it seemed was on the same side, and the argument and division that had been so evident in the past seemed to have been banished into the realms of history. Jacob Lindley was overjoyed. This year the whole town would come together so that people of all faiths and of none, and from many different backgrounds, could all pay homage to the armed forces and jointly remember the brave men and women who had paid the ultimate sacrifice in the service of their country. The young curate felt as if peace was reaching out from beyond the grave and touching the lives of the present day inhabitants of the town and he was deeply moved. This was how it always should have been, the men and women who had paid such a heavy price had fought for a better, more inclusive world, and now at last maybe everybody was beginning to understand how vital a more inclusive world was.

***

"I can't believe it Pete. Tim Bradley's such a passive bloke; he's the last person I would think capable of murder: are you sure that the anonymous informant isn't stringing us along?"

"Well, I didn't speak to him personally so I can't say how he sounded to the call handler, and although I've listened to the tape recording, it's kind of muffled, but he gives so much information that fits the known facts that I think we have to take him seriously. Not only that, he's very precise with his timings and if they prove to be correct, then that will be pretty persuasive evidence so far as I'm concerned. And remember Gov, it's always the quiet ones who end up making the most noise and the timid ones who create the most mayhem."

"I agree with you there Peter. I've met with Stan Hardy to put him in the picture, and I've spoken to our tame J.P. who is prepared to issue a warrant. I'm just off to collect it now, and when I've got it, shall we go and pay Mr Bradley a little visit? I'm hopeful that his computer and his printer will have interesting stories to tell once the experts have unlocked their secrets. If our luck's really in we could strike gold and find the murder weapon and if we do that then its game over so far as our Tim is concerned; even if he refuses to say a dickie bird to us we will still have him bang to rights."

"What if we get to the house and find there isn't any I.T. equipment and that the most modern gadget that he's got is a steam powered black and white twelve inch screen telly?"

"Then we're buggered Pete, we're absolutely buggered! And the person who phoned us will have turned out to be a complete waste of space, but let's just hope that isn't the case."

***

It was just as Tim Bradley was about to settle down to listen to The Archers on Radio 4, which was something he tried to do whenever he had the opportunity, that there was a loud and aggressive knock on his front door; the mug of strong tea he was carrying wobbled in his hand, and some of the contents spilled onto the pale beige carpet causing a large brown stain, so taken aback was he at this very unwelcome interruption to his normal routine. It would require a proper cleaning job to return the carpet to its pristine appearance; Tim was extremely house proud and he felt anxiety and annoyance, in almost equal measure in response to this intrusion into his private space. Who was his heavy handed visitor, and what did he or she want? With a fair amount of trepidation he opened the door to discover 2 large men in suits standing on his doorstep. Outside on the road a marked police vehicle was untidily parked, and behind that was a police personnel carrier containing an unknown quantity of uniform officers.

The taller and thicker set of the two men produced from his wallet a police warrant card. He introduced himself as Detective Inspector Mark Hobson, and he introduced his somewhat less sturdy companion as Detective Sergeant Peter Bennett, both of the Derbyshire Constabulary. He explained that he was in possession of a warrant permitting him to search the premises, and he waved a piece of paper under Tim's nose and told him he had reason to believe that there might be an illegal firearm in the house; he added that he also had grounds to suspect that Tim's computer and printer might contain evidence of serious criminal behaviour and that these would be seized for thorough examination by computer experts. Finally, he informed Tim that he was also suspected of damaging by fire the Anglican church of St Catherine's at Lower Burrdale and that in respect of this and all the allegations being made against him he was going to be arrested and taken to the police station where he would be questioned under caution about all these matters. Tim tried to protest, but the words wouldn't come. He gave a very creditable impression of a rabbit caught in the headlights of a speeding juggernaut, milliseconds before the moment of impact.

For a moment it looked as if he might even faint; his mind was a total whirl. Much of what Detective Inspector Hobson said went straight over his head, although part of the formal caution did register and made him feel sick. He might or might not turn out to be a murderer, but it was obvious to the detectives he would never prove to be a hard man.

But if he wasn't a hard man, in the interview room he became a very talkative one. Contrary to the advice of the duty solicitor, who had been contacted by the Custody Sergeant following the prisoner's request to have legal representation, who felt that he had much better say nothing, Tim Bradley had given the police chapter and verse. He confirmed what they already knew that he had been in

The Black Greyhound from just before 8.30pm on the night of the fire. Seven members of The Royal Albert's darts and dominoes team corroborated his story, as did the landlord of The Greyhound and five of his customers and, most persuasive of all so far as Mark Hobson and Pete Bennett were concerned; retired Detective Sergeant Alan Nadin fully authenticated everything the man in custody had said. This wasn't necessarily a fatal blow to the police investigation; there was a window of opportunity that could have opened for Bradley prior to 8.30pm that might have allowed him to start the fire, indeed the anonymous informant who had contacted the police had said that the suspect had been seen leaving the church at exactly 7pm as confirmed by the church clock and checked against his own wristwatch. Not only that, he alleged that shortly before he did so there had been noises coming from within the church that sounded as if books or piles of papers were being swept from shelves and scattered across the floor. He also claimed that he thought he had seen the flickering light of candles through the vestry windows. Nobody except the police officers and the firemen who later attended the scene could have known these facts. It was possible that one of these persons could have talked out of turn, but Hobson thought this was unlikely; there was a one in a thousand chance that it was pure guesswork, but that was so remote a possibility that it deserved no consideration; both Hobson and Bennett were of one mind; the only way the informant could know so much was because he had seen these things with his own eyes.

All these specific allegations were put to Bradley in interview. He could have made no comment; he could have denied all knowledge of the crimes with which he was accused, which is what he did, but he went much further. Lips trembling and hands shaking, he stammered out an alibi. At 7pm he had been at Burrdale Scout Group's headquarters to pick up the minibus for the evening. He had signed an agreement accepting on behalf of The Royal Albert that the pub would be responsible for any damage caused to the vehicle whilst it was on loan to it. A visual check for pre-existing dents and scratches to the bodywork of the vehicle had taken place, any that were present had been noted on a piece of paper and Mr Bradley and a representative of the Scout Group Committee had signed the list to verify its accuracy. The representative of the Group was Alan Nadin. Normally he would have driven the minibus himself, but he was recovering from a fall and his left wrist was badly swollen, making it painful for him to drive; he was also pleased to have the opportunity of having a few drinks. His right wrist was in perfect condition, so his signature on the paper was its usual bold and swirling self. Mark Hobson had seen this signature many times and instantly accepted it as genuine. He suspended the interview so that he could make a telephone call to Alan, who without any hesitation at all confirmed the truth of Bradley's claims. At this point Hobson terminated the interview and ordered the release of Bradley on bail to attend back at the police station in four weeks time pending further inquiries; he was however now far from confident that these would amount to a great deal.

Events quickly proved him right. After a thorough examination of the computer and the printer seized by the police from Bradley's home the experts were able to state categorically that the printer had not been used to print out any of the anonymous letters and, as for the computer, that annoyingly had no guilty secrets to reveal, unless an obsessive interest in the flora and fauna of England and Wales could be said to fall into that category.

"So, it's another dead end; the Chief isn't going to be best pleased," groaned Detective Chief Superintendent Hardy, "I hate these imbeciles who have got nothing better to do than to waste police time; if I could get my hands on the stupid bastard who sent us off on a wild goose chase right now I'd wring his bloody neck!"

"It's probably a good job then you can't Sir," sympathised Detective Inspector Hobson, "and in any event, whether he meant to or no, our mystery caller has given us a new lead."

"How do you work that out Mark? I can't see how he's done that."

"Well, Sir," replied Hobson, "the caller knew too much about the details of the fire for it to be pure conjecture, that's why we gave his claim such credence in the first place. We worked on the basis that our anonymous informant must have witnessed the crime being committed, but that doesn't now seem to have been the case; the only other viable explanation as to why he possessed such detailed knowledge has to be that he himself was the offender. If that's true, then surely it must mean that our arsonist has to be an enemy of Tim Bradley, otherwise why would he try to drop him in the shit like he has done; and if this logic is correct it opens up a whole new line of investigation."

"There might be some mileage in that theory" agreed a somewhat mollified Stan Hardy, "but it's only a crumb of comfort when what we need is the whole bloody cake."

CHAPTER THIRTY NINE

It was a cold grey day, unusually chilly for early November, but for the moment at least it was dry. Scouts and Guides shivered in the unforgiving easterly breeze and complained that they were not being allowed to wear coats over their uniform shirts and pullovers. They were already lined up waiting for the parade to start. The younger children were still being dragooned into place by hooting Brown Owls and over-enthusiastic Akelas; they had no real idea what Remembrance Sunday actually meant, but it had been repeatedly drummed into them that they had to be on their best behaviour. Only the Army Cadets seemed to fully understand what was about to occur, but they were older than most of the other youth groups, and their khaki uniforms offered them more protection against the autumn chill, so they were less impatient for the procession to start. They waited for the town band to give the signal to move off with a degree of tolerance, which was alas unshared by the other young people herded together in the empty car park waiting for the instruction for the parade to begin.

There was a bang on the big drum, and the march to the Parish Church commenced, although only the cadets actually marched; all the others scurried after them with no real sense of timing or military precision; but it mattered not. Everyone was on display, and everyone was taking the occasion seriously. Nobody was behaving especially badly, nobody was messing about too much; if this level of conduct could be maintained throughout the church service, then the leaders of the various youth groups would be very happy with the impression their young charges had created.

At 9.45 a.m. the parade reached its destination. The Standard bearers were detached from the main body of the procession; they still had a role to play. Then the rest of the boys and girls were ushered into church to take their allocated seats and without mishap everyone was soon in place, and promptly at 10 am the service began.

The Reverend Lindley welcomed the congregation and very quickly the first hymn followed. The format was what it had always been; the hymns and prayers were set in stone. 'Abide with me' and 'Eternal Father, strong to save' were part of the fabric of the service; the prayers for Peace, for Queen and Country and in Memory of the Fallen were taken as read. Past and Future demanded continuity. It would take a very brave or a very foolish priest to tamper with tradition, and although Jacob Lindley did not lack courage, he possessed a great deal of common sense. Well-loved words and tunes brought comfort to the old people who packed the back of the church; innovation on such a special day as this would be entirely out of place.

For the minister time seemed to fly, but for some of the younger children who were not used to having to listen in silence to an oddly dressed man extolling the virtues of a faith they did not understand, time moved more slowly than an Arctic glacier, but even for them it did not stand still. By 10.45 am their incarceration in the church was over, the sermon had been preached, the words of Laurence Binyon so familiar to their parents and grandparents had been read,

The Last Post had been played, two minutes silence had been observed and Reveille had marked the end of silent homage. Now all that was left was to sally forth and repeat the process at the town's war memorial, but this time joined by the ranks of non-church goers who filled the Market Square. It's a bind for the kids thought Jacob Lindley but at least some of them will realise how sad the closing words of this commemoration really are. "When you go home tell them of us and say, for your tomorrow we gave our today." Who could not be moved by the poignancy of those words?

The Clock on the church tower struck 11 am. The Last Post was skilfully played by a young member of the Town Band; the standards and banners of the youth organisations were lowered as a mark of respect and then there was total silence; traffic on the street nearby had been stopped by the police so that it did not disturb the moment, and miraculously even a baby that had been wailing in its mother's arms ceased its crying. With heads bowed the large crowd began to honour the memory of the fallen heroes from two World Wars and several more recent military campaigns. Then it happened.

A loud bang reverberated across the Market Place; there was a gasp of pain followed by a sickening thud as a man's body hit the uneven cobblestones. In a single second the life of The Reverend Lindley had been snuffed out in a ruthlessly efficient way.

What followed was pandemonium. People were screaming, people were crying, people were running, some of them still carrying the wreaths that they had intended to lay. The overweight police officer controlling the traffic with the assistance of two inexperienced P.C.S.O's was rooted to the spot, his role had simply been to marshal the parade; the most bother he could have anticipated was some mild impoliteness from a motorist delayed by the temporary road closure. It was several seconds before he had the composure to radio for assistance, and in that time the person responsible for bringing death to the base of the war memorial had almost certainly got clean away.

Someone in the crowd shouted for a doctor, but in truth his services would not be required. A medical student, Giles Sterndale had rushed forward, ignoring any risk to himself, but there was nothing he could do. The bullet had entered Jacob's heart, death had been instantaneous. On a day when Peace had been prayed for and Heroism had been remembered a cowardly act had destroyed another young life. The unfairness of it all was overwhelming, the sense of shock unbearable and, perhaps most grotesque of all, within minutes of these tragic events occurring they would be making headline news around the world.

***

Detective Chief Superintendent Stan Hardy had been on his way home from a Remembrance Day service at Matlock when he received the news of another shooting in the High Peak. Murders in rural Derbyshire were very rare, but in the space of six months, three killings had occurred and in the most dramatic of circumstances. Instantly he realised that this tragic story could turn out to be the biggest one yet, even eclipsing the murder of Penny Adamson in terms of global coverage. As yet he didn't know whether this death was the latest chapter in the on-going saga of lethal retribution, or an outrage committed by some extremist group, or a stand-alone incident unconnected to anything that had previously occurred; and to be honest, for the moment, it didn't matter a great deal. The tabloid press would splash the story over their front pages regardless. Every Fleet Street hack would have his or her own pet theory to put forward; Derbyshire police could very well do without irresponsible fantasy being tarted up as fact, but they would have no choice. Two principal theories were beginning to do the rounds, and it did not seem to matter to the journalists if either one was actually true.

Theory One was that this ruthless act of slaughter had been the brainchild of some unspecified Moslem extremist group protesting about Western foreign policy in the Middle East and that it could herald the start of a campaign of violence across Europe intended to spread fear amongst Christian communities.

Theory Two was hardly less disturbing. If the Reverend Lindley turned out to be the third victim of an unhinged avenger there would be uproar. "When are these killings going to stop?" "What are the police playing at allowing this slaughter of the innocents to continue unabated?" "Why is it beyond the wit of Derbyshire Constabulary to prevent a lunatic with a gun assassinating people at will?" There was no appetite amongst the press to be fair or objective; all the editors wanted were gruesome headlines; in a state of mounting unease Detective Chief Superintendent Stanley

Hardy changed course and set off immediately to drive to Burrdale Market Place.

Thirty minutes later he arrived; the place was thronged with police personnel. Detective Inspector Mark Hobson was already at the scene and The "Grim Reaper" was in the process of carrying out a preliminary examination of the body, shielded from public view by a hastily erected tent. Wreaths of red poppies were scattered across the floor, abandoned by their carriers as panic set in; the banners of the Scouts and Guides had been trampled underfoot, and everywhere there was evidence of the terror that had gripped the crowd. A woman's high heeled shoe lay close to the Post Office door. An expensive black felt hat which had been worn by the wife of the local M.P. now had the aspect of a muddy football. A collecting tin with notes and coins crammed inside it had rolled across the cobbles until it came to rest at the base of the Market Cross and, behind the outer police cordon, press photographers with long lens cameras were gleefully photographing the wreckage of the parade with no thought about the upset their terrible images would cause, and every thought about how striking the next days' front pages would look. Efforts were now being made to move these happy snappers further away from the scene, but it was proving to be hard work. Scientific Support Officers were already carrying out a fingertip search of the area, and uniformed police constables were mingling with the crowd beyond the outer cordon seeking to find eye witnesses who just might have fragments of relevant evidence which might aid the police inquiry.

"This is a bad job Mark," said Hardy, "and it will get a whole lot worse if it turns out that this is the work of the bastard who killed Penny Adamson and Adam Wallington."

"We'll know that soon enough when Forensics examine the bullet" replied the detective inspector, "but to be blunt, there are a good many factors that already point us in that direction; having said that however there are a number of crucial differences."

"Tell me about them," said the D.C.S.

"Well Sir, if the bullet matches the other bullets that will be pretty well conclusive proof that we are looking for the same killer; also the fact that all three shootings have taken place at a time when large numbers of people have been present is a constant theme, and on every occasion to date the murderer has either used church premises as a backdrop to his crimes or as a place from which to dole out death."

"So are you saying he has done so on this occasion?"

"Yes I am Sir. We won't know for certain until we have received a full report from Doc Grimshawe but he seems pretty well convinced that the fatal shot was fired from above, and the church tower is the highest point around here."

"It would be some shot to kill the vicar from that range wouldn't it Mark?"

"Yes Sir it would, but our man has already proved himself to be a marksman, and the distance this time is a lot less than was the case at Castleton."

"It sounds pretty persuasive stuff to me, but you also spoke of differences," commented Mr Hardy. "What do you think those differences are?"

"Well the main one is that the victim doesn't come from a local family. He only moved to Burrdale about 2 years ago. We've been working on a theory that our killer is native to the area and that he is most probably avenging an event that happened a long time ago. I think the use of a World War II rifle is symbolic; I also still think the theory is a good one. If it is then Jacob Lindley's death doesn't fit the pattern at all. His roots are in Norfolk, he had never even visited the High Peak before he started to work here, but in that time he has become very well regarded, especially by his older parishioners, and it is from that age group we believe our killer has sprung."

"Being well liked didn't do the other two murder victims much good did it Mark? Indeed, being popular was a disaster so far as they were concerned."

"You're absolutely right Sir, and the point's not lost on me. I think Penny and Adam were deliberately selected so that their deaths would make the greatest possible impact on somebody close to them. With Jacob Lindley it isn't like that. I know that this might sound preposterous but I think he was killed because of what he was not who he was. I believe his death is intended to punish the church for some sin that it may have committed in the eyes of our assassin."

"So if we look back in time and find a priest who really pissed off his flock we might be getting somewhere and, given some of the incumbents who have reigned here, that may not be too much of a job to do."

"Oh I agree Sir, but our task has been made much harder by the fire at St Catherine's," commented Mark, "and maybe that's why the place was deliberately torched."

CHAPTER FORTY

"We're just gonna have to find out who your father really was Eddie."

The two men who had been flown over from Los Angeles by the film studio to assist Edward Cartwright seemed utterly unfamiliar with the way the master/servant relationship worked, certainly so far as the beleaguered Hollywood Heartthrob was concerned.

"Well I don't want to," he replied mulishly. "I'm not going to be coerced into some sort of sham publicity stunt in which I embrace an unprincipled rogue or drunken buffoon before the World's Press and look adoringly into his eyes and call him "Daddy", so you can just think again."

The taller of the two men smiled a contemptuous knowing smile as he witnessed this juvenile fit of pique.

You just don't get it do you Dickbrain?" he said, abandoning all pretence of civility. "The Studio has invested millions of dollars in your career, it's not going to sit back and watch all that investment go belly up. You ain't got a fuckin' choice Buster; you'll do exactly what we say; but don't fret yourself about having a sentimental reunion with dear old Dad because that ain't going to happen. We just need to know for sure who put your mother up the duff so that we can take all necessary action if at some time in the future your Pappa starts to cause trouble."

"But surely the trouble has already started?" replied Cartwright, effectively cowed by the forcefulness of the man's reproach, and fearing what the consequences would be if he antagonised him again.

"To a degree it has, Eddie, but nothing's confirmed and if you stay silent and your goddamn mother keeps her mouth closed from now on the story will blow over given time. If there is no hard evidence that any particular individual planted his seed inside your Momma's womb, it could even give you an air of mystery, although of course there has to have been hardness for her to have been made pregnant in the first place, so I have no doubt we will find out that one of the two losers named in the newspapers is indisputably your loving father. When we've established that then we will be better able to prepare for the eventuality that he might one day try to cash in on his family connection."

"How will you set about getting the proof?"

"It's best that you don't know too much Eddie boy, I don't think you could be trusted with such a secret. Let's just say we will need D.N.A. and blood samples from you and we will obviously need samples from the two clowns mentioned in the newspapers."

"But how will you go about obtaining those if they refuse to cooperate with you?"

"We have our methods Ed, we have our methods, but if you think I'm gonna tell you what they are then you've got another frigging thought coming."

"But even if you are successful in everything you hope to achieve, how does that help us at all?"

"Such a lot of questions!" Use your imagination, bird brain. People are like china cups, they can be bought, they can be sold; they can be smashed; everybody knows that. Given a choice between a big bundle of cash in return for total silence or a messy accident with potentially lethal consequences how do you think the average Joe in the street is going to react? It isn't rocket science you know; it's ever so simple, even a dipstick like you should be able to answer that one."

***

The report on the bullet that killed Jacob Lindley was virtually a carbon copy of the reports that had been written in respect of Adam Wallington and Penny Adamson's deaths.

The same weapon, a service issue Lee Enfield rifle had been used on all three occasions, of that there was no doubt; and there were other striking similarities which D.I. Hobson had already pointed out to Detective Chief Superintendent Hardy. In all three deaths the standard of marksmanship had been outstanding, particularly at Castleton and at Burrdale where the distances involved were nearing the maximum range of the weapon. In each case the killer had been firing from above; even at Castleton from his position on the hillside he was looking down on the church tower.

Vengeance from on high thought Peter Bennett, like a Norse God dishing out punishment to his earthly enemies, exercising the power of life and death and capriciously destroying innocent lives.

"There's nothing capricious about it Pete," D.I. Hobson later responded to the musing of his Detective Sergeant, "every incident to date has been meticulously planned and is a tiny piece in a highly complex jigsaw."

But in one respect the Detective Inspector agreed with his DS. Somewhere in the psyche of a murderer a God was featured large, but it wasn't a Norse, or a Greek or a Roman God, but a God whose son had died on the cross and to whom tens of millions of Christians worldwide prayed.

"He hates the Church, Peter. It isn't just coincidence that all three deaths have taken place on or near to church premises and that on two occasions he has defiled the sanctity of the church by breaking the sixth commandment from within its walls. Part of what he is doing is a vendetta against organised religion. We desperately need to discover what it was that could have driven our killer to take such bloody and terrible revenge."

***

The police were slowly building up a profile of their suspect, but in truth it lacked detail. From his choice of weapon and from the slightly old fashioned tone of some of his anonymous letters an assumption had been made that he was not a young man; the best bet to date was that he was a white male, aged somewhere between sixty and seventy years old, living alone maybe as a widower, although the psychologist thought he might be someone who was locked into an unhappy marriage living with but apart from his partner and resenting the situation he was in. To this broad framework had been added, at Mark Hobson's suggestion, the theory that he was either an atheist or a onetime passionate believer in God who had lost his faith because of some catastrophic event. It was also abundantly clear that he knew a great deal about firearms and that he must have received training to be the crack shot he obviously was. Without a doubt he held grudges and dealt with them in a spectacularly dramatic way, but bizarrely none of his three victims were thought to be the cause of his intense anger. He could also be petty and vindictive; his botched attempt to frame Tim Bradley was a striking demonstration of that fact.

Once it had become clear that the anonymous informant had passed information to the police that was patently untrue, and that without this evidence there was nothing to link Mr Bradley to the fire at St Catherine's, Mark Hobson had ordered that he be released from custody and admitted to police bail pending further inquiries, but with the expectation in due course they would come to nothing and that bail would be cancelled. He had then arranged for Detective Sergeant Bennett to interview Tim Bradley as a witness. He had cooperated fully, and tried to be helpful, but had been unable to suggest anyone who might have a grudge against him. Disappointed, but not surprised by his inability to point the finger of blame towards any individual, the police had set about making extensive inquiries. Pubs, clubs, shops and community centres had been visited to try to discover if there were any rumours of bad blood between Tim Bradley and anybody else in town, but these had largely drawn a blank. The only episode that caused even a flutter of interest was a slanging match that had occurred in The Royal Albert between a friend of Frank Oakes and Raymond Baker. Bradley had been drawn into the kerfuffle because of his connections with Oakes, but eventually the whole thing had petered out with all parties realising that they were behaving like overgrown school kids.

"He keeps himself to himself, he doesn't throw his weight about. I'm surprised he got involved at all," said Alan Nadin to Mark Hobson later. "Ray doesn't think much of him because he works for Frank, but Ray is feeling pretty grotty at the moment: I don't think he can see beyond the here and now. I certainly don't believe he would be up to planning something so carefully thought out as this plan obviously was."

***

As had been the case with both Adam and Penny, the coroner, on reading the post mortem report, directed that the cause of Jacob Lindley's death was so obvious and so well documented that there was no need to delay his funeral to await the trial and conviction of his killer. He had made the same stipulation that he had made on the other occasions, burial was permissible because it allowed for the possibility of exhumation in extreme circumstance, but cremation could not be considered. Arrangements were now being made for a funeral service to be held in the Parish Church in ten days' time. Many of Jacob's family would have liked it to be sooner, but had had relatives living in Australia and New Zealand who could not travel at the drop of a hat, and in any event the church had been fully booked for most of the first week. There was also the problem of finding a vicar to officiate given that the man who would have been first choice was the man whose body was going to be carried into church in a coffin.

There were logistical problems too. If Penny Adamson's funeral was anything to go by there would be hundreds of people attending the service; certainly far more than the church could accommodate, and a sizeable number of them would be members of the World's Press. For Detective Inspector Hobson and Detective Superintendent Stan Hardy this was a challenge. Plain clothed officers would be needed to mingle with the mourners, uniformed officers would be necessary to control traffic and to ensure that the paths to the church and later to the graveside were kept open so that the funeral procession was not obstructed by a crush of onlookers.

"He'll be there Sir, I know he will," said Mark Hobson. "It will be too important an occasion for him to stay away, but it will be like looking for a needle in a haystack and we will be incredibly lucky if he does anything to draw attention to himself."

CHAPTER FORTY ONE

The need to examine every scrap of paper that had survived the furnace that St Catherine's vestry had become had been obvious from the outset. It had always been abundantly clear that that task could not possibly take place in the shell of a wrecked building when every gust of wind or drop of rain might further destroy vital evidence. Hence, as soon as it had been safe to do so, all the paperwork had been removed to the old garage at Burrdale police station where in depth examination could take place. That job would take weeks. Even with the additional manpower the Chief Constable had allocated to the inquiry, progress was never going to be quick. The men and women meticulously scrutinising charred fragments of text would do their best, but nothing could be hurried. A single test would be in place, a simple question would have to be asked again and again: "Could what I hold in my hand have any possible evidential value?" and to that question there would always be three possible answers. "Yes," "No," or "Don't know," and the third answer would be the one which would be most frequently given. Second, third and fourth opinions might be required. Detective Inspector Hobson knew from experience that it was highly unlikely that the key to solving this case would easily surrender itself into the investigating officers' custody.

And apart from the bags of evidence, there were also the bags of ash and dust, the contents of which appeared beyond reprieve, and which even the resources of the Forensic

Science Service could not hope to rescue. It was possible five star indicators of guilt might once have been hidden there, but if they had, it was almost certain that they suffered a disastrous sea change to become plant fertiliser or landfill, but just in case this assumption was wrong, and something had survived which could be useful, even this material had to be microscopically examined.

Yet despite all the problems Mark was becoming more and more convinced that somewhere in the ruined vestry answers to crucial questions had lain undisturbed for decades, and he had a strong gut feeling, which he couldn't explain, that some of these answers might still be capable of discovery. He had shared his thoughts with Helena, and had been relieved to find she entirely agreed with him. Her judgement was the judgement he trusted most in the world. He had married both beauty and brains, and there was not a day went by when he didn't rejoice in his good fortune.

Helena had also agreed with him that it was likely that the person he was seeking had a deep hatred of the Church and of the Christian religion, and she volunteered to help him with his search. She had so many social contacts, and a wide range of friends; and people liked talking to her because she was a good listener and had a knack of putting everyone at their ease. All age groups seemed to take to her, but she was especially good when dealing with old people, giving them time and respect, and they loved her for that. It was from this age group that the greatest amount of history could be released if gently coaxed out of them, and Helena said she would ask around to try to find if any past vicar of Burrdale had been a figure of division or controversy.

And as always she was true to her word. Of course, everyone had had particular likes and dislikes, and it turned out that although most of the incumbents at the Parish Church had had admirers and detractors, there was one reverend gentleman who stood head and shoulders above the rest in that regard. Some people saw him as a rock upon which the Church was built, they admired his certainty and lack of self-doubt, they described a man of principle, large of stature with a loud booming voice; and when Helena listened to them, she saw in her head a vision of the Reverend Ian Paisley, but disturbingly with a broad Yorkshire accent, and an unshakeable belief in the literal accuracy of the Old Testament.

Other people, particularly some old ladies, felt very differently about him; they described a bigot and a bully. Several of them expressed sadness about not being permitted to re-marry in church or the anger they had felt when friends of theirs had been denied the right to have a child baptised, or a loved one laid to rest because that person hadn't measured up to the strict criteria imposed by this over-zealous priest.

"He's your man, Darling," said Helena, "I'd stake my life on it. If you go through your records I think you will find a great many examples of occasions on which his intolerance has damaged lives."

***

Immediately after the shocking murder of Jacob Lindley there had been chaos. The only thought on everyone's mind had been safety; safety for themselves, safety for their children, safety for their relatives, safety for their friends. Attention had been focussed on survival; the last thing anyone was doing was taking note of bystanders, unless the actions or condition of any man or woman might have blocked an escape route when it had been a very different story. Old people in wheelchairs or using walking frames had been noticed because they had been seen as hazards; other peoples' prams and pushchairs had registered because they had been viewed as obstructions to be overcome, and for that reason later their presence was recalled, but for the majority of the crowd the casual acquaintance, the irritating bloke in the pub, the woman who you recognised from the supermarket queue had all been invisible and asking questions about them later on was as futile as trying to herd cats. Certainly the police had found nobody who had seen anyone behaving suspiciously, let alone witnessed a man with a gun, but it was unthinkable that the killer would have simply ambled across the Market Place with a rifle so maybe that was not at all surprising.

After a little initial delay the police had acted quickly. A major incident plan had been put into action. Armed officers had arrived at the scene in less than 10 minutes following the receipt of the first 999 call, and uniformed officers had been shouted up from as far away as Chesterfield and Derby to swell police numbers.

It had been immediately suspected that the killer had fired his weapon from above, and the Bell Tower of the Parish Church was the highest point around. Members of the Tactical Firearms Unit had rushed to the church, and they had found the door to the Bell Tower wide open. They had clattered up the steep and narrow spiral staircase to the roof of the tower, but had found nobody, just one shell case had been discovered, it was highly visible; why the killer had left it where it fell so that it would inevitably end up in the hands of a forensic scientist was a difficult question to answer.

After making sure that the roof was clear and that nothing had been concealed there the officers descended into the gallery where the bells were, and every nook and cranny there was searched, including the area under the great bells, but the only things they found were dust and mouse droppings.

The same rigorous search then took place of the Ringing Room but again nothing was discovered, but at least the Bell Tower could then be pronounced clear of any intruder.

A key question that had to be asked was why was the door to the Bell Tower open? Entrance to the tower was only possible through an external door; there was no access from inside the church. The tower had its own key and its own key holders; the keys for the main door of the church were totally different from the tower's keys and could not be used to open it. The door to the Bell Tower was always kept locked, except when the bells were being rung at a service or the ringers were practising, or work was being done on the tower or the bells, because everyone was acutely aware how inherently dangerous bell towers could be. It was an oft repeated anecdote by the Tower Captain that in the medieval times, after Jousting and Archery, Bell Ringing was the next most deadly pastime anyone could engage in.

So why then was it that on this occasion the normal safety procedures had been flouted and the door left unlocked. The answer both key holders gave was the same. When they had arrived at the church to ring that morning the lock had worked perfectly, but during the time they had been ringing something had changed. When they came to try to lock up they found it impossible. Both the keys in their possession proved to be useless. As soon as the Remembrance Day Service at the War Memorial was over it had been intended to find an emergency locksmith and call him out to fix the problem, but neither key holder had thought that there was any likelihood of harm arising during the half hour period when everyone was gathered in the Market Place to pay their respect to the dead of two World Wars.

How wrong they were! But could anyone be seriously blamed? Who could have predicted that some vandal would insert a slither of metal into the Bell Tower lock and then squirt into it a good helping of super glue?

***

"He's a bit of an enigma, Pete," said Detective Inspector Hobson. "He's living in the past, he's stuck in a time warp, he's fighting a battle from 50 years ago, and he isn't taking any prisoners, but at the same time he uses a computer to write his explosive letters and a printer to print them out, and modern quick drying glues don't seem to bother him in the slightest."

"He obviously realised that it would have been impossible for him to have begged, borrowed or stolen a key so he's used his nous. He's assumed, quite correctly, that nobody would be standing guard at the Bell Tower door while the wreath-laying ceremony was taking place. He knew that when he shot all eyes would be on the ground. He had just one chance and he took it, and after he fired the shot he must have been aware that he would only have a very short period of time to get off the tower, get rid of the gun and to mingle with the crowd. He was damn lucky that he didn't break his leg coming down that spiral staircase. I wouldn't want to gallop down it, and I'll bet a pound to a penny I am at least twenty five years younger than he is."

"But you're not driven by hatred to kill, are you Pete? I should imagine nothing gets the adrenaline racing more than an overwhelming desire for vengeance."

"Oh there are one or two people I could cheerfully murder Gov, you included on a bad day, but what's bugging me is how did he get rid of the gun? The lads searched every inch of the Bell Tower and every inch of the graveyard and found complete F.A. He needed to find a safe hiding place for his rifle, unless he no longer had use for it, which I doubt, but we have no way of knowing what his future plans are, and we have to act as if it is going to be a case of "more of the same" in which case he still has need of his weapon."

"You say we searched the tower and the grounds; did we search inside the church itself?"

"We looked under pews and in the entrance porch; we didn't make an extensive search of the church itself. There were ladies coming in and out the whole while, collecting up hymn books, checking nothing had been left behind by anyone, putting on a kettle for the vicar to have a cup of tea when he returned, but of course he never did. They have all been spoken to, they all saw nobody, and although they accept that somebody could have nipped into church for a few seconds without them seeing him, they all feel such a person would have been spotted if he had stayed more than a moment or two."

"But that's exactly what I think he did Pete, and he did it to very good effect. Now let me ask you a question. Where in a church would you think would be the last place to find a weapon?"

"I don't know Gov, I wouldn't expect to find one at all but perhaps I'm just old fashioned. What do you think is the answer?"

"Well, if I wanted to hide a gun I'd hide it under the most sacred bit of furniture in the building. I'd slide it behind the exquisitely embroidered altar frontal if I wanted just a temporary resting place for it; did anyone look there?"

"I don't know Gov, but I'll get somebody onto it right away, but if your hunch pays off I will be denouncing you as a witch."

"Wrong sex Pete, but if it turns out to be correct you'll see just how much of a wizard your D.I. really is and I hope you'll be suitably impressed."

CHAPTER FORTY TWO

"I know we've had a conversation like this before, Alan, but so far as Tim Bradley is concerned, I feel like I'm banging my head against a brick wall. There doesn't seem to be anyone who might have a motive to lie about him; you've known him a long while, tell me again what is he really like?"

"Well, as I've told you before he's not the type of bloke who I would expect to make enemies: to do that you have to be actively unpopular. If I had to use a single word to describe him I would use the word "passive". If I had to expand on that assessment I would also call him "obliging". He is someone who will always say "yes" if called upon for help, but even though people are often grateful to him, he doesn't seem to have the ability to build on that goodwill to create friendships. I'll give you just one example. We wanted a driver to take us to the darts and dominoes match at The Greyhound. None of us wanted to volunteer because it meant we couldn't have a drink, and I couldn't drive because of my wrist in any event, so Tim said he would do it. We wanted to give him a bit of cash for his trouble, but he turned that down. Several of us wanted to buy him a soft drink in the pub, but he always said "No Thanks." We were worried that he seemed to be out on a limb. We tried to engage him, we tried to have conversations with him, but it was an uphill battle; he pretty well kept himself to himself for the whole evening."

"You know, Alan; the man you describe could fit the profile of our suspect in these murder enquiries. We're absolutely convinced that he is also the man who set fire to the vestry at St Catherine's. Are you completely certain that he didn't slip out of the pub when nobody was watching? The church is only a couple of hundred yards from The Greyhound; he wouldn't have had to be gone for very long."

"I'm a thousand percent sure, sorry Mark," replied Alan Nadin, "and I'm equally sure he was with me at the Scout Headquarters at 7pm that evening so he couldn't have been at St Catherine's at that time either."

"Then why would somebody say that he was? He seems to be a totally inoffensive bloke that nobody could take exception to?"

"That's the key question, isn't it Mark? Maybe somebody just sees him as a soft target and is playing a cruel practical joke both upon him and upon the police."

"Maybe so, maybe so," replied a somewhat weary Detective Inspector Hobson.

***

"Do you want the good news or the bad news Eddie Baby?" The men from Los Angeles were almost taunting Edward Cartwright; he felt very ill at ease.

"I'll have the good news, I've had enough shit in my life recently to last me a lifetime, and I don't need any more."

"Well then get the champagne out, it turns out Mick Wallington cannot possibly be your father."

For a fraction of a second a look of relief flickered across Cartwright's face before it rapidly faded.

"So does that mean that Frank Oakes is my dad?"

"Nope! Whoever your daddy was, it wasn't either of those two cretins, and we can prove as much if either of them tries to claim otherwise."

The look of relief re-appeared on the movie star's face.

"So is it the case that we're finally out of the woods and that this bloody nightmare has at last come to an end?"

The men from Los Angeles gave him withering looks, which were a mixture of scorn and contempt.

"Not a frigging chance Hot Shot, it makes the whole frigging situation 10 times worse."

"How do you work that out then?" Edward Cartwright's face was a picture of disappointment.

"Jesus," said the taller of the two men, "haven't you got a frigging brain? We now don't have a clue who it was who impregnated your saintly Momma. Any Tom, Dick or frigging Harry could step into the limelight and claim that you were his long lost son and we'd be wrong footed. Before we could react properly the damage would have been done. It's a Goddamn disaster so far as we're concerned."

"Then what can we do?" Panic had chased away every other emotion from Cartwright's brain.

"Pick up the phone," the men advised. "Call your frigging mother and find out from her who else could have stuck his penis up her fanny at the particular time. She's knows more than she has told you so far, we guarantee that for a fact."

***

The conversation in The Royal Albert was also about knowledge, or rather about a brain slowly shutting down and a man losing his grip on reality and entering into a world of hallucinations and black fog.

"He had a sharp tongue on him if he was in a bad mood, he was arrogant too, and at times his bedside manner left a hell of a lot to be desired. My Old Man detested him as a person, but he reckoned that he was a pretty good doctor and, in fairness, there were times when he was very witty. My Dad said that he once gave a talk at the Village Hall to help them raise money for something or another and he had everyone in stitches; it was made all the funnier because it was so totally unexpected," recalled Bill Adamson.

"My wife's mother didn't like him," interjected Alan Nadin. "She said he was very autocratic. She claimed that he didn't put you at your ease, and that he talked down to his patients; especially the women; she said he could be a sexist pig when he wanted to be, and that seems to have been most of the time."

"Quite unlike his grandson Giles," added a third voice, "now there's a lad who knows how to deal with people. Good hearted too; did you read how much money he and two of his mates raised for the local hospice by running the whole length of the Pennine Way. The weather was pretty foul as well, and they say he got blisters the size of duck eggs, but he kept on going and together he and his friends collected just over £14,000."

"They're local heroes," commented Bill Adamson. "That's why they've been asked to switch on the Christmas lights at Glossop. I wonder if old Doc Sterndale knows anything about that."

"Well Alzheimer's doesn't suddenly take hold, it's a gradual process," replied Alan. "I'm told that at the moment he understands things, but perhaps in 3 months' time it will be a different story. Certainly, if I had any questions about his life that I wanted to ask him I wouldn't be hanging about for too long otherwise it could well become a pointless exercise."

***

"You were right, Merlin, I should have known you would be: I shall have to treat you with a bit more respect from now on in case you are tempted to try out some of your black arts on me," Detective Sergeant Pete Bennett was reporting to Detective Inspector Mark Hobson the results of the latest search of the Parish Church.

"They didn't find the rifle of course, that would have been too much to hope for, but they found an oil stain on the inside of the altar frontal which nobody can explain. It's currently being examined by Forensics; the Church isn't very happy about that, those frontals are very expensive, and this one also has some history about it. We've said that we will do our best not to damage it, and they reluctantly accept an examination has to take place, but I'm told it's an odds on certainty that the oil will turn out to be gun oil."

"So if that does turn out to be the case it will prove that a weapon was hidden there, but that it was removed before we got to it. Nobody saw it being concealed, that much we know, but there is a chance someone may have seen it being taken away, or at least witnessed something or somebody they thought suspicious. Who has had access to the Parish Church since Remembrance Sunday?"

"I thought you'd ask that question Gov. It was locked on Sunday afternoon after the shooting. It stayed locked on Monday, so nobody entered. The brasses were cleaned Tuesday morning and there was a funeral service for Ray Baker's father in the afternoon. Thereafter I believe the Church remained closed until we carried out our search today."

"So whoever retrieved the gun must have done it during one of those times. Sunday in my view is out. The Church wasn't open for very long after our lads had finished searching the graveyard; Evensong was cancelled and even though there may have been moments in the early afternoon when there might have been a chance, it would be too close to the time of the murder and too big a risk to take. The ladies who clean the brasses are in the church the whole time, so I don't think that there would have been an opportunity then. My best bet is that at some time either during or after the funeral service, when I think the church remained open for mourners to pray and to remember, our man saw a chance and seized the rifle."

"I suppose it's possible Gov, but it would still have been a hell of a risk."

"Our man thrives on risks Peter; and maybe there are things happening in his life at the moment that mean he has no choice but to take them."

CHAPTER FORTY THREE

It was the phone call for which Connie had been praying for days. Somehow she knew even before she picked up the phone that it was Edward. She had ached to hear his voice and had cried herself to sleep at night when another day of utter silence had been lived through. Her hand shook as she picked up the receiver. For the first time in such a long time she could see a pinprick of light at the end of the very dark tunnel. If he spoke gently to her, if he was kind, if he forgave her that pinprick of light would explode into a rainbow of iridescent colour, the world would become a beautiful place once more and she would be born again.

But as soon as he spoke she heard the harshness in his voice and the hope that was blossoming in her breast was blown away by a bitter wind.

"This hopefully won't take very long Mother, but I have no other choice, I need you to do something for me."

"Anything my darling, anything at all."

A small portion of her fear started to evaporate; if she could perform a task for her perfect son, no matter how debasing or degrading it might be, and do it well, and help him achieve a desired outcome, he might relent a little bit, and over time she could crawl back on her knees into his affection.

"I want you to tell me who my father was, and this time I don't want any fucking lies, I've had enough of those already!"

"Oh Edward, I wish I could, how I wish I could, but I can't. I'm so sorry. It should have been Frank Oakes; for years and years I thought it was; but he cheated me. People are now claiming that it was that reprobate Michael Wallington, but I wouldn't have let him lay a finger on me, I swear it."

"You claim to have been too drunk to have known who it was who finally had his way with you. If you're telling the truth you could have been fucked by an 8ft gorilla with the pox and you wouldn't have realised it; but, the trouble is, I don't fucking believe you. I think that there were more men than you have admitted to so far; I need to know who they were. I think that you might have been ridden like the village bike; I've got a pen and paper handy in case it turns out to be a long list; so come on start giving me some names."

"Oh Edward that's so unfair and unkind; there was only the one occasion, I swear that on my life."

"Then it should be simple enough to remember it then. If it wasn't Oakes or Wallington or some sexually diseased primate just who the fuck was it? One thing is bloody certain. I'm not the son of God, you sure as Hell ain't the fucking Virgin Mary, and whatever happened that night it was most definitely not Immaculate Conception!"

"Oh Edward, Edward, I don't know. It was such an error of judgement on my part, but I can't say that because it gave me you to love. From the moment you were born your well-being has been my only concern. I love you my darling, I always have, I always will. I'm so sorry I hurt you, I'm so sorry I didn't tell you the truth, but I've learned my lesson. I will never tell lies to you again, my Angel, I promise that on my honour."

"You don't have any honour Mother, you lost that when you entered into a dishonourable contract, but at least you are telling me the truth now. You are right; you'll never lie to me again because you'll never ever see me or speak to me again. I promise you that on my honour."

"Oh, don't say that Edward. Oh God! Oh God! I wish I were dead."

"I wish you were fucking dead too Mother," he said, and he slammed the receiver down, severing the last wisp of umbilical cord that tied the mother to the child.

***

Bishop Anthony sat alone in his study. The letter on the desk in front of him deeply troubled him. It wasn't that he didn't know what to do; he did, and in a few minutes he would pick up the telephone and call the police, but the bitterness of the writer, and the rage with which he denounced the Church was more extreme than anything he had seen before. Bishop Anthony believed in a benign God, and even as a very young man he had implicitly embraced the teachings of the gospels; but now some anonymous person was alleging that the Church that he had tried to serve for his entire life was solely responsible for the death of a fine young man. The accusations contained in this ill-meant epistle both appalled and saddened him.

He had in his time received many letters from people who railed against Christianity and occasionally he had admitted to himself that they had good cause. The pronouncements of unfeeling priests who claimed the moral high ground, and justified every extreme view they promulgated by reference to the Old Testament always filled him with dismay. Faith without humanity, belief without compassion, surely that was not the way God wanted things to be. Bishop Anthony was a devout and kindly man, and he had been distressed to receive this very hateful missive.

He wondered if he would have felt differently if Jacob Lindley had been murdered by extremist adherents to another faith, and he was sure that he would. He would have resisted the temptation to have used the killing as a rod to beat Islam or whatever other creed those responsible for the atrocity claimed allegiance to, which many of his colleagues wouldn't have done, but from a rational point of view he might have seen some advantage. Martyrs to any cause have great value, but that benefit comes at a huge cost. The Bishop knew first and foremost that they were human beings who felt pain and fear and sometimes doubt, and who invariably left behind loved ones who were often scarred by the enormity of the crimes that had been committed. But perhaps on occasions martyrs were part of God's plan, and if so, they surely earned a place in Heaven; but God would not have engineered a situation where a good man could be killed by a madman whose only aim seemed to be to then vilify everything the Church held most sacred. The hand that wrote this letter was steeped in blood, it was the hand of Satan not the hand of Jesus, and even touching it sent a shudder down the Bishop's spine.

It was both brutal and direct. The writer had chosen to set out his accusations in a manner similar to the way in which a lawyer might draft an indictment.

The writer made it clear that the letter had been sent to Bishop Anthony because he was "God's highest ranking representative in the county of Derbyshire." He stated that the work of the Anglican Church was a sham and that in reality, under the pretence of doing good works, crimes against humanity were being committed and then it set out the particulars of the offences as the writer perceived them to be. The relevant section of the letter read as follows:-

In quasi legal language, it alleged that "On many and divers days between the 1st January 1952 and the 31st day of December 1972 and on sundry other days thereafter the Church had shown gross intolerance and intransigence and by so doing had committed countless acts of cruelty". It claimed that acting through its ministers and its lay members it had demonstrated "a total lack of compassion and humanity". It proclaimed that "by a rigid adherence to dogma and a wilful refusal to take any account of human frailty lives had been needlessly damaged and sometimes destroyed". It criticised the Church for "not accepting the realities of mental illness and depression", and it castigated the church for "failing to take care of the most vulnerable members of society." It added that the Church had become "exclusive not inclusive", and that it had exhibited the sins of "pride and hypocrisy", and it concluded that for all these failings, it had had to be punished.

The writer said that the punishment had had to be severe. The only punishment serious enough to fit the crimes had to be the execution of one of its members completely untainted by the prejudice and insincerity of a corrupt establishment. A true disciple of Jesus had to be condemned, and hence it concluded the Reverend Jacob Lindley had to die. The writer taunted the Bishop that henceforward he and self-deluded members of his Church would have to live every hour, every day knowing that people acting in its name had by their actions signed the death warrant of a good and gracious priest. It assured Bishop Anthony that the collective guilt of the spiritual leaders and their flocks would be revealed to the whole World and that as a consequence the steady exodus of people away from organised religion would become a stampede.

And without any thought of fairness, or taking account of how much things have changed thought the Bishop, the popular press will crucify us, and there won't be a thing that we can do to redress the balance. Forcing himself to make the telephone call that he had been seeking to put off, he picked up the handset and dialled the number of his local police station.

CHAPTER FORTY FOUR

I can tell the cancer is taking hold; for the moment it still does not cause me too much pain, but I know I that I am not the man I was even 6 short months ago. When I shot the young vicar, and with that single act sent shock waves around the World my hands were steady and my aim was true, but my joints ached from kneeling on the roof top, and twice as I ran down that awful spiral staircase I thought my knees had locked into place and I all but stumbled on the uneven steps. Still, fear of discovery is a great motivator, and I am not yet so far travelled down the road to Oblivion that I cannot experience the excitement of an adrenaline rush. My descent was all the more difficult because I carried my rifle in my right hand; its work is still not done, and if I had left it behind not only would that have frustrated my future plans, there would also be fingerprints aplenty to condemn me to what little life I have left behind bars.

But for all the difficulties getting down the stairs the main problem was still to come. When I reached the door to the outside world, fighting for breath, wheezing like an old melodeon, needing to find a safe haven for the gun and for myself in the short time available to me before vengeful hordes surrounded the bell tower, I had to think quickly. Fortunately, I already had a plan. I knew the women left behind in church waiting for the vicar and the choir to return were trained in first aid. In a high pitched voice I screamed that there had been an accident upon the Market Place and that somebody who was bleeding badly needed urgent attention. They heard my shouting; I think they thought I was a frightened woman; they rushed from the church to see if they could help; I hid behind the porch; and when they were gone I grabbed my chance and ran into the building. I guessed a search of it would be made, but I trusted to luck to hope that no one would think to look under the altar. Within a minute I had rid myself of the rifle and sprinted back outside the church. My lungs were on fire, my head ached in a way it has never done before, my heart pounded with the ferocity of a steam hammer, and for a second I believed I might be about to die. I was in agony, but then the pain subsided, and when the crowds of frightened people began to congregate in the church yard believing that to be a safe place, I joined the throng. Nobody noticed me, nobody ever notices me, but for once that was an advantage. Seconds after I concealed myself the women returned trembling and crying, and in shock. They were absent for such a short time that they convinced themselves that nobody could have entered into their palace of self-delusion in the time they had been away; later, from a distance, I heard one of them tell a police officer that it would have been impossible for anyone to have sneaked into the church unnoticed on their watch. She believed what she said, and so she was convincing, and the constable who heard this misrepresentation of the truth believed it too. Being part of a crowd and not being seen, hearing the conversations of others but not being a party to them, have served me well, and over the years I have learned many things that have been useful to me.

I know that an old man's reason is fast ebbing away, and that soon his life will have no more meaning than a bag of offal as uncomprehendingly he dribbles out the last days of his life. The information gleaned from that conversation has shown me that before his mind turns to stagnant slime, he must be told how his careless attitude towards others has led to those he holds dear having to cope with unbearable heartache. I intend to act quickly. I must ensure that in his final cogent moments his brain will scream in agony. When that happens my original plan will be fulfilled, but since the time of its conception the need to teach a harsh lesson to a brash youth has become apparent. He will know fear and be told a terrible secret and that will be my swan song. My time will nearly be done. I want no memorial or headstone, but if I did I would want it to carry these words: "He paid his dues in blood." That might cause some to shiver when my unexpurgated tale is told.

But I leap forward. If abandoning the rifle in the church was fraught with risk, reclaiming it was riskier still. I thought I might have had an opportunity to slip into the building unnoticed while the women cleaned the brasses, but the killing of the curate had made them as jumpy as kittens and there was no chance. They locked the door behind them as they worked and access to everyone was denied.

The funeral proved to be my salvation. Although my thoughts should have been on so many grieving relatives and on the man who lay in the coffin and his final months of suffering, they were elsewhere. Nobody batted an eyelid when I returned from the graveside to the church, ostensibly to take time alone to remember, and nobody wondered why I stayed so long. I was waiting for others to leave, that was the sole reason, and when they were gone and I was by myself, I retrieved the gun. I wrapped it in the long black coat I had been wearing, the day had become hot so there was nothing remarkable about a man taking off his overcoat and carrying it to his car. I was parked less than 100 yards from the church door. In less than a minute it was safely concealed within my boot. After I had achieved my purpose I then returned home and confessed my sins to the Bishop in a long and thoughtful letter, but that is not strictly true; I did not confess my sins at all, but I pointed out the sins of others which had led to the killing of the clergyman.

Maybe I am becoming inured to the sight of violent death. I have not once dreamt of the young man since he surrendered his soul to God, but strangely I still have nightmares about the girl Penny. I think that is because I saw the expression on her face the second before she died, I did not see his face, and so it didn't touch me. Also in his case he had become a thing, a token of a corrupt religion, an icon to be smashed, and I am glad my sleep is not disturbed by thoughts of him.

His Bishop and many members of his Church may not be so lucky when I reveal to the World what I have already revealed to them. The knowledge that a life was lost because of their flawed faith may lie heavily upon them and some may find that knowledge nearly impossible to bear.

***

The letter passed to the police by Bishop Anthony had been carefully examined by experts. The paper was identical to the paper used for all the other anonymous letters, and it was also a certain fact that all the letters had been printed on the same printer. The style of writing, although this time adorned with many legal sounding phrases was felt to be the same as in the earlier correspondence and, according to the psychologist who had prepared the profile of the offender, it fitted perfectly with the character of the man the police were desperately seeking.

Detective Inspector Mark Hobson and Detective Sergeant Peter Bennett were discussing these findings, and also anticipating the funeral of Jacob Lindley which was to take place the following day.

"We'll have to have the same police presence that we had for Penny Adamson; we daren't do anything else, but he won't be at the church, I'd bet my eye teeth on that."

"What makes you so sure Gov?" asked DS Bennett.

"Well this shooting is different to the shootings of Adam and Penny. He killed them to cause their families extreme distress and to basically tear them apart. He wanted Mick and Sheila to be blamed by their children and grandchildren for causing a wholly avoidable death. He hoped to witness tears, bitter accusations and everlasting recrimination and he would have needed to be in church to see if his strategy worked. With Jacob it's different. There isn't going to be an individual who has to be made to suffer, there won't be a person for the relatives to turn on; Jacob was killed to punish an institution, no one man or woman has to be taught a harsh lesson. Institutions don't react like human beings, they don't shout and swear they don't burst into tears, they don't throw things in anger or grapple with their neighbours; there isn't going to be a scene inside the church. In time, as a result of criticism from third parties policies may change, but nothing is ever done suddenly, there won't be any high drama."

"So it's probably pointless us being there at all," commented the Detective Sergeant.

"Almost certainly yes, but as we can't say for sure, we still have to be ready for every eventuality."

***

One group of people who clearly did not think that it would be pointless to attend Jacob Lindley's funeral were the men and women who got their livings by dispensing news and scandal and, on occasions, malicious make-believe. Television journalists and print reporters were in attendance in large numbers; and nothing would have pleased them more than for there to have been a dramatic incident inside or outside the church. Had a mad gunman taken the entire congregation hostage, and then threatened to execute one person every 10 minutes until a series of unrealistic demands had been fully met some of the tabloid hacks would have wet themselves in their excitement. Sex, death and tragedy sold newspapers; only the story mattered, the damage done to the real lives of real people did not even register on many of their radar screens.

Unfortunately for the assembled news hounds, fortunately for everybody else, nothing noteworthy occurred. The tears of Jacob's mother were considered to be "mundane" the moving address by the Vicar made no impact, and it seemed to most of the media circus that it had been an entirely wasted day. A noticeable police presence outside the church had maybe deterred a killer from causing trouble, but to the assembled ranks of media personnel it also looked as if it had killed a good story. Then it happened. The reporter from The Sun received a call on his mobile from someone at his office. He was instructed to extract himself from the ranks of his colleagues, and making as little fuss as possible then to go to the Market Place where he was told he would find something of interest. Hot on the heels of an exclusive he tried to slip away unnoticed. Sadly for him his movements were quickly spotted by his competitors, probably because they too had received phone calls from their editors suggesting that they too did exactly the same thing. Whoever the anonymous informant was he had been busy. En masse the body of reporters moved, a slow walk became a trot became a canter as journalists and photographers raced against each other to get to the place where they had been told a news story would be found.

It wasn't much to look at, just a single sheet of A4 paper affixed to a notice board, but it was exactly what the news media wanted to see, and by releasing the information in the way that he had the creator of the notice had guaranteed that it would get maximum publicity.

In essence, it repeated the points made to Bishop Anthony, and the popular press loved it. Here was a chance to pillory one part of the establishment; here was an opportunity for the media to thunder against hypocrisy and to bleat about the betrayal of Christian values. Suddenly the hacks from the tabloids re-invented themselves as guardians of the public good, and forgot the innumerable times they had misled the public with mixtures of innuendo, half-truths and lies. A rogue preacher had preached hate and his actions had damaged lives; that was how they saw the story, and that was how it would be reported.

CHAPTER FORTY FIVE

The Sun and the Daily Mirror had really gone to town. In their different ways they had each tried to paint pictures of a backward looking small town which for most of the 20th Century had been stuck firmly in the Dark Ages, untouched by the cultural and social revolutions that had occurred elsewhere. They were happy to imply that for nearly twenty years after the end of the 2nd World War the local population had been cowed by a puritanical priest who had pursued a ruthless battle against people he perceived as sinners and imposed on them draconian punishments when he located them. They likened Matthew Hardman to a one man Spanish Inquisition, prying into every aspect of his parishioners' private lives and condemning many of them to existences of misery or exile. Both newspapers had found people who claimed to have relatives who had suffered at the hands of this Vicar from Hell. Mark Hobson knew the names of these people and felt that in most cases the revelations which were being made owed more to the quantity of beer the witnesses had been plied with and the amount of hard cash that had changed hands; given the character of some of them he was actually amazed that the claims were not even more outrageous than they had turned out to be.

"If you buy Billy Entwistle a few lagers and then slip him a tenner he'd happily swear he'd seen the Queen bouncing up and down on a pogo stick at Burrdale Heath wearing nothing more than her crown and a silly grin," Mark said to

Helena, "but of course the readers of the tabloids want to believe the rubbish that is printed in them and they'll just accept every word he's said as Gospel, no matter how ludicrous the claims."

"Not all of them Darling," replied Helena, "and even if there is no truth in these particular stories, I think that there are genuine stories out there which will show just how unbending the Reverend Hardman really was. I talked to a lot of people about him and I found real anger and real despair. He wasn't a very nice man; for a Christian, he seems to have been totally lacking in compassion."

"Point taken," said Mark, "but the problem will be in proving exactly what he did, and my job has been made so much more difficult by the fire at St Catherine's vestry. It's such a pity that there still isn't an archive at the Village Hall and that everything had been lumped together in one place, because if that hadn't happened, I would have an alternative source to go to and I would be a lot more confident about getting a result."

"But in one sense," commented Helena, "maybe the fire wasn't altogether a bad thing."

"Why do you say that Sweetheart?" Mark asked. Had the comment been made by anyone else he would have regarded it as crass and not worthy of consideration, but long experience had taught him that Helena was clever and thoughtful and did not make asinine comments or trite remarks.

"It's like this Love," answered Helena. "I think like you do that the killer started the fire because he wanted to destroy evidence. That means he must believe that there is evidence in existence which could harm him; I'm sure if he was confident that there were no letters or photographs or papers that could damage him there wouldn't have been a fire; setting fire to the vestry was always going to be risky; he wouldn't have taken that risk if he hadn't perceived there to be a need."

"Agreed so far my Love, but because the fire was so effective doesn't that mean he has got rid of everything that might incriminate him?"

"No, not necessarily. You've already told me about the thousands of burnt fragments of papers that are currently being picked out of the debris by your officers, and I think somewhere amongst that lot is a key, but in any event, I think that in the world outside the vestry there may be complete photographs or articles hidden away in attics or stored in suitcases under beds."

"You might be right Darling," sighed Mark. "You should be doing my job; you'd be a whole lot better at it than me."

"You'd have got there without me," smiled Helena. "I've just had a bit more time to think than you've had recently, but I'm no match for Burrdale's Number 1 detective."

And the more Mark thought about it, the more he became convinced that that would have been the case, and even though it was Helena who had given him the ball it was now his to run with. A plan was developing in his mind. The next morning he would discuss the case with DS Bennett and then in all probability take his idea to Detective Chief Superintendent Stanley Hardy.

What Mark proposed was not all that unusual, but perhaps it was a little out of the ordinary at this stage in a criminal investigation. Whereas all too often the tabloid newspapers could be a thorn in the side of the police and at times positively unhelpful the same was not true of the "local rag." What Mark hoped to do was enlist the support of the entire community to help in the hunt for the killer of Jacob Lindley and the other murder victims. It would necessitate saying something about the police lines of inquiry and that was potentially a risky thing to do, and as it involved stating that the Reverend Matthew Hardman was a person who was attracting police interest he had to be circumspect in what he put into the public domain. An article giving people a chance to rage against an individual for no good cause would achieve nothing and could harm any relatives of the vicar if any still remained living in the High Peak. Mark Hobson was adamant that there would be no offer of a reward for information and certainly no alcohol would be available to loosen peoples' tongues, and by this means he hoped there would nothing to tempt ne'er-do-wells to invent stories. DCS Hardy had some reservations, but considered that if it was handled carefully and had the prior approval of the C.P.S. it could be an effective tool. So with the senior officer's blessing Hobson made an appointment to meet the editor of the Burrdale Advertiser.

And there was one other step that Mark now felt to be necessary. Already a great deal of material that the officers sorting through the charred paperwork extracted from the stricken vestry felt might have relevance to the case had landed on his desk. He had spent countless hours checking this to see if their suspicions were correct, and all he had achieved was eye strain, but he now realised even more had to be done. He was about to demand that most of the paperwork that had been looked at and classified as worthless be re-examined because it was now apparent that the Reverend Matthew Hardman had potentially become a highly significant person in the build up to the crime of murder. The officers doing the donkey work were going to love him for this but there was no other option. It was now vital that anything at all that might suggest a link between Matthew Hardman, Michael Wallington and Sheila Adamson was identified and then brought to his immediate notice. Nearly six months had passed since the first of these dreadful murders was committed. Christmas was just around the corner and if nothing was achieved by then a lot of people would start to complain. Hysterical bleating by Mr Angry of Buxton was a headache the Derbyshire Constabulary could well do without. Sir Walter Thurlow would start throwing his weight about and that was something Detective Chief Superintendent Stanley Hardy, Detective Inspector Mark Hobson, Detective Sergeant Peter Bennett and all the detectives working long hours to solve the case did not want to occur. Some sort of breakthrough was urgently needed, but unfortunately nothing appeared to be on their horizon.

***

What was on the horizon however for the residents of Buxton, Glossop, New Mills, Burrdale and several of the smaller villages in the Peak District was the switch on of the Christmas lights.

The lights at Castleton were already shining brightly as Castleton was always the first village in the area to illuminate its streets. Tall Christmas trees stand on either side of the main road, bringing colour, wonder and excitement, particularly to the children as they herald the coming of Christmas Eve and presents and magic and Santa Claus. The lights also bring tourists in their hundreds and in their thousands for the big switch on; even cold wind and frost does not deter them and if it snows, providing the roads are passable, then even more people come. The shops selling the famous Blue John jewellery stay open late, and a brisk trade is done. An early start to the festive season makes sound economic sense too, and overcrowded pavements and car parks seem like a very small price to pay.

This year, however, things had been a little different. Memories of the 29th May and the terrible act of murder that had been committed that day were still strong and certainly the police had been desperate to ensure that there was no repeat performance. Since that dramatic day two more murders had taken place, both in front of large crowds of people, and there was a real fear that something might happen again at another popular event. The police had been jittery. Armed police had been present at Castleton, although not in public view, and plain clothed officers had mingled with the crowds. Nothing had occurred but, as Detective Inspector Mark Hobson was quick to point out, Castleton was only the first of such celebrations and the killer still had a great deal of scope.

The one crumb of comfort for Mark was that his actions did not appear to be random, so it was likely the murderer would only make a move if a person, or persons, who he believed to be legitimate targets, were at the scene. Never-the-less he had begged Helena not to go to any of the switch-on ceremonies this year, nor to let any relative or friend take the children to one. He promised that they would go as a family on a later date and he also promised treats for the children if they stayed away. Helena was sad that fear could spoil what should be such fun occasions, but she knew Mark only wanted for her and the children to be safe, so she gladly consented. Daddy would have a price to pay though: two pantomimes and one Nativity Play were the very least he could expect to get away with; but for Mark that was a price well worth paying, and in fact something he would very much enjoy.

CHAPTER FORTY SIX

Fan letters had been a part of Edward Cartwright's life for over fifteen years. Not that he read them anymore; the initial thrill he had felt about being adored had soon waned; they had become tedious and annoying, and often quite frankly ridiculous. Sometimes though a letter would contain such over the top protestations of love and affection that it would be brought to his attention; how he laughed then. The teenage girls who threatened to commit suicide if he didn't send them an autographed photograph or a lock of his hair always had him in hysterics, and the middle-aged matrons who more earthily wanted him to send them items of his intimate clothing made him hoot like a demented owl.

"Write back and tell her if I ever shit myself, then she'd be welcome to my pants," he had told an assistant who had brought a letter to him, before countermanding that instruction and ordering that a signed photograph endorsed with a sufficiently bland platitude be substituted for a pair of his soiled boxer shorts. The girl knew what to do; she excelled at forging his signature, and would write something to meet the need and keep the letter writer gagging for more. Cartwright wasn't stupid, fans meant money, money opened doors, he was not about to challenge that belief; and in any event he could always insulate himself from ever being exposed too closely to them.

But since the article in the newspaper about his mother's escapades the number of letters had started to dwindle; he wasn't yet haemorrhaging admirers, but it was a worrying sign; and when correspondence started to arrive at his house demanding money that was a real cause for concern.

Of course being rich had always meant that he was targeted by charities and by ordinary people with overwhelming problems who had sometimes turned to him in their despair. These letters were never answered, but instead were immediately shredded. He called the writers "parasites" and "leeches", and he nearly spat out the words as he did so. Being charitable was only worthwhile to the donor if it was cost effective; helping some grasping peasant save the life of one of her brood of future dole claimants was never going to be a good investment.

The letters the men from Los Angeles now confronted him with were quite different. There were three of them. It was unclear if they had been written by one person or by more than one person; although the fact that the two typed letters had different fonts and there was also a hand-written note seemed to suggest that these documents were not the work of a single creator. The writer or writers claimed that they had evidence that Cartwright's mother had allowed herself to be deceived by a man who was a known sexual pervert, that she had had intercourse with him many times, even after her child was born, and that she had caught a sexually transmitted disease from him because of the prolonged nature of the relationship: it also suggested that the man who was his father had a genetic defect that could have passed from mother to son. The letters were all appallingly badly written, they were by no means totally persuasive, and the direct request for money to prevent public exposure further undermined their credibility.

"This is just rubbish!" Cartwright bellowed when he read the letters, "It's a try-on, nobody in his right mind would believe this crap!"

"People believe just about anything these days Eddie Baby! You know it's crap, I know it's crap, the bastard who wrote to you knows it's frigging crap, but he also knows that until we can prove it's frigging crap people will listen, and that causes us and you serious problems: somehow you have got to find out who your frigging birth father was or we're all up shit creek without a paddle. Once we know who it was then we have options. We can get him on side, we can pay him off, we can warn him off, or we can find a more permanent solution, whatever it takes. If we can get to that situation without breaking sweat, then so much the better, and thereafter we should be able to explode every frigging myth the greedy bastards throw at us. If we can't do that then I tell you now Buddy it becomes a whole different ball game. The guys in suits back in the States are seriously thinking of cutting their losses. They're this far from just walking away, and if they do that then you'll be frigging history in 10 seconds. You wouldn't like that now would you Tarzan?"

And of course the insolent minder was absolutely right. The thought that he might fall from grace terrified Edward Cartwright. From Hot Shot to Has Been in the blink of an eye, that was too cruel a trick even for malevolent Fate to play. He instantly resolved that under no circumstances was that going to happen to him. He would find the man who was his father; he would deliver him up to the gorillas that looked after him, and what happened to him after that was something that he had absolutely no interest in provided it shielded him from further harm and helped him to preserve the lifestyle he had become accustomed to.

***

There had been long discussions between Detective Chief Superintendent Hardy, the Assistant Chief Constable, and the head of the Tactical Firearms Unit, and later with some of the senior police officers stationed in the High Peak, about what to do in respect of this year's Christmas lights switch-on ceremonies which were to happen later that day. Normally they needed no policing at all, or at most the attendance of a couple of P.C.S.O's to deal with the odd badly parked car or to receive a lost purse or set of keys, but this year might be different. The trouble was that nobody knew for sure if it would be, and everyone had the fervent hope that it would not be; but nobody 6 months ago would have predicted murders would take place in crowded spaces at 3 different locations in front of large numbers of witnesses.

Castleton had been easy because it was the only event taking place on that night and, because a killer had struck there once before, there was perceived to be an enhanced risk of a further incident. Tonight was a nightmare. Tonight Glossop, New Mills, Burrdale and Buxton were all holding ceremonies at more or less the same time as each other. In two of these four small towns murder had already taken place, but which one now presented the greatest risk of a recurrence was anybody's guess and, in any event, statistically it was just as likely that one of the other two could be the scene of tragedy. It was impossible to have armed police in attendance at every one, and probably completely unnecessary and a waste of human resources, but nobody could say there wasn't a risk. In the end it had been decided that a high-powered Police Armed Response Vehicle was the best solution, which in theory meant that it could attend the scene of any major incident in a maximum time of 15 minutes, and hopefully a great deal quicker if it happened to be near to a the particular town when the need arose. A uniformed officer with a radio was to be present at each location whose job was to be alert; he or she would be accompanied by a Special Constable who could deal with any minor problem that might arise leaving the full time officer able to concentrate on the job in hand. This wasn't a foolproof plan, it didn't give blanket protection, but it was the best that could be devised, and DCS Hardy and DI Hobson hoped fervently that it would work. The weather forecast for that night was that it was going to be cold and clear. Frost could be a problem later on in the evening, but not so much early on. In any event all the major roads would be gritted although untreated roads could turn icy by mid evening.

The cold weather was actually welcomed by Mark Hobson. His daughter Lucy had developed a slight cough, and Helena had been feeling off-colour for a couple of days, so the disappointment she had felt about not attending the Burrdale Switch On was mitigated by the fact that in all probability she would have had to come to the conclusion that it was unwise to risk the cold night air and better to stay warm and snug inside, in any event.

***

The police Armed Response Vehicle (ARV) was just entering the village of Hayfield en route to Buxton when the call came. In the sort of manoeuvre that would have seemed routine to viewers of The Sweeney it skidded to a near halt, performed a hand brake turn and set off at speed to travel back in the direction from whence it had just come. The lady waiting with her dog to cross the by-pass from the public car park to walk into the centre of the village was terrified. It was very cold; only a few minutes earlier a council gritting lorry had gone past spreading salt upon the road. She was by nature a cautious driver, particularly so if the weather was bad, and what she had just witnessed seemed to her to be highly reckless. The squealing of the tyres deeply unsettled her and the screaming of the siren and the flashing of the blue lights left her feeling physically sick. For a police car to react in this manner, there had to be a reason. Something dreadful must have happened. Her brain told her that somewhere, perhaps not very far away, a fellow human being was probably lying dead or dying, or horrendously injured and in great pain. She couldn't help herself; she started to shake uncontrollably, and then the tears began to fall.

It was almost exactly 5 miles from the scene of the dramatic U-turn to the very centre of Glossop where a pretty Christmas tree had been erected, but the road through Little Hayfield is narrow and bendy, and there are nearly always cars parked, often at the most inconvenient of spots. The assent to the top of Chunal is steep and winding, and H.G.V's, including gritting lorries, usually can do no more than crawl up the hill at walking pace. As for the descent into Glossop itself that slope is officially categorised as "dangerous." Warning signs instruct motorists to use low gears, and over the years there have been several serious accidents when those instructions have been ignored. If you took into account the fact that the ARV had had to overtake a slow moving Council vehicle, and the cortege of cars that had built up behind it, then the five minutes twenty five seconds it took to arrive at the scene of a crime was nothing short of miraculous; but despite that fact a gunman who had attempted to take another life had slipped clean away.

"His chances are pretty poor," Detective Inspector Mark Hobson was explaining to DCS Hardy news he had just received about the condition of Giles Sterndale.

"It's a wonder that he's alive at all. The only reason he still is, is that he has a habit of swaying on his feet when he's talking and he moved a split second before the gunman fired. The bullet missed his heart by millimetres, but miss it did; his biggest problem is that he staggered back when he was hit, and then fell sideways to the floor. His head struck the bottom step of the War Memorial. He fractured his skull; they've already performed an operation lasting four hours to try to relieve the pressure on his brain. He's currently in a medical induced coma, and will be for some time; there's no guarantee that they will ever succeed in bringing him round; the surgeon was far from upbeat when I spoke to him a few moments ago. Even if they do, he could be left with permanent brain damage, or severe physical impairment, or both. It's not a rosy picture by any stretch of the imagination."

"And you have no doubt that this attempted murder is the latest act by our deluded killer?"

"None at all Sir," replied Hobson. "The bullet actually passed right through Giles's body; it hit the pillar of the War Memorial, and luckily enough we found it. It was fired by the same weapon that has been used every time to such devastating effect. The only difference this time is that this time we have recovered the rifle."

DCS Hardy's eyes opened wide with surprise. "Fantastic!" he said. "Tell me more. Where did you find the gun?"

"Well as you can imagine Sir, it was a scene of total confusion when the ARV arrived; most people were in shock. There were a lot of young kids about, the Christmas Switch-on is designed with them in mind, and a lot of them were crying and upset. Their parents were in a state of bewilderment, and nobody could tell us a great deal about the shooting. It was clear from very early on that the killer had fired down on the victim, which is about par for the course. Somebody noticed a small hole in the window of the room that used to be the Magistrates Court which overlooks Norfolk Square. The place was locked up. The big entrance doors are secured by means of a hasp and staple and a stout padlock. We contacted the key holder, and when he arrived he discovered something funny. His key wouldn't work at all on the padlock securing the first set of double doors, but it worked perfectly on the second set. There was a reason for that. The padlock had been switched on the first set of doors. My theory is that our murderer, sometime in the dead of night used a set of bolt croppers to cut through the original padlock and then replaced it with one of his own choosing. And he was clever. He didn't use a new padlock; that would have been too obvious; he used one of a similar age and appearance to the original, so that a casual observer or a passing uniform beat bobby nothing would appear to be out of place. He clearly let himself in with his own key when the time was right; and I don't think I need to spell out what he did when he was in there, he did what he had to do and then made good his escape."

"But he left the gun behind after he'd used it: why do you think he did that?"

"I don't know Sir. I wish I could say that I think it's a signal that the killing is over, and it might be so, but much as I want to believe that I have a gut feeling that there is still more to come. It could simply be that it was too dangerous for him to take it with him, and it would have been a very risky thing to do, or it could be that whatever he has got planned next doesn't need the same symbolism. I think it's quite possible that a chapter may have come to an end, but not necessarily the whole book."

"There were several hundred people in the Square. I can entirely understand that after the shooting started people would be in a state of panic, but they wouldn't have been before it. Did nobody see anything suspicious before it all kicked off? A man with a big gun has to stand out; surely somebody must have noticed something?"

"Well somebody did Sir, but our man was clever there as well. A witness did see a bloke unlocking the padlock about half an hour before the shooting. He only had a rear view, so he can't give us any description of the face. He is 90% sure that the man was white, probably middle aged and of about average height and weight. He took him to be a cleaner. He was carrying a long hessian sack with the head of a long broom and also a mop sticking out of the top; the witness also believed that the sack may have contained other cleaning tools or products as he got the impression it was quite heavy. He was further persuaded that the man was a cleaner because he was also carrying an old metal mop bucket, and he was wearing a brown shop coat like the one that Ronnie Barker wore in the T.V. comedy Open all Hours. He thought that because the man had a key he must have had legitimate access into the building; he didn't give him a second look. We've recovered the sack and the mop and the bucket, and we've fingerprinted everything that is capable of being fingerprinted; needless to say there isn't a mark on anything."

"Now there's a flipping surprise!" said Detective Chief Superintendent Hardy ruefully.

CHAPTER FORTY SEVEN

A letter was delivered to the home of Mr Alexander Sterndale M.R.C.S. It was a house in turmoil. A decision had been taken that the old surgeon had virtually arrived at the point in his life where he needed specialist medical care because of his Alzheimer's, and a suitably up-market and expensive Care Home had been picked out. It had been suggested that before permanent transfer to it, he should stay there for a brief period of respite care to acclimatise him to his new surroundings and to give his elderly wife a break from her ever more demanding husband. The attempted murder of his grandson Giles had changed everything. The old man was still able to understand the gravity of the situation and had become deeply upset, as had his wife, so now everything had been put on hold. Both needed continuity, both could not cope with further stress; so for the time being the status quo was to continue. Alexander was to remain at home, but a live in carer had been appointed to lift some of the pressure from Mrs Sterndale's shoulders.

The letter, although addressed to her husband, was opened by Mrs Sterndale. It was very clearly typed, and it looked as if the writer had done everything he could to construct a document that even a confused octogenarian could understand.

"Dear Mr Sterndale," it began, "I very nearly made the mistake of calling you Doctor. You wouldn't have liked that, would you? I have heard stories about how you shouted at patients who thought they were paying you due respect by referring to you as "Doctor." You quickly put them right. You never hesitated to let people know how clever you were. The lives of the poor wretches who you operated upon didn't interest you. You treated men and women like broken down cars, and like a good mechanic you removed faulty bits and replaced them with new ones, sometimes I admit with spectacular results, but you never thought about their hopes and fears.

Yet despite your appalling manner you could have become God. You had it in your grasp to make a crippled beggar walk again, but something more important got in your way. My grandmother of cursed memory always believed that you failed to take the opportunity to perform a miracle, and to be worshipped in her eyes, because you rushed an operation to make sure you were not late for a dinner party. Even at a time when ordinary people struggled to find enough food the rich and powerful still ate well didn't they? Did a poor man lose his one chance at salvation because roast pheasant and red wine were calling you? Had you been prepared to devote just a little more time to the job in hand and restored a man to full fitness my grandmother would have put you on a pedestal higher than Jesus Christ himself, but you made a mistake and you condemned him to life in a wheelchair until he took it upon himself to end his misery in a terrible way. By your incompetence she was driven mad, and her insanity poisoned my life. A long time ago I made a vow that I would punish you, and in a way which would destroy your sanity. "An eye for an eye" as the bible says. Madness for her will beget madness for you. Finally two days ago I took my chance. Your grandson Giles now lies near death because of your contempt for the little people you were supposed to heal. His father and mother will by now know that it was you who caused the destruction of their son. Even if he lives his quality of life will be gone. You failed to save a cripple: I have donated one to them to remind them of that error. Every time they look at him they will remember what he was like before, and they will blame you for his and their eternal tragedy.

I know it may not be too long before your brain becomes a congealed mass of grey jelly and you will have to be spoon fed, and placed in nappies like an incontinent child, and behind closed doors nurses will call you names and laugh at your infirmity; and you will not understand. You are on the cusp of oblivion, but you are not there yet. I can promise you that the very last thing you will forget will be your guilt. Pray for a quick death old man, but know that your prayers will be as nothing to those who want to see you dead. Everything that has happened to you and to your family you caused by your contempt for others; a place in Hell awaits you; no man could deserve it more."

***

"It's probably nothing Mark." Former Detective Sergeant Alan Nadin was recounting an incident that had taken place in The Royal Albert the night before. "It didn't strike me to begin with, but afterwards I thought about what you'd said about Raymond Baker and how he could match the profile of your killer, so I thought the best thing I could do is drop in for a chat; I've got another reason for wanting to talk to you in any event."

Alan then explained that Ray had become very withdrawn of late and that his mates felt that was because he was still very distressed about his father's death and also much pre-occupied with his own illness.

"We tried to cheer him up, buy him a couple of beers, and let him know that we were there for him if he needed us, but nothing registered; it was like he was somewhere else; he didn't respond to us at all. Then he said he was not the man he used to be, and he didn't like the man he had become. Then somebody tried to change the subject, although why he thought talking about the attempted murder in Glossop would do anything to improve the mood of an obviously depressed man I can't begin to imagine. Well that was it. Ray gave us such a withering look, and then he stormed out of the pub. As I said, it's probably nothing; I think he was in a lot of pain, he didn't look good and he turned very grey when we talked about Giles Sterndale, but to be on the safe side, as I've already said I thought I should have a quiet word with you."

"You did right Alan. It doesn't prove anything at all, and it certainly doesn't give me sufficient grounds to bring him in for questioning, but he's on our radar screen and now he's moved a little nearer to the centre of it."

"I thought you might feel that. But maybe now I should tell you my second reason for being here today Mark. What would you say if I told you that a 54 year old ex-copper is about to become a dad 23 years after his last child was born?"

"Is Jackie pregnant? I'd say congratulations, you old bugger. It's fantastic news. Please give her mine and Helena's love, and as soon as I've got a bit more time, let's go and grab a beer or three to celebrate your good fortune."

***

I thought I would feel so very different. I thought when the moment came I would be overjoyed or at the very least relieved that a lifetime's ambition had been realised, but instead I feel flat. Maybe if I could have arrived at this point earlier in my life I would feel differently, maybe if I did not need pills to control the pain I could enjoy the moment more, maybe if the girl had been ugly, her death would not still haunt my dreams but I am what I am and for a little longer must live with that.

I tell myself that if I was strong and healthy then I could rejoice in what I have accomplished, but I have never felt that way. Even when I was young something was missing. I have never been happy. My happiness was consumed by fire on a carnival field 50 years ago; where once there was a heart there has always been a void. The only thing that kept me going was a desire for vengeance, and now that has been achieved what is there left to do? I felt inspired when I wrote to the bone-sawyer who messed up my one chance of normality; but even as I typed the words to torment him I knew that there would never be another occasion when I would rise to such heights again. Even when the day comes that I preach my final sermon on the theme of sin and retribution I doubt if I will be so inspired.

 But could there be another reason for the hollowness within me. Maybe there needs to be one more act, maybe after all my work is not done. I thought when I left the rifle behind me for the police to find that all loose ends had been tied together; perhaps I was wrong. The Lee Enfield has done its job; it needs to claim its place in a police Black Museum, but the more I think about it the stronger my belief grows that one more dramatic act is needed to expel the demons from my mind.

He is a vain, shallow, contemptible man. When I wrote to him threatening to kill him I did it to distract the police and for the pleasure it gave me to think how he would squirm. I never intended to end his life, and certainly he does not deserve to share a place in history with the others who have perished. Their worth was universally acknowledged and that was why they had to be sacrificed; he is not fit to keep them company, unless as a yardstick to measure their integrity against his superficiality; but perhaps the World would benefit from knowing how phony this child of Tinsel Town really is. One last act, one spectacular fall from grace, and then maybe I will feel satisfied. Shall I do an act of violence to physically neuter him so that thereafter he can never sow bad seed? His parentage would render this an act of kindness to womankind or shall I be content just to humiliate him in the sight of millions of witnesses; one last defiant gesture before I raise two fingers to God and leave this life to dwell in another place? If I believed the religious mumbo jumbo of the clerics I would say that meeting Satan holds no fear for me, that I have lived in my own Hell for decades and expect nothing else, but I have nothing but contempt for their self-delusion. Worms or flames will devour my body and that will be my end. When that moment comes I will be just like you; the graveyard or the crematorium awaits us all: a finite end to a single life. Believe me, or believe me not, it is your choice, but your fate and mine, be you Priest or Rabbi, Atheist or Agnostic, Infidel or Zealot, will be the same; I rejoice that that is so

CHAPTER FORTY EIGHT

"Same font, same paper, same condescending style, and as usual no fingerprints or DNA to assist us: the letter was posted locally, which might be of some help, although I very much doubt it; he wouldn't be careless enough to draw attention to himself when he was posting it. My bet is that sometime during the hours of darkness, on a deserted street, he just dropped it into the pillar box and walked quietly away. He doesn't make basic errors, and sure as Hell he's not going to do anything to make our jobs easier." Mark Hobson was discussing the letter old Mr Sterndale had received from the killer with D.S. Bennett.

"Having said all that Pete," he added, "there are some things about this letter which are different from the earlier ones, and which I think could be highly significant."

"And what do you think they are Gov?" asked an extremely interested Detective Sergeant.

"Well this letter is a lot more specific than the earlier ones. It spells out, in considerable detail why the writer hates old Alexander, and if anything, it's got an even harder edge to it; even the vicious letter to Sheila Adamson wasn't quite as cruel as this one. He really twists the knife; he gloats about the old man's Alzheimers; there isn't a shred of compassion anywhere to be found; I don't think anyone could have composed a nastier letter than this. Old Mrs Sterndale was the person who opened it. She called us, she wasn't going to show it to her husband because she thought it would do him irreparable damage. However, her son and his wife had been sent an identical letter and when she read it Giles's mum lost it completely. She stormed over to her father-in-law's house and started screaming at him. Does that remind you of Mary Wallington's reaction to her letter? Her husband and mother-in-law tried to calm her down, but she was having none of it. She thrust the letter under his nose, called him a monster, and even though her husband told her to shut up she refused point blank to do so. She shouted the contents of the letter into the old man's face and, Alzheimers or not, he understood every word she said. He started to cry, and as far as I know he is still crying 24 hours later. Giles's mum now regrets what she did, but she can't undo the harm she's caused, and the killer has got exactly what he wanted; Alexander Sterndale has been totally destroyed by his actions.

"The other thing that is different about this letter is that he also tells us something about himself, which he hasn't done before. Now it could be that he just got carried away and let his guard slip, but I don't think he has. I think that very soon he intends to tell his entire story to the world, and then identity won't be an issue, but I think that he's got something else planned first, otherwise disclosure would have already taken place; and given his track records for spectacular assassinations, that is profoundly troubling me."

"So what do think we now know which we didn't know before?"

"Read the letter Pete. We now know he hated his grandmother. To my mind that means for a part of his life he probably had a lot of contact with her; people don't generally hate people they hardly know. Maybe she even brought him up, and if she did that gives us a new lead to follow. We also know that his grandmother adored somebody who had been paralysed; it could have been in the War, it could have been an RTA or a sporting accident, but she pinned her hopes on Alexander Sterndale and he let her down. The grandmother believed he was negligent, and as a result of his negligence, if our letter writer is telling the truth, the victim was left confined to a wheelchair until he took his own life in a truly dreadful way. I don't want to say anything until I have re-checked some of my facts, but I think I have an idea who that person might have been."

***

Connie Cartwright looked a mess, but when your whole life is a mess, what is the point of looking good. Edward had disowned her, the newspapers had ridiculed her, she was sure her neighbours made jokes at her expense, and she believed that even her close friends were secretly laughing at her misery. For nearly a month she had been a virtual recluse, only leaving her house when it was necessary to buy food, and then travelling to places where she hoped no one would recognise her.

The phone call, when it came, shocked her. She had been in two minds whether to answer it; she knew it wouldn't be the one phone call she wanted to receive: if just one more person tried to sell her an annuity or extolled the virtues of the superior double glazing that he was able to offer her at a discount price she was sure that her head would explode;

but immediately it became clear that that wasn't about to happen.

"Mrs Constance Cartwright," said a male voice, "I felt it was at last time to introduce myself to you. I am the father of your son Edward."

Connie was dumbfounded, she almost dropped the handset in her confusion, and then it struck her that this had to be a cruel trick, maybe by some unscrupulous reporter from a tabloid newspaper.

"I don't believe you," she said fiercely.

"Please yourself," the voice replied, "it's your funeral. I'm offering to divulge to you some information that I know your son would be very pleased to receive."

The thought that this might just be true stopped her from slamming down the receiver, but the suspicion that she was being taken for a ride remained very strong."

"What's your name?" she demanded.

"You don't need to know that," came the reply. "All you need to do is pass a message onto Edward."

"How do I know you're genuine?" she asked.

"You don't, you just have to trust me," responded the man, "but I think I can prove to you that I am. Can you remember what you were wearing on the night you became pregnant?"

Connie was taken aback by the question. Over the last few weeks she had played and re-played in her mind the events of the momentous day, and until the wine had taken control and robbed her of her senses, she had perfect recall.

"Yes," she answered, "but..."

The man on the phone cut her off in mid-sentence.

"Good," he interrupted, "I can remember what you were wearing too. I think you wore a white blouse and a pink skirt; you were dressed like a teenage girl, and if I am brutally honest, you looked a little bit ridiculous; and by the way, did you ever manage to get the red wine stain out of your blouse, or did you end up throwing it away? I think the mark was on your left sleeve if I remember correctly."

Every detail was correct, and she had never told anyone. Whoever the man was who was calling her, and she could tell from the voice that it wasn't Frank Oakes or Mick Wallington, he had described her perfectly. All doubt was now gone.

"What do you want me to do?" she asked him.

"Get a piece of paper and a pen; write down the mobile phone number I am about to give you, and then pass the detail on to Edward. Tell him to call me if he wants to learn more; you never know, your little darling may be so pleased with you that he may even allow you back into his coterie of sycophants."

***

 The process of sifting through the material recovered from the burned out vestry was still continuing in the old garage at the back of Burrdale Police Station, and the drabness of the building, and the lack of warmth and comfort, was beginning to depress the men and women forced to spend hours at a time peering at tens of thousands of scraps of printed paper in their search for vital evidence

It was to this place of Purgatory Mark Hobson was going when he bumped into retired Police Sergeant Chris Postles.

Everybody knew Chris. He had been the Station Sergeant at New Mills for almost as long as anyone could remember, and when he retired after 30 years' service he had immediately applied for, and attained the job of driving the new Mobile Police Station (MPS) around the smaller villages and hamlets of the High Peak.

When this initiative had been announced Mark Hobson, like many other officers, had been very sceptical. He had viewed it as a gimmick, a P.R. exercise, a stunt to lessen the anxiety that people living in far flung places felt about the closure of local police offices.

"Why does progress always mean less?" D.S. Bennett had moaned. "Fifty years ago you could travel virtually anywhere by train, fifty years ago every village had a shop, a pub, a bus service and a local bobby, and now all that's gone. Despite all the sodding new technology, and the so called efficiencies of scale you can't say people are better off now than they were then." Many people agreed with him, even D.I. Hobson did, to a degree.

But surprisingly the idea of the mobile police station had found favour among the public, and because Chris Postles was known to so many people he had been trusted as a safe pair of ears. People were willing to talk to him off the record, they had pointed fingers at erring neighbours; they had felt happy to speak to him knowing that he would not treat them as fools, even if sometimes they were hopelessly wrong. As a result, there had been occasions that he had been able to pass on to C.I.D. some nuggets of information that had turned out to be pure gold.

"Afternoon Chris," said Mark, "have you picked up anything of interest today?"

"Not much Mark," he replied. "I've been given the names of a couple of kids thought to be responsible for smashing bottles in the Memorial Park; several people are unhappy about the state of the public toilets in Buxton; there's a bull in a field with a footpath running through it in Edale: it's as soft as a brush, but the locals can't seem to understand that; but the highlight of my day was playing a good Samaritan to a lady in distress."

"A gent like you Chris, I can well believe it; what did you actually do?"

"Well a woman came up to me in Bradwell, she was in a right state. I didn't recognise her at first, then I twigged that she was Jenny Baker, Raymond Baker's wife. Anyway, to cut a long short, it turns out Ray isn't very well at present. She says it's mental rather than physical. He's not in a good place at the moment, so she'd taken his dog for a walk. She left it tied up outside the newsagents while she went in to get him some cigarettes, and it somehow slipped its collar. She was terrified that it might end up being run over by a car or dead in some farmer's field because it had been chasing sheep, and she was frightened to death what Ray would do if she went home without it. I said I'd keep an eye open for the dog, and about 15 minutes later I saw this little black and white dog running loose in a field. I knew immediately that was it. I stopped my van, got out, called it by name, and it came to me. I stuck it in the rear of the vehicle and then phoned Jenny on her mobile; we met up at Tideswell Crossroads and I gave it back to her; she was much relieved, I can tell you that."

"What kind of dog was it?" asked Mark.

"A sweet little Border collie," replied Chris. "She's called Bess; I've actually asked Jenny to let me know if she ever has pups because I would like one."

"And what would you call it? I think Fido might be a good name."

Ex-Sergeant Postles burst out laughing.

"Get real Mark," he said. "Nobody would call a working dog Fido, it would give it a massive inferiority complex."

CHAPTER FORTY NINE

Edward Cartwright was in a foul mood; people were giving him sideways glances. He sensed that plans could be afoot to expunge him from the history of the T.V. Channel. Nothing had been said of course, but when problems had arisen over casting in his much trumpeted bio-pic there had been none of the usual frantic telephoning around to find suitable actors to play supporting roles. He had even heard the producers say fatalistically "if it fails, it fails", and that to Edward was a signal that people were no longer pulling out all the stops to guarantee its success. He had also noticed a change in the attitude of the men from Los Angeles, who were supposed to be protecting his interests. They had always been disrespectful in his eyes, and sometimes downright rude, but now they seemed largely indifferent, which was 10 times worse. Did this prelude a time when they would be moving on, leaving him with a metaphorical label stuck to his forehead reading "Not wanted on this or any other voyage." He wasn't sure, but he was terrified that it did.

When the receptionist at the hotel where he was staying telephoned to say his mother was on the line and wished to speak to him, he had snapped at the poor girl.

"There's no way on Earth that I'm ever going to speak to that bitch again, so you can tell her to rot in Hell so far as I am concerned."

The girl had tactfully refrained from using such language when she spoke to Mrs Cartwright, but had, as diplomatically as possible, tried to explain Edward would not take her calls.

Her clear explanation of the situation had gone unheeded. Over the next 90 minutes there had been seven more calls from Connie, and each time the receptionist had tried politely and calmly to explain to an increasingly frustrated caller that she had specific instructions from Mr Cartwright that she could not ignore. She said repeatedly that she was very sorry, but that there was nothing she could do.

On the eighth occasion the phone rang, she could take it no more. She passed the phone to the Hotel Manager so that he could explain to this "lunatic woman" what the situation was. The Hotel Manager hadn't minced his words. He explained to Connie that from the hotel's point of view what she was doing was at least a nuisance and perhaps even harassment of his staff, and that if she called again, then he would personally report the matter to the police who might be forced to arrest her to prevent further offences taking place. It was at this stage, Connie had screamed at the man, "Just tell him I have been talking to his fucking father on the phone, and that I have some information for him that I know he would very much like to receive." She had then slammed the receiver down in her anger. The Hotel Manager had pondered what to do for the best. He decided that he would pass on the message; he also decided that he would say to the Hollywood star that unless he could control the antics of his mother then he was afraid that he would have to ask him to find somewhere else to stay.

Edward was alone when the Manager delivered his news and also his ultimatum, and he was glad that that was the case. He no longer trusted the people around him to do things properly. Without seeking advice from anyone, he decided that he would speak to his mother and find out what she had to say. If she was now willing to tell him the name of his father then that could be a giant leap forward. If he could find him, if he could buy him off without having to involve anyone else, then single-handedly he might have saved his own career, and at the same time he would have struck a blow against the arrogant arseholes who had been sniggering at him for so long. He picked up the phone and called his mother; she answered after only two rings.

"I hope to God this isn't just another one of your stupid tricks," he said. "If you're going to spill the beans about my Daddy then go ahead; if you're not going to do that then you can fuck off and stop wasting my precious time."

There was a hardness in Connie's voice when she answered him; it was a tone he wasn't used to. He decided that he didn't like it; if he had to speak to her at all then he preferred it if she was a simpering doormat.

"Oh it's true Edward; I have spoken to your father on the telephone, be in no doubt about that; and I do have details about how you can contact him, but if you want those details you are going to have do some things for me."

"And what are they?" he asked aggressively.

"Well, first of all you are going to have to promise me that I will be admitted back into your circle of friends. Do you know Edward, for so long that was the only thing I wanted, but you have been so nasty to me of late that I now want much more.

"You are going to have to build me the house you promised me, and not in this pathetic narrow minded little country; I want a home in Hollywood, and I want the recognition that is due to me.

"I also want a proper allowance, not the pittance I was on before. All this is non-negotiable Darling, you can take it or leave it, it's up to you; but if you sign a piece of paper agreeing to these terms, I will let you have a mobile phone number upon which you can contact your father. He says he is desperate to meet you; he says that is all that he wants. Given the way you have behaved lately, I think he is going to be disappointed, but that won't be my problem.

"Now what is it going to be Sweet? If you sign the paper and get it witnessed, then as soon as it is in my hands, I'll happily enable a touching father/son embrace to take place. If you don't, then what I have been told by your dad will have to remain my little secret."

Edward Cartwright thought for a millisecond. What was on offer was a lot better than the alternative; in any event he was sure that a good lawyer would have no problem getting this "contract" annulled. Promises were made to be broken.

"I agree Mummy Darling," he said. "I'll get the papers you require sent over to your house within the hour."

***

A picture was becoming clearer in Mark Hobson's head, although the meeting with Chris Postles had given him considerable food for thought, and as he entered the garage where all the paperwork from the burnt out vestry was being sorted, he had to admit that he was no nearer to discovering the identity of a killer than he had been before; indeed to a degree the waters had just been muddied; but even so he felt that some pieces of the puzzle were beginning to fall into place.

He remembered that Pete Bennett had discovered that Mabel Agnes Rowbotham, the woman most likely to have been the person who on a joyous night, nearly 60 years ago, had dragged a young Home Guard soldier across the bridge from boyhood to manhood, had died of a heart attack in 1969, and that she had outlived her daughter by 24 years and her son by 16 years. He recalled that it was suspected that the daughter may have had an illegitimate child, but that no trace of that child had been discovered on the Register of Births, Deaths and Marriages. Had the baby been secretly adopted? Had it succumbed to some childhood illness? Was it even possible that it could have been murdered to avoid the stigma of bringing up a bastard? Or had it grown to maturity and become a Serial Killer? Mark had no answers, but he knew that it was imperative that he found some.

Another thing was almost as important, and that was to discover the identity of the person who the killer in his letter to Alexander Sterndale had described as "wheelchair bound." That surely had to be Mabel's son James. Perhaps leaping from a high viaduct, or jumping from a balcony on the twenty fourth floor of a block of flats, or lying across the main Manchester to Euston line in wait for the 20.15 express to sever his head from his body with the ease of a chef slicing through cucumber with a sharp knife might have been more dramatic, but setting fire to himself in front of a vast crowd of people was a pretty spectacular way to go; it amounted to a public horror show, as of course did the three murders currently under investigation.

There was one more significant fact to consider. James Rowbotham and Sheila Adamson had been a couple until James became disabled. A very short relationship with Mick Wallington then followed; in the killer's mind that seemed to make them both culpable; but was there something even more fundamental than that from his point of view? Mark Hobson now realised that it was essential to discover exactly how Rowbotham sustained his injuries; he was beginning to suspect that he could guess the answer.

With all these ideas churning round in his head, Mark started to search through the piles of papers to find any letter, document or report that referred to Mabel by name. He struck gold when he started to leaf through the remains of the Reverend Hardman's scrapbook. In it he discovered the anguished letter she had written to the vicar begging for permission to bury her son in the churchyard. It was barely legible and some of the ink had run, but enough was readable to get a clear feel for the content. The vicar had scribbled a single word "No" in pencil in the margin, and Mark felt this was confirmation of some of the stories that

Helena had been told about his lack of Christian compassion.

He struck silver gilt when he alighted upon the scorched remnants of the Register of Births, Deaths and Marriages. This revealed that Mabel had been married for the first time in December 1918. A letter folded into the register at that page gave him more information. It transpired that her first husband, who had been gassed at the Battle of the Somme, and was in poor health, had contacted flu shortly afterwards in the Great Flu Pandemic 1918/19 and died less than six months later. The name of the husband caused D.I. Hobson to take a sharp intake of breath. Mabel gave birth to a daughter four weeks later; she then married Arthur Rowbotham just three months after that; Mark felt the excitement building as he perused these documents.

Further checks now had to be made; in particular at the archive of the local newspaper, but he had a name to play with, and a person was firmly in his sights, It was imperative to act quickly. Final I's needed to be dotted and T's crossed so that no new evil could take place on the streets of Burrdale and of the High Peak.

CHAPTER FIFTY

If people could have seen him climbing the stairs to his bedroom he knew that they would have thought he had grown old. He thought that too, and he knew it was inevitable. People might also have assumed that his brain was slowing down, but they would have been wrong. Inside his head, his mind was on fire. The end of a journey was in sight; just one more act remained to be done. Excitement almost overwhelmed him; he couldn't wait for the final scene to be played, but he knew that he had to. If he didn't stick to every detail of the plan it would be devalued; and that was something he could not allow to happen.

He entered his bedroom, knelt down on the floor, and then he rolled up the mat that was spread out on the floor beside his single bed to reveal bare boards. Using the broad bladed screwdriver he was carrying, he inserted its blade into a crack and applied pressure. He had done this many times before; there was a knack to it, but when you knew how to do it, it was easy to prise the short length of timber from the floor. With that piece removed it was simple to remove its neighbours on either side, and soon he was able to reach into the opening and pull out the laptop computer and the printer that had been carefully hidden there. He knew exactly where these two items were kept, he did not have to fumble for them, but it took him a little longer to locate the third item he was seeking. It was wrapped in sacking, tied up with string and was quite a bit smaller than its two companions. It was not possible to say what it was until he had untied the string and unravelled the dirty strip of hessian; then it became clear. It was black and ugly, and any expert would have immediately recognised that it was foreign, but that didn't worry him. He caressed it like a baby, even holding it to his cheek in a bizarre act of tenderness, and then he laid it gently on the bed while he searched for a smaller package amongst the sacking. Triumphantly he found it, and it was soon obvious that that contained ammunition. He took two bullets and loaded them into the weapon he had recovered, and then he smiled. Very carefully, he examined the remaining bullets and eventually selected three of them, which he also loaded into the pistol, leaving the rest of the ammunition strewn across the table. What made the bullets he had so carefully selected special only he knew, but they were an integral part of his plan. He replaced the floor boards and re-laid the rug, which was not something he usually did until after the computer and the printer were back in place, and then he carried the computer, printer and handgun downstairs and placed them on his kitchen table.

For the next ninety minutes he laboured. The first document took him a long time to complete even though he had been working on it for weeks, and he had to correct it many times before he was happy with the result; then he printed off several copies of it and placed them into envelopes that he had previously addressed and stamped.

The second document was shorter than the first; but again he was meticulous in his work. When he was finally satisfied, he printed off just one copy and he stuck that onto his kitchen wall with Blue-Tack. When everything was done he did not restore the electrical equipment to its hiding place; there was no longer a need, he would not have a use for it again; and after tomorrow it would not matter if it was found or not.

After his mother had finished speaking to him Edward Cartwright had acted quickly. He did as his mother requested and wrote down his promise to fulfil her three conditions and then he signed and dated the paper, but he knew that that would not be enough for Connie. She had insisted that his signature be witnessed, and that caused him a problem. He didn't want to show the paper to any of the people who surrounded him, he no longer trusted them. They might try to dissuade him from a course of action he knew to be right, but worse than that he would be revealing his hand to them. The game he was playing was best kept secret. In the end he called room service and when a Polish waitress brought coffee to his room, with a little difficulty he persuaded her to sign her name below his. She hadn't a clue what she was signing, which was no bad thing, but she knew what a £20 note was, and she would have committed mass murder to receive such a tip; a similar inducement made to an Australian barman secured a second signature to the paper.

The next problem had been how to get the signed and witnessed agreement to Connie. He didn't want to post it, it would take too long to arrive and, in any event, there was a risk that it could get lost in transit, but he couldn't ask any of his personal staff to carry out the task of hand-delivering it, nor could he do that himself in case he was noticed. In the end he telephoned Connie to tell her he had done everything she had asked. In far gentler terms than he had used of late, he explained his dilemma to her and suggested that it might be better if he left the letter in reception for her to collect, and that after she had examined it, if she was satisfied perhaps she could leave a note for him in return, giving him details of the mobile phone number. Given his mother's decidedly stroppy attitude of late, he was prepared for outright rejection, but Connie was surprisingly docile and readily agreed to the plan. Maybe she wasn't as switched on as he had taken her to be; maybe when all this was over he would be able to extricate himself from her clutches with more ease than he had ever dreamed possible. It was only after he had finished speaking to her, and she had put the phone down that a thought suddenly struck him. What if the number she gave him did not exist, or turned out to be the phone number of the local Chinese takeaway? If that was the case he would have signed a piece of paper giving his mother rights and got nothing in return. For a moment he started to panic, but then he told himself that she wouldn't do that; until very recently he had been her whole life; she couldn't have changed so completely overnight; and if he was wrong, then he was sure out there somewhere he could find somebody who would be able to arrange a permanent solution to his problem; for a hefty price of course.

But thankfully for Edward he soon learnt that he had not been misled. Connie did arrive at the hotel, did collect the envelope with the completed agreement inside it, and did leave him a mobile phone number in return. At 8.30pm, in the privacy of his bedroom, he dialled the number he had been given.

The phone rang for a long time, (or so it seemed to Edward) but just before it went to answerphone a male voice interrupted.

"So your mum did speak to you," it said. "Yes Edward, I am your father, and I think we need to have a long chat."

"How can I be sure that your claim is true?" asked Cartwright.

"I give you my word that it is," came the response, "and remember that I am more than happy to give you a sample of my DNA if you require it, and I can take you somewhere where I can show you a considerable amount of documentary proof."

"And what do you want out of this? I'm not going to let anyone blackmail me; I've no intention of paying you a penny. You can't walk into my life after more than a quarter of a century and expect me to open my wallet and throw money at you like it's going out of style."

"I don't," said the voice quite reasonably. "I just want to meet you. I know I can tell you things that you will find useful, and after our chat I'll just step back into the shadows.

Isn't it the most natural thing in the world for a man to want to be with his only son at least once in his lifetime?"

"Couldn't we discuss things now over the phone?" said Edward. "I've got an awful lot on at present."

"Phones can be tapped," replied the voice, "and in any event if we did that you wouldn't get the DNA sample or see any of the proof that I can show you. Can you slip from under the gaze of your minders for a couple of hours tomorrow morning? A good meeting place would be on the steps to Buxton Opera House. Shall we say 11am? After that I will then take you in my car to the place where the records are kept, and there we will be able to talk uninterrupted and unseen. I know you've got problems looming Son and that worries me; I'm offering you a way to escape them." The man sounded so understanding.

"All right, I agree," said Edward. "Eleven o'clock at the Opera House it is then."

CHAPTER FIFTY ONE

It hadn't been the best of mornings for Detective Inspector Hobson; Christopher had picked up some sort of infection at school and had been sick twice in the night, which had meant disturbed sleep for both his parents. Now it looked as if Helena may also have caught the same thing and she had been sick just as Mark was leaving for work. He too felt decidedly grotty; whether that was just tiredness, or whether he was about to be stricken, he didn't know, but he rather feared that a tummy upset was on the cards.

The evening before he had thought a lot about the case, and had discussed it with Helena, and when he had told her about Mabel Rowbotham's tragically short first marriage she had reminded him of what her Local History tutor had said about children growing up not knowing their true identity, and raised the possibility that that might have happened here.

"Do you think that you could be looking for such a child?" she had said. She was so perceptive, so clever, so marvellously his. He had everything he had ever wished for in life, and in abundance: even with a headache and perhaps embryonic gastric flu he felt on top of the world. Christmas was coming soon, and that would be wonderful, but for him, when he looked at Helena, every day was Christmas Day.

The visit to the offices of the Burrdale Advertiser was even more productive than he had ever dared hope. There were literally hundreds of mentions of Mick Wallington in the newspaper, spread over several decades, but what really set Mark's pulse racing was the report of a fatal accident he had been involved in as a teenager. A court case had followed, and he had been convicted of careless driving. He had probably been extremely fortunate to escape a more serious charge, but there were no eye witnesses. The female passenger and her American boyfriend who had been driving the other vehicle had both been killed outright; the rear seat passenger had been terribly injured; that passenger was James Rowbotham.

Mark then changed the subject of his search to focus on the injured man, and here too he had success. He discovered a picture of James when he was a handsome young man standing with his sister, Patricia, and another attractive young woman who wasn't named, waiting at a bus stop. The strap line beneath the photograph read "New Bus Service Finally Introduced." The fact that Burrdale had been reconnected to the outside world didn't interest Detective Inspector Hobson in the slightest, but the presence of the unnamed girl certainly did. He instantly recognised her. There was no doubt. The girl was Sheila Adamson, and the way her arm was intertwined with James's made it obvious that she was his girlfriend. An important link between Sheila and Mick had clearly been found. If Wallington had physically ruined James's life and if Sheila had mentally ruined it by walking out on him, then it was easy to see how the killer could blame them both for the damage that had so blighted his own life.

Next Mark searched against the name that had muscled its way to the forefront of his brain. Here he was less lucky; it appeared only a very few times in the paper, but he did discover a report of a competition the local CCF had taken part in, which involved a number of teams of Army cadets from North Derbyshire and East Cheshire. The local lads had emerged victorious, and it had been their prowess at shooting that had held the key. The person with the highest individual score was Mark's prime suspect.

Everything was tumbling into place. The one thing that didn't fit was the anonymous phone call made to the police after the fire at St Catherine's. Suddenly Mark realised that Tim Bradley must have made that call himself, deliberately accusing him of committing the arson, but at times when he had cast iron alibis and so would be exonerated. A voice comparison between the tape of that anonymous phone call and the tape the police still possessed of their interview under caution with Bradley had to be made, but he was already convinced that there would be a positive match.

And suddenly there was one final realisation. When Tim Bradley had turned up at Frank Oakes's house just at the point when he was about to be arrested, and had given him an alibi, in fact he had done no such thing.

The clever sod was giving himself an alibi thought Mark, I was convinced that it was true because of Frank's reaction; I never thought that there might be another explanation.

***

It was only as he approached Buxton Opera House on a cold grey December morning that the memories of the tragic events of five months earlier really hit home. He had moved on from them, he had become entirely preoccupied with his own problems, so he had no time to think about anybody else's. What had happened to Penny was history. He had done the right thing at the time, he had sent expensive flowers to her funeral, he had even taken the unusual step of writing an effusive message of condolence himself; there was nothing more anybody could have asked of him.

But as he got to within 50 yards of the main entrance, his body froze. It wasn't the knowledge that a beautiful young woman had been murdered close to the very spot where he was standing that nearly freaked him out; it was the realisation that it could so easily have been him.

I want to get out of this place he told himself, and he felt an overwhelming temptation to turn and run away, but if he did that he lost the chance that he was seeking to put all his recent troubles behind him.

He looked around him and saw nobody. If the bastard doesn't come there will be Hell to pay he thought. If his mother had led him on a wild goose chase then she would suffer. No more Mr Nice Guy, he told himself, you've been too reasonable for too long, now it's time to take a stand.

The tap on his shoulder made him jump like a startled gazelle. He spun round and found himself standing next to an inoffensive, unimpressive looking little man with thinning hair and what his mother might have described as "a very pastry face". Where he had come from he didn't know; he assumed that he had been there all the time and that he had just failed to see him, which given that there was nothing at all remarkable about him, was an entirely understandable oversight.

"Hello Edward," said the man. "My name is Tim, and I am your father."

Cartwright looked at him with disdain.

"Do I really have your genes inside me? What a terribly depressing thought! Can you really be my father?" he asked disappointedly.

"Oh yes," replied the man, "and I'll give you all the evidence you need to prove that fact in just a little while."

"Maybe, maybe not," said Edward, "but for now can we just get out of this place, it gives me the fucking creeps."

"Of course we can," answered the man in conciliatory tones. "Of course it was here that beautiful young woman was shot."

"It was here where a bullet missed me by inches," retorted the brave movie star. "You can't imagine what it's like to live with such a memory."

"Yes I can," responded Tim. "It must give you nightmares, it certainly has done me. My car is parked just around the corner on The Crescent. Would you like to come with me and I will take you to a place where I can answer all your questions, and give you all the evidence you need to prove that everything I say is true."

"I suppose so," conceded Edward; he could put up with a short journey in a horrible little car if that was going to enable him to seize triumph from disaster.

***

"In one sense Sir, it's as if Patricia Bradley never legally existed." Detective Inspector Mark Hobson was explaining his discoveries to D.C.S. Stan Hardy.

"We now know that her mother, Mabel Rowbotham, married twice in quick succession; whether that was because she had been left a widow with a very young baby to look after I don't know, I rather suspect it might have been. She registered her daughter's birth as she was legally required to do in the baby's father's name, but by the time the little girl was 15 months old her real dad had died, her mum had remarried and she now had a little baby brother. From being less than 1 year old, she seems to have been universally known as Patricia Rowbotham, although she wasn't formally adopted by her new father and none of her details in the register were changed. That's what threw people when we searched the Register of Births, Marriages and Deaths. There was no record of Patricia Rowbotham registering the birth of a child; had we looked for Patricia Bradley it would have been a different story; she obviously was aware that things had to be done properly because the world had changed and there was no room for informal arrangements. We know that Patricia, and her boyfriend, an

American G.I. called John Duke, were killed in a car crash caused by the lunatic driving of Mick Wallington; and now everything has fallen into place. Patricia's child Timothy was brought up by a resentful grandmother and by his account of things he seems to have had a thoroughly miserable childhood. For decades, hatred of the people he blamed for his situation has simmered away inside him, and now nearly half a century later he has taken his revenge. I have a hunch that he has acted now because his own time is running short, and he wanted to take retribution before it was too late."

The D.C.S. was convinced; the logic of his D.I. was impeccable. The identity of a killer was now known; all the police had to do was to find him and arrest him, and that was something that needed to be accomplished as quickly as possible, while taking every possible precaution as the man they were seeking had certainly had access to weapons and could very well be armed.

"He's killed three times, he's attempted to kill a fourth time, and he's caused one suicide and provoked one attempt at murder," Hobson said to his boss; "and he's a crack shot. The fact that we have recovered his rifle may not be that significant, he could easily have other weapons at his disposal; we have to proceed on that basis."

An hour later, after the men had been briefed that they were going after a suspect who could be armed and dangerous, and with officers from the Tactical Firearms Unit in support, the police arrived at the home of Tim Bradley. From information that had been provided, it was believed that the man they were seeking habitually had lunch at home, and the presence of his car on the drive way seemed to suggest he had stuck to his usual routine, but when police in body armour forced an entry, and armed officers rushed into the cottage they were disappointed. Bradley was not there, his house was empty, and where he might be was simply not known.

But although he was absent, he had left behind him a number of items that were of great importance to the police investigation. A laptop computer connected to a printer sat in open view upon the kitchen table. Mark Hobson immediately realised that they were not the ones that had been returned to Bradley by the police because they contained no illegal or suspicious material.

The bastard had two computers Hobson thought to himself. He ordered the seizure of both of these items, this time he was confident that there would be much of evidential value to be revealed.

The seven bullets lying in an untidy heap on the table cloth were potentially an even more significant find. They certainly were not rifle bullets, and they were not English. Did this mean that Bradley might be in possession of a handgun? Mark Hobson feared that that was the case.

***

The note stuck on the kitchen wall was clearly intended for police consumption. It was centrally placed so that it could not be overlooked, and it had been printed in big bold type for extra impact. Under the heading "Confessions of a serial killer" Tim Bradley had written the following words:-

I, Timothy John Bradley, freely admit responsibility for the murders of Adam Wallington, Penny Adamson, Jacob Lindley, and the attempted murder of Giles Sterndale. They were all fine young people, none of them deserved to die, but sometimes the innocent must be sacrificed to bring home to the guilty the magnitude of their crimes.

My reasons for destroying blameless lives will soon be widely known. Every National Newspaper has been sent a letter chronicling the sins of those who by their actions drove an ordinary man to become a monster. Lives which are damaged in early childhood remain damaged for all eternity. Emotional wounds don't heal, they bleed and suppurate inside your head, and like a cancer destroy your very existence. With my low grade ancestry perhaps I was fated to have a difficult life, but it need not have been made unbearable by the people around me. Now I am tired, and my life is nearly over and shortly my passing will give the police some rest. Before then, however, one final act of reparation still awaits. A diseased branch needs to be cut from a stunted family tree, and I must be the one who wields the axe.

The valley of the Shadow of Death awaits me; I can no longer delay my final journey.

But apparently, as an afterthought, Tim Bradley had done just that. He had taken a little more time to sketch out a short history of his immediate ancestors. It wasn't done in depth, and undoubtedly a great many details were not covered, but it did show the lineage of the man who believed himself to be teetering on the very edge of existence. It only went back 6 generations and it read as follows:-

1.   Joshua Albert Bradley (one of 13 children) 1803-1841 (agricultural labourer.)

2.   Albert James Bradley (1824-1870) third son of Joshua (mill worker.)

3.   Wilfred George Bradley (1853-1912) only son of Albert. A vagrant. (Died penniless on the streets of Birmingham) his Sister Florence Elizabeth Bradley (certified lunatic) committed suicide November 1903. Absentee father to:-

4.   Sidney Michael Bradley (1890-1919) married Mabel Agnes Newton December 1918. Died of influenza April 1919.

5.   Patricia Mary Bradley (daughter of Mabel and Sid) 1919-1946 killed in a car crash. Mother of:-

6.   Timothy John Bradley 1946-2003 (voyeur and rapist.) A bringer of death and destruction.

7.   Edward Cartwright, an unfortunate bi-product of rape. Vain and useless, a complete waste of space. Unsuitable for breeding purposes and would be best culled.

"It's a suicide note, isn't it Gov?" said D.S. Pete Bennett to his D.I.

"It is Pete," replied Hobson, "but it's obviously much more than that. He's got one more grand gesture left within him before he takes his own life and that clearly involves Edward Cartwright."

CHAPTER FIFTY TWO

The car, which the man claiming to be his father led his long lost son to, was very much a better vehicle than the movie star had feared would be the case. This funny little man, with whom he had absolutely nothing in common, and for whom he felt complete indifference had taste in automobiles, he'd give him that, and thankfully, if he had to have him as a travelling companion they would at least travel in a degree of comfort.

"Oh, it's not mine," said Tim chattily, as if he could read Edward's thoughts. "It belongs to a friend of mine; I didn't think it was appropriate to ferry someone like you about in my old Ford Fiesta." He could have added I also didn't think it would be wise for me to use my own car in case the police are already looking for me, but he chose to keep that piece of information to himself. Edward Cartwright smiled a little smile, at least his father seemed happy enough to accord him the status he deserved; perhaps when all this was over he might slip him a few hundred quid as a thank you; they would never meet again thereafter, and he looked as if he could use a few bob.

"Where are we going?" he asked, as his father held open the door of the Jaguar to allow him to climb in. He was pleased that his Dad seemed perfectly content with the substantial degree of inequality that existed between them.

"I'm taking you to a little church near here, there's a plaque in there that I want you to see; and while we're in there I'll explain everything to you. Meanwhile, would you mind switching off your mobile phone for a little while; I do think it would be better if we can avoid any interruptions when we're in the building."

They quickly arrived at their destination, and within less than 10 minutes they were pulling off the road and onto a small car park at the side of the church; the car park was surrounded by a tall privet hedge which effectively made it a very private place. To be absolutely sure that they could not be spotted from the road Tim drove to the furthest corner of the car park and parked the vehicle in a shady place under the canopy of a large copper beech. Satisfied that their vehicle could not be seen by prying eyes Tim got out of the car and beckoned to Edward to do likewise. When Edward exited the Jaguar, he noticed for the first time that the church had apparently been damaged by fire, and that the damaged area was now fenced off from the car park by a tall wire mesh fence.

"Why have we come here?" he queried. "I've read about this act of arson; surely there can't be anything in here which would be of interest to me?"

"Oh I assure that there can be," replied Tim. "The main body of the church is intact, and it's in there that there is a plaque that you need to see. I think it will also be a good place to present certain documents to you and explain anything you don't understand; I can also give you the DNA samples you require at the same time," and saying that he leant into the rear of the car and picked up a black briefcase from off the back seat.

"Everything we need is in here," he said. He then secured the car and walked with Edward to the church. The door to the building was locked. Tim put his hand in his pocket and pulled out a key. He unlocked the door. Both men entered. He carefully closed and then locked the door behind them.

"Just to make sure we're not disturbed," he said; seemingly trying to put Edward at his ease.

The big time celebrity was not impressed; he had been inside churches in America, for publicity purposes, which had been much bigger and grander that this modest little chapel, and there was also a residual smell of smoke that he found unpleasant.

"Can we just get on with things?" he said impatiently. "It stinks in here, and I suspect there may be rats."

"Oh there are," commented his papa, "and you're one of them. Now sit down if you please in that chair."

"Why you jumped up little shit; who the Hell do you think you are talking to me like that?"

"I'm a jumped up little shit who has the misfortune of being your biological father, and I've got one of these which gives me authority."

Cartwright looked at the weapon, it looked like something he had seen on hundreds of old movies; it was obviously a replica. He started to laugh.

"You don't think I'm scared of you and your toy gun," he sneered, and he took a step towards the upstart who was claiming paternal rights. A bullet whizzed past his ear and embedded itself in the wooden altar screen.

"The next one will be aimed straight at your guts," snarled Tim. "Now be a good boy and do as you're fucking told." The bravado vanished with the explosion. Shaking like a leaf in a hurricane, his complexion imitating that of an anaemic albino, Edward now stood rooted to the spot. He was alone with a lunatic, and a lunatic with a gun; one wrong act or word and that could be it; fear began to grip him tightly; he was within a hair's breadth of losing control of his bodily functions; the situation he found himself in was becoming his worst nightmare.

"Sit down in the chair like I told you to do," ordered his captor. Edward immediately obeyed. Tim reached into his briefcase again and pulled out a set of handcuffs. He threw them into Edwards lap.

"You can just about get anything on E-bay." he said. "Now clip the cuff securely to the armrest, and when you've done that insert your right wrist into the aperture and then tighten the ratchet. Don't try to be clever and leave it loose; there will be consequences if you do."

In a state of terror Edward did exactly what was asked of him. Bradley reached into the briefcase once more and produced a second set of cuffs.

"You get a discount if you buy in bulk," he joked. "Now put your free wrist into these cuffs and make sure that they also grip tight; when you've done that, place your left arm on the left armrest so that I can do the necessary: and no sudden moves; I will be watching you closely, and if necessary I will shoot."

Cartwright had no difficulty in accepting that statement as true and fully complied with the order. He was now shackled to a heavy ornate piece of furniture, and entirely at the mercy of a madman.

"Comfortable?" asked his gaoler mockingly.

Edward was in tears.

"Why are you doing this?" he sobbed pathetically. "What harm have I ever done to you?"

"I'll tell you a story Son," replied Tim. "Isn't that what a good father is supposed to do for his children?

"Once upon a time, a long while ago, a young man called at a lady's house because she had put an advert in the local shop looking for a part time gardener. He'd put on his only decent suit, and he'd done that to try to make a good impression. The woman opened the door, looked at him as if he was dog dirt, and told him to go away. The young man tried to explain why he was there; she didn't want to know. She threatened to call the police if he didn't leave immediately. That stuck up bitch was your own dear mother. She thought nothing more of the incident, but the young man never forgot. Several years later when her biological clock was ticking, the woman decided she wanted a child. She paid a handsome young man to be the father, but unbeknown to her he sub-contracted the job to the village idiot. He was a man who could never keep his mouth shut. The young Adonis got your mother drunk, and then he left it to the sub-contractor to do the spade work. He didn't enjoy the experience, I could see that, but he didn't know I was watching. He said afterwards it was like fucking a dead sheep. After he had done the deed, he left her alone practically comatose; I came in and took full advantage of her stupor, and I left her with a legacy she will never forget. You were her idol, but just recently even she has realised that you have feet of clay; the golden boy has become a very tarnished icon.

"You have inherited all her worst faults and all of mine too; and that makes you too toxic to be permitted to father children. Saving the world from that disaster might prove to be my only chance at redemption."

 "Oh God you're going to kill me!" wailed Edward, closing his eyes to avoid looking at his soon to be executioner. There was another loud explosion, and this time the bullet embedded itself in the padded seat just centimetres away from the distraught young man's groin.

"Not necessarily," replied his torturer, but guess where the next bullet is going. You may die of shock, you may bleed to death for all I care, or you may become the world's most famous eunuch. Obviously, for that to happen, we must have witnesses. Sit back and think about what is to come, I must go and make one or two phone calls.

Edward Cartwright did just that, and then he shat himself.

***

The police had acted very quickly. Urgent telephone calls had been made to Edward Cartwright to warn him to stay in his room until they arrived, but they had discovered it was already too late.

"He went out without saying a word to anyone," his P.A. had said. "We don't know where he is."

Neither do I, thought Mark Hobson, but I do know who he is with.

A telephone call to Constance Cartwright confirmed that she had given Edward contact details for the man she now knew to be his father, and a phone call to his sometime employer Frank Oakes confirmed Tim was not working that day but that he had borrowed Frank's car.

He's taken him somewhere thought Mark, and what he's got planned when they get there won't be very pleasant for our international celebrity.

The million dollar question was of course "Where?" A light flashed in the Detective Inspector's brain.

"I think I know where they might be," he said. "It can't be just anywhere, I think the place has to have some special significance to Bradley. It also has to be away from the public gaze. The only place that I can think of which might fit the bill is St Catherine's Church."

Almost at exactly the same time that he said these words the editor of the Burrdale Advertiser was making a 999 call to Derbyshire Police to pass on some very specific information.

***

Armed police arrived at the church moments before the massed ranks of newspaper people descended on the scene like a plague of locusts. Tim Bradley smiled.

"They're here!" he said tauntingly to his whimpering captive. "I knew that they would come; Showtime is about to begin."

In a police siege situation trained negotiators try to engage with the suspect. "Keep talking" "Keep calm" is the golden rule; the longer the dialogue can be maintained the greater the chances of bringing matters to a peaceful conclusion. Tim Bradley was aware that this would be the tactic. He willingly entered into dialogue. He confirmed that he held Edward Cartwright prisoner, he gleefully described his wretched state; and in the background the terrified heartthrob could be heard moaning; but when conversation turned to what was going to happen, Bradley was unmoved.

There was another gunshot. "He was falling asleep," confided Tim. "I thought I'd better wake him up so he can prepare for the inevitable."

He's mad, thought Hobson, he will do as he says. But then amazingly Bradley appeared at a broken window and pointed his pistol at the police outside. He started screaming at them, telling them to go away and he fired a shot in their direction. This was the opportunity police marksmen had been awaiting. Two bullets sliced through a man's heart. Death was instantaneous. In that one moment Timothy John Bradley became history; he would never kill anyone again.

Tony Read

421

EPILOGUE

With just three days to go until Christmas, things were becoming a little less hectic for Mark and Helena. Most of the last minute Christmas shopping had been done, presents had been wrapped and labelled, and those intended for the children had been carefully hidden away.

Helena had done all the clever, intricate stuff; Mark had been relegated to writing labels.

"You wrap up parcels with all the delicacy of a heavy handed blacksmith," she had teased him, and he had been forced to accept that that was true. Fortunately the special present he had bought for her came in a jewellery box, and even he could cope with wrapping up a small rectangular object.

It had been a good day at work. News had been received at the police station that Giles Sterndale had been brought out of his medically induced coma and that his condition was better than many had feared it would be.

"Physically he will be OK," Mark reported to Helena, "and mentally, although there is quite a lot of stuff he will have to re-learn there seems to be no reason why he shouldn't do that. Given time the doctors are now about 70% certain that he should make a full recovery."

"That's very encouraging news," said Helena. "It's the best Christmas present his family could have wished for."

It had also been a good day at work because it had been confirmed that none of the officers attached to the Tactical Firearms Unit were to be subject to investigation. It had turned out that although Bradley had discharged two live rounds inside the church, all the other ammunition in his gun had been blanks; he could never have carried out his threat to emasculate his prisoner by shooting away his private parts. Since all the ammo recovered from his house had been live, and could easily have been loaded into the pistol if he had so wished, it was obvious that he had no real intention to do this nor had he had a genuine desire to cause injury to any police officer.

"When he fired on us, it was part of a plan," Mark later explained to his wife. "He couldn't harm us, but he knew if he exposed himself we could harm him. That's what he wanted. He was riddled with cancer and his work was done. Rather than place a pistol to his own head, he preferred police marksmen to do the job for him. If an unarmed man gets shot there is always an outcry but this time, thankfully, everyone has accepted that he gave us no choice."

"And what about Edward Cartwright?" asked Helena.

"He's still in a psychiatric hospital," replied Mark. "When we got him out of the church he was covered in his own faeces and gibbering like a hysterical chimpanzee. They think he'll be in there for a few weeks yet, and he may always have flashbacks. He's been dropped by the studio, apparently being the illegitimate son of a homicidal maniac isn't a good pedigree, and public displays of terror aren't too highly regarded by the big boys in Tinsel Town."

"Poor man," said Helena.

"I feel some sympathy for him," said Mark, "but at the same time I have to say that he is one of the most selfish, shallow, vain specimens of humanity that I have ever met."

It was as they sat by the fire later in the evening that Helena became quite serious.

"I've got some news for you Darling," she said. "I went to see the doctor this morning."

Mark's heart started to race. Maybe it was the knowledge that within the last six months the scourge of cancer had destroyed the lives of two people who had been central to the case he had been investigating that caused him to panic. Helena was young and fit, and apart from the last few days always seemed to be a picture of health, but cancer was no respecter of persons, and goodness and beauty were no shields against its destructive power. She hadn't been well lately; if she had been diagnosed with something badly wrong that would destroy in an instant all the joy he had just been feeling.

"And what did he say?" asked Mark, dreading what the answer might be.

"He says I'm pregnant again Mark, you don't mind do you?"

Mark nearly crushed her in his embrace.

"I'm over the bloody moon Love," he said. "I couldn't be happier. It's the best news you could give me Sweetheart."

He kissed her and then he burst into tears.

Tony Read

THE END

Tony Read

www.ingramcontent.com/pod-product-compliance
Lightning Source LLC
Chambersburg PA
CBHW031609180726
48284CB00005B/1470

9 781906 657581